PREMONITIONS

DIANE,
ENJOY READING IT
AS MUCH AS I DID
WRITING IT.)
12-19-14
Frank Mahar

PREMONITIONS

When the Universe Shifts,
Expect the Unexpected

FRANK MCRAE

authorHOUSE®

AuthorHouse™ LLC
1663 Liberty Drive
Bloomington, IN 47403
www.authorhouse.com
Phone: 1-800-839-8640

Published by AuthorHouse   11/12/2013

ISBN: 978-1-4918-2924-0 (sc)
ISBN: 978-1-4918-2923-3 (e)

Library of Congress Control Number: 2013919084

To my wife Donna, and my daughter Jennifer.

*Thank you for your tireless support and assistance, but most of all,
your patience with me as I wrote this book.*

It was all more appreciated than you'll ever know.

CONTENTS

Part One

The General's Wives

"Many that lived deserved death and some that died deserved life."
Lord of the Rings—Gandalf

CHAPTER 1

"We're still in shock ourselves. I was just reaching
for the phone . . ."

Thursday, November 1ˢᵗ, 2012

*F*or weeks now, the air had been laced with a damp chill. The type of chill whose yearly appearance around late October hopelessly attempts to hold off winter just a little longer as it begs for at least one more day of Indian summer.

Children throughout the neighborhood, having put away their Halloween costumes worn the night before, began their seasonal campaigns for more candy . . . . "But mom, I ate all my vegetables and you checked all the candy. Come on mom, please?"

This year the weather had warmed up briefly during their annual quest for treats and the little ones made the most of it. In general, the collections this year surpassed last year's haul by a good margin.

After another long day at his office, Doctor Jim Baker was enjoying a quiet dinner with his wife Lori as they reflected on the previous night's activities with amusement. They recalled watching their next door neighbor Sam and Terry making the rounds with their twins Ally and Pete. The twins had set forth under the guise of Bettie Boop and a rock star this year respectively.

Sam, still wanting his gray Les Paul sunburst guitar to remain playable with the finish intact, convinced Pete to use his plastic guitar with strings thick as pencil lead being his most prevalent prop.

Jim and Lori had stayed home this year, devoting themselves exclusively to candy dispensing duties, for what they knew would be the last time. Next year they planned on taking their soon-to-arrive little girl on her first quest for treats. The baby girl they were expecting, Melissa Ann, would surely change their lives in a dramatic way. They looked forward to her arriving at the end of January and to introducing their new daughter to their closest friends and family members.

This year, however, they had been entertained by and at times concerned with, the variety of costumed visitors that came ringing their doorbell. Every new treat hungry caller had arrived releasing the seasonal chant of "Trick or Treat" before the door could even be opened. Both of the Baker's dogs raced each other all night to meet the treat seekers, barking and sliding into the door before it could be opened.

Of course, they were called upon by the customary pirates, cowboys, gypsies and comic book characters. Spiderman won the popularity contest this year barely beating out green-faced Incredible Hulks with one each of the usual Superman, Batman and Ironman store-bought costumes thrown in for good measure.

This year, once again, the teenagers had predictably gotten into the more bizarre themes consisting mostly of various ghouls and mutilated human forms including the ever popular and haunting Jason style hockey mask. That singularly familiar mask brings to mind many vivid images; none of them being a shoot out between the Chicago Blackhawks and the Detroit Red Wings.

As they watched the parade to and from their door last night, the soon to be proud parents discussed, reshaped and finalized details of the princess costume that they visualized for little Melissa next year.

*

With their dinner finished, Jim and Lori contemplated their options for the night's activities. High on the list was a leisurely, and usually amusing, walk through the neighborhood to assess the number of smashed pumpkins and also to count all the eggs that would never make it to an omelet due to those on the community's more destructive side. Some low impact exercise would be safe for Lori as well as having the additional benefit of shedding a few dinner calories. Their miniature dachshund and tea-cup Yorkshire terrier also seemed in favor of a walk. They both offered up their best hopeful stares complete with inpatient prancing, circling and tail wagging.

With dinner cleanup completed and a walk decided upon, Jim reached to shut off the early evening TV news. As he did so, his attention became riveted to a disturbing report that had just begun. It was being delivered in a very somber tone and it detailed another brutal murder in the area. They moved to the typical crime free suburb of Winnetka on Chicago's north shore within the past year. The area had experienced one other such totally out of the ordinary felony recently.

Surely there were details being kept from the general public, though, what was being released was, very disturbing. The broadcast was particularly disturbing to Jim as it involved the death of another young woman very much like his wife. She no doubt had hopes and aspirations very similar to their own. The report also contained hints of another mutilated body. Unsettling hardly described his feelings. He and Lori just spent the last six months looking forward to an exciting new year anticipating the joys that would surely follow the birth of their first baby.

This year had turned out to be a year of great change and reward. So far it included career advancements, the news that Lori was pregnant and the making of many new friends and associates since moving to their new home.

They had been recently blessed with many new close relationships formed with other doctors Jim now worked with. Regular consultations and patient referrals also kept their collection of twenty plastic surgeons in close social contact.

The Bakers moved to the affluent town of Winnetka after an extensive search for the best place to start their family. He felt proud about being able to move to Winnetka since becoming board certified and accepted on staff at several very prestigious area hospitals including the University of Chicago Medical Center, Loyola University Medical Center and Weiss Memorial.

After enduring the tedious years of medical school, he was rewarded by watching his practice skyrocket over the past year. It was due in large part to his association with the team of doctors that had become known as 'The Surgeon Generals'. Both the success and experience of the group were indeed comprehensive.

They had a rather impressive feature article written on them earlier this year in the Chicago Sun Times entitled, "This team can't be beat— The Surgeon Generals". The study provided extensive background information on the team making Jim pleased to see his and Lori's name associated with such a distinguished group of doctors and their wives.

The team members the piece listed in alphabetical order were Dr. and Mrs.:

John & Lisa Ackerman	Steve & Marilyn Mallard
Jim & Lori Baker	Carlos & Victoria Moore
Mark & Isabella Channing	Tony & Maria O'Connell
Blake & Sandra Falkland	Raymond & Olivia Reed
Keenan & Gabriella Giovanni	Pete & Cindy Reynolds
Franklin & Theresa Griffin	Damien & Jacqueline Ross
Garret & Janice Heaton	Gabriel & Bernice Shannon
Hayden & Wendy Howell	Taylor & Francine Stapleton
Jack & Natalie Kerr	William & Joanna Stevens
Keith & Dana Lawley	Randall & Kelly Wright

Due to the success that sprung from that article's exposure; Jim was not only able to afford his new home in a town that was prominently positioned in the top fifteen richest zip codes in the country, he was also able to purchase a cabin in the north Wisconsin woods where his relationship with Lori blossomed.

Right out of high school Jim knew he wanted to be a doctor and decided on plastic surgery after getting his pre-med bachelor's degree in biology. He had totally shut out the rest of the world during the years of his very-focused medical school education. He was determined to be the best.

He completed eight long years of education. Now he was ready to celebrate the fact that he graduated. Not only that he graduated, but that he wound up in the top five of his class at Rush Medical College in attaining his new MD status.

Enter Lori.

He met Lori 5 years ago during a wild weekend dedicated to the long overdue sowing of oats. They hit it off right away. After two months of dating, they decided to get away for a weekend together. They settled on a cabin in the northern Wisconsin woods. They found a great stretch with no neighbors for miles and a small private lake perfect for skinny dipping and sunbathing. It also offered utterly peaceful sunrises and sunsets with evenings so secluded and peaceful, the insects and owls appeared to make every effort to serenade soothingly to compliment the ambiance.

They found that one weekend at a getaway as complete as this just wasn't enough. They escaped to their perfect little cabin away from it all every weekend they could that summer. There they relished the total freedom the cabin provided to explore each other as they built their relationship into something they knew would last forever.

They would swim together, play silly board games and they dined out at local restaurants with surprisingly good fair for such a remote location. One day while on a hike through the woods, they escaped a summer shower by discovering a cave which turned into yet another exclusive area of their own.

The long peaceful days and nights spent together in this unique retreat of theirs led to utterly spontaneous encounters that told them all they needed to know about wanting to spend the rest of their lives together.

Steamy showers with each other after long hikes and other physical activities in and out of that comfy king sized bed, always found Jim exiting the shower after Lori. He would then find little messages she had written in the fog on the bathroom mirror. The messages always consisted of a heart drawn in the upper left and lower right corners with a different message in the middle that he looked forward to after their long intimate showers together. Messages like "we aren't really finished yet are we?" or "find me . . . quick." or "Free tan line removal at the beach." or simply "Let's cuddle in the puddle"; her cutesy way of describing their intimate times in the hot tub. He looked forward to those messages and to contemplating their meaning as he toweled off.

*

These fond memories were shattered when he heard something he simply couldn't understand. Was the name they just mentioned on the TV really Lisa Ackerman? It couldn't be John's wife who was Lori's closest friend. They had just been out to dinner with John and Lisa two nights ago to celebrate their tenth anniversary. Jim remained glued to the TV as he called out, "Lori. Come in here quick."

"What is it?" she asked, arriving at the TV and becoming alarmed at how glued to it her husband had become.

"I think something terrible has just happened to Lisa!" At that moment, the newscast moved to an on-the-scene reporter giving disturbing particulars to her audience with the Ackerman home in the background.

"Details are still sketchy at this time but Winnetka police have confirmed the discovery of the brutally murdered body of Lisa Ackerman, wife of local plastic surgeon John Ackerman."

"Oh, my god!" exclaimed Lori.

"Mrs. Ackerman's body was found by her husband in the nursery of their home. Dr. and Mrs. Ackerman had recently celebrated their tenth wedding anniversary and have been residents here in Winnetka for six years. Sadly the Ackermans were expecting a child early next year.

"Ed Cassidy, Winnetka's police investigator assigned to the case, had no comment at this early stage of the investigation. Channel 7 news believes this sad story will soon be connected to the other murdered female body found two weeks ago in nearby Evanston. A number of very disturbing similarities to the other murder is sure to shock this usually quiet upscale community.

"Channel 7 news will have more details on the ten o'clock news. This is Susan Peterson reporting live from Winnetka."

They stared at each other in stunned, numbing disbelief as they held hands and slowly collapsed on the couch. Neither of them could utter a word as the shock of this news began to sink in. Jim caught Lori, who began to cry uncontrollably into her hands as she fell forward into his arms.

"Jim, tell me we're not really hearing this! It simply can't be! Not Lisa! This can't be about our Lisa! Poor JOHN! Jim what do we do?"

"I don't know honey. I can't believe it either but that was their house. Lisa was just what, four months pregnant? They were as excited as us about finally conceiving. John must be absolutely crushed! Lisa was his life. His whole life, all he ever talked about. I can't believe what this will do to him. I think I have to go there, but I don't want to leave you now."

She said, "You probably wouldn't be able to get in to talk to him right now anyway. Why don't you try to call him first?"

As he reached for the phone to punch in the Ackerman speed dial, it rang. The caller ID showed 'Raymond & Olivia Reed'.

"Jim. Did you hear the news? It's Lisa. Liv and I can't believe it."

"We just heard Ray. We're in shock ourselves. I was just reaching for the phone to call John."

Ray said, "Don't bother. I just tried. The police are taking all calls to their home right now. We couldn't get through. Jim this can't be."

"We'll just keep trying to reach him. Please let us know if you hear from him."

"Will do Jim and you do the same."

"Ray thanks for calling."

As Jim hung up the phone, he saw Lori still sobbing uncontrollably. He tried to comfort her saying, "Lori there is nothing we can do right now. This is terrible news but please try to calm down. Think of the baby." She looked at him and said, "That's what I'm doing. I'm thinking of their baby as well!"

They held each other on the couch for the rest of the night, lost in upsetting thoughts of their friends who lived a mere two blocks away. One now gone forever; the other more lost and in shock than they were and yet another that would never know the joy and horrors of this crazy world.

*

They had no idea that they were being watched from a short distance away. They had no way of knowing about what was being contemplated at that moment from a short distance away. Tonight he would let the grief take hold. They all needed to feel it.

He wouldn't allow any of them be immune to the pain that was inflicted on him at the hands of the one among them who thought he was so gifted. If the hands were so gifted why was he feeling the terrible pain of his recent loss?

They thought they were so removed from everything his revenge could do, but now they would feel his grief and more. He had only just begun inflicting upon them a small measure of what he felt for the last six months. They needed to feel the loneliness when there should be companionship, feel the silence when there should be laughter, the shattered plans and dreams that will never be realized. He was now set up to inflict this on the ones that truly deserved it.

In his quiet place of observation, he vowed to use all his experience, all his abilities, all his cunning and all his skills to bring the pain he felt from their hands right back to their doorsteps.

So smug were they in their rich little worlds. They are all so cocky and self assured. They were so unquestioningly sure and confident that they were isolated from the terrible things that happened to people without their wealth. But he knew differently. He had a much different experience. This was only the beginning!

CHAPTER 2

"I know where the whiskey is. I'll be right back . . ."

Friday, November 2nd, 2012

*I*nvestigator Ed Cassidy sat at his desk the morning after Lisa Ackerman's murder reviewing his notes on this his latest assignment. The homicide of Lisa Ackerman, 34, pretty white pregnant wife of Dr. John Ackerman, 17 Spruce Street. Her body found mutilated in the nursery of their Winnetka home. She had been out running errands that morning which included a trip to the grocery store and the post office nearby. The house showed no visible signs of forced entry. Her home security system was activated. Her car was found in the garage with the groceries she had purchased earlier still in the back seat. This was very unusual for a number of reasons not the least of which being the groceries included milk, eggs and meat. What could have distracted her from bringing these perishable items into the house immediately and how could it have caused her death in this very extraordinary way?

These same questions could be asked about many of the details surrounding her murder. From the car parked in the garage complete with groceries, to the secured house. Nothing added up. How could she have been killed in the upstairs nursery of her locked home, with the alarm set, no signs of forced entry and no signs of a struggle?

Then there were the details of the murder itself. They were all virtually identical to the murder of Aimee Holden two weeks ago in Evanston. The M.O. appeared to be the same for both. What message was the killer trying to convey by leaving bodies behind for loved ones to find in such a terrible condition?

Both bodies had all of their clothing removed, apparent burn marks made by a very small torch, possibly a pencil torch, up and down the left side of their bodies. They also had a burn mark in the right arm pit and behind the right knee. The left breast was removed, rather cleanly, almost surgically, and the right ankle smashed to a pulp. All had their hair cut

short, sort of like a man's haircut and part of the right ear lobes were cut off. The clothing, hair and make shift mastectomy were all arranged neatly in the cribs that will never see the unborn babies they had been created to embrace.

Another odd part of the impact was the circles drawn around each eye with the fine torch leaving the appearance of a raccoon, or a burglar, or the effect of a bug eyed stare, as well as the unforgettable smell of burned flesh in the room. There was blood at the ear lobe cutting and breast removal site but not nearly what would usually be there had the cutting not been made post mortem. There was no expression of shock on either face. Aside from the burn marks around the eyes, their expressions were rather peaceful. No stab or gunshot wounds. Initial toxicology reports from the Cook County Medical Examiner were negative in both cases and everyone that knew either of the women swore there was no way drug use was a factor.

He was at a loss as to a motive, cause of death and suspects. Ed had reached out to Bill Weller; the Evanston investigator assigned to the Aimee Holden case and had a meeting set up for later this afternoon. He intended to examine the details from both cases and to bounce ideas off each other in regards to motive etc. but he wasn't sure what insights he could bring to the meeting. He was stumped.

He looked at his watch. It showed the day had reached 1:30 pm. He had just time enough for a quick lunch then he'd bring his records to Evanston for his meeting with Inspector Weller. Besides being interested in the Evanston inspector's take on this mess, he desperately wanted to have anything resembling a hunch or an actual development in the case when he interviewed the grieving Doctor Ackerman this afternoon.

*

Doctor John Ackerman had just finished making the dreaded phone calls to Lisa's mom and sister. His pain didn't allow him to make the calls last night. The police had contacted her immediate relatives with the sad news of Lisa's murder and told them there was nothing that could be done that night. Sorrow having been expressed for their loss, they were then told that John would call in the morning.

John would sleep in the den again tonight as the CSI unit had taped off the upstairs, still having more work to do in the nursery. The team had asked him to stay downstairs until they completed all evidence gathering.

So far all they told him was that there were no theories explaining how anyone could have slipped past the security system to do such a thing to Lisa and then get away clean. They couldn't find any footprints around the perimeter of the house that might indicate a window escape or entry. No hair or fingerprints were found other than Lisa's and John's anywhere upstairs. In short, they had no clues that would help the police thus far.

The police had canvassed the neighborhood and discovered that one neighbor two doors down saw Lisa leave the house and drive away around 1:00 pm. No one noticed her coming back home or going back into the house.

John was just beside himself when the doorbell rang. "Hi Jim, Lori, come on in," he said as he welcomed his best friends in. He didn't feel much like talking to anyone, but somehow Lori's hug and tears comforted him. Their visit turned out to be just what he needed.

"John, how are you doing? Is there anything we can do to help you? We just don't know what to say we're so shocked." Lori just kept holding John tightly as she cried with him. Jim joined them but had no words to add. They all sat down. It took several deep breaths to get the sobbing under control before they could speak.

"Thanks for coming over guys, I feel lost, angry, sad and lonely all at the same time. I just called Lisa's mom and sister and none of us could speak really. We cried, and I gave them what little information we have now. It really isn't much more than what the police gave them last night. I had to hang up. We were all just too upset to speak. They wanted to come to Chicago tonight, but I talked them into tomorrow morning."

"John, if it is too soon we can leave, no problem. We just felt we needed to try to comfort you and couldn't stay away any longer," said Jim.

"No, really guys, I think you two are just what I need right now. I don't think I could face anyone else until this has a couple of days to sink in. I feel so helpless, powerless, I don't know, lost I guess. You two are the only ones I feel comfortable enough to tell that I haven't stopped crying since I found her. It was horrible. I will never get the smell of burnt flesh in that room or the image of seeing her like that out of my head as long as

I live. Who would be cruel enough to do something like that to someone as sweet as Lisa? You two knew her.

"She never hurt anyone. She wasn't confrontational. How could she be picked for this? What is the point? Why did this have to happen?"

Then John just couldn't hold it in any longer. He broke down and let his friends comfort him.

Lori hugged John, waiting for the sobbing to stop again.

"I'm meeting with inspector Cassidy today. You can stay if you want. Maybe he'll have some news for us."

Lori asked, "John, when was the last time you ate something?"

"It had to be lunch yesterday before I came home. Last night was like an out of body experience and today I haven't been able to concentrate on much of anything. I keep trying to think of how things will be going forward, but I'm having trouble finding a starting point. I guess eating was about the last thing on my mind."

"I'd go get something but we really want to stay with you. How about I order a pizza and I'll make us some drinks while we wait?"

"That would be excellent Lori. Thanks."

Jim stood up saying, "Lori, stay with John. I know where the whiskey is. I'll be right back with some drinks for us. Then I'll place the order."

The rest of the afternoon, they shared fond memories of their times with Lisa and comforted each other as they ate and drank and waited for the inspector's visit.

CHAPTER 3

'They had never seen anything as flawless as this plan.'

Friday, November 2nd, 2012

*O*n the way to his meeting in Evanston, Ed looked at the Ackerman case details from about every angle he could think of, but couldn't begin to see any pattern other than both victims were the wives of prominent doctors in the city; no, prominent plastic surgeons in the city.

Smashed right ankle, breast removal, hair cut, burn marks what did it all mean? Ed was no psychologist but the fact that the two murders were so close in time and method suggested one sick, heartless bastard that was on what he feared was the start of a serial killing spree. Both cases felt so open ended and pointless that his gut told him neither of them produced any closure for the killer.

The more he thought about it, the facts led him to believe the killer was more than likely a local with some sort of a grudge. He felt sure it was a male probably over 20 or 25 years of age with an ax to grind against doctors, correction against the plastic surgeon husbands of the victims.

That's where the motive logic stopped because they worked out of different hospitals, different towns and they had different specialties. Dr. Holden specialized in cosmetic surgeries, and Dr. Ackerman specialized more in reconstructive surgeries typically associated with accident victims.

The killer would have to be at least that old to be able to think of this sick scenario, let alone pull it off like he did without leaving anything behind for them to go on.

A smashed ankle pointed to an accident possibly. Breast removal pointed to cosmetic surgery he guessed but why two different doctors, from two different hospitals and from two different towns?

And what about the haircuts and four sets of burn marks? It all had to add up to something, but what?

When he got to the Evanston police department, Inspector Bill Weller met him and led him to his office where they spent several hours comparing notes and basically going in circles.

Bill said, "Ed this one has me pulling my hair out. This bastard must really think outside the box because nothing adds up. I've found one thing that I keep coming back to. It makes about as much sense as a fish needing a bicycle. You might check on this with the Ackerman security provider.

"The M.E. put Aimee's time of death at about 2:30 pm. The security company documents showed her disarming the home alarm system at 2:05 pm and then arming it again at 2:45 pm. After apparently being home for forty minutes, she sets the alarm and then is later found dead in the nursery by her husband four hours later at 6:45 pm when he got home. His alibi checks out. He was seeing patients all afternoon during the murder, and everyone I spoke to added more details that painted a picture of the perfect couple.

"No one can remember them talking about a fight, let alone having any kind of family problems. Everything I got on them points to the ideal couple. She happened to be pregnant, as Lisa Ackerman was, but there were no attacks on the unborn babies, so the pregnancy angle seems to be more a coincidence than motive related.

"There was no physical evidence of tampering with the security system, and the codes were entered flawlessly but I can't figure out why she waited forty minutes to set the alarm in the middle of the day while she was home."

"That is unusual," said Ed as he made a note; follow up with the Ackerman's security provider to see if there were any irregularities in the alarm code entry.

Bill said, "Ok. Here's the timeline we've assembled so far on the Holden murder: She left the house at 12:10 pm and set the alarm when she left. Aimee was seen on various security cameras at the grocery store between 12:30 pm and 1:00 pm and she had no contact with anyone anytime she appeared on the security tapes; she shopped like she was in no hurry and didn't look stressed out in any way. She exited the store at 1:00 pm, made a quick stop at her bank at 1:15 pm where she went inside to deposit some checks. She then withdrew $250.00 cash and again she appeared calm and normal on their security tapes. She left the bank at

1:20 pm. She then stopped at the local Caribou Coffee shop for a latte on her way home which was still in the car along with the groceries in the garage with the door closed. Then of course the alarm disarming at 2:05 pm and then curiously armed again at 2:45 pm. Robbery is out. The $250 was still in her purse."

"Any thoughts on why she armed the alarm system while she was home? Was that something she usually did?"

"Not according to her husband. He said they only armed the system when they left the house and at night before going to bed. Yet this time she armed the system while at home. Shortly after that she is found murdered in the nursery by Dr. Holden when he got home from work."

"We haven't been able to pin down an actual cause of death yet either. Like Lisa, she didn't bleed out after the field mastectomy. Aimee's was also made post mortem. She didn't have a look of alarm on her face or any indication of her trauma causing a heart attack. We found no drugs in her system. Just one mutilated, pretty, pregnant Doctor's wife that wound up very dead."

✻

The killer remained concealed outside the Ackerman residence watching Jim and Lori eating their late lunch with John.

'I know who the rest of them will be. I've done all the research I need to in order to get to them when I need to, but the timing still needs a great deal of consideration. It has to be perfect,' he thought.

The sequencing was crucial. All plans were made. He noted that they were excellent except for the timing, and it was almost worked out now. The key was in the simplicity of the method. How did the acronym go again? K.I.S.S. Kill—Individuals—Simply—Stupid.

He could see they were beginning to feel the type of pain he had over the past several months, but he was just getting started.

'Look at them, comforting each other. They have no idea what's coming next.' He knew! His plans were excellent. The simplicity is what made them perfect. The simpler the concept is, the fewer chances there will be for making mistakes. So far all they had was Andy and Barney working the case.

'They had never seen anything as flawless as this plan.'

It came to him on a very informative trip, to where else . . . . the drug capital of the world in South America! He was beginning to think it was providence that prompted his trip to get away and get his mind off the grieving. He wasn't even sure why he chose Columbia, but things just had a way of working out didn't they. There he found the cornerstone of his perfect plan.

'Andy and Barney would never figure it out; not in a million years.

'The next one will get them really thinking, so I have to be especially careful from now on!

'Andy and Barney will probably realize soon enough that they are in over their collective heads and get the Chicago BIS involved. If they aren't considering it yet, they will after the next one.'

He studied that group too. He knew how the Bureau of Investigative Services approached problems like the ones he was throwing at them.

The killer kept fine tuning his plan. He was pleased with the progress thus far and very excited about what was about to happen next.

CHAPTER 4

"I think it's time. I think it's the PERFECT time."

Friday, November 2nd, 2012

*I*nspector Weller decided that it would be best to, accompany Ed on his interview with Dr. Ackerman, and Ed was glad that he did. They were initially surprised to find the Baker's there.

"Good afternoon Dr. Ackerman, this is inspector Bill Weller from the Evanston police department. He's the inspector investigating the Aimee Holden situation and I've asked him to join us. We've both agreed to work together in catching your wife's assailant. I was under the impression that you would be alone this afternoon and I apologize to your guests but this will be more productive if Bill and I were able to speak to you alone."

"Jim and Lori are my best friends. I'm going to have to lean on them a lot, so I might as well start now. They have been helping me wrap my head around this so let's just get this done. And please, call me John."

"Very well John, if it's ok with you then its fine with us. John, Bill and I have reviewed the details in both our cases and they are remarkably similar in . . . ."

"So you think the same person is responsible for both murders then?" John asked.

"Yes that's the assumption we are going on. We have some questions we'd like to get to in a moment but first we'd like to just review the details and make sure we didn't miss anything. I didn't want to go too far with this last night out of respect for your grief."

"John, can you tell us if Lisa knew either Dr. Rick Holden or his wife Aimee?" asked Bill.

"I'm sure neither of us had met the Holdens or heard of them before the newscast two weeks ago."

"Any idea if a friend or relative may have had any associations with them?"

"Lisa and I have very few relatives in this area. Both my parents have passed away and Lisa's mom and sister live in central Florida and have never been to the Chicago area except to occasionally visit us," John replied.

"John, you and Jim here are part of an association of doctors that were recently written up in the paper. You call your group the 'Surgeon Generals'. Does the name have any special significance?" Bill asked.

"Not really. We just started jokingly referring to our collection of plastic surgeons by that name and it kind of stuck. The newspaper reporter that wrote the article about us got wind of it and used it for the title of the article. Our patients found it amusing and began referring to us using the name as well. It was like the old Mash movie coining the nickname 'The Pro's From Dover' but nothing really significant about it."

"We have to ask some sensitive questions as you can well imagine so here goes. How would you describe your relationship with Lisa?" Ed asked.

"It seems everything had just been getting better and better until yesterday. We have made a number of new friends and associates lately and were so looking forward to the arrival of little Johnny. Sorry, we were to going name our son after me." John got choked up and had to stop. Lori went to him and held him. "It's ok John. Let it out. We're here for you."

After a moment John continued, "Sorry inspector but our relationship couldn't have been better. We never fought. We spent every minute we could together doing things, planning things . . . . We just enjoyed each other's . . . . company."

"I'm sorry but we had to ask. Is there anything you can think of that might be at all helpful. We're sure you have been thinking about things intensely since yesterday. Have you received any letters of dissatisfaction from any patients or can you recall any difficult, angry or any particularly unsatisfied patients recently?" asked Ed.

"I'm pleased to say no."

"We understand Lisa didn't work, but did she belong to any committees or community groups? Was she responsible for anything like that where someone could have become disgruntled about something?"

"Lisa wasn't big on being involved in those things. She was never approached and never had the opportunity to turn anyone down," John said.

Jim asked, "Inspectors, do you have any leads or suspects?"

"To be honest with you this case is a tough one. The particulars are truly unique. We had hoped that you might have thought of something since we spoke last night having had a night to sleep on it, but no, in answer to both of your questions. No suspects yet. As you know the Cook County Medical Examiner has been assisting us in collecting the facts in both cases but what you don't know is we have reached out to Chicago's Bureau of Investigative Services to make use of their excellent crime lab facilities and computer data bases."

"We have taken enough of your time this afternoon. Thank you for your patience. We are truly sorry for your loss and we will catch the person responsible for your wife's murder."

"Thank you both. Please call me anytime if you think of any other questions."

"John, I have one other question before we leave. Was Lisa in the habit of setting the alarm when she was at home?"

"No. She set it when she left the house and when we go to bed at night. I'm usually up first and turn it off before I leave for work. Why?"

"We just found it strange that it was set while she was home yesterday that's all. Thanks John. We apologize for the disruption our CSI team has caused in your home. They will be back in the morning to finish their work upstairs, and you'll have your house back by noon the latest.

"Please speak to the rest of the 'Generals' about being extra aware and more diligent than usual with things like setting your alarms, locking doors and keeping in touch with spouses more than you usually would," Bill proposed.

"We'll do that inspector and thanks again. Please let me know as soon as there are any developments."

✻

Ed said to Bill on the way out to the car, "I'll call the security company in the morning and let you know what their records show. It's odd that they both set the alarm during the day while being home since both husbands have now confirmed it wasn't their norm."

*

'Well they have had quite the party in there this afternoon haven't they? We have the sad Dr. A, the supportive Dr. B, his pretty perfect little pregnant wifey and their new buddies Andy and Barney.

'I think it's time. I think it's the PERFECT time.

'What did that song talk about giving them? Oh yeah, a mystery to figure out.

'Actually, I think it's time to give them something to cry about! How about if we were to give it to them right now? Let's see how the Surgeon Generals stack up to the Surgeon Nemesis.'

CHAPTER 5

'. . . Amusement has no place here.'

<u>Saturday, November 3rd, 2012</u>

*T*he next morning after their meeting with the two investigators, Jim invited several of the 'Generals' to their home to fill them in on Lisa's murder.

Lori opened the door and welcomed Garrett Heaton and Blake Falkland each with a warm hug, took their coats and walked with them to the den where Jim was talking with Mark Channing and Keith Lawley. All of them were 'Generals'.

"Garrett, Blake, welcome. Come on in. Mark and Keith just got here as well. What would you like to drink?" Jim asked.

"On a cold fall day with the kind of news we all just got, I think some brandy would be good," said Garrett.

"Works for me as well," said Blake Falkland.

Lori, though very saddened by Lisa's death, tried to remain the perfect hostess. She was dressed in an ivory silk blouse, a rust colored sweater and matching slacks. She said, "I'll be right back guys, please make yourselves comfortable."

Mark started things off, "Jim what can you tell us? How's John?"

"John is about as you'd expect. He's devastated. He's still trying to come to grips with Lisa and the baby being taken from him. The investigators assigned to the case and to the other similar murder two weeks ago in Evanston met with John, Lori and me yesterday. While they seem to be piecing together a lot of similarities between the two cases, there appears to be no reliable leads or connections between the victims so far.

"They're working under the assumption that the cases are related, and are pretty sure that both women were victims of the same killer. There are just too many similarities for them not to be."

"What kind of similarities? There was very little in the way of details in the news reports we saw. They only mentioned the possibility of mutilations," said Blake Falkland.

"Well this is really the most difficult part for John to deal with. Lisa's body was mutilated. Guys, this killer is one sick bastard. Both women were found in their homes, with doors locked and alarms set and no signs of forced entry or footprints around the houses. Both women were found in their nurseries naked with no look of shock or pain on their faces. They were found just laying there mutilated."

"Jim, please. Tell us. How were they mutilated?" asked Mark.

"Both women had their left breast removed post mortem, fine burn marks around both eyes and up and down the left side of their bodies; their hair was cut short like a man's would be cut, and their right ear lobe was partially cut off. Most of it appears to have been made post mortem. Guys it was just terrible. This meeting is not only to familiarize you with the facts of the case; I also wanted to pass along specific warnings from the inspectors. They would like us to be extra careful with safety as both cases involved the wives of local plastic surgeons.

"We also need to free up sometime in our schedules to include John's patients for a while. He's going to need some time off after the funeral."

Lori came in with refreshments for everyone as Keith said, "That won't be a problem. We'll all help cover the appointments for him."

Mark asked, "When is the funeral?"

"It will be on Monday," said Lori.

They talked for a while longer reflecting on their memories of Lisa and all vowed to be extra careful in the coming days until the killer was caught.

Jim & Lori went to see a feel good movie on Sunday that didn't quite work for them. They were trying to get their minds off Lisa's murder by spending a very close weekend comforting each other.

Monday, November 5th, 2012

On Monday; the weather had turned bitter cold for Lisa's funeral services. Lisa's mom and sister insisted on coming to Chicago to stay with John for a few days and together they decided on a closed casket.

The article on Lisa's death contained all the funeral arrangements. A great many friends and patients that thought so highly of John came to the services to lend support for his loss. At the services, the 'Generals' learned that John was going to spend two weeks in Florida with Lisa's mom and sister to get away from the house for awhile. What they didn't learn was that one of the guests at the funeral was getting a first-hand look at the entire team of 'Generals' and their wives.

✲

He knew them all by sight. He knew all their names due to the article written last July.

'Look at them, all in one place. How tempting it is to wait outside and finish them all off at one time, but no, where's the personal suffering in that? This needs to be drawn out and painful for them as it was for me,' he thought.

Everything was going according to plan. He carefully left them clueless. He knew that once they got a high enough level of forensics resources involved, they'd probably figure out how he was able to perform the murders so easily.

He hoped to be done with his retribution by then.

Every murder he committed seemed to be appeasing the anger he felt toward that despicable group of self indulged twits just a little more. As he reflected on this simple fact, he knew he was doing the best thing for her. Yes, she was gone. Yes, she had suffered horribly. He would never forget her. Her soft touch and never ending desire to please.

He would always miss her being in his life. That hole, that enormous hole that was left in his life would be avenged.

Plans that had been perfected were being continuously fine tuned. Items that Andy and Barney hadn't even thought of yet were being tweaked to stay even further ahead of what their simple little inexperienced minds could conceive. They had so little actual experience in solving crimes bigger than missy's stolen tricycle or getting aunt Bee's cat out of the local maple tree.

It had been so easy to stay ahead of them that he almost considered dropping a misleading clue to watch them go in even bigger circles, but, 'no, let's not get sloppy. Amusement has no place here,' he reminded himself.

This is serious business. Dates, sequence, items needed for the crime scene and the method of execution were all meticulously planned and so far executed flawlessly. He refused to distract himself with petty amusement. There would be plenty of time for reflection after everything was finished here.

Columbia would be his home for a year after he was done here. After all, there was nothing left for him here now that the love of his life had been taken from him. He may just open a new business down there for a while after he had a chance to settle in. He could also toy with the locals for amusement. They are so laid back and backward there that toying with the peasants would probably yield plenty of fulfillment to appease his need for continued amusement. Especially watching their local yokels try to keep up with him through it all. After all, he was beginning to enjoy the execution of the revenge quest he was on.

Maybe after he continued on to Greece he might try his hand again if his need for appeasement returned.

For now, the Nemesis hungered for more appeasement here.

CHAPTER 6

"I never felt so dirty getting clean."

Tuesday, November 6th, 2012

*I*t was time for the rest of them to return to their regular routines.

Jim went back to his practice and like many of the others; he took on many of John's patients until he returned from Florida.

Under these extreme circumstances, John had agreed allow Inspector Ed Cassidy to see a summary of patient files so the inspectors could review current procedures and results with the promise of maintaining confidentiality in the eyes of the patients. As long as patient names were kept confidential, he could see no harm in assisting them in this unconventional way and felt the backgrounds might provide a lead on a potential suspect.

Inspector Bill Weller, however, wasn't having the same luck with Dr. Holden. He refused any information on patients and insisted that his judgment on patient satisfaction would have to suffice.

The neighborhood canvasses had produced nothing, and Bill had hoped for more cooperation from Dr. Holden. He had an uncomfortable feeling about his lack of cooperation but understood the doctor's reasoning behind it. He had to respect his doctor-patient confidentiality. He was actually surprised at the amount of information that Dr. Ackerman was willing to give to Ed Cassidy. Even though it produced no leads thus far, it showed a tremendous amount of faith in his patient's satisfaction with his work.

The last few days turned out to be thankfully uneventful. Everything had settled back down into regular routines with a few exceptions. The 'Generals' and their wives took to heart the advice given to them by the police. They made every attempt to be more in touch and aware; looking for anything out of the ordinary or even slightly suspicious.

Wednesday, November 7ᵗʰ, 2012

On Wednesday, Lori was reflecting on John and Lisa's lives together, having been cut short like they were, and decided that she would do something special for Jim. She was feeling wonderful and blessed to have their futures to look forward to, so she decided to prepare one of Jim's favorite meals and have a special night together. He was a steak and potatoes kind of guy and always said he can get that anywhere, but a home cooked meal was special to him. He had simple tastes. He wasn't big on fancy meals that took a long time to prepare and pronounce. So she decided on a meal consisting of meatloaf, corn on the cob and garlic mashed potatoes with home-made buttermilk dinner rolls. She enjoyed baking for Jim because he appreciated it as much as he did. The dinner preparations in the kitchen smelled good along with the cinnamon and apple scents from the home-made apple pie she baked for dessert.

She put out her best dishes, wine for him, sparkling apple cider for her, champagne glasses, table cloth and matching napkins. The chilled bottle of champagne she had on hand and the bouquet of flowers she picked up that afternoon nestled in a pretty vase finished the setting just perfectly.

Dinner wound up being easily well timed since Jim now called regularly to check up on her and to let her know when he would be home. She did the same; calling him to let him know every where she planned to go and when she expected to be home.

When Jim came home from work, the lights were turned down low. Dinner needed a half hour more to finish cooking and Lori had some soft romantic music playing.

Even though she was seven months pregnant, she waited for him in the bedroom, poised on their king-sized poster bed dressed only in a sheer black teddy with light beige lace trim and a smile.

"Are you too tired to perform one more exam doctor?" she teased.

"Not at all," he said. "And I don't think I'll need my little black bag for this house call."

She was a welcome sight after an extra long day's work. His days were going to remain longer until John got back to work. Neither of them minded helping John out while he got some much needed time away.

Jim looked around and saw the work she put into preparing the evening and her playful smile.

"Dinner won't be ready for at least a half hour. Is that enough time to determine my state of health?" she asked coyly.

He quickly got more comfortable and answered all her questions without saying a word.

Dinner was delicious and afterward Lori suggested they get away this weekend to relax at the cabin and give him a chance to unwind after his week of unusually long work days.

"That's a great idea hon. I'll take off work early Friday afternoon; we can head up there and spend Friday night through Sunday afternoon at the cabin. I'm not sure how much skinny dipping we'll be doing this time of year but quiet evenings with my favorite mommy to be, a nice fire, the smell of fresh popcorn, watching a movie or two while cuddling under a warm quilt for an evening or two sounds like the perfect way to unwind after a hectic week."

Saturday, November 10th, 2012

It turned out to be a great weekend. They hadn't been up to the cabin since the just after the 4th of July.

The leaves had all fallen from the trees but the area was still secluded and they took a nice long leisurely walk along the lake, through the woods and to their favorite cave.

They brought some chairs up to the cave last summer. On this hike, Jim carried a back pack with a couple of blankets, some snacks and apple cider. In her condition, the chairs were very welcome as she was tired, and the baby was very active during the entire walk.

Jim made a small fire just outside the cave and they snacked, drank cider and talked about the baby until the sun went down.

It was a little spooky getting back to the cabin but they followed their familiar path and found it with no trouble. They fell back into the cabin laughing, hugging, kissing and ultimately stripping on their way to the shower. The warm water removed the chill they brought back with them from the hike and she exited the shower with the cleanest back and cleanest everything else that Jim could give her.

Before she went to start up the popcorn, she left Jim a little message on the mirror. When he came out he smiled at the mirror. In between the two hearts she wrote, "I never felt so dirty getting clean."

They didn't make it halfway through the popcorn or the first movie before falling asleep in each other's arms on the couch. The abundance of fresh country air from their extended exercise throughout the day eventually emerged victorious in their battle to remain awake until the end of even one movie.

Sunday, November 11th, 2012

Sunday morning was bright and sunny. It really was beautiful at the cabin but after a simple breakfast they decided to straighten up, cover the furniture and pack up the cabin for winter. They would head back home early and grab some lunch on the way. This would allow Jim time to relax for awhile after the four hour drive, insuring that he would be rested for what promised to be an unusually long and trying week of surgery and seeing patients.

✧

The Nemesis had quite the extensive log on the actions of the 'Generals' and their wives, their schedules and their practices. He had been collecting this kind of information for the past six months since she died. It somehow appeased his need for revenge to be inching closer to the perfect plan. The gathering of critical bits of information that allowed him to continue executing the pain he intended to inflict on the targeted doctors definitely seemed to smooth out the rough edges of his anger. That intense anger he carried with him all the time lately, could cause him to rush toward another milestone. Instead, he wanted to apply the tact and discipline necessary to remain one step ahead of Andy, Barney and their new growing community of crime professionals.

He knew who went shopping when, who took kids to school, and who picked them up, who went to church and who didn't. He had charted each wife's actions meticulously.

While their impromptu little trip out of town was unexpected, it didn't impact his plans at all. He knew Doctor B and his wife would get back to their routines. He would return to his medical practice, to helping out good ole Doctor A and she would return to the weekly routine that never seemed to change.

Monday: stay at home (probably soap operas and bon bons) (Done, check)
Tuesday: house cleaning (probably more soap operas and bon bons) (Done, check)
Wednesday: laundry and maybe a little yard work (afternoon more soap operas and bon bons)
(Done, check)
Thursday: it's time to start our new schedule of bi-monthly appointments at the OB GYN.
(And of course it was shopping day in the afternoon afterward.)
(Blah, blah, blah)

'How did that old song go?
I believe it was something about 'time coming today.'

CHAPTER 7

'Why was he doing this to these pretty young women?'

Thursday, November 15th, 2012

*L*ori picked up the ringing phone. The caller ID showed 'Dr. Rittenhouse'.

She answered, "Baker residence, Lori speaking."

"Good morning Lori, this is Dr. Rittenhouse's office. This is just a reminder about your appointment this morning."

"Yes, I'll be there. It's getting close now and exciting. I'll see you at 10:00 am."

She felt really good and couldn't wait to check on Melissa's progress to confirm that everything was ok after their semi-strenuous weekend at the cabin. All the advice she had received told her to pretty much continue with regular routines but to avoid anything overly strenuous or "bumpy".

After a quick shower, Lori put on her new gray and white loose fitting top trimmed in pink with black slacks and reasonable shoes. Jim had picked out the outfit on an impromptu shopping stop last Sunday and she couldn't wait to wear it. All the moms-to-be wore unique outfits for their visits to the upscale doctor's office trying to win the casual glance competition in the waiting room.

"Jim, don't forget I start my bi-monthly doctor's appointments today. I'm going to drop off the dogs for their annual teeth cleaning before my appointment and then I have some grocery shopping to do this afternoon; I should be home by two o'clock."

"Thanks for calling babe. I didn't forget. Call me afterwards. I can't wait to hear how great Melissa's doing. Hopefully we didn't overdo it last weekend."

"Yeah, and the hike was strenuous too!"

"I love you Lori. Talk to you this afternoon. Bye, Bye."

✻

At 2:30 Jim asked his secretary if she had heard from Lori yet and she replied, "No, nothing since her phone call this morning."

This wasn't like her, so he called her cell phone and got no answer. Then he called home and got their answering machine message: "You've reached the Baker's. If we aren't answering the phone, we are either out of the house or playing house. Leave a message, and we'll get back to you when we can. {Giggle} 'Jim, stop'. Bye-bye!"

He became very worried very quickly. "Angie, I need to step out for about an hour, late lunch. Please ask Dr. Reed to cover my three pm appointment."

"Will do Doctor Baker," said his receptionist.

✿

He couldn't get home fast enough. When he arrived, he saw Lori's car pulled around back in the carport. He went in the rear entrance and was greeted by the alarm warning beeps. Something didn't feel right at all. He keyed in the alarm code disarming the security system and began to panic.

"Lori? Honey are you home?" he ran upstairs and found her lying on the floor in the nursery.

His worst fears confirmed.

"OH, MY GOD NO!"

"LORI, LORI . . . LORI!"

He reached for her but stopped. She looked so peaceful, so unbothered by everything he now saw and smelled in the nursery.

This was Lisa all over again! Aimee Holden all over again! "No, No, NO, LORI NO!"

Jim collapsed to his knees in shock. This wasn't real. At first he refused to believe what he was seeing and began to sob uncontrollably. "Lori, Lori, Lori, honey, my god, not you too."

As much as he wanted to pick her up and hug her, he resisted.

His whole world had just changed. He couldn't think of what to do next, so he sat there crying uncontrollably for how long he didn't know. He had to call the police. He couldn't call the police. That would mean that this was all real. It couldn't be real. Was it true that Lori and Melissa were both gone? If he didn't call, it wasn't real. It wasn't real. This wasn't real.

None of it . . . . but it was. He knew now that it was real. He had to make the call. He knew now that he had to make the call.

"Winnetka police department 911; what's your emergency?"

Jim said, "It's my wife. She's dead. Someone killed my wife, and she's dead. My baby is dead. They're both dead. Please come quickly,", then he let the phone slip from his hands to the floor. He heard the operator somewhere off in the distance or perhaps it was his imagination. It didn't matter; he couldn't hear the words themselves anyway. He was a doctor. He recognized it. He was in shock!

He knelt down next to Lori and let his emotions go. He was there when the police arrived. He barely noticed them. He was numb, in a trance. He was numb and shaking.

✲

Inspector Ed Cassidy was notified to respond to the 911 call at the Baker residence at 3:30 pm and arrived there by 3:50pm. The scene was organized chaos. The crime scene tape was being spread around the perimeter of the Baker property; the M.E. was just going into the house as a female police officer was leading Dr. Jim Baker to a living room chair and attempting to calm him down. His initial shock had turned to anger by now. He was now beyond livid. He told the officer, "You'd better find him first because if I do there won't be a trial!"

Ed went to him and attempted to calm him down. "Dr. Baker, please don't talk like that. We know you are upset, but you've got to trust that we'll do our jobs. We will find this bastard, and he will pay for this."

Jim replied, "There isn't a price big enough for him to pay that would bring back Lori and the baby." Then trying to make sense of the murder he asked, "Why is he hurting innocent women Ed? Why? He clearly has some sort of problem with us doctors. Why not go after us? What's his problem? What could Lori or I have done to deserve this?"

"Doctor, you're trying to make sense out of the senseless act of a coward. I know that doesn't help much, but there is no logic that will comfort you thru this. This person is a heartless killer, and there is no good reason for any of this.

"Do you have any sedatives in the house, Jim?"

He nodded his head in the direction of the downstairs bathroom.

"Please get the doctor some water and check out the bathroom for something to help him calm down a little while I go upstairs," Ed instructed the officer looking after Jim.

At the top of the stairs in the nursery, he found an all too familiar scene waiting for him. In the middle of the floor lying face up, naked and mutilated was Jim Baker's pretty wife Lori. What made the scene in the nursery especially bizarre was the utterly peaceful look on her pretty mutilated face. The open eyes missing any hint of pain or distress and those damn burn marks around her eyes and the smell of burning flesh!

'Why was he doing this to these pretty young women? Why was he doing this to any of them and how was he getting to them AND getting away so clean? 'Hell,' Ed thought, 'while we're at it, are we even sure it's a 'he'. It could be a 'she' I guess, but I doubt it.'

He looked around briefly knowing what he would find. Sure enough, like in the other two cases, he found Lori's outfit folded neatly with her hair that had been cut off, resting on top of it, all in the unborn baby's crib. She had such radiant blonde hair that was always pulled back making her look so classy. Now it was chopped off and discarded like some no longer needed article of clothing. On top of the clothing and hair was her left breast just like at the Ackerman crime scene. Nothing else in the room seemed to have been disturbed in any way. The room was impeccably decorated and orderly with not a chair or bed spread out of place or visibly disturbed. The windows were locked from the inside and the curtains were neat and perfectly in place. There were no drag marks on the carpet so she must have died right where she laid and once again there was some blood but the volume was very minimal for such a violation to the human body. The mastectomy trauma was once again seemingly made post mortem.

How were such violent acts being performed with no visible disturbance at the crime scenes?

This guy needs to go down! He needs to go down hard, and Ed vowed that he would be the one to do it.

There wasn't much else he could do here, so he went down to talk to Jim.

"Jim, do you feel up to a few questions and a statement?"

Jim replied, "Ed I'm so pissed right now that . . . . Ask me anything you want. We need to find this son of a bitch before he does this to anyone else."

As fast as his anger had risen, it now left him just as fast. Then Jim's resolve cracked and he just broke down. Ed spent some time with him and waited before asking any questions giving the sedative a chance to do its job.

*

The reporters were beginning to amass outside along with the neighborhood curiosity seekers. He recognized Susan Peterson from Channel 7 news outside starting to give her report when he turned his attention back to Dr. Jim Baker.

"Jim, tell me what you can about today."

He told the inspector about Lori calling to let him know she was dropping the dogs off at the vet before going to her bi-monthly maternity appointment, her planned trip to the grocery store, her promise to call him around 2:00 pm, his concern after his last patient had left at 2:30 pm without his having heard from Lori yet, and the rest of it leading up to finding Lori.

"Have you touched anything in here? Also was the door secure when you got home?"

"As much as I wanted to, I didn't touch anything. When I got home her car was where it is now, the back door was locked, and the alarm warning went off when I opened the door. I entered the code to shut it off and started feeling sick. Then I went upstairs and found her."

"That's enough for now. I'll come back in the morning. Jim do you want to call anyone or go stay with anyone for tonight?"

"I don't know right now. I can't think. I probably will need some calls made in a while. I don't feel like talking to anyone tonight. This has to sink in some first."

"The CSI unit will be working upstairs, downstairs and outside for a couple more hours, then the M.E. will take Lori's body out. I can stay if you'd like some company."

"Thanks Ed but I just need to absorb this by myself for tonight. I guess I do need you to make a couple calls for me after all. I really can't call Lori's parents with this news right now but they should know as soon as possible. I'll also need you to call my brother Jerry and ask him to break the news to my dad. Tell them I'll call in the morning and there is nothing they can do tonight. Also call Ray Reed. He's one of the doctors in our group. He will inform the rest of them. There's a phone book on the desk next to the phone in the den."

Ed made the difficult calls for Jim and left him to his grief over Lori's murder.

CHAPTER 8

'Oh! Looky there. Time for lunch.'

<u>*Friday, November 16th, 2012*</u>

The self-proclaimed "Nemesis" reviewed his extensive logs full of information on the 'Generals', their wives and their activities, schedules and habits. The time he had spent gathering, disseminating, and organizing this information was paying off as he continuously reshaped the ideal strategy to exact his revenge. He was amazed at how the simplicity of his plan had Andy and Barney so baffled and also how rewarding it was personally.

He had nothing but disdain for his targets within the 'Generals' and no remorse for their wives. The decision to turn up the heat and not give them time to fully react to Lori Baker's demise came to him as he watched the TV cameras being put away after this evenings news cast from the Baker's front yard.

✻

Isabella Channing had just dropped her son off at school the morning after Lori's murder and stopped at the local Starbuck's for her favorite coffee, caffé mocha and a blueberry muffin.

As she sat down in the only open seat, next to a man reading a book, she was distracted by the plans they had for a birthday party tomorrow afternoon for their son Mikey. He was doing so well in the second grade this year and she wanted to reward him with an exceptional party.

The man next to her got up and held a piece of paper out to her with some writing on it, caught her attention, and began asking for directions to the post office. Before she could respond, he sneezed. She gave him, unknowingly, the most inappropriate response possible, "Bless you," and began with the directions. Halfway through them he interrupted her and said to her, "Isabella, look at me as if you see forever in my eyes and smile."

She immediately did so without even thinking. In fact, she didn't think anything on her own for the rest of her life which wound up being a very short period of time.

✧

Dr. Raymond Reed didn't get around to calling all of the 'Generals' last night after hearing about Lori's murder. There were six more to call this morning. Not wanting to pass off the breaking of such terrible news to his secretary, he had decided to make all the calls himself throughout the morning, in between appointments.

After his 10:00 am appointment; his last call was to Dr. Mark Channing, who was seeing a patient at the time, so he left a message with his receptionist to have him call back.

"Hello Ray, it's Mark what's up?"

"I hate to be the bearer of bad news Mark but . . . it's Lori Baker, Mark. Jim found her yesterday pretty much like Lisa was found. It appears to me that there is a psycho on the loose and he seems to be targeting the wives of doctors in the area."

"First Lisa, now Lori? Ray what's this all about? It can't be about the girls. The common thread has to be us somehow but what could it be?"

"No Mark, first Dr. Rick Holden's wife Aimee, then Lisa and now Lori. This is no coincidence. It's definitely about us doctors and I can't imagine what could trigger this kind of confusion.

"Mark, call Isabella and make sure she stays extra careful for the time being."

"I will Ray thanks. Man I feel terrible for Jim. Lori was due in January wasn't she? I can't believe how ripped up he's got to be right now. Is there anything we can do for him?"

"There's nothing we can do right now. Mark we must do everything we can to keep our wives safe."

"I'll call Isabella right now and give her the news about poor Lori, and thanks again Ray."

✧

The Nemesis was just about to set the house alarm on his way out the back door of the Channing home on 14 Oak Lane when the phone rang. He decided to stay and listen to the message that would be left by the caller.

'I'll bet this is the charming Dr. C. calling to speak to Mrs. C. Problem is, she can't come to the phone right now but you'll figure that out soon enough,' he said to himself.

"Honey it's me pick up . . . . Izzie are you there?"

'Oh she's here alright but she's not picking up anything anymore doc. In fact, you better pick up the kid because she's going to have a little trouble driving to the school to get him this afternoon in her current condition.'

"Izzie when you get this please call me right away. I'll try you on your cell", said Mark as he ended his message.

'Well doc, it's been fun but . . . gotta run. Oh! Looky there. Time for lunch.'

He reset the house alarm as he left, then locked the rear door and at a safe distance from the house, he made a few adjustments to what he was wearing then walked several blocks to his car. It was now time to pick up some lunch and reflect on his busy morning that had just brought him one step closer to his retribution goal.

*

After trying Isabella's cell phone Mark became worried. Especially after the news Ray just had given him about Lori this morning. This wasn't like his wife at all.

Ever since Lisa's murder, they had been staying in very close contact on the advice of the police investigating her death.

He decided to call his next door neighbor. Isabella said she planned to visit her this morning after dropping the kids off to school. They were both coordinating Mikey's birthday party tomorrow. She must be there and probably left her cell phone at home.

"Georgia? It's Mark. Are you and Izzie going over the last minute birthday party plans?"

"No Mark, but I believe we will be shortly. I've been waiting for her to come over. I saw her car pull around back about 9:30 but she hasn't come over yet. She told me she'd be here no later than 10:00 am."

"Thanks Georgia. I'll try the house."

Now Mark suddenly felt panic rising through him like a storm swell lifting a ship at sea. She was home when he called and she didn't answer the phone. After what happened to Lisa and Lori, Mark called the police, briefly telling them his concerns and then he raced home.

The police were there when he arrived and were looking around the outside of the house. Having heard no response after ringing the bell, they then checked the front and rear doors. Both were secure.

"Officers, I'm Dr. Mark Channing."

"Hello Dr. Channing. Your wife's car is out back, but she's not answering the door. The house is secure. Please open the door and let us check out the house before you enter."

Mark unlocked the rear door and the alarm began to sound its warning to disarm. After entering the security system's code, he stepped aside and let the officers enter to examine the house. Two minutes later one of them came down and didn't need to say anything. Mark's worst fears were confirmed by the expression on the cop's face.

All he said was, "Dr. Channing, you'd better sit down. I'm afraid we have some very bad news."

CHAPTER 9

"It's Déjà vu all over again."

<u>**Friday, November 16th, 2012**</u>

*I*nspector Ed Cassidy was reviewing his crime board. He wanted it updated when Bill Weller came over this afternoon. A large blown up map of the North Shore area dominated the board. He had highlighted the Evanston murder site and the two Winnetka murder sites, numbered and connected the dots looking for any patterns. He had police reports, murder scene photos with time lines all captured there.

Over to one side he listed a number of threads that were common to all three murders:

1. Wives of plastic surgeons.
2. Murdered and found in their home.
3. Identical mutilations—mostly postmortem.
4. No apparent signs of a struggle in the house.
5. House alarms set and doors secure with the murdered wives in the house.
6. No trauma expressions on their faces.
7. Tox screens were negative.
8. Husband's all had alibis—their devastation appears real.
9. No histories of domestic violence.
10. No forensic evidence of anyone but the husband and wife at the crime scenes.
11. Nothing suspicious in spouse background checks.
12. No indications of robbery.
13. Cars, groceries etc. abandoned on premises.
14. No apparent motive or cause of death.
15. No suspects.

He and Bill had focused on the husbands first. They ran the usual background checks, looked for recent increases insurance policies, bank accounts, etc. but there were none of the usual indicators of foul play. Ed had ruled out the husbands themselves. It was remotely possible, but not likely, that they could have started some sort of murder club and were assisting each other in this killing spree. But no, everything truly pointed to their being loving-grieving husbands.

Plastic surgeons weren't like heart transplant surgeons. They were enhancement type doctors not life and death doctors. Not that they couldn't have pissed off the wrong kind of patient. The scope of retribution here was much larger than what would seem justified by a botched nose job.

The motive was eluding him especially with no insight from Dr. Holden's patient backgrounds. Something there probably had more to do with motive than anywhere else. After all, this extreme behavior was initially directed there. What could have pissed off or in any other way motivated this sick individual to wreak the havoc that he or she was to these obviously innocent women. He made a mental note to go at Dr. Holden again for his records.

As Bill arrived for their meeting, the phone rang at Ed's desk.

"Inspector Cassidy," he answered as he waved Bill in. "I see. We'll be right there.

"Don't take your coat off Bill. There's just been another murder. Dr. Mark Channing's wife Isabella was just found in their home. Bill it's the same M.O. all over again. This just gets crazier by the minute."

"Looks like another long night Ed. I have a few ideas we can talk about on the way to the Channing's."

*

In the car Bill said that, in his last conversation, the M.E. confirmed that she could find no needle marks on any of the three bodies. They were all seen in public, minutes before their deaths, so she was ruling out drugging of the wives by injection or oral intake to gain control of them. Also, something else didn't quite make sense. He reread the article on the 'Generals' written last summer and noticed that the doctors were listed in alphabetical order and so far Lisa Ackerman, Lori Baker and now Isabella Channing had been killed in alphabetical order. Could his pattern be this transparent? The alphabetical angle, however, didn't explain the first victim Aimee Holden. She didn't fit the pattern at all. In fact, her husband wasn't one of the 'Generals'. Of recent anyway, the wives of the 'Generals' seemed to be being taken out in order.

"Ed, all three victims were pregnant so far. I'm wondering if that's another connection we'll find to the others with Isabella Channing."

"It's something we'll know soon enough. Let's go meet another devastated doctor."

*

They arrived at the Channing's 14 Oak Lane home to yet another all too familiar crime scene involving yet another pretty, young, naked and mutilated wife of a plastic surgeon. Ed was thinking that there has never been this much activity, more accurately this much murder activity, in his quiet little north shore suburb's history. It was amazing how quickly a community's identity can change.

Flashing lights, crime scene tape, M.E.'s van, camera crews and nosy neighbors were a combination that he was seeing too much of lately. What was waiting in the house for him and Bill would be as well. He felt like he really didn't need to see the murder scene, didn't want to see the murder scene again.

He wasn't looking forward to the smell of burned flesh that was present at each crime scene so far. He couldn't imagine being one of the doctors finding not only their mutilated wives, but also to have that smell in the air. That had to have made it especially horrific for them.

The reason he was able to endure what he knew was waiting for him at the crime scene was the possibility that maybe this time there would be a clue. Maybe this time the killer would have slipped up enough finally to leave them something so they could start going somewhere in this case besides the next house and the next victim.

As they approached the Channing home, they could hear Susan Peterson who had become the reporter exclusively covering this story. ". . . Winnetka police don't like to use the words but these murders can only be described as serial killings. Serial killings are indicated by typically three or more murders with similar modus operandi. There has also been what the police define as a requisite cooling off period in between all of the murders. All of the customary indications of a serial killer, or killers, have been observed in these recent homicide cases. The holidays will be a much lonelier; a much sadder and quieter place this year in four north shore doctor's homes. This is Susan Peterson reporting live from the Channing residence in Winnetka for Channel 7 news."

Ed walked into the house and as he expected, there she was, another pretty doctor's wife lying naked and mutilated with that horrible smell of burning flesh in the air. All he could think of was an old Yogi Berra saying, "It's Déjà vu all over again."

✿

Well there's Andy and Barney now! My but they are a prompt couple. They remain a prompt and clueless couple. Even they must be starting to catch on to a bit of my pattern by now.

I'm thinking it would be prudent to lay low for a while before I confuse them a bit more. There's nothing more rewarding than confusing that crack investigating team from the north shore by leading them down the wrong beaten path.

I think it's time for a break. Perhaps it's time for another leave of absence and a trip to my favorite little drug capital, Columbia.

His drug habits weren't getting any worse, but they certainly weren't getting any better either. The Nemesis had found that a line or two of cocaine took the edge off his anger which got out of hand without it. He couldn't afford to get too emotional about what he still had to accomplish in the revenge arena.

A little R & R completely away from things would be best. He was looking forward to the thrill of staying ahead of what he was sure would be increasingly resourceful members of the law enforcement community. After all, it was becoming rather boring being pitted only against Andy and Barney. He wanted to make sure his next moves were especially well thought out because the rules were about to change due to too much current repetition.

He expected increased surveillance on a number of the doctor's homes due to the way he constructed his pattern of selecting the wives. Misdirection is an excellent tool for a serial killer. He enjoyed the thought as he reflected on how predictable the simplistic minds of inexperienced inspectors could be.

✻

Saturday, November 17th, 2012

Inspector Bill Weller's meeting on Saturday with Dr. Holden started out about as expected. Neither the mounting body count, the horrific pattern that kept repeating nor the cooperation of the other doctors in maintaining their doctor—patient confidentiality while providing background information seemed to faze him at all. He remained steadfast in his refusal to give any patient information.

"Doctor Holden, while we certainly respect the privacy of your patients, Inspector Cassidy and I feel strongly that there must be something you could give us to help prevent this string of horrible murders from increasing. Please try to remember how you felt when you discovered Aimee. The terrible loss you felt. The same feeling of emptiness is now being shared with three other doctors in the city at an especially bad time of year. How many more beautiful, young, innocent, doctor's wives need to be mutilated with their lives cut short before you'll give us some cooperation here Doc?" asked Bill Weller.

"I don't want this to continue. I just don't see how I can reveal my patient records and maintain their confidentiality. If handled incorrectly, it could ruin my practice."

"Doctor, please consult with Doctors Ackerman, Baker and Channing as to how we managed their interests. We feel strongly that there must be something that can help us since it all began with Aimee. We are confident this isn't about the wives. There could be something in your patient records that could help stop this madness. Please help us any way you can."

"I will call the other doctors to see if there is a way I can provide you with patient case information in a way that won't jeopardize my practice or my patient's confidence in my practice."

"Thank you Doctor. That's all we can ask. Please do it fast for the sake of the other wives."

Part Two

Lori's Essence

*"There are other forces at work in the world Frodo
besides the will of evil.
And that is an encouraging thought."*
Lord of the Rings—Gandalf

CHAPTER 10

Everything that is, except . . . 'The Flowers'.

Sunday, November 18th, 2012

*L*ori's funeral services were held on Sunday and consisted of a short wake with a closed casket. It was very somber especially in light of the murder of Isabella Channing only one day after Jim found Lori in their nursery.

There were only 17 of the 'Generals' in attendance as John Ackerman hadn't returned from Florida yet and Jim certainly understood when his friend Mark sent his condolences. He was he just too devastated over Isabella's murder to attend Lori's services. It was too soon. He couldn't face everyone yet. The remaining 'Generals' tried to comfort Jim to no avail. This was all just insane. There wasn't sufficient time to reflect and mourn one heart break before being forced to focus on the next one.

The sorrowful looks from one person, after another, after another, was almost more than he could bear.

After the gut wrenching moments that followed his final separation from Lori at the cemetery chapel, he went home to mourn with Lori's mother Beth and her sister Jenny. There simply weren't words that they could give to each other. They had a simple dinner then held each other and cried well into the night.

Monday, November 19th, 2012

Monday morning's dismal overcast skies did little to lift anyone's spirits as Beth and Jenny tearfully started their trip home to Florida. Promising to return in two weeks to help with the packing up of Lori's things they said their goodbyes and headed for the airport.

Jim heard the phone ring and wasn't in the mood to talk to anyone so he let the answering machine pick up. It was Ray Reed, "Jim, just calling to see if you needed anything; . . . a shoulder to lean on, or just a friend to keep you company for a while. Hey, just call if there is anything I can do for you buddy. Take care." Still too saddened and in a daze, Jim sent him a text back thanking him but declined. His dad and brother stopped by before they returned home to northern Wisconsin. After they left he started packing for an extended trip to the cabin.

He knew it wouldn't do a thing to get his mind off of Lori but he just couldn't stay in the house where it happened any longer for now. No matter what he sprayed in the nursery, he swore he could still smell her burned flesh in the air. He had to get away to clear his mind and try to start putting it all behind him.

As he was on his way out the phone rang. It was odd because he could only hear the upstairs phone ring. None of the downstairs phones reflected the impending call, then the upstairs phone stopped before he could begin his ascent to answer it. Dismissing it as an electronic burp of some sort he packed the car and headed up to the cabin.

✻

The aroma of grilled burgers was in the air as he passed their favorite diner three miles before reaching the cabin. The entrance to Jake's Sky Diner was at the top of sixteen steps designed to resemble the air stairs seen at most smaller airports. They led up to the diner which was shaped like an old world war two bomber. It was complete with a two engine wing section and with glass gun turrets on top, front and underneath. Next to the star on the side was the slogan 'Home of the Hangerburger'.

Both his mouth watering and stomach gurgling reminded him that he had skipped breakfast. Climbing the stairs and holding on to the hand-hold chain, he caught himself reaching out for Lori's hand to make sure she didn't lose her balance on the way up. Inside the diner was like a museum crowded with memorabilia and scaled versions of the fighter planes from that era. The surroundings soon blurred from sight through the tears that welled in his eyes. He was seeing her sitting across from the table as she had last summer. She looked great wearing that yellow and white striped shorts outfit that so reflected her sunny disposition. He couldn't shake the image of her movie star beautiful face, million dollar smile and the love she had for him that was always there in her eyes.

The trip to the local supermarket to stock up on groceries after lunch dampened his spirits more than the diner. They always enjoyed shopping together and as the cart began to fill he could envision her playfully skipping and twirling up and down the aisles as she tempted him with her meal plans. She loved to cook for him and was always surprising him with new recipes.

Once he arrived at the cabin, everything there also reminded him of Lori because she did most of the decorating and her warm homey touches were everywhere. Was this trip going to be a good idea? As much as it all reminded him of Lori, he realized it would be this way everywhere he went for a long time.

He understood that going through Lori's personal items back home was going to be nearly impossible. This realization came to him as he considered doing the same task here at the cabin. Getting started was half the battle, and he realized that it was necessary to start putting everything behind him, but that conflict would have to wait a little while longer. At least there were no baby items here to deal with.

Then he began reflecting on what Melissa would have looked like, what a beautiful woman she should have grown into and the things she could have accomplished. His recent career successes gave him the ability to enroll her in any school she chose. He could have provided her with any training she desired, which was now just one more sad part of this whole mess. It was time to clear his mind.

The pine needles crunched beneath his steps on his way to the beach as they offered a welcome change in smells from those still lingering in the nursery. The long hike around the lake and through the woods found him thinking about Lori and the baby with every step. This was part of the grieving process that would continue for months, probably years. Would he ever be able to move on and start a new chapter in his life without Lori and the baby?

The sun was down about an hour before he got back to the cabin. Before preparing a quick dinner, Jim decided on a shower to wash away the day's hiking activity. It felt good to get out on the long hike and breathe all that crisp clean winter air but now as he entered the shower; it also reminded him of Lori. When he stepped out to towel off the shock of his life was there on the steamed up mirror.

There were the all too familiar hearts traced in the steam at the upper left and lower right hand corners with the message 'The Flowers' written in between.

He couldn't breathe. He dropped the towel and stared at the mirror in disbelief. Could this be? Was he imagining the message?

A very close up look confirmed that the message was definitely 'written' in the steam like Lori used to do. It even looked like her hand writing.

What did it mean?

'The Flowers'.

He must have stared at the message for twenty minutes before it began to fade as the temperature and humidity evened out between the bathroom and the bedroom. Eventually, he realized it was gone and that he was still standing there staring at the mirror.

'The Flowers', it had said.

It had been there. He was convinced. It wasn't imagined. A closer look couldn't find a trace of the message there. Breathing on the mirror to fog it up didn't bring any part of it back. Closing the door, running the hot water in the shower until it fogged up again didn't bring any part of it back and yet it had been there, but the message made no sense.

What could it mean? How did it get there? A search of the cabin confirmed that all windows and doors were locked and that no one could have gotten in during his shower and yet the note got there somehow. Now that it was gone, he remained convinced that it had been there.

After toweling off, he wandered around the cabin, searching, mostly looking upward like a child seeing the world and walls around him for the first time. Something unimaginable had happened. It was beyond explanation. That note kept running senselessly in his head.

'The Flowers'.

Tuesday, November 20th, 2012

After a restless night's sleep, he decided on a hike to the cave the next morning. The crisp early winter air had a way of making yesterday seem very distant. Everything that is, except . . .

'The Flowers'.

During his hike, he settled on a trip into town to the local book store. He really needed a shower but was obviously hesitant. Finally he decided to take the shower.

At the end of it he peeked out of the shower door at the mirror sheepishly and only found steam. No hint of a message, just steam.

Relieved and almost disappointed in the lack of reaffirmation, he grabbed his cell phone on the way out to the car. The screen showed a missed call and after dialing to retrieve the communication, Lori's voice was there. Initially, the thought was that it must be an old message.

"Jim, it burns but I can't cry. I'm . . . ." then there was nothing but static.

Then details began to register through the shock. It couldn't have been an old message. There were no old messages on his phone after the funeral which was when he cleared them all. That was definitely Lori's voice. It sounded urgent. What burns? Lori had been found with burns on her body and around her eyes. How could he forget that smell when he found her in the nursery. The odor reminded him of surgical laser burn odors or the cremation smells sometimes evident outside animal hospitals.

He replayed the message, but there was nothing but static.

What's going on? Has he lost his mind?

He went to replay it again but the repeat key yielded, "That is not a valid choice. Please select from the following options:" he pressed the new message option but nothing. "You have no new messages, zero saved messages."

Wait Jim. Take a breath. This couldn't be right. There was no message. After redialing voice mail he again heard, "You have no new messages, zero saved messages."

It was gone just like the note on the mirror. Get a grip Jim. Slow down. Think. Think. Take a breath.

A check of the phone's missed call log showed nothing.

"That's it. I'm losing it."

The glass of straight Jack Daniel's didn't change a thing. He was shaking all over and couldn't stop.

Ray. Call Ray. John is in Florida and I can't call Mark. Call Ray and talk to him.

Finally, after several more drinks, he placed a call to his friend Ray Reed.

CHAPTER 11

'Talk about making people an offer they couldn't refuse!'

<u>Monday, November 19th, 2012</u>

The satisfaction overwhelmed him as the Nemesis checked up on his two new widowers, Jim and Mark. One wasn't leaving his house as he continued to wallow in grief. The other one now all packed up to go to his cabin to try and 'deal with his grief.' How wonderfully satisfying it is when things go according to plan and without a hitch.

The basics of his plan of revenge came to him in the middle of a very emotional time last winter. He had decided to get away. He needed a total break from the grief and the images burned in his memory that he could never forget. He would never forget the pain he felt after seeing his lover suffer a death so terrible that a closed casket was needed at the wake.

She was so sweet and innocent. She didn't deserve what she received at the hands of that doctor. He was paid to perform better than that. To get proper results, not the butchery that wound up happening to such a sweet wife & mother of two. That damned doctor should have been trained better than that.

He had watched her go through the botched surgery that resulted in a condition called Capsular contracture, a condition that required removal of her left breast implant. The quack that performed the augmentation said that the Capsular contracture she developed could have happened to any one and was not due to any negligence during the surgery. She had begun to feel such pain. She shouldn't have had to suffer that.

She had just wanted to make herself sexier for her husband, Bobby. She had felt that her breasts were too small and had always wanted to please him in any way she could. The Nemesis couldn't understand the fact that she still wanted to please her loser of a husband. When she decided to give it one more try was when everything started going south. Everything that went so wrong would never have had a chance to get started if not for her wanting to please Bobby. The Nemesis was so close to proving to her that he made a much better provider and caretaker for her than Bobby did. Anyone could see that.

She shouldn't have had to undergo the second surgery to remove the left implant let alone endure the embarrassment she experienced during the six month waiting period required before it could be re-implanted.

It was the third surgery, the one to re-implant, that caused all hell to break loose.

By all accounts that he had been able to gather from doctor acquaintances of his, the local anesthesia used at the quack's independent surgery center led to all her problems.

It was the local anesthesia combined with the anesthetic gasses that caused a condition known as Malignant Hyperthermia. They simply weren't prepared to deal with this unique set of conditions that could prove fatal when combined with her rare hereditary sensitivity to anesthetics.

That damn doctor is supposed to be a professional. All the schooling, all the knowledge, all the seminars to keep up with the latest medicines and risk factors and he still was unprepared to help her when the symptoms began to present themselves.

Oh he had the very expensive drug needed to counteract the problem. He even had the very large amount on hand that was necessary, but according to the Nemesis' friends, that medication is very rarely called for. It more than likely had passed its expiration date and wasn't replaced.

Of course the quack would never admit to that. Every effort to prove it was stonewalled and eventually covered up with conveniently-found paperwork that showed up just in time to head off the lawsuit they were preparing.

That's why he needed to pay. She paid with her life. She trusted them. She put her health in his hands, his experienced, well-paid hands. The terrible pain he wound up inflicting on her over the two days it finally took her to pass would be inflicted on him, and on his new targets, all of them. They will all pay the same price.

Now he had a new bunch of targets within this group called the 'Surgeon Generals'; they were JUST as bad. How many lives had THEY messed up.? They were all alike, hurting innocent people with no consideration for anyone but themselves. They thought they were better than people like him because of their degrees and wealth.

Yes, they had the degrees, the notoriety, the fancy houses and all the money they needed to have whatever life they chose. They had articles written about them. Well the ones he planned to target, for his personal reasons, were going to know what a life turned upside down feels like. They were going to experience, as he had, the absolutely irreplaceable loss of someone close and very dear to them and undeserving of that kind of death.

A trip back to Columbia would do him some good. He needed to get his mind off things for a while and make some adjustments. The doctors were upgrading their security systems as anticipated. Adding more cameras, light activating motion sensors, etc. on the exteriors of their homes like that was going to prevent anything. His plan was unstoppable! All they were accomplishing was driving up sales at the security companies. Oh well, what ever made them feel better, for now.

Tuesday, November 20th, 2012

Tuesday morning he arrived in Bogota and that afternoon he took a small chartered flight to one of over seven hundred unpaved runways in Columbia. This runway in particular was approximately four hundred miles north of Bogota and just outside Cartagena. He could have flown into the Rafael Nunez International Airport which was only ten minutes from his favorite resort but he preferred a leisurely chartered flight so he could see the Columbian countryside on his way in, which also left no paper trail of his arrival.

Before taking this trip, he had taken care to grow a beard thick enough to mask his general appearance, just in case. You could never know when you might be caught on camera these days with surveillance everywhere. For this reason, he also never went anywhere outside his room without his sunglasses and hat that covered a good part of his face from the typical location of cameras. What wasn't covered remained mostly in the shadow of the hat.

He preferred the Caribbean shores to that of the Pacific Ocean shores in Columbia. On his last trip to Cartagena he discovered its history dating back to four thousand BC, its Caribbean seaport beauty and especially how easily one could buy just about any drug imaginable. Also many drugs a person couldn't imagine, he found out, were readily available. It was one of those that he needed more of.

After booking a room at the Occidental Grand Cartagena Resort he took in the sights around the pool. He loved this thirteen acre beach resort as it was one of the most exclusive and elegant places he'd ever stayed at. When he tired of one pool, it was a short walk to either of the other two. The scenery was always spectacular in and around the resort.

The 'Generals' weren't the only ones with the financial means to enjoy places like the Occidental Grand. He was fortunate to have made a number of very good electronic and internet stock decisions that set him up for life.

He and his brother Bobby were ten years old and knew nothing about stocks when his dad invested $10,000 in Apple Corporation. Fifteen years later when he died, each brother received half of the shares. Bobby never could see past the end of his nose and sold his shares a couple years later, making over $300K. It was too much money for his short term thinking to pass up.

"After all", he had said, "the stock could plummet and be worth next to nothing. At least now I can pay cash for a new house and new car". Of course he didn't mention paying off loan sharks that he was indebted to for the money he borrowed to support his growing drug habit. This was as far ahead as Bobby could ever think and was the reason that whenever he was able to get anything worthwhile, he usually lost it just as quickly.

The Nemesis was a much better planner and could always see the bigger picture. He did some research and realized the potential for some of the planned product releases and wound up tripling his stock value. From there he started playing the day trading game and found he had a knack for investing in promising young internet businesses. His wise and timely investments in many of them left him in an enviable financial position. The term 'not hurting at all' pretty well summed up his economic status.

Wednesday, November 21st, 2012

On Wednesday afternoon he had just pulled up to his drug contact's secluded digs. His friend Alejandro Mendez was nicknamed 'El Mensajero Negro Del Diablo' which meant 'the devil's black messenger'. From him any drug was available. He was also a major supplier for local prostitution. Something resort areas like Cartagena had an unquenchable thirst for.

"Ah my American friend! It has been too long. Come, sit. We must drink to old times and good days to come."

He shook his hand and gave him the respectful forearm taps as he said, "Alejandro my friend. It has been a while. So good to see you look well."

"Mamacita bring whisky for me and my friend. Have you enjoyed the fruits of our last time together Mi Amigo?"

"Yes, I have enjoyed them very much. It works wonderfully and no one back home has ever seen such a drug. It suits my plans very well."

"Good. Good. I am glad you are pleased. What brings you to my humble hacienda today, ah?"

"While I enjoy relaxing at the resorts your country has to offer my friend, I've come to visit because I could use some more of your products. Some more cocaina and some more fruit of the Borrachero tree."

"Aahh, this I can do for you, Mi Amigo, but of course the price has risen as all things do with demand. Yes?"

"Very well then tell me Alejandro, what are the new prices?"

"The cocaina, it is the same but the Burundanga price she goes up. Cocaina is available everywhere and has little value in my country as it is so plentiful. The Burundanga is available nowhere but here. As you know, in the drug business, there is no, how you say, 'volume discounts'? When the fruit of the Borrachero tree are seen by gringos and its many uses are appreciated, the price she goes up.

One gram is now 350,000 pesos."

He knew the all American negotiating method known as the 'flinch' wouldn't work here but he felt like it was almost expected. So out of respect he said, "That is ten times the price I paid one year ago. Has the price of Cerveza increased so much this year? If I had known, I would have brought many cases to my good friend in Columbia."

Even at this price, which went from $20 US per gram last year to $200 US per gram this year, it was unbelievably cheap for the cornerstone of his plan. Especially since one gram went so far.

"Americans have such humor. I am keeping the price respectable for such a respectable return customer. As you know, when dos amigos discuss business too many times, the wrong people notice these things. The price goes higher as my risk goes higher. The local policía de drogas watch me very closely. I take risks to just talk to gringos here. This is acceptable for you Mi Amigo?"

"Of course Alejandro, this is good. I would like twenty grams of cocaina and ten grams of Burundanga."

"This you will have tonight my friend. It will be delivered by two of my finest mamacitas who will pleasure you well into the night if you so desire. Hector will handle the business on your way out and will give you a little cocaina for your long trip back to the Occidental Grand. Now come. Walk with me. We talk too much and drink too little."

Alejandro researched his customers well. That's how he remained in business as long as he had and how he enjoyed his obvious success. Mentioning where he was staying or even his room number was unnecessary with 'El Mensajero Negro Del Diablo'. He knew these things before he invited a guest to his hacienda along with how long he has been in Columbia, information on his private charter and hell, probably how many pieces of luggage he snuck into the country.

With business concluded, they walked through his expansive gardens with all their breath taking colors and the incredible variety of his exquisite landscaping. They drank and enjoyed the spectacular view of the Caribbean from the highlands of his estate which was located in a very secluded area of the Columbian countryside.

He could see himself investing in property like this after his plan was complete. It wouldn't be in Columbia though.

The combination of scenery, food, smells and warm Mediterranean Sea air found only in Italy was much more to his liking.

'I wonder how Don Vito Corleone would have used such a drug in his day if it were available.

'Talk about making people an offer they couldn't refuse!'

These thoughts amused him as he returned to his suite.

CHAPTER 12

"What do I recommend? How quickly can you get home?"

Tuesday, November 20th, 2012

octor Raymond Reed was glad to hear from his grief-stricken friend.

"Jim, how are you doing up there? Are you getting any sleep?" he asked.

"I'm about as good as can be expected I guess. God I miss her Ray!"

"I'm not going to lie to you Jim. Expect it to be tough for a long time. Now is the time when you need to lean on friends and family. Would you like some company for a while up there Jim?"

"No Ray, I'm fine I guess, but I need to talk to you about a few things."

"Sure Jim. Whatever you need, just fire away."

"There's been a few weird things happening since I left home," he said then started explaining about how everything reminded him of his time together with Lori, how each event hurt more than the last, etc.

"Ray I miss her smile, her wit, her sexy flirtations whether they were the messages on the mirror I'd told you about, the notes she'd leave lying around or on the answering machine. I miss being with her and I miss how I felt coming home to her after being away from her. I miss how we used to enjoy going out together. I miss how she used to pick out my clothes and arrange them on the bed like a little flat person complete with the shoes on the floor before we went out anywhere . . ." Then after a long pause, he began to explain about what he experienced with the mirror and the cell phone message he found and now could no longer retrieve.

"Wow, Jim. I don't know what to say. Listening is the easy part I guess but I'm not sure what to say otherwise. Please don't take this as condescending but, are you sure about the messages?"

"Ray, I know how it sounds and I really couldn't see myself sharing this with anyone other than you or John but yes, I'm sure. I'm not as crazy as this probably makes me sound. They were real!"

"I'm honestly at a loss for words. Again please don't view me as insensitive either. I think our friendship is strong enough for what I'm about to say to you. Did you hear what you just told me about the things you miss? I'm not a psychiatrist Jim but it sounds a bit like you may be looking for what you are missing from Lori. Are you sure these messages aren't manifestations of the things you miss most, buddy? Are you absolutely sure about the messages?"

"Ray, I'm not offended at all. I know how this must sound. I assure you I'm not losing it. People that are losing it don't question their own sanity to themselves and are usually offended when others do. I'm just not sure where to go from here. I had to share this with someone because it's starting to drive me nuts thinking about it. With John in Florida trying to wrap his head around losing Lisa, you're the only one I could think of to talk to about these things.

"I know how much you care about Lori and me, so I'm asking you Ray. What do you think I should do with this?"

"How committed are you to staying at the cabin for a while yet?" he asked.

"I have to admit it has been good to get out of the house and away from trying to walk past the nursery without looking inside. I found myself steering clear but that just brought back those horrible images in my head of finding her there like that.

"She was so beautiful, such a beautiful person inside and out and then that monster had to do that to her. I can't get them damn images of her out of my mind. No matter where I look or what else I try to think about, it always comes back to what I saw when I found her there.

"She is in every corner of our life together in the house, cabin, car and everywhere we used to go together. When I see the couch in the cabin, the chairs we left on our last visit to the cave we found, the beach, in every familiar place I see her smiling face, then I see the nursery!

"How committed am I to staying here? It's not the getaway it used to be but it's definitely better than staying in the house right now I guess."

"I know you're first reaction to this will be to think you're putting me out by accepting, but nothing could be further from the truth buddy. How's that for a lead in? Anyway, how about if I take a day or two off and join you at the cabin to help you get your mind off Lori? I've never been up there so you could show me around the property, we could grab some dinners out, drown some sorrows.

"It's not putting me out at all, partner. Do us both a favor and consider it seriously before you respond," said Ray.

"That may be a good idea Ray. We could spend quite a bit of time hiking and maybe with someone to talk to, even knowing the conversation will probably turn to Lori and Lisa quite a bit, and it would be a distraction from what I'm going through now.

"I'll tell you what Ray, let me see how the rest of the day goes and we'll talk later this afternoon. By then I'll know which way I need to go. Friend or home."

"Jim, if you need more alone time out there I certainly understand. I just want you to know you have an option and I could probably use a little getaway time myself. We have a lot to talk about.

"If you'd rather I didn't come out though, I think you need to come home and share this with the police and your shrink first if you feel like it."

"The shrink may not be such a bad idea but I don't think so. Not yet anyway. Yeah, I'm sure there will be some benefit in sharing with a therapist at some point but not right now. I just have to sort things out on my own for a while.

"I thought about sharing it with Ed Cassidy first obviously, but this is just so odd that I'm not sure he'd take me seriously."

"There's only one way to find out. Jim, we've all heard stories about how people have had unexplainable premonitions. More often than not they are linked to sound emotional situations. Certainly you, John and Mark have experienced extremely emotional events. Hell I don't know how these things come about or how much stock to place in them when they do, but I know you. I can tell how shaken these things have made you.

"What do I recommend? How quickly can you get home?

"I think if I was you and in your current situation, I'd sit down with Cassidy and see what he says. He seems like a level headed guy and I'm sure he'd be interested in anything you have that could shed any light on the situation.

"I must admit, I can't think of what that flowers reference could mean but I'm sure he's more interested in solving the case than looking a possible gift horse in the mouth. No matter how unusual a horse it might be."

"Thanks for always being my friend first and my analyst last Ray. I'll probably come home tomorrow and try to see him on Thursday," Jim said.

"If that's what you'd prefer, then it sounds like a plan. Good luck buddy. Thanks for thinking enough of me to call. Promise to call me again anytime. I mean it; you'd better not hesitate to call me out there if it'll help you. Please call me anytime Jim."

"I will Ray and thanks again for being there when I needed you."

Jim hung up and headed out to the bookstore feeling much better having talked to Ray.

CHAPTER 13

He had never let one get away yet and this wouldn't be his first.

<u>Wednesday, November 21st, 2012</u>

*T*he Nemesis relaxed poolside in a long row of comfortable lounge chairs set into the water on a ledge in the large resort pool. So far this afternoon all he did was take in the sights mostly around the beautiful pool area. Families with their kids, obvious honeymooners, young men and young ladies looking to score abounded, but soon he realized that boredom was overtaking his relaxed mood. He felt the edge he had developed for staying ahead of Andy and Barney slipping away.

He had gotten used to the excitement that went with his master plan. Here, despite the incredible beauty of the first class resort, he missed the thrill of the hunt. The planning, the risks, the execution of a plan and the sense of reward that went with those things were missing from his fun in the sun.

Aside from the beautiful resort he was enjoying, the country in general was really quite poor, backward in most respects, and the population in general was uneducated. There was nothing much to do outside of the resort as he wasn't into site seeing, boating or parasailing.

He decided that if he was going to stay here for a week he needed to entertain himself somehow. His mental wheels started turning and blending his agenda back home with the potential for local amusement.

After dressing for dinner, the expected knock came on his door. Two very stunning women approximately twenty years old came strolling in, placed his anticipated package on a nearby table, and started immediately draping themselves all over him as they were obviously pre-programmed to do by his local business partner 'El Mensajero Negro Del Diablo'.

The first one, the more well endowed of the two, wore ivory short shorts with a powder blue-nearly sheer top that left very little to one's imagination. The second one was much more athletically built and was dressed similarly only the colors were reversed. Amused but hungry, he put a halt to their advances and suggested some dinner first.

Then like little trained puppies they both quickly shifted gears and were all about the meal. He acknowledged the behavior and was a bit jaded by the lack of conquest. He preferred some company at dinner however mindless it would be and appreciated the 'gifts' from Alejandro.

Dinner went as expected with the two girls doting over him and in agreement on everything he said or suggested. Their behavior was exactly what he expected from them. They were both very attractive and also, he knew, very disposable if Alejandro sent them to him as he did.

He decided to make the night an exciting one as he drove the two girls out to a secluded spot that was not far from the resort. He found they were sexually very experienced for their age, and it had been a long time since he was cared for so well. He intentionally avoided sex with the wives of the 'Generals' as that wasn't what it was about. He needed to keep his focus there at all times.

This was different. Here it was all about the sex. It was time to satisfy his sex draught. It would then be time for amusement.

"Maria my dear, what are you doing?" he asked of his well endowed partner. "No need to get dressed, I want you to bite Rosa very hard, and Rosa; I just know you're really going to enjoy it. After all, you'll never have this much fun for the rest of your life."

She immediately went to Rosa and bit the lower part of her left ear completely off and Rosa only sat there and smiled as she bled profusely down that beautifully athletic chest of hers.

"Rosa, you look like you're having fun. Please take that branch and hit Maria seven times and Maria, I know you will enjoy this too. Trust me; this is the most fun you'll have for the rest of your life as well and as athletic as Rosa is built that should be a very short time."

Maria started smiling immediately, and the smile never left her face as Rosa without hesitation picked up the rather large branch he pointed to. She showed off her athletic abilities as the Nemesis expected. She started beating Maria's head first this way then that way with the branch. Maria smiled throughout the crude batting practice until there was no light left in her eyes. Three more swings completed Rosa's assigned seven. She dropped the branch, and moved toward him with her sexiest strut, still smiling and bleeding from her ear.

They were truly mindless. What a drug! He ended Rosa's life with one A-Rod type swing-for-the-fences hit in the head with the branch. Leaving the bodies for the local wild life to clean up, he returned to his room with his appetite for amusement completely satiated for now.

He liked the way he was spicing up his vacation and for the time being decided to take in the sights poolside again. After another day of pure relaxation, he would fulfill his need for conquest. It was so easy and safe to do here as people turned up missing all the time. It was the norm in this country. Very little explanation needed. It was a known fact that one third of the kidnappings in the world happened here in Columbia. It was no great mystery to him how they accomplished that amazing statistic.

In a word, Burundanga! Or the most scientific name, Scopolamine. The locals liked to call it Datura, or Black Breath. By whatever name you chose, what a drug!

Thursday, November 22nd, 2012

It was another promising day in the drug capital of the world and he planned to enjoy every minute of it. After a couple hits of Alejandro's best cocaine and he was off driving south on highway 90A to Carrera Route One down the Caribbean coastline all the way to the southern end of the peninsula. Arriving at the Hilton Cartagena, he parked his rental car in a lot next to the lavishly landscaped resort and ate a fantastic lunch to offset the Thanksgiving Day dinner he was missing back home. Another reason tied to taking this Columbian excursion at this time was his lack of family to spend the holiday with.

After lunch, he made a short walk to the Bocagrande Hospital next door which looked like a great place to hunt. There were doctors and very attractive nurses coming and going everywhere at such a quick pace that nobody had time to notice him.

He viewed it as a human shopping mall of opportunity. He was dressed very well and looked like a doctor in a hurry to make rounds at the hospital when he came upon a nurse just getting into her car. Hospital people are so trusting on a hospital campus. This was just the kind of mistake that would prove fatal.

A young nurse looked to be the perfect mark. She looked very tired and her guard was down as she started her car. When he walked up to the car, she gullibly rolled down the window to see what he needed.

"I'm sorry to bother you nurse, but I'm new to the area and need to get to a patient's home right away. This is the address," he said as he bent toward her with a paper in his hand and discreetly blew the fine powder on it into her face as he tripped slightly.

"Oh, I'm so sorry. I guess I'm in too much of a hurry. Do you recognize this address?"

She looked at the paper which was empty, then looked at him and said, "Nurse, look at me as if you see forever in my eyes and smile."

She immediately smiled for him. It was a beautiful smile below a curiously blank stare.

At his request, she drove them three blocks to her house for an afternoon of the best, albeit mindless, sex of her short remaining life.

Her neighbors saw them arrive, smiling and walking arm-in-arm and thought nothing of the young attractive nurse bringing a doctor looking gentleman home with her. They also thought nothing of him leaving as he walked the short distance back to the Hilton for his car to head off for another practice run.

He knew his approach needed to change due to the added security being installed back home on the doctor's houses. He must practice snaring someone out in the open on the street to round out his repertoire of abduction techniques so this afternoon it would be all about the hunt.

It wasn't long before his short walk found him catching up to a strikingly beautiful, dark skinned, Columbian woman, wearing a banana yellow top with dark brown slacks and matching scarf, walking along the line of parked cars. The yellow top brought out the blonde highlight streak in her hair which was unusual for the conservative way Columbian women usually wore their hair. She was walking leisurely along a row of three story buildings just off a small park, where children were doing quite well flying home made kites in the gentle Caribbean breeze. With his escape route previously set up, he walked casually up to her with his 'address sheet' as he adjusted his stride to match hers.

"Excuse me miss, could you help me. I'm not from around here and, well, I'm actually a little lost. I'm trying to find a lawyer's office at this address." As he lifted the paper to blow softly on it, a cross breeze suddenly lifted the paper and emptied its contents between them off to his right side. It almost backfired on him but what was worse; she noticed the powder fly off the paper and was hip to this trick.

Damn locals. "Policía, Policía. Detenerlo, Detenerlo" which meant "Stop Him, Stop Him."

It was just his luck. A cop was walking toward them from his left about a block away. She reached out to detain him but he pushed her off and ran past three buildings then turned down an alley. Toward the rear of the last one, he picked up a bag that he stashed there earlier and replaced the tan shirt he was wearing with a red one from the bag as he continued to move along the back alley.

He put on a Chicago Cubs cap and a pair of Ray Ban Clubmaster sunglasses from the bag then threw it behind some nearby bushes. With his outward appearance sufficiently altered, he began calmly walking back toward the front of the building. Just as he rounded the rear corner of the building he saw the policeman and pointed back towards the alley at the rear of the building and said, "That way. A man in a tan shirt was running that way."

He turned up the sidewalk and calmly walked passed 'blonde streak' who was watching the opening of the alley with much anticipation, hopping up and down like she needed a restroom. He continued two blocks further to his car and watched the scene until 'blonde streak' gave up her vigil, found her car and drove off.

He followed her back up Carrera Route One all the way back to his resort where she parked in the employee lot. She was now apparently running late as she dashed into the resort and headed toward the poolside bar. What a small world!

It took him less than fifteen minutes to change into trunks and order lunch under the thatched roofed lounging area along the side of the pool. There he relaxed and had several drinks as he watched his new favorite female bartender with blonde streaks in her hair. She was making more conversation with the guests than drinks for them. She looked stunning in the resort uniform she had changed into and he noticed the name tag that declared her name; Elena.

He also observed that she was a very flirtatious thing that warmed up to mostly the older more distinguished looking guests. Her technique was very profitable and her tip jar remained filled to the brim except for the three times he noticed her discreetly lightening its load a bit.

He had never let one get away, and he was not going to allow this one to be the first.

Her shift lasted only four hours after which she went into the store room behind the bar and emerged a short time later clad in a very revealing red and yellow bikini designed to show off her best assets. She wasted no time scouting out the landscape of the pool. They made the kind of eye contact that lingered long enough to tell him all he needed to know about her intentions for the night.

This was almost going to be too easy.

CHAPTER 14

". . . there are no rules and there are no bounds
to these kinds of things."

Thursday, November 22nd, 2012

Jim decided to go it alone for a few days finding peace at last in the solitude of the cabin property. Besides, he wanted to stay out of all the Thanksgiving Day celebrations that he was invited to back home. It was especially noticeable as the holiday approached that all his friends were kindly and too exuberantly inviting him to spend the holiday with them. While he appreciated the compassion they displayed, he couldn't face the unspoken message that went along with each invitation. The invitations all said very clearly, "We don't want you to be all alone on this holiday that's so close to your loss of Lori."

He got home early Thursday afternoon and had just hung up his coat when the phone in the bedroom rang only once and no more. It stopped him in his tracks as none of the downstairs phones rang. He immediately thought of how the same thing happened on Monday before he left for the cabin and how he dismissed it as an electronic glitch. Now, curiously, he started upstairs trying to think of what could be causing that phone to ring independently of the other house phones.

At the top of the stairs the blinking red message light could be seen on the bedroom nightstand answering machine indicating that there were four messages.

'You have four new messages, first message, Monday 8:01am', "Jim, just calling to see if you needed anything; . . . a shoulder to lean on, or just a friend to keep you company for a while. Hey, just call if there is anything I can do for you buddy. Take care." 'End of message'. He automatically pressed 'nine' as he always did and heard 'message will be saved for twenty one days'. Ok that was the message he heard before leaving for the cabin when he sent a text to Ray declining his offer.

'Next message, Monday 10:05am, "Jim, he asked me to take off my clothes and lie on the floor. I don't want to but I have to. Now he . . . .", then there was just static and a beep. 'End of message'. Stunned at the incredulous message, his reflexes kicked in and he pressed 'nine' once more and heard, 'message will be saved for twenty one days', 'Next message'. Diving for the stop button he almost knocked the answering machine off the nightstand, dropped to the bed and suddenly realized he wasn't breathing.

It was Lori's voice! It was definitely Lori's voice! No mistake there! He not only recognized her voice but also the edge of panic it carried in her message. 'The time stamp was about the time the phone rang as I was heading out of the house for the cabin.' 'I remember leaving around 10:00 am that morning.' 'That was when I thought there was an electronic glitch.' 'That was when the phone rang upstairs but nowhere else in the house.' 'That was when I left the house still in a daze and beside myself with grief from the funeral.' 'What's happening to me?' 'Am I losing my mind?'

Two messages to go! 'I can't lift my arm to press play!'

His trance lasted over twenty minutes as he sat there on the bed and tried to rearrange these facts into some semblance of order, trying to make some logical sense of what he experienced here. There was simply no way to break down and reassemble this to make any sense at all.

Stunned, motionless, trembling and staring at the machine which now blinked a red '2', he managed several quick gasps of air before his regular breathing could began again. Numbness and a chill came over him before he could finally summon up enough courage to hear the next message.

'Tuesday 8:45pm, "Hi Jim, we just realized we never called to tell you we reached home ok. We love you Jim and want you to know that you and Lori are always in our thoughts and prayers as we all try to move on and make sense of something that we know will never make sense. Sorry I guess I'm rambling here. Hope you're doing better than we are. Please call us any anytime. Talk to you soon." 'End of message.' It was Lori's sister Jenny. Again he pressed '9' and heard, 'message will be saved for twenty one days', 'Next message, Thursday 11:02am'. Now his pulse began to race again as he realized that was the time that the upstairs phone rang only once today when he got home.

'Jim he crushed my ankle and he's burning me. Why, Jim, WHY? It hurts, but he asked me to smile, and I have to. Jim why is he . . . .' then again, just static and the beep. 'End of message.' This time he consciously and very deliberately pressed '9' and heard, 'Message will be saved for twenty one days', 'End of new messages'.

He started talking to himself again. 'Think Jim. You're not crazy. You're a doctor. You're mentally competent. It doesn't make sense but you heard it. Did I? Play it again, so you know you're not nuts.'

The answering machine sounded off announcing, 'You have two saved messages, no new messages.'

'WHAT? I just saved four messages. I heard the confirmations. There has to be four messages,' Jim thought.

'First saved message, Monday 8:01am, "Jim, just calling to see if you needed anything . . . a shoulder to lean on . . . . or just a friend to keep you company for a while. Hey, just call if there is anything I can do for you buddy. Take care." End of message'.

Ok.

'Next saved message, Tuesday 8:45pm, "Hi Jim, we just realized we never called to tell you we reached home ok. We love you Jim and want you to know that you and Lori are always in our thoughts and prayers as we all try to move on and make sense of something that we know will never make sense. Sorry I guess I'm rambling here. Hope you're doing better than we are. Please call us anytime. Talk to you soon." 'End of saved messages.'

NO. NO. NO. NO. NO.

"There were 2 more messages. What happened to the other two messages? There were two messages from Lori. I heard them. I HEARD THEM", he yelled to the machine.

Now he really was stunned. 'I know I heard them. I saved them. It was Lori's voice. I heard the save confirmations. What the hell is happening?'

Pressing play to hear the messages again yielded the same results.

Suddenly the answering machine appeared to be floating under water as tears started down his cheeks.

"It's just not right. None of this is right. WHY LORI? HOW CAN THIS BE POSSIBLE?" he screamed with every ounce of breath he had left as he fell back onto the bed shaking his head and sobbing.

<u>Friday, November 23rd, 2012</u>

The next morning was a sunny one, but it did nothing to lift his spirits or remove the stunned feeling that lingered from yesterday.

"Get a grip Jim, focus." "I have to discuss this with someone."

"This is the Heaton residence. Garrett speaking."

"Garrett. It's Jim. Do you have a minute?"

"Of course I do Jim. How are you?"

"Quite frankly Garrett I've been better, even right after Lori's passing."

"What's happened Jim?"

"I need to speak to you in person Garrett, as a friend and I guess professionally as well."

"Would you like me to come over?"

"Actually I was hoping to see you at your house. It seems as though I like to get out of this house as much as possible these days. How about I come over in half an hour?"

"That would be fine Jim. I'm looking forward to it."

He wasn't sure how to even begin relating the events of the last few days to his good friend Garrett, but after almost draining his glass of very fine brandy, he found himself blurting out everything from the cabin mirror messages to the answering machine messages that were there, then weren't. Garrett had always been easy to talk to. He was the only 'General' who completed a second major in psychology. That helped make him a great listener as well as a trusted friend. The team referred patients to him when they needed help dealing with significant reconstructive plastic surgery issues.

"Garrett what do you make of this?" Jim asked.

"Jim, first off you're not crazy if that's what you're asking me. I'm not sure if you know this about me or not but I have studied various forms of 'strange phenomenon' for quite some time. The one thing I've learned is that there are no rules and there are no bounds to these kinds of things.

"There are well documented cases of extremely difficult to understand events that, besides being quite beyond comprehension, turned out to be inexplicably accurate."

"Garrett, I know this sounds weird even unbelievable. I shared the cabin incidents with Ray Reed after it happened. He was as unconditionally supportive as you are right now. He didn't call me crazy either but man, I feel like I'm at least on the edge of it."

"I refuse to believe you are experiencing what shrinks refer to as 'Grandiose Delusional Disorder' on any level. That's when a patient believes he has some great but unrecognized talent or insight, a unique identity or knowledge. You are much too grounded for any of that. I know you Jim. Besides, you'd be absolutely stating these things as a fact or trying to convince me these things are real and that you have no doubt about any of it but you are obviously here doing quite the opposite.

"I truly believe in you Jim and I believe something is happening here that neither of us can explain. Hell I wish I could. All I can offer to you as a friend and amateur shrink is that you should believe in you and your sanity. Keep believing in what Lori represented in your life and believe in the love you had for her and let that guide you through this tough time. Trust your gut Jim. Definitely talk to Ed Cassidy and don't be bashful about the facts as you see them, as you experienced them, proof-be-damned."

"I've been leaning that way all along Garrett. I guess I just needed a couple of friends to tell me to go ahead and do it," Jim said and left with a new resolve to meet with Ed Cassidy.

CHAPTER 15

"I don't like to use the term freaky Ed but . . ."

Friday, November 23rd, 2012

*J*im checked his watch as he entered the police station and noticed he was right on-time for his meeting with Inspector Cassidy.

"Please have a seat dere, Dr. Baker. Inspector Cassidy is expecting you and will be with you forth with."

Recognizing the New York accent and slang, he nodded, took a seat and began reviewing in his head just what approach he would take to lay out all he had experienced to the inspectors.

✻

"He should be here any minute Bill. So to review, we've concluded that the CSI reports on the Channing murder coincide with the other three cases conclusively. Mutilations, M.O., lack of hair, fingerprints or any foreign fibers and despite our warnings and increased security by the 'Generals' themselves, we apparently have another flawless home security breach," Ed said as he wrapped up their findings.

"Connie took and preserved more tissue samples before releasing the Channing body. So far we have been able to keep the crushed ankle and the burn marks in the right arm pit and behind the right knee that was found on all the victims from the grieving husbands. It really wasn't too tough what with all the other more visible mutilations and the shock of the expressionless nude bodies with the burn marks around each eye making them look like a raccoon found at each scene," said Bill.

"It's a small consolation, Bill, but the Chicago BIS is as stumped as we are. Their crime lab tech Rick Newberry has reached out to a data tech contact he has at the FBI named Cory Seaver who has been searching their extensive records for anything resembling this M.O. but so far nothing.

"We need some sort of break on this one Bill, and we could use it sooner rather than later. Since we passed the magic number of three murders, the Chicago media have ratcheted up their coverage and are now officially referring to our dirt bag as a serial killer. You haven't been getting the same grief in Evanston as we do here because we are being labeled the epicenter of the killing spree. They have been running little mini-series type updates almost every night on the Chicago news channels, and recently it's gone national. It's getting kind of crowded around here as not only has the local and Chi-town media been camping out, but now a number of out of town press groups are beginning to feed the story to their outlets. They are driving the LT nuts.

"Unfortunately for all of us, this 'guy' is good. So far he has been so meticulous that we have nothing from Connie, state or the FBI labs," said Ed as he seemed to stare right through the crime board they had assembled.

"Well we might as well get it over with. Shall we talk to the good doctor?" asked Bill.

"Sure. Officer Bellows, please bring in Dr. Baker," said Ed as he flipped over his crime board.

*

"Dr. Baker, so good to see you again, please sit down. Let me get you something to drink," Ed offered to his guest.

"No. I'm fine thank you. Have there been any developments since we last talked?"

"I'm afraid not. No significant change in direction from last week. This is where we are so far:

"The forensic evidence gathered in all four murders is positively similar enough to conclude that they were performed by the same individual or individuals. We now know for sure that most of the significant injuries were inflicted on each victim postmortem but with some of injuries there is simply no way to tell.

"I'll be using a gender 'he' in our discussion generically as we don't know if the perpetrator is male or female at this point. Everyone on our team is fairly sure these types of crimes are most likely to be performed by a male rather than a female. They are apparently being directed for some reason at local plastic surgeons only and most recently they are obviously targeting the wives of your team of 'Generals'.

"Now, while we have had very liberal cooperation from the 'Generals' as far as private insights into patient records, we only recently were able to convince Dr. Holden to do so. He is now collaborating with us to enable the private review of cases within the past year or so to possibly flush out a motive. We think that this is significant because his wife's murder was the origin of this spree. As such, we expect that one of his cases would be most likely to yield some insight to this sick person's motives.

"There is also the obvious fact that with the exception of the original victim. Aimee Holden, it seems that the wives of the generals are being attacked in last name alphabetical order just as the names were listed in that Sun Times article last summer. Following that logic, we have increased patrols in the Falkland's neighborhood with Sandra alphabetically being the next name on the list. We've been out to the Falkland's home and have seen the new super HD security system Dr. Falkland installed, and it is a beauty.

"Since we last spoke we have expanded the scope of the investigation significantly. We have joined forces with Chicago's Bureau of Investigative Services, Illinois State Forensic Science Center in Chicago and have been working with a number of contacts at the FBI field office here to tap into their incredible lab and database resources looking for patterns and possible profiles.

"Dr. Baker, I know to the victim's survivor this must seem like we're all vine and no tomatoes at this point, but this is the most frustrating and least productive part of this investigation. Once we get a little direction from the profilers, and inevitably a lead or two from the scenes, the investigation will gain some traction and the puzzle pieces will begin to fit together," said Bill.

"You're right it is frustrating, and I realistically don't ever expect the frustration to go away entirely because none of these innocent women deserved to die. None of us can imagine what could justify this kind of violence in a person's head. The main reason I asked for a meeting today is that I have some information to share with you that I don't completely understand.

"You see, I've had a few things happen to me in the last couple of days. I've discussed this with several of my associates, and they all think, as I do, that I need to share this with the two of you."

"Please Doctor. By all means, if there is anything that can possibly shed some light on this research it would be most welcome," Ed said.

Jim went on to describe the message he found on the mirror at the cabin and his history of receiving messages like that from Lori when she was alive, the weird phone rings, the answering machine messages he heard that were no longer there and the timing of them.

Once he started he was like a machine with the switch stuck in the on position. He felt that if he were to stop before he got it all out that he would be looking so foolish that he wouldn't be able to continue with the rest.

When he was finally finished he said, "Thanks so much for not looking at me like I'm nuts. Because ever since all this happened, that's the way I feel every time I think about it. You guys are men of science like I am, but I know what I heard, and a lot of it makes no sense to me. I mean, what kind of message is 'The Flowers' anyway? How do you explain the way the singular phone rings coincide with the timing of the messages I heard, that are no longer on the machine of course. Every time I try to rationalize how these events could possibly have happened, I think that all I'm doing is telling myself rational lies. Anyway I'm past all that and have just been trying to make sense of them."

"Dr. Baker we, and a number of our colleagues have gotten some pretty strange clues through the years and honestly these felonies have been remarkably absent of clues so anything you can share with us will be looked at from any angle we can," Ed assured him.

"I understand that and please call me Jim."

"All right, Jim, what do you make of the crushed ankle reference that you heard on the answering machine?" Ed asked.

"Not sure. It's just another thing that doesn't make any sense to me," said Jim.

"Jim, please; this doesn't leave the room, but all of the victims had evidence of a crushed ankle, the right ankle specifically. In Lori's case, it wasn't quite as severe or noticeable as some of the others but it was apparently crushed nonetheless. We don't mean to add to your grief by sharing this additional information about your wife's condition, but this is the most exciting aspect of all your revelations to us, and we assure you we will look into the other things as well," said Bill.

"Thanks for all your efforts. We all appreciate them. I know you will keep us informed of any new developments."

"We'll definitely be in touch Jim, and soon," Ed promised him as they walked out of the conference room.

Ed put his arm on Jim's shoulder and assured him, "Jim I will personally review these clues you've given us today strenuously and please keep us posted if you come across anything else."

"I will Ed," Jim said as he left.

✳

Cassidy and Weller went back to the crime board and did a little updating.

"I don't like to use the term freaky Ed but . . . that was freaky. The references to having no control play well with what we found but now are we getting back to them being drugged and with no evidence of drugs in their systems? Let's pull the good doctor's phone records and see what they reveal. Also let's see what Rick, or his buddy Cory at the bureau, have to say about the phone rings.

"That leaves the 'The Flowers' message. Meaning what exactly? How many of these can we really take seriously?" asked Bill.

"I mean, they have all been surrounded by flowers especially with all the funerals they have been attending. Some of them have received flowers after the funerals, but nothing unusual about them was reported. No, weird or out of the ordinary messages or senders were noted. I'm not sure what it's supposed to mean."

"Well, I tell you what Bill, I'd be more ready to dismiss the whole visit if it weren't for the ankle. All in all, I'd say the good doctor has given us a couple of chunks of mud to throw at the wall. Let's see if any of it sticks.

"I'll check the phone records; you talk to Rick and Cory then we may want to get a team of techs out to the Baker home to run some tests on their phone system," Ed suggested.

"Let's catch up over a beer later what do you say?"

"Sounds good," said Ed and their meeting ended.

CHAPTER 16

"Elena, look at me as if you can see forever in my eyes and smile"

Thursday, November 22nd, 2012

*H*e wore his best poolside eye candy to get her to notice him and she didn't disappoint. She picked up on his $7,500 Rolex Submariner Blue watch, Ray Ban sunglasses and $400 Gucci Speedo trunks. She dove in and swam underwater until she 'accidentally' bumped into him.

She then rose out of the water quickly, intentionally too high and in front of his face giving him a close up view of just how tough a job that skimpy red and yellow bikini had holding all of her in. He wound up staring at the cornerstones of an absolutely spectacular body which she kept fit and tanned to a deep bronze well beyond her naturally brown colored skin.

"Oh, I'm so sorry!" she exclaimed.

He was amused and played along. "Don't be. I'm delighted that you swam into me. I was beginning to get bored with the lack of company in the pool. Everyone else seems to be paired up or with family and here I am all alone and with no one to talk to or drink with."

She tilted her head to the side and forward looking at him under her very lush eyebrows, batted her eyes, smiled and said, "I'd just love some good conversation and a drink . . . . to begin with."

The playful banter continued for a short time and then she moved in so close that he could feel her body heat even through the warm pool water and direct heat of the sun.

He could tell that she was a very shallow girl, and that she definitely knew how to take advantage of the gifts that mama gave her. He was becoming aroused as he adeptly prolonged their conversation and was delighted at the way she never stopped her underwater seduction of bumps and tugs.

They danced their underwater dance until it reached the point of needing a room, but they decided to first lounge poolside for a while with a few drinks.

The sun and breeze off the Caribbean Sea was the antithesis of the weather he left in the Chicago suburbs a week ago. They laid there soaking it all up and watching the sea gulls until he was sure his sun block was about to fail him.

Just then she asked, "How about we get changed and then grab some dinner to start what I know will be a sinfully wonderful night in Columbia?" He liked her play on words and replied with a smile, "Funny, I was thinking the exact same thing." They left the pool area in search of dry clothes, arm in arm. To anyone else at poolside they looked as if they were there on their honeymoon.

She grabbed a bag from the employee room behind the bar that she packed earlier in anticipation of a steamy night with a rich American tourist.

As they passed through the lavish lobby, he bought her a yellow and white flower for her hair. She placed it just above her left ear and it complemented her blonde streak. Unfortunately, it didn't stay there long once they reached his room.

They were both hungry for more than just supper and their passion exploded even before the door had a chance to fully close. Soon all they had on was the ceiling fan as they reached the king sized bed adorned with turned down white, brown and creme colored satin sheets with the classic OGC resort logo embroidered on the pillow cases and sheets.

Once they hit the bed she broke their embrace and changed the pace. She began to slowly and seductively explore his body in a way that almost made him change his mind about how the night would wind up. Almost—but not quite. There would be other girls. There always was.

*

As the late afternoon turned into evening, they were relaxing after round three and he couldn't take his eyes off her incredible body as she slithered out of the oversized hot tub. Their very athletic afternoon had wound up there. He watched her chest heave as she began to towel off, short of breath. "Man does not live on sex alone. Shall we grab a bite to eat?" he asked her virtually out of breath himself.

"Sure lover. I am starving. May I suggest we eat at the Barbacoa—Steak House here at the resort? They have an elegant menu and desserts to die for."

Once again she amused him with her innocent foreshadowing. He replied "Perfect! I'm all in."

*

She was right. Dinner at the Barbacoa was extraordinary. Everything from the service, to the chef's attention to every plate presentation detail, made this a dinner he wouldn't soon forget. It gave him time to make sure the two of them were utterly comfortable with each other. Then the opportunity presented itself!

"John, please order more wine. I think you will like what a good wine does to me after I drink enough of it. I will be right back," she said in her most seductive voice.

The full complement of personal documents he had made for travel used the alias 'John Deramore'.

"I can only imagine what that transformation will be like after the afternoon we just shared. You may rest assured that I do my best to see that all of your desires are fulfilled tonight my dear," he replied as she left the table.

Looking back over her shoulder she smiled and said, "Surprise me with dessert!"

Smiling and fully intending to do just that, he nodded and waved a beckoning finger to the waiter as he watched yet another of her fine assets sachet to the restroom.

"Waiter, may we have another bottle of Chateau Lamothe Guignard and some Raspberry Meringue Gateau dessert for both of us please."

Once the waiter left, he discreetly sprinkled some very unique powder into Elena's glass of wine and swished it around. He remembered that she was hip to the usual ways his new favorite drug was dispensed locally so he resorted to another just as effective way to obtain all the control over Elena, and the night, that he needed.

*

Friday, November 23rd, 2012

"Ed? Rick Newberry, Chicago BIS, hey listen I pulled the phone records for the Baker residence and just emailed them over to you. We have CT's scheduled for tomorrow; I'm sorry communication technicians, at the Baker home, for tomorrow. So far Cory's got Nada on the M.O. search. I'll keep ya posted. Call me if you need anything else. Talk to ya. Bye."

Ed's choppy communication from the BIS tech was the only message on his voice mail. He downloaded the 'Local Usage Details' for the Baker home and saw the call from Dr. Raymond Reed Monday at 8:01am but the next call listed was Lori's mother Beth Conner from Florida on Tuesday at 8:45pm. There was no call in between the two calls as described by Jim Baker nor was there one after the Conner Florida call.

While the phone record evidence was contradictory to Jim's account of the answering machine messages, it was certainly not unexpected. Jim was absolutely insistent about actually hearing, and trying to save the two messages from Lori. If not for the particular message about the ankle that Jim mentioned to them he'd be willing to dismiss it as maybe wishful thinking, delusions from his deep grief or something else.

Doctors are generally more used to dealing with highly stressful situations than the average person. They were typically more stable emotionally. Despite the horrible tragedy of his wife's death, he still wasn't ready to write Jim Baker off as delusional or worse yet actually beginning to exhibit a mental breakdown.

This was a tough one to figure out every way he looked at it. Boy could he use a break, the start of a break, the start of a clue, hell even Jim's supernatural messages were welcome but so far they weren't helpful either.

Focus Ed. 'Ok, let's totally accept the 'Lori messages' for now,' he thought. 'What's the meaning of the messages? How the hell is our perp getting the women to cooperate? Something in Lori's message was indicating a consciousness but also a lack of ability to resist. Was it some kind of deep hypnosis? That could be it. It sort of makes sense. It's either that or drugs. Negative toxicology screens keep pointing away from the drugs though. Besides, how could anyone have the chance to hypnotize now four women who were going about their regular routines? How could 'he' possibly intervene and gain the control that would be needed for such horrific crimes.'

While Connie's report showed the field mastectomies were performed post mortem, she found evidence of the burning and ankle crushing being done before they died. Burns are about the most horribly painful thing you can experience short of amputation let alone the pain that must have accompanied the smashing of an ankle.

'I can't imagine controlling those women through the pain they must have felt from all that burning of their bodies only with hypnosis. It fails the means & opportunity test. Hell while we are at it, what's the motive?'

Ed relentlessly continued on his circular path to nowhere trying every angle he could imagine and still not getting anywhere. He was intrigued by the 'Lori messages' and filed them with every other seemingly pointless fact of the case.

He updated his crime board adding 'missing answering machine messages', 'ankle reference', 'singular phone rings', 'steamed mirror message' and finally 'The Flowers'.

✻

Thursday, November 22nd, 2012

It had been at least fifteen minutes and she hadn't returned from 'powdering her nose' yet. No matter, he was enjoying the live music and watching the very colorful and scantily clad dancers roaming from table to table and performing for the restaurant's patrons.

Eventually Elena sauntered back to the table, sat down and took a sip of her wine. She looked seductively over her glass, smiled her sexiest smile and said, "Are you ready for a wild night señor?"

It seemed like she was a little spacey now compared to when she left a minute ago. 'Elena what have you been sniffing out of your purse my dear?' he thought.

He was in the middle of savoring another fork full of Raspberry Meringue Gateau. After which he added a healthy sip of wine. He wasn't about to let idle worthless verbal foreplay interrupt this moment. He always felt that Chateau Lamothe Guignard and Raspberry Meringue Gateau were simply exquisite on the palate together.

Finally he replied, "You have no idea. Tell me what you think of the Raspberry Meringue Gateau, then finish your wine and we shall begin our night together and I promise it will be one that you will never forget."

After dessert was finished he said to her, "Elena, look at me as if you can see forever in my eyes and smile," then he thought, 'because your forever won't last past this night.'

She did exactly as she was told and he knew he had her.

"Now I think it's time to retire to my room my dear."

She rose quickly, smiled that sexy seductive smile of hers again and said, "I would like nothing more."

He offered her his arm, which she took. Then she tilted her deep chestnut colored head of hair with the blonde streak and matching yellow flower that had found its way back into it, onto his shoulder. She put her arm around him and nestled that phenomenal body of hers as tightly against him as she could and they started out of the restaurant.

'This is going to be fun but also an incredible waste,' he thought as they headed to his room.

And the band played on.

CHAPTER 17

"I have lots of toys there. We will have much fun"

Saturday, November 24th, 2012

Jim couldn't get used to being in the house alone. The life he had shared with Lori kept flooding back to him whenever things got quiet. Tonight would be different, however, because Ray and Olivia were coming over to keep him company. They were also going to discuss his meeting with the police. This would be the first time he would be entertaining guests since Lori was taken from him.

He couldn't cook and Olivia knew that. She suggested bringing over Chinese take-out so they could spend as much time visiting as they could on this visit to the Baker home and helping Jim to take another step towards dealing with Lori's death.

"Liv, Ray, come in. Thanks so much for coming over. I really need this time with good friends. Let me take your coats."

"Not before a proper greeting," said Olivia as she gave him her warmest, extended length hug after which she held both his cheeks with her palms and gave him a firm but quick, friendly kiss.

"Jim, it's great to see you. How are you doing?" asked Ray.

"Well each day gets a little better but I've got a long way to go. I can tell you one thing though. I'm going to plan more evenings like this with friends because seeing you guys has me feeling better already! Come on in. Sit down. What can I get you to drink?"

"Wine for Liv and brandy for me would be great. We didn't bring the food in so we could chat a while. It's being delivered in about an hour," said Ray.

Jim poured the drinks and brought them all up to date with his visit to the police station earlier.

"Don't you feel better now that you shared all that with them, especially since it appears that they are taking you seriously?" Olivia asked.

"Yes, I thought . . . . ; guys do you hear something?" asked Jim.

They all listened and sure enough it sounded like a faint phone ringing upstairs. Setting down their drinks they all went upstairs together slowly and curiously as none of the regular house phones were ringing. At first they couldn't pin down where the ringing was coming from but ultimately they zeroed in on a closet in a spare bedroom.

The shelf in this bedroom is where Lori had kept old electronics; clock radios, answering machines, cell phones etc. One of the abandoned cell phones was ringing.

It was an old blackberry that Lori had given up a year ago in favor of a smart phone. They had stopped service on it when she got the new phone. The three of them looked at it lit up and ringing on the shelf in stunned silence, then looked at each other as if answers would be written on one of their foreheads.

"I guess I'll get it," Jim said and picked up the phone. The screen's caller ID showed XOXO as he pressed the speaker phone button. It was Lori's voice that they all heard next saying only, "Black Breath," then fairly loud static, and the phone went dead in his hand.

Jim pressed several buttons, but the phone had gone dark, and there was no response from any of the buttons.

"Welcome to the club guys because if I'm crazy, you both are right there along with me. You did hear that right?" asked Jim.

Olivia started first, "Jim there's no mistaking that for anything but Lori's voice. It was Lori. She said, 'Black Breath'. You heard it too didn't you Ray?"

"Yes I definitely did. Jim I'm speechless. This is obviously, beyond explanation. I'm looking at the phone in your hand and it was lit up, I heard Lori's voice and for lack of a better word, now it's dead," said Ray.

"Bear with me sports fans because you're really going to love this," Jim said as he turned the phone over. He took off the rear cover, and there was no battery in the phone!

Jim said, "Lori always recycled old batteries before storing old electronic equipment in here. There are four phones on the shelf, and none of them has batteries in them. The one that just rang was the one Lori had last before she got her latest smart phone."

Ray and Jim exchanged a wide-eyed stare of disbelief.

"I need my drink," said Olivia. It turned out they all did after that, and as they all started downstairs to get them, the door bell signaled the arrival of dinner.

✿

Friday, November 23th, 2012

The restaurant was just off the far end of the resort's open air lobby. As they passed through its entrance, his plans for the night crystallized. They were passing the floral stand as he said, "One moment Elena. I would like to by another flower."

"I already have the beautiful flower you bought me earlier in my hair. Where am I to put that one?" she asked him seductively.

"Oh it's not for you my dear. It's for the most beautiful and sexy girlfriend that you are going to invite to our little party tonight," he told her.

Twenty minutes later she arrived at his suite and she was a very close second to Elena. Not only was she spectacular to look at through her rather skimpy attire but she also had that wariness that most local girls naturally had due to the high rate of disappearances germane to the area.

"John, this is Graciela, my very good friend and companion. Graciela, this is my new friend John."

"Graciela, unless my Spanish fails me your name means pleasing or agreeable yes?" he asked as he bowed at the waist, noted the irony of how true that would soon be, and offered her the flower he purchased and prepared for this meeting.

'John' was glad that he had selected the exact same Taormina flower for Graciela that he had bought for Elena. It was a pure white flower with a soft yellow center. She wouldn't be quite so suspicious now that she saw the same flower in Elena's hair but he knew he needed to work fast before she noticed any possible behavioral changes in Elena.

He welcomed the challenge of gaining control of this beautiful young woman who was obviously checking out the room for anything indicating there might be a threat to her safety. She appeared to be a party girl looking for an opportunity herself as she very confidently sauntered over to face him.

The pure white area on the flower was dry and waxy so the powder didn't dampen and absorb into the pedal and its color hid the powder very well.

"A beautiful flower for a beautiful lady," he said as he offered it ever so slightly toward her face knowing a woman's tendency to enjoy a flower's fragrance. Her initial fears having been successfully allayed by the oh-so-gracious 'Wealthy American Tourist'; Graciela didn't fail his plan. In fact, she must have read the script because she took a healthy sniff and placed in behind her left ear exactly like Elena had. Mission accomplished!

He went for some wine making a show of popping the cork and pouring directly into glasses that were sitting rim down on the bar. As he offered the wine to them, he looked at Graciela and said, "Graciela, look at me as if you see forever in my eyes and smile."

Gradually a very seductive smile grew on her face which on its own meant nothing, but when her eyes gained that quality of a non blinking star struck stare that never looked away; he knew she was locked down tight and ready for their night together.

"Ladies, I feel like leaving the resort. Let's go to Graciela's house and have us some fun, what do you say?"

"We would like that John. I have lots of toys there. We will have much fun," said Graciela. With that, he grabbed a small bag of goodies on the way out and 'suggested' that since it was such a wonderfully mild night with that refreshing Caribbean breeze blowing in from the sea, it would be nice to walk the three blocks to Graciela's house.

✿

When they arrived he realized she was right about her obvious desire to please her guests.

"What a naughty girl you are Graciela!" he exclaimed once he saw her rather impressive array of adult novelties.

"I am a good hostess. I like my guests to have the kind of fun they don't get at home," she said.

"Well then let's have us some fun," he said as he watched them shed what little clothing they were wearing. Graciela put on some salsa music, pushed him backward on to her king sized oval bed. The girls paired up for an extremely suggestive vertical dance to begin with. Soon the real entertainment began as the dancing switched from vertical to horizontal. They were immediately all over him. What one didn't do to him the other did until he felt it was finally time for the main event.

Maybe he was feeling a little home sick. Perhaps he was finally satiated with how easy and unchallenging sex was to come by here. Maybe he just wanted to get back in the saddle again.

Suddenly he shifted into professional mode and had the girls get dressed. Since Elena lived only two blocks from Graciela they walked the short distance but first he had the presence of mind to ball up the sheets and took them with for that extra measure of forensics safety and dumped them in the bottom of a garbage can on the way. He remained completely within the confines of the sheets from the time he was pushed down onto the bed ever mindful of not leaving any DNA items behind in the room. It felt good to be 'back in the saddle' once again.

The bag he kept with him since they left his room contained what he called his 'clean kit'. He stopped just outside Elena's rear door on a cement entry and pulled it out after both girls went in. It contained all the items that allowed him to keep the crime scenes so clean back home.

It consisted of the turtle neck shirt, very thin body suit with elastic bands on the sleeves, neck and pant legs, booties, rubber gloves and hair net all of which he put on in the back yard then slipped into his smooth soled shoes.

He had been very careful to step only where he would leave no foot prints on the way to her back door and kept his soles dry until he got to the cement area leading to her back porch where he changed.

The pencil torch, scissors and hammer remained in the bag as they all went in for some real fun out of the sun.

He left after about an hour of familiar mutilation and butchery, finally ready to put this trip to Columbia behind him.

He would leave in the morning with all his next steps mapped and his supplies replenished, through his usual private charter to an abandoned airstrip in southern California. There his contacts would meet up with a refueling truck he had arranged to be there. Then they would continue on his next charter straight into the Chicago Executive Airport in Wheeling, IL. He couldn't wait to get back home. He longed to sleep in his own bed, confound his own police departments and murder his own choice of women to make his point.

CHAPTER 18

". . . a coffee drinking chain smoker with halitosis . . ."

<u>Saturday, November 24th, 2012</u>

Connie Bristol wrapped up her conversation with Ed Cassidy saying, "Sorry I wasn't more help. I thought your idea might have had some potential, but unfortunately based on all the details I just mentioned; I'm sure it's a dead end."

"Well thanks for checking and keep me posted if you come up with anything else," said Ed.

He had a theory about the killer possibly using some sort of muscle relaxants or nerve blocking agent to achieve the results he'd been able to obtain with the victims. Perhaps that was allowing him to get away with the excruciating pain he inflicted on them, and still maintain control of the crime scenes as he did. Connie ran a series of tests that conclusively eliminated them as a possibility. Not only were they not present in the tissue samples she collected from each victim, but a number of details involved in using those types of drugs simply didn't add up.

There were many factors that proved impossible for 'him' to be using those kinds of drugs in this case. She took into consideration the very broad scope of CNS (central nervous system) relaxants and scenarios such as Baclofen, carisoprodol, cyclobenzaprine, serotonin syndrome, etc. All of them would have required much too large a dose, and it would have had to have been administered very swiftly. None of these types of drugs could have been administered quickly enough to fit the murder timeline of any of these murder cases. It wasn't only getting the drug into their blood streams in some form which was quick, but the response times on top of that definitely put them out of the ballpark.

No, somehow our little mystery boy is getting big time control over his victims in an extremely short period of time. In fact, it's the only thing that adds up to what's in evidence in each case. But how?

They had immediately thought of an injection to get something into the blood stream quickly, but there was no evidence of injections on their bodies or drugs in their systems.

Besides Connie told him that these kinds of drugs would have had any number effects on the victims that didn't wash with the facts from any of the cases. Symptoms such as drowsiness, confusion, dizziness, fatigue, seizures, hallucinations, nausea and in some cases urinary retention would be affected. None of these symptoms was observed in any surveillance video they had, which admittedly wasn't much, or by observing any of the victims at the crime scenes.

They also would cause a response directly contrary to the peaceful looks on each of the victims' faces in light of the mutilations they each experienced.

There was also no evidence of petechial hemorrhage. Despite all the TV crime story characters making this determination with one simple glance, in real life this situation was much harder to determine and required very close observations.

Damn it all, nothing made sense in this case so far.

✻

Sunday, November 25th, 2012

If it were anybody else but Ray and Olivia Reed, Jim would be feeling very much like a third wheel with a big sign on his forehead saying 'Lonely'. They made him feel anything but as they arrived at Morton's Steakhouse for a nice distracting dinner out. Since Jim turned them down for Thanksgiving Day dinner at their place, he found it difficult to refuse this offer. He was in the mood for a good dinner away from the house anyway.

They announced their reservations with the maitre d' and were escorted to the bar area where they met Blake and Sandra Falkland.

They had all decided to dress somewhat formally with the guys staying this side of a tuxedo but the ladies decided not to hold back at all and both were stunning.

Sandra was wearing a spectacular ivory and rose-red colored dress that was simple, but very elegant in design with a diamond earring and necklace set that would have paid for Jim's first year at med school. The ivory swirls, and straight band type highlights on the gown were very stylish and eye catching as they accentuated Sandra's impressive figure.

Olivia was similarly decked out having had her hair done up in swooped back style with a very tasteful white Asiatic lily placed perfectly on one side. She wore a royal blue velvet dress with silver highlights that was very low cut and exquisitely adorned with well placed sequence. She wore a simple diamond and sapphire necklace and earrings which matched the dainty wrist and ankle bracelets.

Liv and Sandy greeted each other with a hug in which they scarcely touched. At the same time, they each kissed the air next to each other's cheeks so as not to spoil their impeccable make up. All Jim could say was, "WOW!" As the hugs came his way he said to the guys, "Blake and Ray, you are two lucky dudes. Boy did you two ever marry up!"

"We are trained beauty connoisseurs, and lucky ones at that to be able to accompany these two handpicked beauties," said Ray.

"Oh PALEASE," said Sandy. "Ok we accept the compliments. Now can we get some drinks? These two 'beauties' are parched!"

Jim was sufficiently distracted from the moment he arrived and throughout their dinner which was excellent. Not only the food but the company of good friends was just what he needed.

As perfect as the night was, they couldn't help drifting to the topic on everyone's mind. That being the details surrounding the killer that remained at large who had impacted the life of everyone gathered at the table.

"That's about all I can tell you at this point. I really appreciate the way Ed Cassidy has been actually taking me seriously. He was anything but condescending or dismissive when I presented him with what I've been experiencing lately," Jim concluded as he brought the Falklands up to date.

"Also during my conversation with Inspector Cassidy yesterday, he said they were working on a theory involving some sort of muscle relaxing drugs, but it didn't pan out due to response times versus established timetables. Besides, there was nothing at all notable found in the tissue samples taken from any of the girls," said Jim.

"Can anyone say 'Square One'?" said Blake.

"Yes it's very frustrating, but the police are assuring me that this is the most exasperating and least fruitful part of most investigations. It is all the more pressing in these situations as the victims, for the most part, are all known by each of the survivors," said Jim.

"Well they certainly have that one right. We're all afraid to say it, but the reality is we are all waiting for the next shoe to drop and are equally afraid that it will do so before the police find this menace," Blake said.

"True but we all must remain ever vigilant until they do find whoever this is," said Olivia.

"They just finished installing that new super HD monitoring equipment at our house that we just found out about this past week," said Blake. "It not only does it provide an incredible amount of detail which will be picked up by the cameras, but the bloody thing also sweeps each section periodically and has night vision capability as well," Blake continued.

"I was thinking of getting ours upgraded to that one too Blake. It can't hurt. I guess I'll call them Monday," said Ray.

Jim felt Lori's loss again, despite the camaraderie, as he realized that there was no real reason for him to upgrade his security system and remained quiet for the remainder of dinner.

✻

Monday, November 26th, 2012

Jim made the decision to return to his regular surgery regimen, but put it off until the next week. This week's step in the direction of normal behavior for him would focus on getting back to handling regular patient consultations and follow-up routines. Monday morning he got a good jump on that plan, but during a morning hour long lull in his comeback schedule, he had another uncomfortable call to make to Inspector Cassidy.

"Jim, it's good to hear from you. How are you doing?"

"I wish I could say fine. I guess I'm doing better, but Ed I've had another, dare I call it, communication or message or whatever from Lori," said Jim.

"Oh? What type of communication or message?"

"Don't get me wrong, I feel just as strange telling you this as I did the previous messages, but this time I actually have two witnesses. Ray and Olivia Reed were over for dinner on Saturday and . . ." he paused here feeling almost too awkward to continue but he knew he must. ". . . we all heard the faint telephone ringing sound coming from upstairs. Understand that none of the house phones were ringing on the first floor. When we ALL followed the sound it led us to the closet in the unused bedroom where Lori stored old used electronics. What was ringing was Lori's old blackberry. It was lit up and ringing!" he said remaining hesitant to continue.

"And who was it that was calling?" asked Ed.

"Well that's just it. I hesitate to categorize it as a call, but I 'answered' it and immediately placed it on speaker for all to hear. I didn't want to be the only one to hear like the last times. Especially since I couldn't prove anything on any of them," he said.

"What made you suspicious about the call?" asked Ed.

"Here we go . . . . not only did we discontinue the service on her blackberry once she got her Droid phone, but Lori was in the habit of removing the batteries from all the old devices she stored and recycling them. Ed, there was no way this old phone of hers could be ringing."

"Anyway, once I placed it on speaker we ALL heard Lori's voice and all it said was, 'Black Breath'.

"After that, we all heard a kind of heavy static and then the phone went dead in my hand. I mean lights off and not another sound. Once we all stopped staring at each other and confirmed that we each heard the same thing, I opened the phone and showed the Reeds that there was no battery in it!

"Ed, this just keeps getting stranger by the minute."

"I have to admit Jim, I'm equally speechless. Does the message mean anything to you? Any idea what the 'Black Breath' message could be referring to?" asked Ed.

"I can't begin to understand that one. Could it possibly mean . . . . I mean could she possibly be referring to the person that overtook her was close enough for her to smell his rotten breath? Was he a coffee-drinking-chain smoker with halitosis and possibly rotten teeth? That doesn't seem like the, in all probability, sharp person that's been outsmarting us all with his lack of clues at each crime scene does it? I don't know what it could mean," said Jim.

"I'll run it by the rest of the team and see if anyone can draw the meaning out of it from this end. Thanks for calling Jim and please don't hesitate to call. Anything that may lead to a clue or direction in this case would be welcome no matter where or how it got to us. I'll be in touch," said Ed as he hung up the phone on one of the strangest conversations he's ever experienced in working a case.

CHAPTER 19

'I won't ask if they missed me.'

Tuesday, November 27th, 2012

*A*fter his uneventful private flight from Columbia to the now deserted air strip outside of Imperial Gables, located in the remote southern California desert, he awaited his connecting 'ticket' back to Illinois. This 'ticket' was a tanker truck that would allow him to take off without needing to file a flight plan as required by all airfields operating in the US.

Although he didn't believe in mirages, Elena's spectacular body appeared from memory just outside his window. She was beckoning him to join her with that sexy smile and that incredible blonde streak in her hair catching the sun in a way that made him wish he had brought her home with him.

What a waste that was. Too bad they didn't meet under different circumstances. He could have controlled that incredible beauty to be his little slave for years, but there would be others and they would take his mind off the one true love that was taken too soon from him.

He shook off the thoughts as a smoke trail in the distance marked the arrival of his 'ticket' back home.

'Time to refocus on current events people,' he thought to himself. He really couldn't wait to get back in the saddle again in Winnetka.

'We have some twists and turns coming boys and girls! I wonder what Andy and Barney have been up to. They probably have some new playmates now because they are just too damned incompetent on their own and probably have been getting a lot of heat from daddy, the big bad chief of the wussie Winnetka police department. They wouldn't know what to do with a real challenge. They couldn't handle this one on their own if the solution were posted on a billboard on I-94.

'Revenge can not only be sweet; it can also be its own reward.

'Hell I've already rewritten Confucius' old saying, "Before you embark on a journey of revenge, dig two graves."'

'There have been four graves dug so far and three more to go to properly honor you my love,' he thought as that all too familiar melancholy feeling over took his mood once again.

Once the refueling was completed, he was back in the air and four hours from home.

✻

"Hey Bill, its Ed. Listen there has been another development in the Baker case. I hope you're sitting down."

"Let me guess, another trip to the Twilight Zone?" Bill mused.

"I'm sorry. I don't mean to be disrespectful, but I'm just having a lot harder time swallowing Dr. Baker's medicine than you are Ed," Bill said trying to bring it back to professional and barely succeeding.

"Can't say as I blame you Bill but for some reason I believe him. I don't know why but, perhaps it's a sincerity in his face when he's been telling us these stories of his. I just have a feeling about these Lori clues, or messages, or hell what do we call them anyway Bill? Dr. Jim had the same trouble with defining them. Maybe that's why I'm so inclined to believe them. He's not all about the hard sell with them. Anyway here goes . . ."

As Ed finished relating the latest phone conversation he had this morning with Jim Baker. Then he received the expected long period of silence at the other end of the phone.

"Bill? Are you there?" he asked.

"Now there are three of them in on it? Ed, really, are we supposed to put any real credence on any of this? It's starting to feel more and more like a distraction from what we really should be doing with our time. There's a goddamned killer on the loose out there Ed; we don't have a piss ant sized clue on any of this yet, and you want to be chasing Casper's new buddy Lori for answers?

"Again Ed, I'm sorry but it's a bit much for me, anything more from Connie or the boys from BIS or state?"

He knew enough to drop it with Bill. Right now even the unanswerable ankle revelation would mean nothing to him, "Not since she threw the CNS relaxants out the window and no, it's been all quiet from the boys' front as well.

"On a positive note, many of the 'Generals' are upgrading to that new super HD surveillance system that just came out. Let's hope that one of them can provide us with something resembling a clue before the chief has us all walking a beat and gives our badges to the local rent-a-cops working the nightshift at Wal-Mart."

☆

As previously arranged, once the Nemesis' private charter landed at the Chicago Executive Airport, his 'friend' in the tower promptly wiped his arrival from all logs. Ten thousand dollars will do that for you if you have it and know the traffic controller that's upside down in his mortgage.

Tomorrow he would be back to spying on his favorite widowers to see what's been going on since he left for his R & R . . . . 'rest and restocking'. He was looking forward to working once again with the laser microphone he had picked up a month before he left for his first trip to Columbia. What an awesome tool! From the street, undetected, he could pick up conversations in a room by bouncing a laser beam off a window which magically converted inside conversations to electronic signals which were then filtered, amplified and pumped right back into his headset as if he were sitting in a chair in the room with them!

This was his favorite toy in the rather extensive arsenal he had assembled for the sole purpose of keeping ahead of the keystone cops working on the case, as well as following any new developments from the 'Generals' themselves.

It had allowed him to pick up on a number of pattern changes they instituted lately like calling hubby before going anywhere and reporting in every fifteen minutes if they were out of the house for any reason, blah, blah, blah. None of it would do them any good anyway.

He was feeding their assumptions and playing off their paranoia as he constantly adjusted his plans to stay three steps ahead of the lot of them. Most times he felt almost cheated out of a better challenge.

He was constantly fighting a sense of it all being too effortless. This he knew could bring him down quicker than Andy and Barney ever could. His mantra was, 'don't forget the three Cs, complacency = carelessness = caught' and so far it served him well.

Fortunately for the 'Generals' side, he missed all the recent conversations between Jim, Ray Reed and Ed Cassidy regarding the 'Lori clues'. He was blissfully unaware that the tide was possibly turning ever so slightly away from his favor.

'I won't ask if they missed me. I know they did, albeit like the plague, but it's nice to be missed just the same. Speaking of the plague, it's about to continue spreading once more,' he confidently mused to himself.

With the new security systems now in place at many of his target homes, he needed to shift his M.O. somewhat. He knew he couldn't afford to lure the victims into a cozy encounter inside their homes any more so next up . . . . time to think out of the box.

That night he set up outside the home of his next victim to see if any more adjustments needed to be made before he spread the plague to victim number five.

'Oh, this strategy is a thing of beauty that I can't wait to share with my good buddies the 'Generals',' he thought.

Part Three

Mourning's Glory

"I wish none of this had happened."
Lord of the Rings—Frodo
"So do all who live to see such times
but that is not for them to decide."
Lord of the Rings—Gandalf

CHAPTER 20

". . . a little something extra for Mrs. Falkland; double check."

Tuesday, November 27th, 2012

After a couple of uneventful days, Jim headed for an early morning shower. His mind was consumed with how the return to his work routine was progressing, patient issues and the fact that his buddy John Ackerman had returned from Florida and would meet him for lunch this afternoon.

That was when the routine that he was so accustomed to; the routine that had been slowly creeping back to make his life closer to normal again, suddenly left the building quicker than the air from a balloon popped by a pin. He had not been looking at the steamed mirror when he first exited the shower, but he eventually, and reluctantly did glance that way. His arms locked suddenly when he finally checked it out.

There, as clear as stars on a frosty night, was another message written in the mirror's steam. Sandwiched between the two hearts, one in the upper left and one in the lower right corners of the mirror, was a written message; "Sun Dancer—Sandra."

"Lori, can you hear me? Are you here? Lori, what does all this mean? Lori, Lori, Lori . . . ," he sobbed as he clutched the towel to his face and fell to his knees and back against the shower door, temporarily unable to move from the room and the sight of the mirror.

After a few moments of staring at the message, he gathered his senses and rushed to the bedroom and grabbed his cell phone. Before it had a chance to disappear this time, he took a picture of the mirror. Not that anyone would believe that he didn't put a message there, but perhaps Olivia could verify that it looked like Lori's writing.

Just that quickly, the possibility of returning to a regular work routine and a quiet lunch with John had vanished.

✻

The stack of patient records reflecting one year's worth of patient treatment was impressive. There were, however, twenty 'Generals' and the good doctor Rick Holden made twenty one. Ed and Bill had no idea they were involved in that many peoples' lives within a year's time.

After completing their initial cursory review of the stacks, they noted very little in the way of suspicious cases from the files that the 'Generals' provided. That is, any issues that could lead to angry or vengeful patients or relatives of patients.

Dr. Richard Holden, however, was quite a different story. No wonder he was hesitant to provide them to the investigators. Ed & Bill found at least twenty cases that they could easily file under 'Less Than Desirable Results' or hell for that matter; they more realistically deserved to be filed under the heading of 'Botched'.

"I'm no doctor Ed, but it sure doesn't look like a very good batting average for 'ole Doc Holden now does it? I mean shit, he's been doing better during the last six months but before that; I can easily see at least fifty cases that could set Ricky boy in the winner's circle for the 'Malpractice Poster Child of the Year' award. My god, some of these poor women must have gone through hell," said Bill.

"I'm with you," Ed agreed. "Let's get a little deeper in on the twenty worse situations we singled out beginning with the ten from the front half of the alphabet. Meanwhile, I've reached out to Jack Sullivan at BIS for his own independent search through the files from the first half of the alphabet. I'd be interested to see if he comes up with the same group of disgruntled patients as we did.

"Ok, from the first ten we have three apparently botched nose jobs, four boob jobs, one facial reconstruction and two liposuction procedures gone wrong. Let's start with the Liposuction situations. Connie produced some interesting research regarding the potential for complications and risk factors.

"This is from an email she sent me: 'Major risk factors for severe complication development are inadequate hygiene standards, the permeation of multiple liters of wetting solution, disproportionate postoperative discharge, and selection of poorly qualified patients. A lack of surgical experiences was a very common contributing factor, particularly in the timely identification of complications as they developed.' She goes on to say that some of these contributing factors sometimes can be deadly!" Ed read as he set the email down and started digging in to the short stack of documents they had singled out.

"Wow, imagine going in for liposuction and coming out counting worms," said Bill.

"That's colorful. He did have a fatality involving the Fairholm liposuction case and plenty of complications in the other. Why don't you take Mr. Barringer and I'll take Mrs. Fairholm's case?

"Fairholm's case has some real sour grape potential," said Ed.

"I know I'd be pissed if he were the reason my wife started pushing up parsley at Mother Nature's Acres. The Barringer case seems to have had unusual infections that were dealt with over several months as well," mused Bill.

"The Morley facial reconstruction case seems, to the untrained eye, a very botched surgery as well. Five months of follow ups and four minor procedures following the original surgery rings the old alarm bell for me," Ed supposed.

"That leaves us nose jobs and boob jobs. While the nose job circumstances weren't the worst of the group, there were two law suits filed out of the three we picked. I'll follow up on those Bill.

"I suggest we split the boob jobs and take two each, you can take the Girvan and Holbech cases and I'll take the Cobern and Collamore cases" said Ed.

"Keep in touch with any results Bill and I'll do the same. Maybe we can dig a lead out of one of these situations. Doc Holden definitely has some patient contentment issues."

*

"Let's see: Bouquet of flowers; check. SFC cap; check, SFC jacket; check, mustache disguise; check, Special designed gym shoes adding three more inches to my height; check, Out-of-town rented van; check, A little something extra for Mrs. Falkland; double check."

The Nemesis had discreetly purchased a bouquet of flowers that no self absorbed 'Generals' wife could resist. They were all so used to being pampered and getting everything their little hearts desired, that she wouldn't suspect a thing. Especially with all the extra attention they were all getting recently, since his little revenge campaign began to drop their counterparts like flies.

'Time for one more confirmation of pedestrian traffic at the old park of choice and tomorrow will be all set,' thought the Nemesis as he triple checked his itinerary for the next step in his plan.

There were several scheduled activities in the Elder Lane Park community center building. It was just off the playground which contained a swing set, slide, horse on a spring, exercise climbing area and park benches for the moms to watch the little ones get some exercise and pull out each other's hair in warmer weather. That section would be vacant in this late fall/early winter season, though, and it was of no interest to him. The timing of the craft fair and youth basket ball game scheduled for tomorrow was a primary consideration in timing his plan.

Once those were over, the usually vacant winter season scene at the park would return. This was the perfect cover for the deserted area of beach below the park that was bracketed by piers going out one hundred feet into Lake Michigan. Yes, this was the perfect spot for his next installment.

It would serve the community right for placing that ugly bronze "Sun Dancer—Jackie" statue like that along the side of the kid's park up above his planned murder scene. It probably scared off more than one rich little brat with its ugly hat and cape. What was that supposed to represent anyway? No matter, the real action would happen tomorrow down on the beach. Down there it was nice and hidden from the park due to the retaining wall between the sets of stairs on either side connecting the park above to the beach below.

At each side of the beach, community center building and park above, were those overly gaudy houses, no, estates. House didn't do them justice. These estates were very common along the lake front in this part of Winnetka. Poised up over their own retaining walls and walkways connecting them to their own little private beaches, each of them had a spectacular view of the lake. None of them, however, had a direct view of his selected little stretch of sandy beach. Hell a number of those estates belonged to the 'Generals' but not for several properties down in either direction.

Plan, review, re-review and then re-review again. The setting and timing were perfect for this much needed shift in direction. There was virtually no boat traffic within sight, save for an occasional barge that passed too far from shore to be of any interest in broad daylight let alone on the overcast gloomy day that tomorrow promised to be.

Perfect. Perfect. It couldn't be more perfect.

CHAPTER 21

". . . I'd be asking you for a ride to the funny farm"

Tuesday, November 27th, 2012

*A*fter the way his morning started out, Jim decided to call his friend Ray Reed and invited him to breakfast. He found once again that he needed a friendly shoulder and ear.

"Sure Jim that would be excellent. I have a free morning until 11:30 today anyway. Do you want me to see if Liv can make it also?"

"I'd really like it if she could Ray. Something else has happened that I need to speak to the two of you about but not on the phone," said Jim as he hung up and headed out to their favorite diner.

Finding himself with an unusually light schedule of patient appointments as well, with nothing until mid afternoon, Jim arrived early to contemplate the sum of all the unnatural things he had recently experienced.

There was a lot for his mind to absorb and still maintain a semblance of sanity.

What was happening to him lately? Doctors are supposed to be logical men of science that deal only in facts which inevitably lead to reliable conclusions. Recently, it seemed that random ideas were bouncing around in his head like a BB in a boxcar, leading nowhere and making no sense. The clues, or messages, or whatever the hell it was that kept coming in a steady stream of late, seemed to defy logic, at least so far. They must mean something, collectively add up to something or point to something, someone, somewhere, somehow.

Was he misinterpreting them?

He remained truly lost and hopelessly frustrated when it came to drawing any kind of meaning from them. His gut told him that there was some sort of meaningful insight that he should be extracting from all this.

Just then the sight of his beautiful friend Olivia, followed closely behind by Ray, broke his train of thought. It was just as well because all he was managing to do was drive himself nuts thinking about it all anyway.

"Hi Jim, how are you?" she asked as she swooped in with one of her warmest hugs.

"Quite frankly Liv, I think I'm going nuts, but I'm once again much better now that you and Ray are here."

They all sat down after Jim got his breath back from Ray's bear hug of a greeting. Jim just stared at the two of them, paused a bit, then the tears began to form in the corners of his eyes as he said, "I don't know where I'd be without the two of you right now."

Liv reached out and held his hands, tearing up herself and said, "You won't ever have to worry about that Jim. We will always be here for you."

"Well I wish they'd turn the heat down a little in here. My eyes are sweating," Jim said.

"Yeah, mine too," said Liv as she dabbed the corners of her eyes snickering.

"I have a pot of coffee and a glass of orange juice for each of us coming for starters. It looks like the waitress is coming back now. Why don't we order and then I have some things to discuss with both of you."

After the waitress left, Jim began, "Well first it was the 'Flowers' message, then the cell phone message about burning, then the information about having to do what she didn't want to, then the crushed ankle message, then the one about the 'Black Breath' that we all heard and now this morning there was another one."

"There was another one? What happened this time?" Ray asked.

"If you two start noticing an odor coming from my direction in the near future it's because I'm scared to go into the shower anymore. This morning I was just beginning to feel good about things returning back to normal when I exited the shower and found this." With that, he pulled out his phone and showed them the photo he took of the mirror this morning.

"Oh my god Jim, that's Lori's writing! Look at the way the S's are made, just like she used to. I'm thinking of various notes I've received from her with the S's written just like that," exclaimed Olivia.

"I was thinking the same thing when I found it and fortunately I was able to collect myself enough after the initial shock of seeing it and snapped a picture for you two. It is so much more telling than simply relating the message to you verbally."

"You almost didn't make it out of the mirror's visual reach in your birthday suit there, Mr. Photographer," Olivia snickered.

"You noticed!" exclaimed Jim as Ray returned the conversation's tone back to serious.

"Jim, I can't begin to describe any of this, but I'm with Liv on this one. That is Lori's writing. It is definitely her handwriting and as exciting, humbling and eerie as that is, I guess, we are back to our favorite topic of 'What can it possibly mean?'" said Ray.

"Ray I'm exhausted. I have been kicking all these things around in my head all morning right up until the moment you two got here, and it's always the same. I wind up with nothing. I guess the harder I think about it all; the more I keep going back to visualizing Lori and her playful spirit. Then my mind wanders off track. I suppose my concentration on the subject suffers in the bargain.

"While I'm betting it's the same for you two to a degree, I'm counting on you and Ed Cassidy to help me make some sense out of this before I go insane. I say Ed Cassidy because I get a weird vibe from Bill Weller whenever we speak. Ed seems to be taking these 'unexplainable things' better than Bill. I do believe Bill thinks I've lost it, and there are plenty of times lately that I'm close to agreeing with him," Jim explained.

"What has Ed said about this latest message Jim?" Olivia asked.

"I haven't related it to him yet. I feel more bizarre every time I go to him with yet another of these 'unexplainable things'. Oh, I will tell him this afternoon but I wanted to ask you two for one more favor," Jim said.

"Ask away buddy, anything; you know that," said Ray.

"I know you have appointments later on this morning but could you pry yourself away to join John and me for lunch?" asked Jim.

"I have so much catching up to do with him, and I think it would go much better with the two of you there with me. It is an awful lot for him to absorb so early back from his visit with Lisa's mom and sister in Florida. We'll be meeting at that new Italian restaurant in town at 1:00 pm," said Jim.

"Olivia has a doctor's appointment this afternoon but I'll be there. I've been anxious to spend some time with John since he left for Florida," said Ray.

"I wish I could be there with you two. It will be great to see John again. We all need to get together again soon. It's been a while and so much has happened," offered Olivia.

☆

After breakfast, Jim returned home to make yet another of those uncomfortable calls to Inspector Cassidy. As usual he took the information in stride, promised to look into it and like Ray and Olivia; he had no immediate explanation for what it could mean.

"Jim, please don't shy away from bringing anything to me regarding any of these cases no matter how awkward you feel about them or how insignificant you think they may be. Sooner or later it will all start to make sense. We will without a doubt be glad we received them, and you'll be glad you shared them," said Ed.

"I'm glad you think that way Ed, but I'm not so sure Bill shares your feelings."

"Well no two people are alike and no two detectives are either. I'm finding out that Bill and I are complementing each other. We've been working together well since our lieutenant reached out to his lieutenant and got him assigned to our task force. It's still grunt work time around here, but something will break soon, I'm sure of it," said Ed.

☆

The luncheon with John went about as expected. After the initial awkward pleasantries that skirted the two six ton elephants at the table, namely Lisa and Lori's murders, Jim brought the conversation around to where he needed it in order to start relating the incredible things that had happened since John left.

He didn't hold back once he got started. The more he told of his bizarre tale the more he felt the renewed strength of their friendship as John absorbed everything Jim had to tell him with sincere interest

"John I'm having a hard time with all this obviously, but if not for Ray and Liv hearing the cell phone 'Black Breath' message and the photo I took this morning of the mirror, I'd be asking you for a ride to the funny farm," Jim said.

"Jim, I've just spent nearly four weeks absorbing Lisa's death and the terrible news about Lori and Izzie. There certainly has been a lot for all of us to consider, but all this . . . . Jim I'm not sure what I can give you in the way of making sense of any of it," John concluded as he tried to come to grips with what he was just told.

"I don't expect anything from you but what you've already given me John and that's confidence in what I just told you. We are all struggling with that one, the confidence part that is, but I just wanted you to be up to date with everything on the home front."

After that, Jim and Ray related all they knew in the form of progress and lack thereof from the investigators as well.

*

'Well isn't that cozy! Too bad I don't have my surveillance microphone with me to hear the chorus of "Kumbaya" they must be singing in there. Soon enough they'll be singing a different tune and so will my brother.

'He's going to pay for not taking better care of her. He's the one that made her feel so inadequate that she was driven to the surgery from hell. He did very little due diligence before allowing that hack to cut her up and ultimately take her away from us. He was just too busy starting up that damn flower pit that he keeps shoveling money into. Even now he doesn't spend half the time he should with their two boys. They'd be better off in foster care than with him.

'The wheels of destruction are rolling your way too brother! They'll get there soon enough,' the Nemesis contemplated as he began the next step down his path to revenge.

CHAPTER 22

'Have fun with the dead ends, boys,'

Tuesday, November 27th, 2012

That night the Winnetka Police Department had a surprise 'racket' planned for retiring Lieutenant Michael "Cuffs" Gorten. Lieutenant Gorten earned his nickname by amassing one of the best arrest records from virtually every city he worked in. Inevitably the most perplexing situations found their way to his desk where he not only welcomed them but attacked them with an unrelenting vigor that always got the desired result.

He had planned this retirement before the recent string of serial murders began and was calling it quits after forty tough years on various major city police forces.

Like every cop before him; graduating from the academy landed him squarely on the streets walking beats. In his case, the starting blocks were nailed down in Atlanta. After which he transferred to one high crime rate city after another including tours in Boston, New York City, Philly and Chicago. Along the way, he earned his detective's shield and was never quite able to find the time to work on a family. Recently he decided to slow his tempo down and transferred to the Winnetka PD for an utter change of pace. He thought it would be the perfect place to wrap up his career in law enforcement. The whole slow down thing had been working great but as of late, not so much.

Everyone knew LT "Cuffs" wanted to catch this serial nut job and was postponing the signing of his retirement papers until it was done. This didn't stop the planned 'racket', though.

Once most of the 'pleasantries' in the form of witty, not so witty and just plain vulgar greetings, tributes and gifts were presented, things began to settle down a bit. "Cuffs" cornered Ed and Bill for an update. He just couldn't leave it alone not even at his own party.

"I'm honored to meet the famous LT 'Cuffs' in a more relaxed setting. I hope you don't mind that Ed didn't put up a fuss when I asked to crash your party," said Bill.

"Not at all Weller; not at all. We've been seeing so much of you around the house recently it's almost as if you're part of our squad," said Gorten.

"Yeah, well no offense but it's not by choice. This bastard is proving to be a slippery one for everyone right up to the Feebs. I'd like nothing more than to be the one that makes this guy no longer eligible for the census," said Bill.

"Lew, Bill and I have spent the last few days going through the files we received from the good doctors."

"And the bad doc apparently by the look of the files Doc Holden gave us," interjected Weller.

"Yeah well," Ed continued, "We threw some shoe leather at ten of the twenty worse cases we found and got nothing solid from the effort. We also sent the first half of the files we sifted through to Jeremy Cowan, the Feebs' profiler, to see if he can find anything interesting that we may have missed."

After a few more details and various interruptions from rowdy party participants, they were eventually able to put the string of murders out of their conversations long enough to enjoy the rest of the party.

Wednesday, November 28th, 2012

The next day found Ed and Bill back at the stack of case files. After an exhaustive day of study they had once again pretty much eliminated every file they evaluated from the 'Generals' but found plenty that warranted a closer look from Doctor Rick Holden's stacks.

"There's no two ways around it Ed, this guy is a hack. I mean his office is located on the corner of Incompetent Street and Negligent Avenue. Did he even graduate from medical school? Perhaps we should start there," said Bill.

The study of this stack left them even more astounded than the study of the last stack of Holden cases.

"Just when his batting average was getting a bit better, bang it goes right back down in the shitter. He must have the highest malpractice premiums in the suburbs, maybe even in the city. It'll take a week to follow up on all these situations. Don't forget we have ten more left over from the last group," Ed reminded Bill.

"Here you take this stack of greatest hits, and I'll take the other one. I hope you have on comfortable shoes, a full tank of gas and no plans for the rest of the week and weekend," Ed said as they started perusing their stacks of files.

"Whoa, it looks like this time I get one wearing a pine overcoat at the Horizontal Hilton," said Bill continuing to go overboard with his off color references to another victim's demise.

It was definitely time for some grunt work.

✻

'So this is what it feels like to dress up like a loser every day,' thought the Nemesis as he finished donning the outfit he deemed perfect for an afternoon of revenge.

The outward appearance of the Nike running shoes completely hid the elevators he placed inside them to increase his height three inches. A pair of plain navy blue uniform type pants complemented the jacket he was wearing which bore the colorful yellow, red and blue 'SFC' logo on the back and right lapel area with the name tag removed from the left breast area. Of course the matching 'SFC' logo on the baseball type cap he wore and the clipboard with delivery slips from 'Shaw's Floral Creations' rounded out the appearance of a 'SFC' delivery guy.

He took the beautiful bouquet of three dozen red, yellow and white roses with sprays of baby's breath around them still wrapped in clear plastic to the van he had waiting outside. The plain white panel van's only outward markings were the stolen license plates he had switched yesterday at a shopping mall which he placed on the van he rented in North Chicago.

'Yeah, the North Chicago Express Rental office is not going to see the switched plates on their van until well after I'm gone. Then Andy and Barney can play a little game of connect the dots. The incredibly inept duo will trace the stolen plates on the van rental back to Antioch where I switched them with that rust bucket.' He only wished he could be there to see the look on their faces when they reviewed the North Chicago Express Rental surveillance tapes and found the bald headed old black dude with white hair and mustache that appeared to limp in to the store to rent the van with cash. 'There's a bunch of sterling clues for ya! Have fun with the dead ends, boys,' he reflected to himself.

The weather was perfect and just as predicted. It was a dismally overcast and dry day with temperatures in the mid thirties and winds of less than five miles per hour. All in all it couldn't have turned out to be a better day for a special delivery to the Falkland residence.

After a short fifteen minute trip he pulled off Sheridan Road on to Elm Street and stopped short of Hoyt Lane. There he parked the van on the side of the road and crawled into the back to put the finishing touches on his precious cargo. Removing the clear plastic from around the flowers and taking the vial from his shirt pocket, he lightly coated a couple of rose petals with some of the precious cargo he had brought back with him from his latest trip to Cartagena Columbia.

"It's Showtime!" he exclaimed as he returned to the driver's seat and drove on to meet with the lovely, and soon to be his next victim, Mrs. Sandra Falkland.

CHAPTER 23

"Fish and chips it is then."

Wednesday, November 28th, 2012

*H*e parked the van at the end of the long winding driveway in front of the deceptive two car garage door. Deceptive because after his usual thorough inspection of the property building plans he found a lift in the center of the garage floor that lowered two cars at a time to a six stall vehicle storage area beneath the street level garage. From there, a selected vehicle could be driven on to the lift, raised to street level, by remote control of course, and driven away.

'I really need to get me one of those. Six stalls wouldn't be enough, though; I'd need at least a ten stall lower level. I do like my toys!' he thought as he left the van and walked up the front walk to the door. On his way, he noticed the security camera to his left at the far end of the long front porch and discreetly kept his face mostly angled away from it. Then there was the overhead camera towards the door next to that obnoxious hanging flower pot now devoid of flowers. He kept the big bright bouquet of flowers he was delivering blocking this one until he got his head past it; then he let the bill of his cap take over the facial blocking duties.

He remained careful not to look too obvious about giving them only as much of a facial shot as he wanted them to have. 'I do hope my mustache remained on straight,' he mused to himself.

Ding dong. The exquisite sound of the doorbell did the elegant estate proud.

'This is definitely NOT Avon calling Sandra,' he joked to himself as he waited for the door to open.

The look on her face couldn't have been more priceless. She took one look at that huge bouquet of flowers and was instantly delighted at the sight of them. Her face transformed and her guard went down, both were reactions that he counted on.

"Are you the lucky lady of the house, ah, let me see here . . . Sandra Falkland?" he asked her in a somewhat monotone, mundane delivery guy demeanor.

"I certainly am. Oh, they are absolutely beautiful!" she exclaimed. He sensed that she wanted to get them into the house as soon as possible, so he needed to act fast.

"Yes they are beautiful and fragrant. You should smell the inside of my van about now," he said as he moved the bouquet closer to her face guiding the 'sprinkled' petals specifically toward her nose.

She leaned in and took a good whiff and said, "My, they do smell wonderful don't they?"

He smiled, agreed and looked her in the eye to confirm that the blank look of resignation had found its way to her face before he said, "Sandra, look at me as if you see forever in my eyes and smile." She immediately did so as all the other wives had without even thinking.

She looked directly at him, went deep into his eyes as if he were the love of her life and gave him a seemingly endless smile accompanied with that expression of love.

He nonchalantly tilted his head just right so the cameras couldn't see that he was talking to Sandra now and said, "Ok Sandra, you can go back to admiring the flowers now while you start signing my little clipboard here. I want you to pay close attention to what I'm about to tell you.

"After I leave, take the flowers inside and put them on the dining room table, wait until four pm and then call Blake to let him know you will be leaving the house for about an hour to run to the grocery store and that you are going to prepare a special dinner for him tonight. Be very calm, relaxed and normal during your conversation with him. This is very important to me.

"Then I want you to put on your coat and take your time driving to Elder Lane Park, leave your car parked on Elder Lane just before you get to Sheridan Road. Then walk across the street through the parking lot and take the left set of stairs down to the beach house below by the lake.

"I'll meet you there, and we'll have lots of fun. Now you can smile, take the flowers and say good bye."

She finished signing for the flowers, nodded, took them from him, smiled, said goodbye and went inside closing the door. All very normal looking for the cameras he noted as he turned to his right dipping his head to the left and down a bit looking perfectly normal for watching his step. Then he got back into the van and drove off like he did this every day.

'Well I doubt that could have gone any better!' he thought as he decided where he wanted to go for lunch until his rendezvous with Sandra late in the afternoon.

✻

After the delicious plate of meatloaf, potatoes and carrots he ordered for lunch, he reflected on his progress so far. He was thinking that after this business with Sandra was finished, it would probably be a good time to start putting some serious effort into finding a new companion. After all, he was getting close enough to the end of his little adventures to do so. These thoughts were fed by the rather attractive waitress that had been eyeing him since he sat down in the restaurant.

'Very pretty. I can get used to the athletic body complete with all the right curves in all the right places. She is very well proportioned. Yeah, I could wind up quite satisfied with a package like that,' he told himself.

'Note to self; I think this one deserves a test drive.' He then left a very generous tip, made some additional deliberate eye contact with her that was complete with a suggestive smile, and left to enjoy the rest of his afternoon.

✻

"Blake? It's Sandy how's your day been so far?" she asked when she called her husband right on time at four pm.

"It's been hectic love. I've had a particularly heavy work load as it were and could easily be persuaded to call it a day this very moment. That would be the most splendid idea I've heard to date. I would be able to rush home for a hot bath, and some quality time with the most beautiful companion a bloke could ask for. I'm afraid, though, that my frightfully vain patients that remain in the waiting room will keep me here for two more hours at least."

"Well honey; you just finish out your day, make them all happy and I promise you I will ease the tension out of each and every tense muscle you've got once you get home. In fact, since I have some time until you get here, I'm going to make a quick run to the market and start the night off by personally making the meal of your choice. What would you like for dinner?" she asked.

"Why don't you just keep it simple love? We wouldn't want you to run out of energy later after dinner now would we? Humm? Just prepare some fish and chips with that incredible tartar sauce you used to make when we very first were wed. That should do just fine don't you think?" he asked sounding really tired. She could hear the exhaustion in his voice.

"Well whatever my dashing Englishman wants! Fish and chips it is then. I'll see you home around 6:30 for dinner and a very special dessert, ok?" she asked.

"A team of wild horses will be dreadfully insufficient at detaining me from such a magnificent offer as that my love."

With that they exchanged an intimate goodbye and she began reaching for her coat when the phone rang again.

She stopped and instinctively turned to answer the phone, but she had her instructions, and they immediately overrode her usual inclinations. So she ignored the phone and turned to leave the house; not setting the alarm she reached for the garage door at the end of the butler's room.

Before she reached the door, the answering machine picked up and she heard Lori's voice saying, "Sandy don't go!"

Again she hesitated slightly minus the tear that would have usually formed in the corner of her eye, and she said quietly to herself, "I must go to the beach!" and shut the door behind her.

Her Mercedes SUV was there waiting for her as she started the car and drove off leaving the garage door open. Very unlike her but so was just about everything she thought to do since receiving the flowers earlier.

Since receiving that beautiful bouquet of flowers that, she would never set eyes on again.

CHAPTER 24

". . . that hair must be a real bother to comb every day."

Wednesday, November 28th, 2012

At four pm the Nemesis found himself driving east on Winnetka Avenue toward the lake then turning north onto Essex Road driving between the tennis courts and the football field at New Trier High School. He pulled in amongst the sparse gathering of cars along the north side of the tennis courts, parked the car, removed his little bag of tricks from the trunk and walked the three blocks to Elder Lane Park.

Once there he took the right set of stairs down toward the beach stopping halfway down just out of sight of the road and still on the hard stairs so as not to leave any footprints just yet. There he put on his clean suit, hair net, gloves and smooth soled shoes which effectively contained his DNA, keeping any of it from being left at a crime scene. After removing himself from clue dropping status, he continued down the rest of the stairs, walking through the sandy beach over to the bath house at the start of the pier and waited for his date.

As was the case on all his previous reconnaissance missions; there was precious little traffic on the lake at this time of day. A barge was floating lazily south, well off shore probably heading towards the industrial cargo ports in Gary Indiana as many did.

'Sandra, Sandra. Oh, where for art thou my dear, beautiful Sandra? I can't think of a single song with Sandra in it, so I guess that tired old worn out line will have to do my dear,' he mused to himself as he waited.

☆

As previously instructed, Sandra Falkland took her time on the short trip to her designated parking spot on Elder Lane just outside and across the street from the Elder Lane Park parking lot. There she locked and left her car as previously instructed, walked across the empty parking lot and through the kid's park which had no activities on this night. The weather being what it was this time of year; there were no takers for any of the park's amenities or walkways with its barren trees. The trees were the only witnesses to her trek to the beach, interrupting their diligent watch over the leaves which previously grew and flourished on them but now began to rot on the ground below.

She took the left stairs down to the bath house where she recognized the floral delivery man who was now the only thing on God's brown earth worth listening to. She was oblivious to her surroundings; the season of slumber that had now overtaken all other living things around her, and all sounds except the sound of his voice which she hungered for.

"Hello Sandra, I see you found the beach just fine, and I'm quite sure that you followed all my instructions to the letter. The water is a bit brisk this time of year, but I'm sure you'd find it very exhilarating. Would you like to go for a swim?" he asked.

"If you think that's a good idea, I'd love to," she replied as she looked out to the lake and started walking to the water's edge.

"Well I'll tell ya hon, on any other day I might have enjoyed watching you skinny dip in the icy cold lake but not today. I have much bigger plans, and you know what? I just know you're going to be absolutely thrilled with them!" he told her with phony exuberance.

Sandra stopped walking immediately and turned toward him as an absolutely excited look came over her face showing she could hardly wait to participate in anything he would suggest.

"We can start by reminding you that you will thoroughly enjoy everything we do here ok?" he asked, nodding to reinforce his suggestion.

"Sure. Anything you say is fine with me. What would you like me to do first?" she asked with a happy, hopeful, almost puppy-dog smile on her face.

"Why don't we start off by removing all your clothes, folding them neatly and placing them there up against that retaining wall in a nice neat stack?"

"Sure no problem," she said and instantly began removing all her clothing without any inhibition, much like she was preparing for a shower.

'Wow,' he found himself thinking, 'what a beauty and what a waste.'

"That's great Sandy, now lie down in the sand like a good girl," he said as he approached her with his little bag of very select toys. His body began a series of movements that had become so automatic, he no longer even needed to think about them. He had now come to enjoy the thrill of flawless execution. He was reveling in how this latest episode would move him incrementally closer to completing his tribute.

✡

With the light having all but left the shore, the captain of the passing barge named the Greta Marie, could barely make out the figure going down the left side stairs to the beach. His attention was drawn to watch the faint figure when he first noticed a set of headlights approach in the parking lot above the beach.

A short time later, he was vaguely able to see someone descend the stairs through the barren tree branches at the right side of the beach near the bath house. Then the approaching darkness all but swallowed the person up. He couldn't even tell if it were a man or a woman.

His curiosity got the better of him as he began to realize that there was precious little time left before losing sight of the beach. He looked at his watch, and it was 4:45pm. Seeing anyone on the beach this late in the year and this late in the day had him thinking he may catch a little tryst in the sand. So he grabbed his very pricy night vision binoculars with video recording ability and looked for the figure on the beach.

These binoculars could see a person up to 450 meters which was about the length of five football fields, and he was certainly within that distance. Peering through the lens, he found that there were, in fact, two people there; one apparently dressed for the weather and the other had a very curvy nakedness about her and had just lain down in the sand as he pressed record.

Just as he suspected, it was probably some college kids completing a sorority pledging or something similar. 'The more money they have, the crazier they get,' he thought to himself as the clothed figure appeared to be waving his arms over the one on the beach.

The next thing he knew he was almost blinded as the night vision binoculars picked up a very bright light in the dressed figure's hand. He lowered the night vision binoculars and through the recurring stars now in his eyes; he could vaguely see the light in a person's hand being waved over the figure lying on the beach like some sort of ritual. It was sharper and brighter than a flashlight and appeared to be some kind of torch. If he weren't seeing stars at the moment, he might be able to tell.

Just as his eyes began to see normally, the light went out. Picking up the binoculars again, he noticed that the dressed figure had a very weird kind of hat or bonnet of some sort on and was still leaning over the naked figure on the sand. After quickly re-aiming the binoculars on the scene, he closed his eyes tightly needing a few moments to get the stars out of his eyes from a very bright light.

He finally opened his eyes again as his barge had carried him to the point where trees on the shoreline had come between him and the beach, so he stopped the recording. The show was over, but he did get some footage involving at least one very well endowed nude gal that he couldn't wait to assess after he docked tonight.

The very brief green glimpse of that gal's superb body through the night vision glasses made his night. As he thought about her, he couldn't help wondering about the torch or whatever that light was that had blinded him temporarily and what it was being used for. Whatever it was, all of it would make for interesting speculation when he showed the beach video at his local watering hole tonight after docking in Gary Indiana to deliver his cargo.

*

She immediately did what she was told as he removed the hammer from his bag. "Remember now Sandy, nothing from here on out will ever remove the pleasant image of sunny blue skies on a warm beach like this. This is the calmest day of your life. Nothing can ever disturb you again for as long as you live," he said and immediately thought, 'Which will be about 15 minutes or so.'

A very quiet peaceful look came over her face that shook momentarily each of the three times he struck her right ankle with a hammer, but it remained there, calm and seemingly unaware of the damage being inflicted, just as instructed.

He then took out the small pencil torch, fired it up and started scoring up and down the left side of her previously unblemished body then raised her right arm to add a little dot in her arm pit. Next was a small burn he had to leave behind the right knee and then the circles were carefully drawn around each eye.

This was the essential part of his ritual that disturbed him the most, not because of the intense pain it would usually cause a person to feel, but due to the smell that lingered until he left with another notch in his torch. It also reminded him of the pain endured by the love of his life when similar marks had appeared on her body.

"I know all that hair must really be a bother to comb every day. Well the good news is you won't ever have to wash or comb it again," he said as he cut her beautiful, long, straight blonde hair short like a man's cut carefully placing each lock of hair on her clothes that she had folded so neatly just moments before.

It was then that he pulled out a vial containing the unique drug that he sprinkled on the rose petals earlier in the afternoon. One very small dose ingested, and his victims simply had their free will eliminated while leaving them awake and articulate. In a matter of seconds, they were left mindless and completely under his control. A control that would last several days if he would allow it, but he hadn't yet.

To anyone watching they looked fine and showed no outward symptoms of being drugged at all! A second dose, before the first one wore off, would prove to be fatal. The second dose made the body basically stop working, instantly shutting down without giving it a chance to register shock or stress that death would usually impose on a body. It was that second deadly dose that he sprinkled onto one of the scissor blades and then tapped it carefully into her nostril.

She stopped breathing almost immediately. Except for the burn marks around her eyes, her face looked at peace with the world. He blew sharply on her nose to remove any possible traces of the drug which finished the first part of his ritual.

He reflected on the incredible waste of life that had become necessary due to the careless hands of that hack Holden. While the loss of life here didn't sadden him, he realized that it would not have been necessary if only Holden hadn't killed the love of his life. Now tribute must be made to her memory. This was simply another installment, another piece to the puzzle, one step closer to completing his revenge for the one he loved.

Once she stopped breathing, he began his meticulous clean up placing the hammer, pencil torch, scissors and vial back into the bag and removed a scalpel, just as he had done with the others.

Then using the surgery skills learned in med school and previously only used to save helpless four legged patients, he carefully cut around and completely through the ample left breast and put it on the hair he had placed on the folded clothing along with the piece of her right ear lobe.

His night was now complete. After wiping the scalpel on a paper towel from his bag, he carefully placed the scalpel back in the bag. Then he removed first one rubber glove pulling it completely over the bloody towel, then the other pulling it completely over the first glove. Then he did his usual cursory look around one last time for any mistakes but as usual his routine was perfect. There were no clues left for Andy, Barney or any of the others that would be soon crawling all over the beach with their magnifying glasses and cameras. Later he would deposit the rubber gloves in a garbage bag inside a dumpster behind the restaurant after it closed for the night. The area had no security cameras to capture this last part of his routine.

He then pulled on a clean pair of rubber gloves and took Sandra's car keys placing them in a clean plastic sandwich bag and then in his pocket.

He then slowly and carefully ascended the stairs watching for any potential observers and saw none. With his 'clean suit' intact, he reached the top of the stairs and made a beeline through the park towards Sandra's car again checking the vicinity carefully before he approached it. After realizing the area was clear, he quickly went up to the car, got in and started it up. Then after driving several miles away from the park and the lake, he parked it in the far end of the previously chosen supermarket with the driver's door facing the dark end of the strip mall and locked the keys inside.

Ducking behind the end building of the strip mall he removed his 'clean suit' and replaced it back into his bag. Then he left the shadows of the buildings and storage fences behind the mall and began nonchalantly walking a mile or so back to his car. He found it sitting right where he left it in the school parking lot which was now deserted.

Even if someone noticed the vehicle left in the lot after the last person drove theirs off, it was too far removed from the crime scene for anyone to connect the dots. The brisk night air had invigorated him during his walk. He recapped the day's activities in his mind taking pride in his planning and satisfaction in the execution of his plan.

That night he slept like a baby realizing he was yet another step closer to his goal.

✿

The second thing Blake noticed when he got home that night, after the garage door being left wide open with no car in it, were the flowers on the dining room table.

"Sandra? Sandra my dear, are you at home?" he called out as he became more and more worried at the dark silent house he walked through as he looked for his wife.

A sense of dread was quickly replacing his initial excitement at the thought of Sandra making some seductive game out of his arrival home from work. Something just didn't feel right. Certainly if she were being coy with him, she would have left a trail or some obviously visible clues for him to follow. The dread completely overtook him as he noticed no cooking smells that surely would have been present if she had completed the plans they discussed not three hours earlier. She should have been back from the store an hour or two before and should have been done cooking by now as well, but all he saw was a dark empty house with a blinking red light.

'A blinking red light?' he thought as he snapped out of his distracted thought long enough to press play on their answering machine. He did so thinking that she must have had an accident or been otherwise detained or perhaps that would be her 'clue' to start him in her planned direction for their intimate night together. The message would clear it all up.

'Wednesday, four o two pm,' "Sandy, don't go!", 'end of new messages.'

What!!?? What was that? It sounded like Lori Baker! It couldn't be! Lori's been dead for two weeks now, and there were no messages on the machine this morning when he left for work.

He pressed play to listen to the message again but all he heard was, 'You have no new messages,' as he stared at the red zero on the display.

"Wait just a minute. There was a message there. I heard it. It was there. It said 'Sandy, don't go', and it was Lori Baker's voice I'm absolutely sure of it!"

He sat down in one of the dining room chairs and started to recall the strange things that Jim had just told Sandra and him about, when they went out to dinner last weekend with Ray and Olivia. A stark realization caught up with him, and he just let go.

Numbness overcame him as he began rubbing his face with both hands, suddenly realizing that the worst thing that could possibly happen to him probably just did, as it had to several of his closest friends.

No, he refused to think like that just yet. The recent tragic events that happened to his friends were clouding his thinking. He needed to make some calls. There were things he needed to do before he had to resign himself to thinking that way. This he knew, but who to call first he didn't know.

Police, friend, who first?

He wasn't sure how much time passed while he sat there, but he realized he was focused on listening to his heartbeat and the sound of each breath as he took it. Then that ugly thought brought him back to reality at once as he again began to revisit that sinking feeling in his gut. That feeling that said Sandy might have fallen prey to the monster that took Lisa, Lori and Izzie from them. Then he lost it. His British stiff upper lip went right out the window. After about fifteen minutes of shock, he called Ray Reed.

He couldn't call Jim or Mark, and John had just gotten back from Florida after spending weeks grieving over Lisa.

Ray, yes Ray was the call he needed to make.

"This is Ray. Blake, is that you? What's up buddy?" said Ray.

"Ray, I don't know how to say this, but I just got home, Sandra is missing and I couldn't think of who else to call but you!"

Somehow he surprised himself and got a whole line out without breaking down.

"Oh Blake, is she with a friend? When was the last time you two talked?" he asked.

"We last spoke at about four this afternoon, and she sounded fine. She called to ask me how my day was going. Then she told me she was going to the market to pick up a few grocery items to prepare dinner. Ray, she was going to make me fish and chips. We were going to have a warm, intimate evening after a long weary day. We made plans Ray, but she's not home, nowhere to be found.

"There is a big bouquet of roses on the dining room table, and she's gone Ray. Gone! I don't have the slightest idea where she could be at this late hour. Ray, she's gone!"

His friend at the other end of the line could hear him break down after that short rant.

"I'll be right over Blake," he said as he hung up the phone and dialed Ed Cassidy's cell number on his way out.

CHAPTER 25

. . . his semi blank stare was virtually absent recognition.

Wednesday, November 28th, 2012

*E*d Cassidy got to the Falkland residence ahead of Ray and did a quick check of the exterior looking for things like footprints in soft dirt areas, broken shrub branches or other obvious clues before going up to the door.

With that done he headed for the front door. It was time to face another distraught husband in a holding pattern for the worse possible news about his wife.

'Well with this high end security system we may actually get our first clue,' he thought as he made mental notes regarding Blake's security camera locations before ringing the bell.

An obviously distraught Dr. Blake Falkland answered the door and anxiously ushered the inspector in to begin the process that he still hoped would bring his wife back to him.

"Inspector Cassidy, do come in, please," invited Blake.

"Good evening Dr. Falkland. I got here as soon as I could. Where would be the best place for us to talk?" asked Ed.

"Let us retire to the sitting room and, look at me. Where are my manners? What can I get you to drink inspector; coffee, soda, water? I'm afraid I could do with a scotch about now myself," Blake said.

Anticipating that this may be a lengthy discussion, Ed replied, "If it's not too much trouble a soft drink would be great and please, if it's scotch you need by all means, don't let me stop you."

After Blake left for refreshments, Ed looked around their beautiful home. Everything from the pictures, no, art work on the walls, to the furniture, window and floor treatments were exquisitely coordinated in a traditional style. He could see into the dining room from where he was and couldn't help but notice the big bouquet of flowers on the table. Ray had clued him in about a few things during his brief call including Blake's references to the market trip, flowers and her being gone when Blake got home.

He got up and examined the flowers briefly noticing there was no card and that they appeared to be rather hastily tossed on the table close to the edge without removing the plastic wrapping around the vase.

Just then Blake returned with their drinks and noticing that Ed was studying the flowers said, "Those were on the table when I arrived home this evening just as they are right now. I hadn't touched a thing in the house except the answering machine and the phone when I called Raymond Reed," he said.

"Excuse my curiosity and wandering Doctor. Let's go back, sit down and start from the beginning. How about starting with the conversation you had earlier with your wife."

They returned to the sitting room where Blake related everything from Sandra's call to him at four pm this afternoon right up to his call to Ray.

"Are you sure about the answering machine message you thought you heard? We have had several relatively strange ones lately in and around these recent cases," inquired Ed.

"Inspector, just as I'm sitting before you in this very chair, I can assure you that there is no doubt in my mind I heard Lori Baker's voice on that answering machine not an hour prior to this discussion. She said, 'Sandy, don't go!' but it wasn't on the machine at all after that single play back. I don't know quite what to make of it, but I can assure you that I did indeed hear that message! I have pondered hearing that message every moment from the time I heard it until now," insisted Blake.

"Right, then I surely cannot explain its absence but none-the-less to my recollection, the message contained quite a sense of urgency. You'll have to excuse me, as at that moment I was relatively shocked to hear it," said Blake.

"Dr. Falkland, I need some information on the car your wife drives. I'd like to get out the APB before we go any further," said Ed.

He collected the information required and gave it to one of the officers that had arrived on the scene after Ed. Ed also left him instructions to allow Dr. Reed in upon his arrival.

"Dr. Falkland can we review the security tapes for this afternoon?" Ed asked. He was anxious to spot anything that might resemble their first clue from any of the recent murders.

"Please inspector, call me Blake and yes, right this way. I'm as anxious as you must be to review the tapes as well," said Blake as he led the way into his den where the security monitoring equipment was kept.

✻

As they passed the foyer on their way to the den, Ray arrived. Ray had never seen Blake look this helpless. The afternoon's events felt like a gut punch to this very educated, talented and skilled surgeon. Ray couldn't help comparing his distraught friend's appearance to that of a confused little boy lost in a foreign country. After his best attempt at comforting and expressing optimism to his associate about the return of his wife, he was brought up to speed on their way to the den.

There were now numerous squad cars parked outside the Falkland home. Once the APB was put out, the camera crews began arriving as sharks would if they smelled blood in the water. The police were forced to unroll the crime scene tape that had become all too familiar in the formerly crime quiet town of Winnetka. In establishing a perimeter, they provided fodder for the reporters facing them and the newly set up cameras and lighting equipment.

All the usual local feeds had their satellite vans there but what distinguished this newly designated crime scene were the two new additions. The rather large white double rear axle ENG trucks with CNN and Fox News logos on the sides respectively.

These huge 'Electronic News Gathering' beauties were equipped with dual satellite dishes. The smaller of the two for K band transmissions similar to the local station news vans and its big brother for C band transmissions. They were rolling productions studios set up for complete electronic field production of any event whether it was news, sport, reality show or in this case serial murder crime scene coverage and were quite a sight to behold.

The Falkland lawn quickly assumed an atmosphere resembling a circus minus the livestock and fire eaters. Many clowns were clearly represented, however.

The local news channels set up their smaller equipment very quickly. All of them were eager to be the first station breaking the story on this latest development.

✻

"We are live in Winnetka outside the Lake Michigan shoreline home of Dr. Blake Falkland. His missing wife Sandra Falkland is feared to be the latest victim in a string of unsolved murders involving the wives of several prominent local plastic surgeons. The last three murdered women were all wives of a team of very successful doctors living and practicing in the Chicago north shore suburbs who had an article written on them last summer calling them the 'Surgeon Generals'.

"If this winds up being a related case, it will mark the fourth wife of the team. Channel Seven News team investigators have learned that so far the only pattern appears to be that formed by the last names of the victim's husbands. It's too early to tell but if the pattern holds true, Dr. Falkland's wife would be the fourth victim whose last name appeared listed in alphabetical order from that Sun-Times article. The serial killer still on the loose is now being called the 'Plastic Wife Killer'."

That was it! Whether he was 'being called' that or not, now he would be. The name was just catchy enough to stick in the media, and had just rolled off the tongue of Susan Peterson, anointing the at-large killer with his new name. From that innocent moment on, if you didn't refer to the murderer as the 'Plastic Wife Killer' you simply were not credible and not in touch with the details of the case. Hell you must be talking about some petty case from Hoboken instead of the one in the bright lights of the big city as she was.

The buzz got around to the other local feeds and by the time the two big boys got up and running; word had reached the ears of their team on the scene and the phrase was pumped out of the north shore suburb to a national audience and soon would be viral on the web as well.

"'Channel Seven News' has been covering this developing story which appears to be related to the serial murders of four wives so far starting with Aimee Holden wife of Dr. Richard Holden, who practices plastic surgery in Evanston Illinois," Susan reported, as a picture of Aimee Holden and her husband appeared on TV screens throughout Chicagoland that were being fed her report.

"Aimee Holden was the first victim in the 'Plastic Wife Killer's' rampage that began approximately one and a half months ago on October 18th. Her pregnant body was found murdered in the nursery of their apparently secured home in Evanston with no signs of forced entry.

"Since then the serial killer has remained at large having also taken the life of Lisa Ackerman, wife of Dr. John Ackerman, on November 1st in their Winnetka home. Lisa was also found murdered in the nursery of their home which was also secured by their activated alarm system and once again with no signs of forced entry.

"Then on November 15th the pregnant body of Lori Baker, wife of Dr. James Baker, was found under the same circumstances also here in Winnetka and most recently the body of Isabella Channing, wife of Dr. Mark Channing was found and again in the very same way.

"This scene is beginning to take on all of the same characteristics of the previous heinous crime scenes which would make it number five in this very sad string of murders. So far the 'Plastic Wife Killer' has left the local, state and federal authorities baffled and without a suspect. We will continue to update you on this heartbreaking story as it develops. This is Susan Peterson reporting live from Winnetka for Channel Seven News."

*

Once they reached the den; a brief pause precluded their watching the security tapes during which Blake mercifully missed the newscasts now beaming across the country. Blake seemed almost twitchy as his head and eyes kept looking side to side with that hopelessly lost look that had been on his face like a steady companion since Ray got there. It was as if he were trying to look through the walls for answers lying beyond them that would complete the questions he couldn't yet comprehend asking. He was looking right at Ray, and his semi blank stare was virtually absent recognition.

The seriousness of the situation was brought home to Ray after seeing this drastic transformation on Blake's face. The tear that began to form in the corner of his eye reflected not only concern for the good friend in front of him who was already lost in grief, but also for the fear developing in his mind of what might have actually happened to his very beautiful wife Sandra.

They watched the security footage starting from three pm then skipping ahead during blank areas until at approximately 3:40 pm when a delivery van pulled up the drive. The driver produced the bouquet of flowers, which now graced the dining room table, from the side door of the van, brought it to the front door, and rang the bell.

Sandra was seen approaching the door and unlocking it after checking the peep hole. She then answered the door, and her face was instantly transformed into a wonderful expression of surprise and joy at the sight of the flowers. There was no audio, but you could read her very expressive lip movements as she mouthed, "Oh, they're absolutely beautiful." At that point, she looked the delivery man in the eyes as he told her something. He was wearing a baseball type hat that covered his eyes but the cameras, while incredibly bright and clear with vibrant color, did not afford a clear view of his mouth so they couldn't get a hint of what he was saying to her. The camera at the far left end of the front entry porch area lined the top of his head up exactly with the bottom of the hanging flower pot which gave them a height reference.

What he told her must have been something about how nice the flowers smelled because, at that point, they could see Sandra lean forward and sniff them.

A few seconds later he was holding his small delivery ticket clipboard out for her to sign for the bouquet. He might have paid her a compliment then because she looked at him and smiled. After continuing to talk for a short while yet, he turned to leave and Sandra could be seen smiling as she brought the flowers inside the house and closed the door, locking it behind her.

After setting the flowers kind of haphazardly on the dining room table, which seemed to be the only thing slightly off about her actions, she eventually went to the phone obviously to call Blake. The time of her call on the video was 4 pm. The call ended, and she hung up the phone at 4:15 pm.

She went for her coat and grabbed her purse on her way to the garage door. She locked the door behind her but did not arm the security system. Along the way, the phone must have rung because they could see the answering machine light suddenly blinking red in the background as she walked out the door.

This confused them all, and they looked at each other puzzled for the first time as everything else about Sandra's movements, expressions and actions appeared normal.

She must have heard the phone's ringing throughout the house but chose to ignore them. There was a slight hesitation on her way to the garage door. That must have been when the phone rang. It was just before the red light started flashing, but she appeared to be in no particular hurry to leave the house as her movements seemed quite nonchalant.

But the question remained; why did she ignore the phone?

CHAPTER 26

" . . . please check out the beach below the park . . .
I'm freaking out here"

Wednesday, November 28th, 2012

Who was it that called Sandra on her way out? Ed could not figure out why she didn't pick up one of the phones before the answering machine registered the call. She passed several between picking up her coat and reaching the garage. What was so important that she didn't have time to answer the phone? Surely the trip to the market she told Blake about wasn't that pressing.

Suddenly the same sense of anxiety that came over Blake when he got home to his empty house, started to drench Ed Cassidy as if he were suddenly walking through a waterfall. What washed over him once again were those familiar feelings of dreading another tragic outcome and the desperation of being unable to stop this monster.

"Excuse me gentlemen I need to make a quick call," said Ed.

He placed a call to his assistant at the police station and set her to work getting the court order necessary to obtain the Falkland phone records for the past week. There was so much pressure to solve these cases that the chief had a judge pretty much on call for court orders as long as they were relevant to solving the serial murders.

His assistant assured Ed that he would have the documents in his hand by morning.

When he returned to the somber pair of doctors, they were pondering the answering machine dilemma as well.

"Inspector, now I know how Jim Baker must have felt upon his disclosures to you regarding the unexplainable voice recordings he witnessed," said Blake.

"Blake, I can promise you that I will take your statement about the message you heard very seriously. How can anyone dismiss it after the visual evidence that your home security system is showing us? In fact, it bolsters Jim's statements all the more in my eyes, as difficult as they would usually be to acknowledge.

"I'll take a copy of the video back to the station with me on a flash drive to examine further and will keep you posted on our progress in finding your wife Blake. Rest assured; I will find her," said Ed.

He left after making a copy of the security video. Mentally Ed knew his statement to Blake was true, finding his wife was inevitable. What he wasn't sure about was a growing suspicion that she would probably wind up being victim number five in this mess.

Just as Ed got back to his office at about eight pm and started reaching for the phone to call Bill for an update, the sergeant on duty for the night shift burst in saying, "One of our patrol cars just found Mrs. Falkland's Mercedes SUV at the south end of the parking lot just west of the Grand Food Store on Green Bay and Pine."

Ed said, "I'm on my way. Get a forensics team headed out there pronto."

✻

He could have practically walked the four blocks from the Winnetka police department to the food store. In retrospect, it would have helped the already developing traffic jam there. Besides the six police cars already on the scene that were flashing lights throughout the area surrounding her car, the local news vans had picked up the police chatter and began to arrive as well.

Upon his arrival Ed handed out pictures of Sandra Falkland to all police personnel on the scene and immediately began assigning sectors of the local area to several of the officers to start canvassing for any information on the doctor's missing wife. The rest of them, as they had done so many other times recently, began establishing a crime scene perimeter and went to work on crowd and media control.

The forensics team began what would turn out to be yet another futile attempt at collecting clues from the scene as Ed made the call to Blake Falkland with the news of the car's discovery.

✻

Blake arrived ten minutes later with Ray Reed and the keys to the Mercedes SUV allowing the forensics team to finish processing the vehicle's interior before moving it to the police station's secured lot.

Ed did his best to assure Blake and Ray that this was not necessarily a bad sign. The conversations they had on their way back to Blake's home danced around the edges of the unspoken truth that neither one of them wanted to admit. How could this be anything else but worse news?

"Blake, let me call Olivia so she can meet us at your house with some dinner. You haven't eaten this evening yet, and you need to keep up your strength buddy. Maybe some time with friends would be helpful right now."

Ray spoke the words as he realized the déjà vu of his role tonight. He had just helped another close friend who reached out to him with a desperate call for help. Then he drove over to comfort his friend with empty words that ultimately would mean nothing once his beautiful wife was found horribly mutilated. Those two acts would inevitably be followed by the redundant series of inadequate words and gestures of comfort aimed at diminishing that horrible final image that was destined to be burned in his memory for the rest of his life. In the end, he and Olivia would be left with yet another widowed friend who would be but a hollow shell of his former self, emptied by his loss and mentally aimless at seeking a new direction for his life.

"That's a wonderfully warm suggestion Raymond, but it's one that I must turn down I'm afraid. As much as I do value the friendship you and Olivia have always given us, I find myself in need of alone time this night. I must allow some of this madness to sink in. I really wouldn't be able to focus on anyone in the house this evening but do accept my thanks for your offer," he said sadly.

*

The Nemesis was thoroughly enjoying the 10 o'clock news coverage this evening as he switched from channel to channel confirming how little the news media was able to report in the way of actual details on his latest little escapade. He had once again buried it beautifully. His attention to detail and focus was paying off.

He was also very proud of the fact that significant national news outlets had found the previously crime free, sleepy town of Winnetka. They rehashed the old confusion as to how all of this could be happening here as they tried to rationalize and sort out what little details they actually had about the recent events. Their graphics were spectacular, though; he had to give them that. Next the lot of them would be trying to make sense of it all using their inane conjecture.

Yes, there is the physically and for the most part mentally perky Susan Peterson who was still trying to advance her career to possibly a national news station from her coverage of the stories. She incessantly kept proclaiming herself as some kind of authority on his efforts.

Truth be told; they were all individually struggling to find an angle that the others didn't think of so as to differentiate themselves and make their coverage appear somehow superior to the rest. They had already worn out the holiday season, prominent doctors and innocent wife angles. In their own way, they were just as pathetic as Andy and Barney.

Where had investigative journalism disappeared to recently anyway? All this current crop of self serving reporters wanted to do was interview and spew redundant clichés. What happened to 'uncover the facts that the police often missed' and then finding corroboration through second sources? He speculated that it was probably too much bother, and not enough TV face time which was where the real money was and what news was all about these days.

Well the attention was welcome anyway. He felt all of it was a fitting additional tribute to the lover torn so prematurely from him. If his efforts happened to contribute to the career of a budding little news starlet, so be it.

✻

"Jim, its Ray do you have a moment?"

"Sure Ray what's up?"

"Jim, I just left Blake's house. I've been there most of the night. Jim, Sandra is missing, and Blake is beside himself with worry. He got home at around six tonight, and the house was empty. He had talked to her earlier and was expecting a quiet night and a cozy dinner they had discussed earlier, but when he got home, the house was dark, and she was nowhere to be found. The police just found her car abandoned at the parking lot next to the Grand Food Store. Jim it doesn't look good," he respectfully reported to his friend.

"Did any neighbors see her leave? Did they check the local hospitals? Do they have any idea where she could have gotten off to?" Jim started nervously firing off questions to Ray.

"We just left Ed Cassidy after meeting him at the lot where the vehicle was found. We brought the car keys because the car was found locked and abandoned. Jim, there was no sign of Sandra. The forensics team is going over the car as we speak. Blake, Ed Cassidy, Bill Weller and I spent the night reviewing his security video.

"What we saw was a bit unsettling but inconclusive. The video showed her receiving the delivery of flowers and also showed the delivery guy leave after chatting with Sandra probably a bit longer than usual.

"The cameras inside the foyer then showed her taking the flowers into the house and we could see her calling Blake. He revealed that, during that conversation, she told him she was going shopping to pick up a few things to prepare dinner for him. He came home to a dark empty house with the flowers on the dining room table and no card on the flowers by the way. Then about 8:00 pm her car was found abandoned at the food store. Blake is in a panic," said Ray.

"I'll be right over to talk to him,"

"No Jim, don't. I tried getting him to agree to Olivia bringing dinner over and offered to spend time with him but he refused saying he needed some alone time to absorb everything so I left. I just wanted to let you know that's all."

"Thanks Ray. I'll say some prayers for him and Sandy. I would prefer to go talk to him but . . ." He left it at that, not finishing his sentence.

Thursday, November 29th, 2012

When he woke up the next morning, Jim turned the water on extra hot in his shower then peeked out at the mirror when he was done and all he found was an unbroken veil of heavy steam on the mirror with no message.

"I know it probably doesn't work this way Lori but we could use a little help with Sandra today," he said more to the ceiling than the mirror. He was unaware of the message Blake heard when he got home. All he could do was finish getting ready for what he knew would be a workday filled with distraction and concern for Blake and Sandy.

*

When Ed arrived at work the next morning, he was handed the Falkland phone records for the past week on the way to his office. After a quick study, he noted the 4:00 pm outgoing phone call to Blake's office from the Falkland home, which lasted nine minutes, then there was no incoming call after that. The next entry was at 6:05 pm from the Falkland home to Ray Reed lasting five minutes. Nothing in between!

'Why did I expect that this would be anything other than another dead end,' he thought as he reviewed the details in the missing person case so far;

1. Fact: Blake spoke to Sandra at 4pm and she sounded perfectly normal.
2. Fact: Blake arrives at 6pm to an empty house and an open garage absent Sandra's car.
3. Fact: Blake swore that he heard an answering machine message that was no longer on the machine.
4. Fact: The surveillance tape clearly showed the answering machine recording a message about the time Sandra left the house but she didn't answer the phone.
5. Fact: The phone records show no incoming call that would have left the message on the machine in between Sandra's outgoing call to Blake's office and Blake's outgoing call to Ray Reed.

This could only mean one of two things; either Blake erased the answering machine message, which there can be no possible reason for him to do, or the incoming call which was not on the phone records but clearly caught on video tape erased itself. There also can be no physical explanation for that or the red light they saw appear on the tape.

'So, here we are, great; now that's real progress!' he thought as he stared out his window at a sunny and unseasonably warm late November day.

*

"Billy, don't hit your sister! Do you want to stay for a while longer or would you like me to take you home right now?" Billy's mother asked as several seagulls swooped over the children on their way back over the beach.

Billy's response to his mom was trying to catch up with the flight of the birds in an effort to avoid the question and extend this rare warm late fall day's activity in the park. He stopped at the short row of bushes on top of the retaining wall overlooking the beach and followed the bird's flight. They were circling down toward the beach which was just outside of his view. He called out to his mother, "Mommy, there's really a lot of birds down there look! What kind of birds are those mom? Can we go down to the beach and watch them?"

On her way to joining him at the parks edge, she said, "Those are seagulls Billy." Once she got there to join her son's bird watching, she was able to look further down the retaining wall than he could due to her additional height and was frozen by what she saw.

"Oh, there's too many birds here Billy I don't want any of them to bite you. They're probably just looking for some fish to eat. Let's go back to the swing set with your sister. I need you to play nice with her Billy, ok? Come on now, let's go," she said.

Once she got him settled on the swings with his sister, she dialed 911 on the way back to a park bench seat to steady her now shaky legs. She found herself calmly giving her name, location and information about the gruesome sight she just witnessed on the beach below to the operator that answered through the phony smile she offered to the kids.

*

It took all of three minutes for a squad car to arrive. No siren was heard, but the lights were flashing as the officers hurried toward her and the kids.

"Mommy, look! The police are here. Are they going to punish me for pulling Rachael's hair?" asked Billy.

"No dear they're just going to make sure the birds don't hurt us. You stay on the swings with Rachael while I go talk to the nice policemen ok?" she replied as she went to meet them.

"Good morning, are you the lady who called?" the officer asked as he briskly made his way toward Billy's mom.

"Yes officer, please check out the beach below the park. I would like to take my children home and away from here as soon as possible. I'm freaking out here," she said.

"Please remain calm, you're doing fine. Yes, please take the children home. Is there someone you can leave them with? Obviously we need to talk further and take your statement without upsetting the children. What's your son's name?"

"His name is Billy, and yes I can leave them with my neighbor. I'll be back here in half an hour to help all I can. I don't think I'll ever forget the sight of that poor woman down on the beach left like that," she replied.

The officer then slowly went over to the children smiling and asked, "You're Billy right?"

Little Billy's eyes lit up at the name recognition and said, "Yes, that's me."

"Hey, would you mind taking your sister home with your mommy? Your mom's a little worried about all the birds, and she could use her brave little man to calm her down."

"Sure officer, I can do that!" Billy said proudly, pleased to play a big boy and help his mom.

"Great Billy thanks. That would help us a lot. Meanwhile we'll go check them out and make sure they don't hurt anyone ok?"

"Thanks officer, I'll make sure they get home all right. Come on Rach, it's time to go," Billy said as he grabbed his little sister's hand and led her to his mother.

With that settled, the two officers descended the stairs where they found an all too familiar scene.

The naked and mutilated body of another physician's wife only this one sadly must have been here a while as it had a number of birds perched on and pecking at her open chest wound.

CHAPTER 27

*"Sir, what was your name again and
when could you get us that video?"*

Thursday, November 29th, 2012

If there is anything worse to a police officer than being one step behind
a killer on a string of murders with no clue as to how the perpetrator
is able to stay ahead of you, it's the feeling of being powerless to stop him
from doing it again.

Unfortunately Inspector Ed Cassidy was wearing both these feelings
like wet on water this morning and he hated the emotions that went along
with wearing them.

This all hit him hard after seeing that all the local and major Chicago
papers today carried a variation of the headline, 'Missing wife feared latest
victim of Plastic Wife Killer'.

If things weren't frustrating enough, his next call was from the mother
of the two kids who were playing in Elder Lane Park and apparently just
found Sandra Falkland's naked body on the beach below.

Bill Weller was on his way over so Ed called and told him to just meet
him and Connie at the beach. He also threw out a shout to the boys from
the Chicago crime lab.

After parking his car in the lot at Elder Lane Park, Ed headed
toward the left set of stairs on his way down to the beach and froze in his
tracks before he reached them. There at the north end of the children's
playground was a bronze statue of a young girl with an outdated swimsuit,
a hat and a cape over her shoulder with a plaque beneath it which read,
"SUN DANCER—Jackie"!

He instantly thought of the mirror message that Jim had shown him
a picture of which read; "Sun Dancer—Sandra." He also thought of
the 'Sandra don't go' message that Blake swears he heard in Lori's voice
yesterday on his answering machine. Then the 'Flowers' reference seen by
Jim Baker written in the steam on the bathroom mirror at his cabin in

Wisconsin came to mind, and he realized that in some weird way they all pointed to the situation on the beach below where Sandra Falkland now laid dead.

Once again all he could think to himself was, 'TOO LATE!!' He kept screaming 'ONCE AGAIN, TOO GODDAMNED LATE AGAIN' over and over in his head as he tried to file all this away and prepare himself to examine the gruesome dance that had played itself out on the beach.

It seemed like half the town of Winnetka was now sporting that attractive, eye catching yellow crime scene tape. There was so much of it in fact that it was beginning to spread the news vans too thin to be able to cover all the taped scenes. Several members of Winnetka's finest just added Elder Lane Park and the beach below to the list.

The CSU team had completed their preliminary analysis and photos of the area immediately around the body as Ed reached the bottom of the stairs. It was worse than usual. This time the overnight guests of the beach added to the pathetic sight of Sandra's already nude and mutilated body by nibbling on her until his patrolmen got there some fifteen minutes before. Even through all the unnatural markings of mutilation her body now wore instead of clothes, he could see that she was a very attractive woman and dreaded the call he must now make to Dr. Blake Falkland.

*

Connie arrived right after he did shaking her head slowly with a big 'Not Again' sign clearly etched on her forehead. She went to work immediately taking body temperature, checking rigor and the rest of her usual on-site examinations of the body.

"Ed, I know I'm not telling you anything you don't already know, and I know it doesn't help, but you have got to stop this bastard whoever he is. This just keeps getting sadder and more depressing with each victim. He must be the sorriest son of a bitch ever to shit between two shoes to do this to these women," she said. This was so out of character for her and showed just how frustrated she was as well. It also spoke to her disgust at the graphic nature of the murders; this was coming from a medical examiner with over twenty five years of experience in big city crime.

"I see he's expanding his M.O. Now he's helping them kick the oxygen habit right out on a public beach," said Bill as he also arrived on the scene.

"Even though it's secluded down here, someone must have seen something related to this one. We have to figure out how he's getting the women to cooperate enough to pull these off so successfully. Bill, Connie, what are we missing?" Ed asked out of exasperation.

They wrapped up their analysis of the crime scene unable to provide Ed with any answers to his sad question. Then Ed decided on what was going to be released to the media, and what might solicit a clue from any of the locals as they headed back to their cars.

✻

The cameras had just begun rolling as Inspectors Ed Cassidy and Bill Weller got to the top of the stairs which connected the kid's park above with their latest crime scene on the beach below.

"Inspector Cassidy, can you confirm that the body found on the beach is, in fact, that of Mrs. Sandra Falkland who turned up missing yesterday?" asked Susan Peterson. She leaned as far over the crime scene tape as she could shoving her microphone in his direction and stepping directly in front of his path as he exited the Elder Lane Park crime scene where police men and women otherwise contained the media.

"The only comment I will make about the situation at this time is yes the body found dead down there on the beach is Sandra Falkland's. The condition of the body, how it got there, how it was found etc. is all part of our on-going investigation and we cannot discuss any of it with you at this time. We will be holding a press conference back at the station in about six hours from now at roughly 4:00 pm. We will have factual information for you at that time.

"There will be no further comments made here, and we ask respectfully that the members of the press remove themselves as fast as possible back and away from this park as you are interfering with the investigation that we all hope will soon lead to the apprehension of the person or persons responsible for these heinous crimes. There is nothing for you to see here and we will be filling you all in the best we can, always keeping in mind, once again, that this is an on-going police investigation. Thank you in advance for your cooperation," Ed said.

He kept shaking his head 'no' and using the 'sweeping the air in front of him' gesture which looked like he was shooing away pesky flies as he dismissed every question they bombarded him with on the way to his car.

Susan Peterson had just gotten brushed out of their way after her very short interview with Ed on the way to his car when her camera man zoomed in for the brief report she was about to give.

"That was Inspector Edward Cassidy of the Winnetka police department as he left what has just been confirmed as the crime scene where the body of Sandra Falkland was found.

"This is now officially another addition to the brutal serial murders involving the wives of a prominent plastic surgeon group known locally as the 'Surgeon Generals'. You heard the inspector tell us that a press conference will be convened later this afternoon at the Winnetka police department. During that conference, more details on this morning's discovery are expected to be revealed to the press.

"Only moments ago, Inspector Ed Cassidy confirmed to this reporter that the body found down below on the beach this morning is Sandra Falkland, wife of Dr. Blake Falkland, and she was found dead on arrival by the Medical Examiner. This is all the information we have at this time. Stay tuned to Channel Seven News for more details as they become available.

"If anyone out there has any information they feel may be pertinent to this morning's discovery here on the lake front, please call either the number shown on the lower portion of your screen which is a hotline to this reporter, or the Winnetka police department. This has been a special report updating the progress of the 'Plastic Wife Murders'. I'm Susan Peterson live on the scene at Elder Lane Park in suburban Winnetka for Channel Seven News.

"And that's a wrap," she said to her cameraman as he finished the session.

＊

"Great, that's all we need. Now we're going to have every crackpot out there that's looking for their five minutes of glory calling in and tying up our phone lines," said Lt. Mike Gorten at the end of Susan's telecast.

☆

Captain Gilbert Schellden was just getting back to the land of the living after his late night drinking binge on the docks with his shipmates and dock hand buddies. He had just tuned in to channel seven trying to find the local weather forecast for his trip back to Traverse City Michigan tomorrow when Susan Peterson broke in with her special report.

He couldn't help thinking about the video he shot late yesterday afternoon and shared last night with his drunken little group. It didn't get the reaction he thought it would, but truthfully the video was very dark and cut short by a blinding light that appeared just as it was getting going.

As he picked up the phone to call the Winnetka police department, he heard the phone's ringer and found a member of his crew already on the phone calling him, "Captain, were you just watching the news by any chance?"

"Yeah Jack, I'm about to call the police to offer up my little beach scene video to see if it has any connection to what happened yesterday," said Gil.

"Let me know what they say. I'll let you go."

☆

"Winnetka police department, this is Sergeant Tattersall speaking. Can I help you?"

By the time Captain Gil got it together and dialed the Winnetka police department, it had only been a half hour since the channel seven news cast had aired that solicited information from the public. The Winnetka police department had already logged 175 calls from people reporting everything from 'very suspicious neighbors' that they probably had a grudge against to 'strange lights in the sky last night'. They needed to assign anyone not working on a priority to man the phones.

"Yes this is Captain Gilbert Schellden I was sailing past Winnetka yesterday afternoon at about 4:30 pm and noticed some action on a beach there. My barge is equipped with night vision binoculars with a built in video recorder which I grabbed and started filming what I thought at the time, I'm a bit embarrassed to say, was a tryst in the sand about to happen."

At that news Tattersall almost hung up as it began to seem like another crank call. He looked over to one of the other deputies on another call, tilted his head up, rolling his eyes and twirling his index finger in a circle around his temple as the deputy did the same and they both smirked.

"When I looked through the binoculars, I got a better look and it appeared to be more like some pledging activity or ritual. There was a bright light like a torch or something that almost blinded me through the night vision on the glasses, but I thought someone may be interested in taking a look at the video," he said.

That last part got Tattersall's attention as he quickly sat up and almost spilled his coffee as he grabbed a paper and pencil.

"Sir, what was your name again and how soon could you get us that video?" he asked.

"That was Captain Gilbert Schellden, S-c-h-e-l-l-d-e-n and right now I'm in a motel in Gary Indiana until tomorrow, and I reckon it's about an hour and a half drive to Winnetka from here. Problem is I don't have a car having just sailed into port here last night."

"Give me the address of where you are staying and we'll have a Gary patrol car there in ten minutes. They will bring it to us. Captain Schellden, when were you planning on returning home?" Tattersall asked.

"Well, the plan was to leave tomorrow around 6am," he replied.

"How about you ride up here with the Gary police and we'll set you up for the night and get you a ride out to your barge when it passes through here?" offered Tattersall.

"I guess that would work. I sure hope the video helps you some after going through that much trouble," he said. After hanging up with the Winnetka police, he immediately called his first mate to give him the change in plans which put him in charge for the first part of their trip home.

CHAPTER 28

". . . a trial, or twenty five cents for a 9mm bullet.
Yeah I'm going with the bullet"

Thursday, 10:15 am, November 29th, 2012

Back at the station Ed said to Bill, "Say what you will about swallowing Dr. Baker's medicine Bill but several totally unrelated occurrences are now adding up beyond debate.

"First, the obscure 'flowers' message; second, that photo Jim showed us of the mirror message that read 'Sun Dancer—Sandra'."

"Wait just a minute Ed. How does that make sense? Just because we just found Sandra Falkland?" asked Bill.

"Didn't you see that bronze statue in the park of 'SUN DANCER—Jackie'? Clearly the message's intent was about Sandra being found near the Sun Dancer statue. Then there's the 'Sandy don't go' message that Blake says he heard on the answering machine. Then there's the other one that I think we really need to look into and that's obviously the 'Flowers' message which is now, more relevant than ever," said Ed.

"Wait a minute here Ed. Something's not passing the smell test. I'm not sure what the 'Flowers' message has to do with anything, other than she coincidentally received flowers before leaving for the market, but, we're getting most of these 'convenient Lori messages' from Jim Baker and they are beginning to look a bit too coincidental to me. I mean really, don't these 'messages' look like maybe the good Dr. Baker might just know more about these murders than he's telling us?" speculated Bill.

"Surely you don't think Baker has a hand in these do you? That doesn't smell right either," said Ed.

"Well let's do a little thinking outside this box for just a minute. What if Baker really ain't so chummy with the former Mrs. Baker and gets the idea to copy cat the Aimee Holden murder on his own wife. Then, well you know how friendly all the good doctors are with each other, so maybe they concoct this scheme of doing a little house cleaning of the

'General's Wives' variety. I mean that would explain a number of things we've been pulling our hair out over. Things like the security alarm being set with doors locked from the inside and the killer's being able to get close enough to the wives to start handing out reservations at the Chateau Eternity. Then there's the fact that the murders are being committed in alphabetical order to make it look like it was one killer instead of a coordinated effort of a number of men. That would be a perfect misdirect right there. Even you'd have to admit to that one Ed."

It was times like this that Ed wondered not only what it would be like to work these cases alone but also how Bill ever got his inspector's badge in the first place.

"I can only say that there's keeping an open mind, and then there's that theory Bill. No offense, but no way that theory gets off the ground let alone flying anywhere; there's way too many holes in it. First, absolutely every indication we have points to each of the husbands being devastated by the losses of their wives. True, doctors have their 'Money faces' when they need to break bad news to families and such, but this would have to be one academy award winning performance stacked on another Bill. We simply have too much corroboration independent of the 'General's' themselves on that.

"Second, how can he copycat the Aimee Holden murder right down to the burned dots behind the knees and in armpits and other details that were never released? They didn't have access to any of that information, and the M.O.s were all identical from the Holden murder right into the 'Generals' murders. Third, all the 'Generals' have alibis. Every one of them was seeing patients all day during the period each murder was committed. I just don't see motive or opportunity. Means maybe, hell they're all rich but that's about the biggest stretch I've ever heard. Can't buy it Bill, just can't buy any of it. Hell two of the wives were pregnant. Where's the motive in the husbands killing the unborn kids as well, not just from one family but from two? It's just asking an awful lot to line that much up without any conceivable motive," Ed concluded, not buying into Bill's bullshit philosophy.

"You can't always get totally in the head of a psycho and figure out what makes them tick. What seems far-fetched as a motive to you and me makes perfect sense to a psycho that's bent on scheduling dirt naps for a bunch of innocent wives.

"If it's all the same to you Ed, I'm not dismissing the idea just yet and I plan on taking a little closer look at the good Doctor Jim Baker," said Bill, still clinging to his paper thin theory.

"You do what you've got to do Bill, but for me that dog don't hunt is what I'm saying," concluded Ed with utter finality.

Thursday, 11:00 am, November 29th, 2012

They finished up their pointless tête-à-tête and made several of their easy phone calls to the various agencies that were now part of their team from the Chicago BIS, state and FBI bringing them all up to date, setting up a meeting with several of them.

Now it was time for the tough call to Blake. Only this one they needed to make in person before any of this reached him through the media. First, he thought, it may be a good idea to soften the blow by inviting Blake's friend to join them.

"Ray, its Ed Cassidy. I'm afraid we just found Sandra Falkland's body murdered on the beach in front of Elder Lane Park similar to the other wives."

"Oh no Ed, have you talked to Blake yet?"

"I'm on my way there now. I thought you might want to be there when I did."

"I can be there in ten minutes and Ed, I think it would be wise if I called Jim Baker for support as well," said Ray.

"I agree. Go ahead and do it. Bill and I will see you at Blake's house in ten."

✤

There was nothing that needed to be said once they got there and Blake opened the door. He looked at the four of them on his front porch and knew what was coming. All four of them were finding it hard to make eye contact with him and all of them looked like nobody wanted to speak first.

It was Ed's responsibility so he broke the ice getting in only three words before Blake lost it, "Blake, I'm sorry."

Blake stood there looking just as numb as when he opened the door and seemed to lose three inches in height right before their eyes. Then as he fell against the door, Jim grabbed him to keep him from hitting the floor and they all walked him into the den to finish with the bitter news.

None of it was easy, but they owed him the details. One half hour and one half bottle of scotch later, Blake regained some of his composure as the scotch worked its magic.

"I was expecting this you know. Since I dropped off the keys to you last night, I knew it was only a matter of time. Sandra has never just gone missing like that. It could only be tragic news to follow," he said.

"Blake there is a number of things coming into focus now; I'm sorry to say, since we found Sandra," Ed started.

"There are also some things we need to take a much closer look at as well," continued Bill as he started watching Jim's reactions discreetly but more closely.

After relating all that they could about Sandra's discovery on the beach, Ed began lining up the recent clues they had all given him in the now more relevant light. "Unfortunately after finding Sandra's body this morning we think there can be little doubt left that the perp is picking his victims alphabetically right down the list of 'General's' names from that article the Sun-Times wrote on your group last summer.

"We've already had discussions with Dr. Keenan & Gabriella Giovanni this morning, who happen to be next on the list, to explain the detail assigned to watch their house and all of Gabriella's movements. Dr. Giovanni refused to allow us a police presence inside their home which we think is a mistake. Their security system isn't as modern as yours Blake and we are very concerned for Gabriella's safety. Maybe one of you can talk to them and change their minds. I don't think there can be too much protection in light of current events," said Ed.

Jim assured them, "We'll certainly have a talk with them Ed."

"Like I told you when you came to me in doubt Jim, we had planned on taking the information you gave us very seriously. If we take a step back and look at the, whatever you'd like to call them, clues, insights, let's go with 'the messages', a number of them seem to line up in an obscure way now.

While we couldn't make sense of them before, several of them point to a number of the aspects of Sandy's murder.

"Then there are those that seem to give some insights to Lori's abduction and the confusing one about 'Black Breath'. We have no idea what that one is about, anyway in light of these we need to re-visit that surveillance tape and take a much more serious look it. We may be missing something relating to the 'Flowers' reference.

"We will be reviewing it more closely and showing it to some other members of the external agencies this afternoon at the station as well. Due to the fact that these 'messages' were centered on the 'Generals', we're hoping that maybe there's something that might look odd to one of you if we consider some of the facts surrounding them," Ed laid out.

"Let's start with the timing of the flowers. The flower delivery had come an hour before she left. She didn't leave before deciding to call you Blake. It was a very normal call by your account in which she appeared calm and was planning a loving dinner and a quiet night with the two of you. Blake did you order the flowers for Sandra?" asked Bill.

"No, and they appear to have been delivered absent a card. I had noticed the lack of a card when I first arrived home. I was curious, knowing that they were not sent by me. At first I thought the card may have been removed or perhaps it had dropped off the bouquet but one does not appear on them from the time of delivery as shown on the tapes. Who would be disposed to sending flowers without a card?" asked Blake.

"That's exactly what we were thinking. Also, there's the fact that Sandra didn't seem to look for a card from the time the flowers arrived until the time she left the house. Do you have an anniversary or any special date you are celebrating or an event coming up that would warrant someone sending you flowers?" asked Ed.

"None what so ever I'm afraid," responded Blake.

"Well again there seems to be red flags all over those flowers but we needed this background from you to eliminate some of the more obvious considerations.

"The FBI tech is meeting us at the M. E.'s office this afternoon and we will be all over these tapes like a fat kid on a cupcake," said Bill.

"We'll need to take the flowers with us to the lab Blake if that's ok with you," Ed requested, once again ignoring Bill.

"Do what you must inspector. At this point I'd be better off with them gone from the house," said Blake as the meeting ended and the inspectors prepared to leave.

Ed donned a pair of rubber gloves and handled the flower vase very carefully as he took them out to his car and later into their meeting at the M.E.'s lab.

*

Upon their arrival, they found the Medical Examiner, Connie Bristol; the Chicago Bureau of Investigative Services crime lab tech, Rick Newberry and the red-headed-freckle-faced FBI data tech genius Cory Seaver, already there and waiting for them.

After reviewing the surveillance tape several times with no comment, Ed stopped it and asked for observations from the group.

"Well I don't know about anyone else but I think we all just got our first look at our elusive dirt bag," said Bill.

"I agree, and we need to run through the list of local floral shop names to find out what that 'SFC' on his cap and coat stand for," said Rick.

"There's more and more that stinks on this tape and this delivery guy every time I watch the thing," was Ed's reply.

"Yeah, it doesn't look like there would be much in the way of his finger prints on that vase by the look of those gloves he's wearing. What kind of flower delivery guy wears gloves anyway?" asked Cory.

"The kind that had better hope one of you guys find him first because if I get him in my sights I'll save the tax payers in this county a lot of time and money when I drop him like a one foot putt. Let me see, tens of thousands of taxpayer dollars for a trial or twenty five cents for a 9mm bullet. Yeah I'm going with the bullet," said Bill.

"Look at the way he keeps the bill of his cap just enough in the way of the camera so we can't get a good look at the upper half of his face or enough of his mouth to read his lips. That's no coincidence. The camera at the far end of the front entry area puts his height right at the bottom of that hanging flower pot there," Ed pointed out to the group.

"Yeah, and is that a real mustache or a phony do you think?" asked Cory.

"Looks real to me even in this high def video," said Rick.

Connie asked, "Ed could you dispatch someone out to the Falkland home to measure the height of that hanging flower pot and the height of that far camera?"

CHAPTER 29

*". . . we just witnessed a good portion
of the Sandra Falkland murder"*

Thursday, 12:00 Noon, November 29ᵗʰ, 2012

*A*fter requesting Connie's measurement and research on the floral shop name, he returned to the room to find the others in the middle of a new discussion after viewing the tape again.

". . . and his walk seems a little stiff to me," said Bill.

"What did I miss?" asked Ed.

Rick informed him, "We were discussing the whole drawn out kind of floral delivery we are witnessing on the tape. I mean, a delivery guy usually would ring the bell, then ask the person to sign his ticket, give them the flowers and leave. We're talking about a process that would usually take all of about 30 seconds or on the outside one minute tops, once she answers the door. Not this guy. He talks to her for forty seconds, then pushes the flowers toward her to smell, like she needed proof that they smelled good or something.

"Then he chats with her some more, about what we can only speculate, then he must say something romantic and funny by the dreamy look in her eyes and the smile on her face that follows, all before he finally asks her to sign for the flowers. We are at a minute and a half already. Now they chat for another minute and forty five seconds more before she actually takes the flowers and goes inside. That's a total stranger standing there, talking all told four full minutes before leaving. I mean; this guy is either the most charismatic delivery guy in the world, or he just finished an agenda of some kind."

"And that starry eyed look she gives him is almost creepy. Could he be hypnotizing her or something?" asked Cory.

"Not with that little interaction; and not in that short time. Besides, her actions look normal after he leaves and according to Dr. Falkland; she didn't speak robotic, slow, spacey, controlled or anything else that would indicate hypnosis. I do agree that the entire delivery is fishy. It's not that she smelled the flowers but that they talked a while and then he almost offers them up for her to smell that's got me thinking. The delivery guy smells flowers all day in the shop and in the delivery truck on the way to all his destinations. The smell of flowers has got to be almost unnoticeable to him, kind of like the smell of fries to a McDonald's short order cook after smelling them all day," said Connie. She then made her way to the vase full of flowers and began turning them, so they were in the same orientation the delivery guy had them in his hands on the tape.

They all stopped talking and just watched her go through her motions as she was obviously following a train of thought in her head that none of them wanted to disturb.

✿

Captain Schellden had just finished packing up and checking out of his room when the Gary Indiana squad car pulled up to the motel lobby. They made it to the Winnetka police station just before one pm and he was ushered in to a room, with a very extensive audio/visual set up, where he met Lt. Gorten.

"Ah, Captain Schellden, please come in. We want to thank you for being so flexible with your schedule on our behalf. Can I offer you something to drink?" asked Lt. Gorten.

"Yes, please, anything soft would be great. Here's the video I told you about," he said handing the compact chip to the tech in the room.

"Why don't we let Jason here play with that while I ask you a few questions in this adjoining room?"

The captain took the hint as the lieutenant's comment was more direction than a question.

✿

"Well bless my bloomers I think I just found a little something gents," Connie said as she scurried off to retrieve several items from another room.

"A little something? What little something Connie?" Bill asked to her back as she left the room full of guys with blank stares and bunched up eyebrows.

"Patience people, patience, please," she said as she returned to the room wearing a breathing filter protective eye wear, gloves and carrying a magnifying lens.

"Great oaks from little acorns grow," was all she'd say very slowly and softly as she moved the flowers under a bright light and concentrated intently in on the rose that would have been closest to Sandra when the delivery man offered her a sniff.

"I noticed two things. First flowers delivered to someone from a florist generally are more buds than open flowers like these. That got me looking closer at the flowers. After orienting them as they were in the video, I noticed that there appears to be some kind of barely visible residue on this red rose petal here. Again, usually I wouldn't have noticed it because the flowers wouldn't be as open as these are. I thought I saw a slightly lighter coloration in that area on the petal closest to Sandra the last time I watched the tape. God bless hi-definition video!

"I'll need to do a little work on this once you guys leave my humble crime cave today," she said.

The way she brightened up at even the hint of a clue at long last, prompted Rick to say, "It almost looks like you're having fun there Connie."

"Oh, I've had fun before guys, but this ain't it," she said as she departed with the flowers holding the vase with minimal contact touching only the rim edges and leaving the guys to finish their video examination and discussions.

"Well that didn't take long," said Rick as a deputy entered the room handing Ed a sheet of paper with the name of the floral shop and the flower pot measurement as requested.

"Well let's see here, apparently 'SFC' is the abbreviation for Shaw's Floral Creations on Central Avenue in Wilmette. This report also puts the camera at the far end of the front porch and the bottom of the flower pot both at exactly six feet up from the front porch floor.

"So, we have a very suspicious six foot tall delivery man from Shaw's Floral Creations in Wilmette that has brown hair, a medium build, sports a mustache and walks a little stiff legged when he delivers flowers with no greeting card. He delivers said flowers that nobody we know of ordered, one hour before our latest victim leaves her house to buy groceries for a romantic dinner with her husband that they never had, because she winds up dead and mutilated on the beach below Elder Lane Park. Is that about it gentlemen?" asked Bill.

"That would about cover it except for the delivery van with no company markings on it," added Cory.

"We do have a license plate number, however," added Ed as he handed the paper back to a deputy with a scrawled plate number to run on it.

"While they're running the plate number, I can think of nothing I'd like to do more than take a trip over to Shaw's Floral Creations to see if we can catch up with our new buddy the scumbag delivery driver," said Rick.

"You boys go have some fun. I want to take the tape back to my lab and examine it some more. You never know what you'll find with a close enough look," Cory said as he made himself a copy of the flash drive and left.

✢

It was now 2:00 pm, two hours before the scheduled press conference. Ed tracked down Lt. Mike Gorten in the interview room next to the A/V lab and coaxed him into the hall for a brief meeting. He brought his lieutenant up to speed with what the five of them had found on Blake's surveillance tape and told him they were off to the floral shop to look for the delivery guy who qualified as their first suspect. Ed left his brief handwritten statement with the lieutenant telling him to read it to the news media in case he didn't return in time for the four o'clock press conference.

As Ed was turning to leave for their trip to the flower shop, Mike grabbed his arm stopping his exit. Then he steered him and Bill back into the interview room and introduced them to his new guest, Captain Schellden. Ed was told that he was possibly their first real witness and told him about the video he produced for them.

"I need you to interview him before you go Ed. Jason is doing what he can to clean up the video next door. The captain said it was getting quite dark, and the tape was made through night vision equipment, but his initial comments seem as though he may have captured our perp on his video," said Mike quietly before they reached the Captain's earshot.

☆

"Hello Captain Schellden. I'm Inspector Ed Cassidy, and this is Inspector Bill Weller of the Evanston police department who has been temporarily assigned to work with us. Could you start from the beginning and tell us what you saw and what prompted you to make that video of the beach yesterday?" asked Ed as he eagerly sat down and began the interview.

☆

In short order, the tech had ported the video to the huge flat screen at the front of the room. The video was dark, green and short just as Captain Gil had described it, but these things were his specialty. Through an extensive series of video tweaks, he was able to alter the video reducing the heavy green tinting and lighten it up considerably, so they had a much better view of the episode on the beach. He also blocked out the brief blinding light, and the seconds after it that jerked to the deck of the barge temporarily.

When he finished his adjustments to the video it became much more revealing. He signaled to Ed and the lieutenant through the glass, indicating that the video was ready for viewing as Captain Gil finished answering Ed's preliminary questions.

☆

After Captain Gil had finished telling his story, Ed became intrigued. He and Mike left Captain Gil in the interview room with a deputy while they joined Jason, Bill and Rick for their first viewing of the enhanced video.

What they saw stunned them all. They could clearly see Sandra Falkland lying naked on the beach with a man wearing a mustache who was kneeling over her. His fully clothed appearance was in sharp contrast to Sandra's nakedness. Not only was he completely covered by his clothing from head to toe but he was also was wearing gloves and a hair net. The video next showed the man reach into a nearby bag and taking out a hammer, after which he took 3 savage swings at Sandra's right ankle. They were stunned as she simply laid there and took it apparently without protest.

This was unbelievable! They were all watching Sandra Falkland's murder. No doubt about it!

The man's movements were clearly rehearsed and machine-like as he then put the hammer back into the bag, pulled out a very small pencil sized torch and lit it. Jason was able to control the glare from the torch enough so they could continue watching the man's movements. He moved very quickly with very efficient strokes as he completed the burn mutilations. Next he replaced the torch in the bag removed a pair of scissors and proceeded to give Sandra Falkland the last hair cut she would ever receive, placing the clippings on her neatly folded clothing.

Then he reached into the bag once again and removed something small that wasn't visible at all, did some small movement and returned whatever it was back into the bag. Next it looked like he was about to cut her nose with the scissors. He brought them very close to her nose, but appeared to think better of it and returned them to the bag.

That's when he clearly removed a scalpel and starting removing Sandra's left breast as the camera became blocked from the scene on the beach by trees due to the barge having moved to a position that no longer had a clear view of the crime scene, and the video ended.

They each looked at one another, one by one, stunned to silence by what they had just witnessed!

Bill was the first to speak and said, "I've seen enough. Oh, I've seen plenty. We need to follow up on our lead at the floral shop pronto. If we find this bastard at Shaw's Floral Goddamn Creations, I want to be the one to give him the lethal injection that permanently plants his ass in a Granite Garden."

"I don't think anyone can dispute the fact that we just witnessed a good portion of the Sandra Falkland murder. Does anyone disagree?" asked Lt. Gorten trying to bring the emotions of everyone in the room down a notch.

Jason said, "I agree. He looked prepared for the crime and had his body totally covered up to prevent any of his DNA from being left at the crime scene, right down to a hair net on his head. There's no way Captain Gil had the time, skill or equipment to doctor his video. It's genuine all right, and there is no doubt as to what we all just saw. That ritual on the video matches up with the mutilations done to each body we've found so far. There's no way he could have known about those details. Sad but true. Wow!"

"Ed why don't you grab the boys here and a couple of black and whites, drive over to Shaw's Floral Goddamn Creations and see if anyone there resembles the dirt bag we just saw in that video. I'm with you Bill. I can't wait for that bastard to assume room temperature. Keep me posted," said the lieutenant.

Thursday, 3:00 pm, November 29th, 2012

He didn't have to tell them twice. On their way out Bill said, "We're off like a prom dress," before the lieutenant could say another word. As Mike entered the interview room next door to thank Captain Gil, he couldn't help being amused by the shocked look on his face as he watched the men tear out of the A/V room next door.

"I take it the video helped ya'll in some way?" he said.

"Yes Captain, it did. We can't thank you enough. I'd like to count on your integrity as the Captain of a sea going vessel to keep what happened here today strictly between us. Would that be a fair expectation?" Gorten asked him.

"Yes sir, I surely will. Just knowing I was able to help is satisfaction enough."

"Great. Please come with me and we'll discreetly make arrangements for a meal in one of our best restaurants here in town and a place for you to spend the night that will soon have you forgetting that motel you slept in last night. My desk sergeant contacted the local coast guard on your behalf and arranged to have you brought out to meet the "Greta Marie" when she passes through tomorrow.

"In fact, since I don't have any plans for the evening myself, how about I get you set up in a hotel so you can relax and freshen up a bit. Then after my press conference at four pm I'll take off a little early today to join you for a little elbow exercise; that is if you'd like some company. It's all compliments of the Winnetka PD," Gorten offered.

"That sounds perfect to me lieutenant. Where do I sign up?"

Part Four

Missing Direction

*"All we have to decide is what to do with the time
that is given us."*
Lord of the Rings—Gandalf

CHAPTER 30

'Yeah, don't hold your breath on that one princess'

Thursday, 2:45 pm, November 29th, 2012

*H*e had just gotten home from returning the rented van to the North Chicago store and removing his old man disguise he wore that afternoon when he decided to check up on his favorite cops. The Nemesis started spying on Andy and Barney outside the Winnetka police station to see if they made any discoveries on any of the cases yet. He had wanted to listen in on their preparations for the press conference to see what they weren't going to tell the media and to see if the dream team of law enforcement was able to get a bead on Bobby as a suspect yet. Hell they better have after the show he put on for Falkland's new security system.

After training it on several windows until he finally found Ed's voice in the AV room, what he heard through his high powered microphone, took his cockiness level down a few notches.

'I don't think anyone can dispute the fact that we just witnessed a good portion of the Sandra Falkland murder. Does anyone disagree?' an unknown voice in the room said and that almost shocked the breath right out of him.

'What? What in the hell were they talking about witnessing Sandra's murder? That little stretch of beach was totally out of sight with the beach house blocking the left side, the high bank up to the park behind and the trees and stairs up to the community center on the right,' he thought as he went over the beach area again in his head.

'That only left a view from the pier which was empty or the view from . . . .' then he paused, as a shocking realization came over him. He remembered the barge passing by yesterday. '. . . . the barge on the lake! What are the odds on that one boys and girls?'

Next he heard another unfamiliar nerdy sounding voice say, "I agree. He looked prepared for the crime and had his body totally covered up to keep any of his DNA from being left at the crime scene, right down to the hair net on his head. There's no way Captain Gil had the time, skill or equipment to doctor his video. It's genuine alright, and there is no doubt as to what we all just saw. That ritual on the video matches up with the mutilations done to each body we've found so far. There's no way he could have known about those details. Sad but true. Wow!"

Then the first voice said, "Ed why don't you grab the boys here and a couple of black and whites, drive over to Shaw's Floral Goddamn Creations and see if anyone there resembles the dirt bag we just saw in that video. I'm with you Bill. I can't wait for that bastard to assume room temperature. Keep me posted."

Well at least they picked up on the Bobby clues and would soon have him in custody. However, the barge captain's video, now that wrinkle took him totally by surprise.

'That's why I must maintain a high level of diligence. I have to stay on my game. Fortune is still smiling on me. I got back just in time. I almost missed that little discovery of theirs. It sounds like Andy and Barney are heating up a bit or more likely getting lucky. No matter, I'm still way ahead of them. Man, what are the odds on a barge happening by and capturing my dance with Sandra on video? That video couldn't have been very good and had to be with night vision equipment and some wicked magnification to be able to pick up anything from that distance off shore. Especially with it getting as dark as it was at that time of day.

'Shame on you Captain Gil, do you take that kind of equipment on a commercial barge to spy on pretty little north shore house wives like Sandra Falkland having their inevitable affairs or do you just comb the beaches?

'In this weather and at that time of day you really got lucky Gil baby. Actually, now that I think about it, this could work in my favor. The keystone cops won't be able to search Bobby's shop until they can get a search warrant. That's a process they won't be able to start until they can confirm Bobby's appearance in person and get him back to Winnetka for a few questions before they will be able to demonstrate probable cause to a judge.

'That will give me enough time to plant a hair net in his back room locker. The only question is should I put anything else in there while I'm at it?'

After a few moments of consideration, he decided that all they needed was a few crumbs right now. No sense hitting them with the whole loaf just yet.

*

Rick rode the short distance to the Wilmette floral shop with Ed and Bill escaping notice by the media personal who had begun gathering for the four o'clock press conference. Ed also requested that the two back up patrol cars meet them in Wilmette to avoid a caravan type exit from the police station, to assist in cloaking their escape from the prying eyes of the press.

On the way to 'SFC' Bill said, "Back in the tiny border town where I come from in Texas, you get a guy as low as this one, you bring him in, sweat him like a whore in church, then beat him like a rented mule until he confesses. Up here you people do things a little different. I guess you all have more patience than we did."

Ed replied, "Maybe, but there's also that little thing called the victim's rights. You know that annoying chunk of legislation that keeps lawyers driving cars better than ours, going on French Riviera vacations with busty blondes that are all paid for by the local drug dealing scumbags that laugh in your face on the way out of the courtroom if we do it wrong. That's life in the big city."

"Where in Texas did you grow up Bill?" asked Rick.

"It was about the most remote part of Texas there is on the southwest border with Mexico. It was a little town called Presidio located about 250 miles south of El Paso," he replied.

"What made you want to leave a garden spot of the world like that?" asked Ed.

"Why didn't I leave a hell of a lot sooner would be a better question. It's not as if Presidio Texas is dripping with opportunity. I got into law enforcement early because it was one of the better paying jobs out there and there wasn't a whole lot of crime anyway. I needed the money because I had just gotten married to about the only gal that wasn't taken and that was a big mistake," he said.

"Why so?" asked Rick.

"Well first off she was so ugly she could make a freight train back up and take a dirt road, and she couldn't cook worth a damn. She was alright in the sack I guess but with what little else she had going for her and the limited opportunities in Presidio, I decided to get out of Dodge before I did something stupid like get that gal pregnant. I started hopping from one big city to another and finally got tired of Texas and decided to see what snow looked like, so I moved up here with you fine folks eight years ago and I haven't looked back since."

Thursday, 3:30 pm, November 29th, 2012

Their idle chit chat ended as they pulled up to the flower shop which was right on the edge of town.

They avoided a grand entrance when they arrived at the center of the retail strip mall where 'SFC' was located. After parking, they entered and started looking around like anybody else wanting to purchase flowers. The patrol cars took positions to the rear of the shop and just down the block in front. Both were told to watch for a white full sized Ford van with no external company markings and were given the license plate number from the Falkland surveillance video.

The rear squad car team noticed a small Ford Transit delivery van parked next to the store rear entrance. It was all white with a smaller version of the FTD logo of a man holding a bouquet of flowers with wings on his hat and shoes. It also had the 'SFC' logo prominently placed above it. Under it all was their company slogan, 'Your perfect arrangements—there when you need them'.

There were no white vans in the front area of the shop.

A tall, thin and very attractive young girl, probably in her late teens, greeted them at the sales counter. She had short brown hair, was conservatively dressed with an apron sporting the now familiar 'SFC' logo above her as yet underdeveloped right breast.

"Can I help you gentlemen?" she asked them as they continued looking around at various store displays and positioning themselves for a better look into the back room.

Satisfied that by now the two teams were in place outside both store entrances, Ed replied, "Yes, there was a floral delivery made from this store yesterday to the Falkland home in Winnetka and the lady of the house was very impressed with the delivery man. She said he really knew his flowers and we were wondering if we could consult with him on a project we've been working on."

She replied, "We have two guys that deliver our arrangements. Brian only works with us part time after school and knows very little about flowers I'm afraid. It must have been the owner Bobby Shaw. Now he knows flowers!

"Give me a moment to look up the order and I'll confirm that for you. Did you say the Falkland home in Winnetka yesterday?"

"Yes that's right," replied Bill.

"Let me see, Falkland, Falkland, huh. I don't see it here. Are you sure it was delivered yesterday?" she asked but then not waiting for an answer she said, "Let me get Bobby. I'm sure it had to be him."

*

She then disappeared into the back room and was back shortly with the owner Bobby Shaw who was about six feet tall, medium build and a very familiar looking mustache.

Then in a carefree voice sounding like he just finished playing with his three year old daughter Bobby asked, "Can I help you gentlemen?"

With Bobby's appearance being just what they were looking for, Ed took a half step in front of Bill signaling him to cool his jets. At the same time he pulled out his identification and badge, "Bobby Shaw we are with the Winnetka police department. We'd like you to come with us to answer a few questions. We think you may be able to help us with an investigation we're working on."

"I'm not sure what I can help you with, unless it was floral arrangements for the policeman's ball but how about I come over to see if I can help you after we close in three hours," said Bobby.

Bill could contain himself no longer, in fact Ed was shocked that he kept his lip zipped this long, "Look Mr. Shaw," he started out virtually spitting out the name, "Police investigations are the sort of thing that can't afford to wait for flower shops to close. Are you with me on that? We need you to close your shop now, send your little helper here home to text her friends all about how her boss was escorted out to help the nice officers with a police investigation that is more important than building Aunt Bee's wrist corsage.

"See what we're politely suggesting here BOBBY?" he said over emphasizing the name as his impatience showed through.

"Am I under arrest here? I didn't do anything to warrant you two coming into my shop and treating me like this in front of my employee. Do I need a lawyer?" asked Bobby.

"You tell us. Done anything recently that puts you into the 'lawyer needing category' there BOBBY?" Bill continued.

Ed tactfully moved Bill aside and said, "You'll have to excuse my partner here Mr. Shaw. It's been a very rough few weeks. What he's trying to say is we need you to come with us to answer some questions now, you can call an attorney if you'd like which is usually what people do if they have something to hide or are knowingly guilty of a crime.

"I have no reason to read you your rights, and I am not accusing you of any crime. We will be taking you to the Winnetka police department to ask you some questions and Mr. Shaw, this really can't wait."

"Very well. Robin I'm going with them for a while. Just lock up at 8:00 like usual and hopefully I'll be back by then," Bobby told his employee.

'Yeah, don't hold your breath on that one princess,' thought Bill.

"If I'm not back in time, I'll call you later on when I get back about what time to come in tomorrow," said Bobby.

Bobby was then escorted to the Winnetka patrol car parked out front for transport back to the station house minus the cuffs that Bill would have preferred to have slapped on extra tight.

✲

'Well the party is finally over. Have fun in Winnetka Bobby, I hear it's lovely this time of year,' thought the Nemesis as he watched the car at the rear of the shop assume a watchful position out front. The three detectives followed the patrol car with Bobby as they headed back to the station.

CHAPTER 31

It was love at first sight but for the wrong brother.

<u>Thursday, 4:00 pm, November 29th, 2012</u>

As badly as he wanted to follow them back to Winnetka, he couldn't be in two places at once. He needed to stick to the most pressing priority; that being planting the hair net before Winnetka's finest returned with a search warrant in hand to rifle through SFC.

Bobby had needed him to co-sign on the loan when he bought the shop and the Nemesis had insisted on a key and the security codes. They would come in handy now as he planted some very damning evidence against his brother.

✻

After pulling into a secluded spot out back, he put on a pair of gloves and took out a new hair net from his 'clean bag' and waited at the rear shop entrance until he heard the front door chime signal a new customer.

Once Robin's attention was completely consumed with helping a customer, he snuck in and carefully opened Bobby's locker and grabbed his delivery cap. With the hair net inside out on his gloved hand, he rubbed it around on the inside of Bobby's cap to get a little DNA and hopefully a hair or two on it. He then returned the cap, laid the hair net on top of a gym bag at the bottom of the locker and retreated quietly out the back door to his car.

Then he drove back to his favorite observation area outside the Winnetka police station. There he would soon see the show he had been waiting for since the love of his life died so cruelly six months ago.

✻

Ed phoned ahead and by the time they arrived back at the station, the warrant was waiting for them. Their on-call judge came through for them once again. It was always Ed's intention to execute the search warrant before seriously interrogating Bobby and things were finally starting to fall into place.

On his way out the door, the desk sergeant, John Tattersall, stopped him with new developments.

"Inspector, we ran the plates on the delivery van. They were stolen from a blue Chevy van in Antioch yesterday. You're also going to love this one. Our plain white delivery van was rented from the North Chicago Express Rental Company in North Chicago also yesterday and returned earlier this afternoon by a John Deramore. After Mr. Deramore had returned the van, the rental company was cleaning it up when the attendant noticed the license plates had more dirt on them than the rest of the van and reported it to management. Then they found that the plates didn't match their records for the van and local police ran them and, wait for it, wait for it, that's right, they were the ones stolen from the blue Chevy van in Antioch, which had the white rental van plates on it."

"Our Mr. Deramore has been a busy little boy," concluded Sergeant John Tattersall.

"Did you check for security tapes at the rental company?" asked Bill.

"Yes we did, and they sent us this photo of Mr. John Deramore," Tattersall said as he handed the picture to Ed.

"What a surprise. John Deramore is not only a lot less than six feet tall; he's quite old, stooped over, bald and a black man without a mustache," said Rick as they all looked at the photo.

"Obviously Bobby hired this guy to rent a van for him. It can't be a disguise. Bobby's mustache is real and too long to grow back in a day," said Bill.

"Well then there's also the fun fact that North Chicago police were unable to find John Deramore's Illinois issued driver's license number. His license is apparently a forgery," said Tattersall as he finished his disappointing report to the group.

"Great, that's just what we need, another dead end. I swear, if dead ends were dirt, we'd have about an acre," Bill said sounding very depressed.

Lt. Gorten had just personally taken a statement from the mother of the two kids that found Sandra's body when the deputy handed him the search warrant they had been waiting for.

"Here you go Ed, tear that place up and find something will you?" implored the lieutenant as he handed him the papers.

"We'll begin the background check on our scumbag from Wilmette while you're tossing his shop."

✢

As he waited for Andy and Barney's return with the gift he left in his brother's locker, the Nemesis went over the next step in his plan. That step would catch everyone flat footed while they were busy playing cops and bad guy with Bobby.

Bobby. Bobby. Bobby. His mind kept wandering back to the rift that had developed between him and his brother.

'It's time to pay the piper little brother,' he thought as he remembered the reasons for the intense hatred that he now had for Bobby.

'He's going to pay right along with them for not taking better care of her. He's the one that made her feel so inadequate that she was driven to the surgery from hell. He did very little due diligence before allowing that hack to cut her up and take her away from us. He was just too busy starting up that damn flower pit that he just keeps shoveling money into. Even now he doesn't spend half the time he should with their two boys. They'd be better off in foster care than with him.

'The wheels of destruction are rolling your way too brother! They'll get there soon enough,' the Nemesis contemplated as he began the next step down his path to revenge.

✢

The relationship wasn't always bad between the Nemesis and his brother. They grew up the best of friends really with each having the other one's back through the tough school years when siblings usually were in various competitive struggles be it sports, with girls or in fraternities through college.

They gravitated to fairly similar pursuits out of high school. Med school was tougher on his brother though, and he wound up dropping out while the Nemesis continued on and wound up completing a degree in veterinarian medicine.

After Bobby had dropped out of med school, his path turned decisively for the worse. He became a very angry young man that was hit hard by his failure in medicine. It was especially tough on him since his brother's sharp intellect kept getting remarkable grades as he breezed through the undergrad schooling which is where Bobby first got bogged down. Clear differences in concentration and comprehension abilities became apparent as they both tackled the biological and physical science aspects of their educations. Bobby simply didn't have a head for it or the desire to put himself through the four year veterinarian school commitment.

Bobby was nothing like his brother who graduated with honors seemingly always at the top of each of his classes. It was his brother who also toughed it out through an additional four years of specialty training for surgery certification and the eight hour exam that went with it.

College separated the medical men from the boys in the Shaw household and Bobby didn't take it well. Jealousy and bitterness developed while his brother was off becoming a successful vet and it took him down a path that the Nemesis could never relate to. He knew his brother's potential but started losing respect for him when he demonstrated a lack of drive and dedication to succeed.

Bobby fell out of med school, into trouble and immediately went to work developing a rap sheet of petty robbery and assault charges as he tried to support his growing drug habit. This continued until their dad passed away and left them each a large amount of Apple Computer stocks. Bobby burned up the profits of approximately one quarter of them and stopped just short of being a three time loser and throwing his life away completely.

It was at that point that he finally started cleaning up his act, and that's when he met her. The Nemesis was just finishing up his schooling when he found that his brother was actually settling down and starting a floral business with his new wife Allison.

It was love at first sight but for the wrong brother. He begrudged Bobby finding her before he did and always thought that she was too good for Bobby. They nonetheless went on to build a family having one boy then two years later another one.

Meanwhile, the Nemesis met his wife Denise, who he always felt was a settle-for partner after being infatuated with Allison for years. He never really grew close to Denise, and she proved unable to give him the one thing that would cement his feelings for her; children. More specifically heirs to carry on his name like Allison did for Bobby.

He would have a legacy to pass on to his kids unlike his brother who proved less competent as each year passed. His veterinarian practice became wildly successful due to his skill not only in surgery, but also to his keen mind which would routinely foresee business challenges ostensibly before they occurred, and he was always ready with successful remedies.

It seemed he couldn't fail while his brother struggled to keep out of the red in his floral shop.

He didn't need the money because he held on to his stock shares and they did quite well. He didn't tap into them and diminish their value during the years of their greatest growth like his brother did.

These and many other differences that developed between them led to a period of years where their relationship became strained and they continually grew apart. It was during these years when the Nemesis developed the greatest animosity for Bobby, and not only lost respect for him, but began to focus on how Allison was being short changed on the things in life he felt she deserved.

It was also during this time that he began to take a personal interest in her well being and started seeing her when Bobby was forced to spend crazy hours at the floral shop.

Late nights during holidays and on weekends provided ample opportunity for him to become close with his brother's wife. He learned a lot about how sensitive she was and the many ways she tried to please her husband only to be neglected by Bobby, which infuriated him all the more.

She deserved better than Bobby. He should have treated her right. She deserved better vetting of the surgeon that would be ultimately chosen to do such a potentially dangerous and, at the end of the day, life threatening operation. It was a procedure that led to such sacrifice and pain on her part. She endured all of it to make herself more pleasing to him.

His brother had a good thing and didn't appreciate it. He had a beautiful, sensitive, caring wife who bore him two heirs, and he didn't recognize the gifts he had in the three of them.

Things are finally coming together now. Things would be very different soon, then maybe he could leave this all behind him and start over again with the right woman in a country far away from all the memories that the north shore of Chicago held for him.

✻

After joining up with the Wilmette police force, it didn't take the combined team long to find the hair net in Bobby's locker. Besides the three from Ed's team, four more had joined them. The newly formed squad thoroughly searched the floral shop and the delivery mini-van, but they were unable to find anything else that was relative to any of the wives' murders. They felt they had enough though, to cut off the rest of the flower sales for the night and send Robin home early after sealing the shop with crime tape.

When they arrived back at the station in Winnetka, they had with them several items of Bobby's clothing and the hair net. They bundled these items up with the glass of water he had been drinking out of while the three of them were tossing SFC. All bagged items were sent with Rick to BIS for DNA testing and comparison with the hair net/bonnet seen on Captain Gil's video. They would now pursue a new search warrant from their on-call judge to search Bobby's home and car for the bag of items and the rest of the clothing seen on the video.

It had been a very long day. After everything that transpired during that very long day, they were all equally hyped up to make it a very long night as well for Bobby Shaw.

CHAPTER 32

"Well gentlemen I think we have enough witnesses to that one!"

Thursday, 7:00 pm, November 29th, 2012

The interrogation went about as expected with Bobby claiming innocence and offered a weak alibi about visiting with his cousin who was watching the kids for him during the time of Sandra's murder. She had since taken them for a visit to relatives in California until the middle of December.

The interrogation quickly landed somewhere between agitated, and heated when the bonnet detail was introduced and a still image taken from the beach video was shown to him. Although it was a bit grainy, it clearly showed a close enough match to his appearance and that coupled with the fact that he coincidentally wasn't into work the day before kept Bobby's tension and stress mounting to the point of near panic.

None of this was helped by the rap sheet they read to Bobby which included petty robbery, minor assault charges and drug possession. Even Bill had to admit in his head that these were all minor offenses that didn't include anything at the level of the brutal murders they had found strewn across Winnetka's landscape of late.

While they didn't paint a picture of Bobby with a halo and wings, they adequately documented a troubled past which could always escalate with the right motive. That was an element they still hadn't made any progress on, motive. It would have to be the main thrust of their efforts now that they had their suspect at long last.

Bobby was told that he was being placed under arrest and would be further questioned tomorrow and possibly be arraigned for the recent murders of the 'General's' wives.

✻

He was flabbergasted beyond belief as he was led away to his cell for the night protesting, much to the delight of the Nemesis. He caught the whole show courtesy of the microphone he had trained on the station from his front row seat in a dark parking lot across from the station.

It was time to pull the shade down on this very busy and satisfying day. He was basking in the warm fuzzy feeling of having achieved what he had planned, and then some thanks to Captain Gil.

Yes, it had been a very successful and satisfying day indeed. After some sleep tonight, he should be ready start wreaking havoc again tomorrow.

Friday, November 30th, 2012

Bill started his day's activities by stopping by to see the M.E. on his own.

"Good morning Connie, how's it going today?" he asked her.

"Fine Bill, what's on your mind?"

"Connie, I've had a thought creep into the back of my brain that I have discussed briefly with Ed, and I'd like to run it by you as well. Now to listen to Ed you'd think my wheel's spinning but the hamster is dead, but I want to run it by you real fast," said Bill.

"All right, you've got my attention. Let me have it."

Bill laid his flimsy theory of how he thought Jim could possibly be the killer having got the idea after the Aimee Holden murder. Other factors that contributed to his theory were that he was skilled at surgery, would have access to the alarm system, could have reset it and could be in league with the other general's in eliminating the wives for some reason.

"In your opinion doc, were the bodies cut up like a plastic surgeon would do or not?" he asked.

"Well Bill I have to admit that's a lot to digest this early in the morning. I'm afraid I have to shoot that theory down from a number of angles.

"First, medically speaking, if any plastic surgeon I know cut a woman like these were cut when they had their field mastectomies I'd be on a personal crusade to have their license to practice plastic surgery on a human revoked. While they appear to the untrained eye to be a clean job of removal, a plastic surgeon would have naturally made their cuts in different locations simply due to their knowledge of anatomy. These breasts were removed cleanly but surgically speaking, crudely.

"Then you have the rest of the details in the cases involving a motive, opportunity, etc., which I'm sure Ed reminded you of. Not to mention the specific details that have carried from murder scene to murder scene that were never reported. Dr. Baker and the rest of them would have no access to those facts. Doesn't wash at all from my perspective Bill if that's what you're asking me," said Connie.

"Yeah, I'm afraid that is what I'm asking. That's exactly what I was after Connie. Ed mentioned a lot of the same things, but I wanted your medical opinion. Thanks for your brutal honesty. I don't like sugar coating, so thank you for that, and forget I ever mentioned this ok?" He said as he left with his tail between his legs to go meet Ed as he finally threw his flimsy theory aside.

*

After arriving at the Winnetka police department, the first words out of Ed's mouth were, "I just heard from Connie."

"Oh, what about?" asked Bill trying to maintain his ignorance of what he was sure would be another embarrassing moment with Ed.

"She found a foreign waxy substance on the rose closest to Sandra as Bobby handed her the bouquet to sniff. However further testing revealed no drug substances on the wax. She's puzzled at the wax but can't find anything sinister about it," Ed was sad to relate.

"This is turning out to be a frustrating day Bill. You're going to love this. ADA Pelham just left here and after hearing that Bobby Shaw's alibi was confirmed by his cousin she feels we don't have enough to hold him!" he told Bill.

"What? You have got to be kidding!" he said. "We have this dirt bag practically dead to rights. What about the hair net? Did Connie find any of his DNA in it?"

"Yes she did, but Pelham says hair nets aren't that uncommon on flower shop workers, and there is not enough reliable evidence to hold him.

"Bill we are going to have to cut him loose unless we find something before this afternoon," said Ed.

✢

The Nemesis just had to pass by the Giovanni home to get a chuckle at all the new 'inconspicuous' officers that were keeping a watch on their house needlessly.

His selections thus far had the desired effect of leading them to guess the next victim would be chosen alphabetical by last name. They had it half right. His next victim would be alphabetical but not according to the last names from some silly Sun-Times article written last summer as they now believed.

He smirked then continued on to the home of Dr. Raymond Reed for a little stake out of his own.

They had the easiest home to spy on. All the best rooms, such as the living room, family room, master bedroom, etc were all facing the direction of his little hiding place in a park that was close enough to use his microphone successfully.

He was picking up details about the dinner being planned by Mrs. Reed for Saturday night which was to include Jim Baker, John Ackerman and Blake Falkland. This would be an intimate gathering of husbands that he'd moved to widow status recently. How SPECIAL!

'It's a great idea 'Liv,' he thought. 'To bad it'll never happen, but it will provide me with the opportunity I was looking for to catch up with you and briefly chat. I mean chat really briefly about my plans for you, blah, blah, blah.'

✢

"No Ray, I don't need you to go with me. I'm going to make a few calls, invite the guys, and then I'll run over to Johnson's catering after lunch. I should be back by two o'clock ok?" she asked Ray, who was still at work.

"Great, I have a couple more patients to see this afternoon but I should be home by five."

"I'll see you then dear, love you!" Olivia said as she hung up.

✢

'That should be enough time to scout out the area and get the night rolling,' thought the Nemesis.

His head was swimming as it was turning out to be another very active day. First he got the news earlier that they were releasing Bobby because the numb-from-the-shoulders-up ADA didn't think they had enough to hold him. What did he need to do, photo shop an 8 x 10 glossy of Bobby at the scene with a scalpel in his hand before they'd hold on to him?

He knew his brother well enough, though, to realize that the stress of being arrested and accused of murder would drive him to his old drug buddies for something to take the edge off his anxiety.

In his mind, understanding how Andy, Barney and Bobby all thought, would make this easy. There were unmarked cars both down the block from the flower shop watching the front door, and at his home. They would be assigned to pick up the tail on Bobby as soon as he showed up at either location because he probably already ditched the tail they put on him when they released him. He also knew that Bobby, being the model father that he was, wouldn't show up at either place. After scoring some cocaine, he'd lay low at his drug buddy Doug's house for a day or two especially with the store being closed.

After all, the weekend was here, and the kids were with their aunt for a week, so he didn't have to worry about Bobby for a while.

After arriving at Johnson's catering, he discreetly checked out the security system that was in place, to pick out the perfect camera dead zone. This is where he would initiate his little chat with Olivia tomorrow, but tonight he felt like a good steak and a quiet evening of relaxation, reflection and fine tuning.

✢

"Thanks for seeing me this afternoon Jim. I just wanted to bring you two and Blake up to date with the investigation," Ed explained as he took a seat in Jim Baker's richly appointed great room.

"No problem Ed. We're anxious to hear the latest news. Can I offer you something for lunch and a drink?" asked Jim.

"No, thank you Jim, I can only stay a few minutes. Inspector Weller and I have a lot to do this afternoon and I'd like to stop over at Blake's house later as well."

"Sorry, we weren't able to get Blake over here. His schedule is a bit hectic this afternoon and right now that's a good thing. He needs to get his mind off Sandra any way he can, and he prefers the diversion of seeing patients to seclusion or a retreat somewhere," said Ray.

Ed got about halfway through his news of a suspect, the fortunate and timely video, and the disappointment of having to release Bobby when the phone rang.

"I'll let the answering machine get it Ed, please continue. I can't believe that wasn't enough to hold him. It's especially disappointing after all this time without a suspect and virtually no clues," said Jim.

The phone stopped ringing, and the answering machine speaker immediately began spewing static noise which stopped their conversations. The next thing they all heard was Lori's voice saying "More tests Connie" then more static, and the machine stopped recording the message.

All three froze and looked at each other's face for any sign confirming what they had just heard. Jim dropped his glass, and Ray had started getting up but stumbled back into his chair as each doctor stared at the other in disbelief!

"Well gentlemen I think we have enough witnesses to that one!" said Ed.

"I don't get it," Jim said in a shaky voice. He kept staring at Ray and said, "Who's Connie?"

Ray replied, "I don't know Jim."

"Well I can answer that one for you; Connie is our medical examiner, and I was just about to tell you my last bit of news before, before . . . . that.

"During our intense review of Blake's HD surveillance video, Connie oriented the bouquet so she could look specifically in an area where

Sandra smelled the flowers and found, we don't believe coincidentally, a slight waxy material on the flower that was closest to Sandra. After testing the waxy surface, Connie concluded that there were no suspicious substances on it.

"Ok boys, I have to admit here that I'm as freaked out as you two appear to be but I heard what to me sounded like Lori's voice saying 'More tests Connie'. Just for the record, is that what you two heard as well?" asked Ed. Not much rattled Ed but this did.

The two doctors, too shaken to speak at the moment, merely nodded their heads in agreement.

Ed got up and went to the answering machine with Ray and Jim both on his tail. They all saw the blinking red '1' in the message counting window. Ed reached out, pressed play and all three of them heard the mechanical machine voice announce, "You have 1 new message; Friday 1:10pm," after which they all heard the message a second time.

Ed requested, "Jim, please save the message." Jim slowly pressed the correct button but as was the case with previous messages he reported, when they went to hear it again all they heard was, "You have no new messages. You have no saved messages."

Again freaked out glances were exchanged by all three of them. Nobody found the words to speak first, so they just slowly sat back down trying to comprehend what had just happened.

CHAPTER 33

"I guess we can all make our grand entrance together"

Friday, November 30th, 2012

Finally Jim broke the silence, "Ok, now we know 'Connie' is the M.E. but hasn't she done all the appropriate testing that she can in trying to find clues for you Ed?"

"I'm as shaken and confused as you are Jim. Connie has always been one of the most conscientious people I know at doing her job. I'll ask her if what we heard holds any meaning for her.

"Meanwhile I think we all got about as much out of this meeting this afternoon as we can so I need to get going," Ed told them, anxious to leave the house quickly.

✳

"Ed I appreciate your growing regard for these messages or clues or whatever and I'm not taking any professional offense at the suggestion contained in your latest one. Having said that, I can tell you with absolute certainty that I have performed every substance test that would usually be run to determine toxicity in this kind of situation," said Connie.

"I don't know Connie, are there any tests that are not usually run?" Ed asked her grasping at straws.

"The only other ones I know of are run looking for a particular substance. Tell me a particular substance and I'll check for it. Mind you it's a very large substance universe out there. Absent that information, we run tests that cover a very broad spectrum of known substances that could possibly have a detrimental effect on a person," she said starting to become professionally frustrated not only with the line of questions but also with her lack of discovery.

"No offense Connie, I just wanted to keep you as much in the loop as I could here."

"No offense taken Ed, I guess this situation is exasperating all of us. I've done everything this side of specifically testing for what would be virtually an unlimited number of random substances."

"You're the best Connie. I'll get back to you if I get a lead on anything specific."

*

"Inspector, come in please it's quite cold out there," said Blake reflecting on how much the temperature had dropped in just twenty four hours.

"Can I get you something to drink?"

"I'll have whatever you're having Blake, thank you," Ed replied as he noticed Blake's cup of coffee. He needed to shake off the chill brought on by the late afternoon's freezing rain.

They sat in Blake's family room as Ed brought Blake up to speed with the investigation and also with what he experienced at Jim's house earlier.

"All in all it sounds like it has been an alternately hopeful, disappointing, weird and confusing day thus far. Am I right?" asked Blake.

Ed was about to respond when he noticed a suddenly wide-eyed and terrified look on Blake's face as he looked past Ed at the window behind where he was sitting. He quickly turned to see what had transfixed Blake's gaze and soon found his own gaze locked on the frosted window. Actually it was on the frosted window with the writing on it. That storm window was still up halfway from yesterday's warm weather. The writing was on the inside of the storm window in between it and the interior window.

The writing was faint but clear enough to read. There were two words, 'Liv Now' with one word being written above the other.

Ed turned back to find Blake's still gapping eyes and said, "Well this day keeps getting better and better doesn't it?" He took out his phone and made several attempts before he could capture the writing at the right angle to be readable in a photo.

Blake finally spoke asking, "I suppose it's missing the letter 'e' and suggesting that I should get on with my life then, is that it?"

"Blake I don't quite know what to make of it but all I can say is that it definitely IS there!" he said, having just about enough of this unexplainable day.

"Besides the window; how have you been Blake? You went back to work rather quickly after Sandra's death. It's only been two days Blake, is that wise?"

"I've made the necessary arrangements and this is the only way I can deal with being alone Ed. I have no immediate family here in the states and beside my 'General' friends. It's all together too quiet around here now, and of course THAT didn't help a damn thing," he said pointing at the window which had now cleared up.

"I've never seen the point in pity wallowing. Don't get me wrong Ed, I loved my Sandra dearly. She was an absolutely beautiful and charming woman. I am finding myself dreadfully unprepared for her sudden loss. I guess I never considered the need to . . . Look at me, wallowing after all," he said as his upper lip began losing all of its usual stiffness.

"That's quite alright Blake. These last few weeks have been very challenging for all of you. Now is the time to lean on friends and let their kindness and support help you through it all," he said.

"Raymond and his lovely wife are putting together an informal dinner tomorrow night that I am quite looking forward to. They have invited John Ackerman, Jim Baker, Mark Channing and I will be joining them as well. I should think that it will be a very welcome break for us all."

"Sounds as if it will be Blake. Listen, thanks for the drink and I have taken enough of your time this evening. I will keep you posted as to any further developments. I can assure you that none of us will rest until this business is cleared up," he said as he took his leave of the Falkland home after one last look at the window from both of them.

When he got to his car he verified that the photo was still on his phone. "Well with the way these things have been disappearing so fast recently, I had to check," he found himself saying out loud.

Saturday, December 1st, 2012

"Don't know about you Bill but I needed a break after yesterday. It's one thing to be told freaky things by witnesses but it's quite another to be one of those witnesses," he told Bill as they updated the crime board at the Winnetka police station.

"I needed to not only discuss what I witnessed yesterday at the Baker and Falkland residences with you but I wanted to take another serious look at these, what did we decide to call them?"

"Messages I think, or was it clues? I don't know, pick one it's a new day," said Bill.

"As several 'messages' have shown an uncanny relevance, I thought it would be a good idea to isolate the ones that we can't relate to anything. Now if we update our board with the new ones I find this group here that we still don't have a clue about in regards to their meaning or whatever.

The list on the left contained; 'Jim, the flowers', 'Sun Dancer-Sandra' and 'Sandy, don't go' messages.

The list on the right was longer and contained: 'Black Breath', 'Jim, it burns but I can't cry. I'm . . . .', 'Take my clothes off, lie down, don't want to, must', 'More tests Connie' and the 'Liv(e) Now' messages.

At the bottom and in between them both was 'Crushed ankle, burning me, asked me to smile, I must'. They could relate two parts of the message to the victim M.O. but the two phrases were as yet unexplainable.

"Let's look at the list on the right. Is there any way we can piece anything together and create something that we might have missed?" asked Ed.

"I don't know Ed. You know I believe you and all but I sure wish I was there with you yesterday when you visited the good doctors. Perhaps it would help me hit the belief button a bit harder, but I'm still struggling with this whole section on the board," said Bill as he drew an air circle around the weird clues section.

At a loss for any new direction, they sadly looked at the growing list of names in the center which now included Sandra Falkland as they stared in silence. Just when they thought they were getting somewhere with the video and a suspect, they found that ugly square one feeling creep over them like a heavy wet blanket that was robbing them of oxygen.

They didn't like the feeling of having to wait for another shoe to drop before they could realize any new developments in the case.

As fate would have it, they wouldn't have to wait very long.

*

'There she is. Right on time as always,' he thought as he watched Olivia Reed park her Balmoral Blue, Autobiography model Range Rover. She did have taste. He had to give her that.

His arrival at the camera dead zone was timed perfectly as he met her and went into his "new to the area" spiel sneezing appropriately and accurately right in the middle of it. He really had that one down now.

Her surprised look quickly subsided and he said to her, "Olivia, look at me as if you see forever in my eyes and smile." When she did, he gave her his instructions which were to be followed to the letter. She had to because he had a relatively tight window to prepare her for the arrival of her husband from work and their dinner guests!

He returned to his car, confident Olivia was up to her tasks as he followed her home.

*

Their house was well off the road and the lavish trees, evergreens and bushes blocked any view of the house from the street. He waited a block away until he saw her turn into their driveway and gave her sufficient time to park her car, unlock the rear door, disarm the alarm and turn off all security cameras.

He had changed into his 'clean suit' in the car while he waited, then drove to the end of the driveway and entered at the rear of the house where he found Olivia waiting for him, still with that hopeful smile on her face, clearly pleased at his arrival.

A quick visual check confirmed that she completed everything he'd asked of her so he said, "Shall we retire to the dining room my dear?"

"Sure, I'd love to," she replied with the last words that would ever leave her lips.

"Olivia, please take off all your clothes, fold them neatly on the dining room table and lie down beside them," the Nemesis told her as he lifted his bag to the table shifting once again into autopilot for the procedures he needed to perform on Olivia Reed.

✿

Ed personally visited the stake out to check the men he had in place to protect Gabriella Giovanni. They were both hidden and visible in their locations as they planned out earlier.

"Any activity at all so far officer?" he asked.

"None sir, Mrs. Giovanni has been in the house all day and we see her movements occasionally. All exits are covered. We checked in with her about an hour ago, she related that she has no plans to go anywhere and her husband should be home at 4:00pm," he replied.

"Thanks officer. Call me if your team notices anything at all, no matter how insignificant it may seem," he told him as he drove off.

✿

Blake picked up Mark Channing on his way over to the Reed home and as he got to the eight-car-wide end of the driveway they pulled up next to Jim and John Ackerman who had just arrived and had also ridden there together.

"I guess we can all make our grand entrance together," said Jim to Mark as the four of them got out of their cars and ran to the house to get out of the freezing rain.

When they got there, Ray was visible through the glass panels along the side of the front door and he was just standing there with the door slightly open.

They all entered and were instantly aware of the scene that had frozen their friend when he arrived ahead of them only moments before.

There on the dining room table laid Olivia's nude and mutilated body. The clothes she had worn earlier were folded and stacked neatly next to her, the hair that had been cut off to give her the man type style was on top of her clothes with her severed left breast on top of the hair. A scene previously witnessed only by three of the five doctors was now on display for all five.

Blake dropped to his knees as he visualized for the first time how his beautiful Sandra must have looked when she was found on the beach. That, combined with the heavy smell of burned flesh that hung in the air like a fog, and the sight of Olivia's mutilated body was more than his trained stomach could handle as he emptied it on the floor.

Mark turned out to be the strongest of the group and called the Winnetka police department who connected him to the late working Ed Cassidy. With that call, the victim list in the center of Inspector Ed Cassidy's crime board had just gotten one name longer.

CHAPTER 34

"How about some English for us pavement pounders"

Saturday, 5:30pm, December 1st, 2012

D amn this guy. Ed was beside himself with frustration.

"Yeah Ed, what is it?" asked Bill.

"Bill he's done it again, we have another victim."

"What the hell. Did someone fall asleep at the Giovanni stake out?"

"No Bill, it isn't her. It's Olivia Reed."

"You're shitin' me! What, do we need stake outs on everyone on that damned list to find this guy?" asked Bill.

"I don't know Bill. Maybe he skipped his pattern because of the heavy security we put on the Giovanni's. I just put an APB out on Bobby Shaw. He's dropped off the grid.

"All I know is that I'll have ADA Pelham's ass on a platter if we find Bobby is involved in this one in any way at all. Can you meet me at the Reed home in twenty?" asked Ed.

"Sure, see you there."

⚜

'Well let's see if they can wrap a brain cell or twenty around this. I should clue them in to check all the flop houses in the near north shore area so they can find my dumb ass brother.

'How obvious! Couldn't they at least use something other than a black and white to keep watch on the flower shop?' he thought noticing the Wilmette stake out vehicle out front as he circled around the block to the rear entrance of 'SFC'.

After letting himself in, he opened the locker next to Bobby's which was used for storage, carefully placed the pencil torch against the rear corner, left a small amount of shredded canvas fibers just in front of it and left the locker door cracked open. Then he turned on the closet light in the back room as he noticed one of the cops walk up to the front door for a security check on the lock.

Peeking discreetly out of the back room he knocked over a vase just as they tugged on the door. That woke them up! Dashing back into the back room, he shut off the light, slipped out the back door and ran across the short distance to the dumpster area just as the two officers were rounding the rear corner of the strip mall. It was a very close call, but he made it past the dumpsters and through an opening in the back fence just as the cops walked up. They started scanning the immediate area with their flashlights, found the rear door to the shop opened slightly and called it in.

He made it the half block to his car and was off before they began combing the block outside the shop's back lot from their vehicle. The search lights were swinging like light sabers in his rear view mirror as he calmly put some distance between him and the incriminating scene he left at SFC.

✻

"Put a lid on that place sergeant. Nobody goes in until we get there with our forensics team, got it?" Ed demanded as he grabbed his keys. Ed and Bill were just on their way out to the Reed crime scene when the call came in from the Wilmette stake out team reporting a disturbance at SFC.

"Bill we need to split up. I want Rick Newberry from BIS out there to thoroughly check that place out. If you don't mind, you could meet him and our boys out there while I cover the Reed's house with Connie and CSU," Ed suggested, wishing he could trade places.

✻

Rick Newberry actually beat Bill and his team to the flower shop and started examining the rear of the store while the CSU team started from the rear door and worked their way in with Bill on their tail. They dusted for prints as a formality expecting to find Bobby Shaw's prints, and then they flipped on the lights looking for anything seeming out of place. Noticing the broken vase and the locker door ajar, they zeroed in on them.

With several cameras flashing from multiple angles, they opened the locker and easily found the torch that was planted by the Nemesis.

"Let's see him wiggle out of this one Rick. It looks like our murdering scumbag of a florist got a little nervous and clumsy when our local boys in blue tugged on the front door. He knocked over that vase there and pulled out in a hurry. Left us one of his little toys it seems huh Rick?" he asked the BIS tech as he continued his examination inside the locker.

"His bag might have been tattered. There are a number of canvas fibers here just in front of where the torch dropped. This torch is small enough to be the one we saw on the Captain Gil video.

It's all adding up Bill," Rick concluded.

"I'd say we about got his ass this time. How did he manage to stay ahead of us this long Rick? I mean this is some sloppy shit here. Couldn't he afford a bag without a hole in it? Then the dumb son-of-a-bitch thought we wouldn't be watching his shop? I think our boy is getting rattled by us catching up to him, and he's slipping. I'd bet we've about got him to the point where he doesn't know whether to check his ass or scratch his watch," speculated Bill.

"I'll bag what we found Bill. The fibers may wind up being the biggest nail in his coffin so far. We need to find him fast, search his car and house again, then find that goodie bag of his," said Rick.

*

"Why Olivia Ed, why her?" asked Ray, racked with emotion.

"I have been trying to answer that question at each crime scene so far Ray and I don't have an answer. None of us does. In fact, him choosing Olivia comes as even more of a shock to our team as his past patterns had indicated he was selecting his victims alphabetically from the 'Generals' article. I don't know Ray. Maybe he jumped off his pattern because Olivia was so close to Lisa, Lori. Isabella and Sandra or because she was such a help to Jim, John, Mark and Blake or he may have just took a detour due to the unusually heavy security at the Giovanni residence. Hell I don't know what to tell you Ray. I really don't, other than how sorry I am for your loss," was all Ed could think of to say. Then a thought came to him.

"Blake! The window message, remember? You thought it might be a message telling you to move on and 'Live Now' but clearly it must have been referring to Olivia's being next!" he said.

At that moment, Ed nearly became physically ill as he realized once again, obscure as it was; there was a message that should have helped them prevent another senseless murder if only his team could have deciphered it better.

There wasn't much that he expected to find different on this all too familiar scene that wasn't on any of the others, but he did his usual diligent search for clues alongside the forensics team who dusted everything in sight including all entrance ways.

They found the same array of abuse to the naked body on the table in front of them. The usual burns, amputation, crushed ankle, hair cut and arranged on the neatly folded clothing, everything right down to a tee!

He accomplished everything he needed to at the scene, leaving Connie to finish her on-site examinations before she took the body back to the morgue. He just made it past another yellow crime scene fence when the media vultures started pulling up to exploit and sensationalize yet another grieving doctor's misfortune.

He made up his mind first to see what Bill found at the SFC shop. Then he decided to call the entire team in to try to figure out what they were missing from the remaining clues they had received thus far.

These things he would do after adding another name to the list on his crime board.

☆

Less than an hour later he had the team assembled at the Winnetka police station. Present were Ed, Bill, Rick Newberry the BIS crime lab tech they'd been working with all along and Cory Seaver the FBI Tech head. Also in attendance were Connie, Jeremy Cowan the FBI profiler, Lt. Mike Gorten, John Halifax from the Illinois State crime lab, Jack Sullivan a BIS investigator and ADA Pelham.

They started from the first murder of Aimee Holden and tediously reviewed each case and each 'message' they received well into the morning before calling it quits on connecting any more dots.

They all liked Bobby for all the murders. ADA Pelham even had to agree now as she sheepishly kept to herself and about as far away from Bill as the room would allow. Even with keeping her gaze focused down on her lap she could feel Bill's eyes burning a hole in the top of her scalp.

· With a portfolio report on each murder placed in each team member's hands, the meeting broke up and was scheduled to reconvene on Monday.

Sunday, December 2nd, 2012

Cory was especially motivated to find a connection as he had always prided himself in his ability to wrap his computer skills around any mystery. He stayed at it all weekend long before finally putting the 'Black Breath' message in a new light. He found an obscure reference to a drug prevalent in Columbia nicknamed 'Black Breath' which was a particularly nasty variation of Scopolamine.

From there he was off to the races. One thing led to another for the rest of the weekend. He did extensive research on the drug, how it was prepared, into what forms and methods of delivery and effects of the drug etc. and prepared a detailed presentation for the next team meeting.

Monday, 8:30am, December 3rd, 2012

At their morning meeting, he brought the fruits of his weekend labors in the form of a report and handouts for everybody there.

"The drug scopolamine," he started off, "is generally used for the prevention of motion sickness in its more traditional and controlled application. However, there is another form of the drug that is most widely abused in Columbia South America. In this form, the locals have given it the name 'Burundanga' or 'Black Breath', that's right 'BLACK BREATH', because they say it turns your soul black and it can't see or be seen by the light. The scientific name for the drug is Datura.

"The effects of this form of the drug are frightening. It basically eliminates your free will while leaving you awake and articulate. To anyone watching a person after the drug has been administered to them, and I'll get to how that's done in a moment, that person will look fine and won't look 'drugged', spacey or sluggish at all. They walk, talk and look totally normal. The one exception being their lack of independent or unguided thinking. If someone were to ask them a question they have full use of their mental capacity and can recall anything asked of them.

"Columbia is responsible for approximately one third of the world's kidnappings. After this report boys and girls, I think you'll agree with me when I recommend not going there anytime soon if you prefer keeping your wits about you.

"It starts off looking like a cacao fruit. They get the drug from the seeds inside or they can extract the drug from the roots of the plant just as easily. The seeds are so toxic that they'll kill you immediately if swallowed. The seeds are easily processed into powder or liquid form and are utterly tasteless, odorless and colorless. Usually they are dried, ground into a powder, bleached and then dried either into a pill, powder or liquid form. Once processed into any of these forms, it can be put into a drink, on food or in a mist quite easily to achieve the desired effect.

"In order to get that result, which is usually a kind of mind control, a very tiny amount is needed. In fact, the drug from these seeds are so potent that just 1 gram administered correctly can kill 10 to 15 people, and it is so common down there that it is sold on the streets for about $25.00 a gram!

"Criminals in Columbia commonly use the drug to rob or rape people without their knowing it. Think of it as a date rape drug on steroids. There are reports of women waking up from the effects of the drug that were walking down a street after having been beaten and not knowing how they got there. They didn't know how long they have been out of it and were looking for their missing child. Speaking of that, the drug as administered down there for their purposes usually lasts about three to four days!

"Others have been reported waking up in empty apartments with bank accounts drained and when they ask their landlords how they could let someone take all their furnishing, they are told that the victim was helping load the trucks and appeared quite normal!

"Folks, this is the most sinister mind control drug I have ever run across in all of my years of research and it explains just about everything we have been experiencing on these cases. All a person has to do is sprinkle a little on a piece of paper, a business card or a greeting card or even the palm of their hand, walk up to a person asking for directions, sneeze and that's it. In less than a minute, 'Game over man'!

"Our local perp has probably been using one or more of these techniques to administer the drug to our doctor's wives gaining total control over them. They would be completely unable to differentiate reality from fantasy and would be totally under the control of anyone throwing a suggestion or directive at them. They could for instance suggest that this feels good and say . . . smash an ankle, without leaving a look of distress on that person's face. Sound familiar? If a second dose is administered in the same day as the first, it is instantly fatal. I mean the next breath is the last, and the brain doesn't have a chance to process any of it!

"Is a peaceful look absent any signs of distress coming to anyone's mind besides mine?

"Connie, I feel bad for you because this drug doesn't show up on any standard blood or urine screening tests but I did find out that it shows up if you subject it to targeted HPLC testing," Cory told her.

"Ah, little help here? How about some English for us pavement pounders Cory?" suggested Bill.

"HPLC stands for 'High Pressure Liquid Chromatography' without getting into a lot of specifics. It uses an explicit set of conditions, chemicals and equipment to separate the drug from where ever it was applied," explained Cory.

"Ed, this is the direction we were looking for and puts a new light on the 'More tests Connie' while thoroughly explaining the 'Black Breath' message. Way to go Cory! I'll get right on testing that wax I found on the flower petal as well as the nose, throat and stomach tissue samples I've collected from all the victims so far," said Connie.

"We have a HPLC set up in our lab that you can use Connie," offered John Halifax.

Lt. Gorten said, "Cory I don't know how to thank you for your research. It looks like we've all got a lot of reevaluating to do. Let's get on it now!"

CHAPTER 35

". . . and probably saved him a fitting date at
Mr. Malloy's cement shoe boutique."

Monday, 1:30pm, December 3rd, 2012

*I*t was all making sense now. The big blank mystery that hung over the recent murders like a massive dark cloud was finally dissipating and the sun was beginning to shine thru brightly.

Now they needed to locate Bobby Shaw, put a solid case together that he couldn't pay a lawyer to wiggle out of, then they could start getting back to normal. He longed to drive around his town without seeing those tacky yellow crime tape fences around all those beautiful estates.

"How in the hell did he find a drug like that anyway? Besides that, we still don't know what Bobby has against the 'Generals'," said Bill.

"Well at least we can now figure out how he was pulling them all off. He must have caught Lisa Ackerman as she exited her car, which would explain the groceries left in it. It also explains how he was able to disarm all the home alarm systems and then arm them again after he murdered the wives. All he had to do was ask for the codes and they willingly gave them to him. That's what allowed him to go in and out cleanly and leave each house secure when he was finished. Lori Baker must have got caught in the same scenario having met up with Bobby at the grocery store.

"Same with Isabella Channing, who was seen talking to a man in the Starbuck's that morning she died. I'm sure now that Connie knows how to detect it she will come back with proof that Bobby also laced the flowers with that drug. That also explains the problem Rick had resolving the length of time Bobby spent talking to Sandra Falkland when he delivered the flowers to her. There was that forty seconds or so that he talks to her and then the minute and a half after he convinced her to smell the flowers. It all adds up to the drug response times that Cory outlined," Ed concluded.

"Yeah and the son-of-a-bitch must have been giving her detailed instruction about dumping the car and meeting him on the beach for her last dance with the devil during that last minute and a half conversation," said Bill.

"As we found out by his stumble at the flower shop Saturday, he may not be the sharpest knife in the drawer, but he was smart enough to have found the one area at Johnson's catering where they wouldn't be picked up by the surveillance cameras. After following her into that 'no video zone' he must have drugged Olivia Reed because we found them enter that area, then the next thing we see on the tapes was them leaving again separately and this was on the exterior cameras. Bobby must have parked his car a short distance away because he's seen just walking out of camera range giving us no vehicle photos.

"It's a good thing we don't run into that drug more here in the states. Since it's grown and produced in Columbia and virtually not seen here, you have to figure Bobby made a trip to Columbia at some point. Let's get the boys working on that and on digging deeper into his background.

"Meanwhile we still need a motive so let's start looking for a connection with the 'Generals' and Rick Holden. There must be a reason he chose their wives," suggested Ed.

"Then we need to continue where we left off reviewing the rest of Dr. Holden's files," said Bill as he split the remaining folders between them.

After about an hour of going thru the files, Bill exclaimed, "Well piss on the fire and call in the dogs, the hunt's over! Look at this Ed. This file is on a Mrs. Allison Shaw, wife of a Mr. Bobby Shit-For-Brains Shaw, who had a boob job that went so far south that she got her halo on and is currently playing harp duets with Jimmy Hoffa."

"Let me see that Bill," he said as he grabbed the folder from Bill.

"Patient Name: Allison Shaw. Procedure: Breast augmentation surgery and asymmetrical breast correction. Initial procedure performed on June 6th, 2011. December 15th, 2011 patient developed complications known as Capsular contracture in her LEFT BREAST and required removal of the implant. Mrs. Shaw was admitted with significant infection having spread throughout the left side of her body during which she BROKE her

RIGHT ANKLE on the way into a hospital emergency room apparently delirious with pain.

June 23rd, 2012 patient recovered sufficiently from the implant removal and was scheduled to undergo re-implant surgery.

June 29rd, 2012 patient succumbed to complications arising from re-implant surgery. Death ruled accidental and not due to professional negligence.

"Formal findings: Several hours into the procedure involving breast re-implantation, patient Allison Shaw, developed Malignant Hyperthermia and suffered a fatal reaction to anesthesia. Malignant Hyperthermia is deemed a sufficiently rare metabolic condition, a severe sensitivity to anesthetics that was triggered by anesthesia and is known to be hereditary. Mrs. Shaw experienced a sharp increase in heart rate and skeletal muscle oxidative metabolism which caused her body temperature to exceed 118 degrees, overwhelmed her body's ability to supply oxygen and remove carbon dioxide which ultimately led to circulatory collapse and her premature death.

"MH can occur with IV sedation or with local anesthesia which is combined with anesthetic gasses. The only known treatment for MH is the use of dantrolene sodium which has an explicit shelf life needing to be replaced periodically. Most cases of MH have been recorded at small out-patient facilities, as opposed to larger surgery centers.

"Take a look at these file photos Bill. Allison was a rather pretty lady in her before picture. Notice the short hair style and partially missing ear lobe. Oh, my god, look at the post mortem photos WOW, she went through hell Bill.

"Her body looks like it went through a war zone with no protective gear. Notice the red skin from the infection they described up and down the entire left side of her body and her face! Now where have we seen those circles around the eyes before, making her look like a raccoon? Only thing is, they weren't red like the ones on Allison in these images. Man she did go through hell before she died," Ed said as he finished with the file's report.

"I'm at a loss for words Ed. That's about the saddest looking picture I've ever seen. The look on her face is quite the opposite of the dead women we've been finding around here. That woman went through some severe pain and look at these pictures; there's the explanation for the burn

severe pain and look at these pictures; there's the explanation for the burn marks imposed on our victims, there is a mole or birth mark behind her knee and one under her arm.

"If I knew for sure that someone was directly responsible for doing something like that to my wife, I'd be hotter than a goat's ass in a pepper patch too, but Bobby boy is taking it to a wholly different level. Hell, he's trying to wipe out half the plastic surgeon's wives on the north shore apparently for some kind of retribution. Man that picture of Allison is just plain nasty," said Bill.

"You're right Bill, and I can see why Dr. Holden was so reluctant to release this file in particular but it wraps up Bobby's motive in a pretty box with a great big bow doesn't it?" asked Ed, and then looking at their crime board he added, "I guess we can move all the clues on the right side of the board to the left because Cory's research busted this clue thing wide open as well."

At that point Sgt. Tattersall brought in the results of their most recent background search on Bobby.

"Let's see here; Active in high school sports, mostly football, made the varsity team with his brother Mark. Enrolled in med school but dropped out after one year, couldn't cut it in the grades department. Then got a job as a factory worker for two and a half years, various disciplinary reprimands on his employment record, this would be about the time he began working seriously on his rap sheet. He has a history of frequent drug possession charges; most of them were minor and dismissed. Then he seems to have developed a gambling problem and significant debt to our good buddy Mr. Malloy. We all know his reputation for advanced debt collection techniques.

"Then he apparently decided that instead of running up a tab with Mr. Malloy's excellent accountant, it would be easier to support his habit by merely taking the money from a number of sources. Those included arrests for everything from robbing convenient stores to grandma walking her dog.

"Then his rap sheet entries stop about the time their father died, and he inherited a good deal of Apple Computer stock which must have supported his habit quite nicely and probably saved him a fitting date at Mr. Malloy's cement shoe boutique. He also paid cash for his house at that time and started a flower shop shortly after that. He didn't have enough left to start SFC though, because his brother Mark needed to co-sign on the loan which he's still paying on and is, in fact, six months behind in payments," concluded Bill as they were interrupted by an excited deputy that burst into the room.

"We've got him! They just picked up Bobby Shaw a block away from his house, and they'll be here in ten minutes!"

CHAPTER 36

*". . . he'd have had to fall from the very top of the stupid tree
and hit every branch on the way down"*

Monday, 7:30pm, December 3rd, 2012

"So, where have you been BOBBY?" asked Bill as he started circling around their newly arrived guest.

"I still haven't done anything wrong. I was just hanging out with a couple buddies of mine," he said.

"Those wouldn't be your buddies with the excellent ties to the drug community would they, BOBBY?"

"Look, I want to wait for my lawyer. You guys don't have anything better to do than harass me. Why, aren't you out looking for the guy who really killed those five doctor's wives instead of messing with me?" Bobby asked.

"Oh, we've got the guy that killed those five doctor's wives, and also the guy that killed the sixth doctor's wife last Saturday night, BOBBY," said Bill who was starting to enjoy badgering their suspect.

"No, wait a minute. You're wrong."

"What do you mean, I'm wrong. Did I stutter, BOBBY?"

"No, but that proves it. I couldn't be the guy 'cause I was with my buddies last Saturday night. It wasn't me, see!" he said.

"Ok, I'll be right back. I didn't realize that you had such a solid alibi there BOBBY. Let me have a quick chat with your drug buddies and we can probably have this whole misunderstanding cleared up in a jiffy. If you are so innocent then why are you sweating like Mike Tyson in a spelling bee, BOBBY?" Bill asked.

"While we wait for your lawyer Bobby, you are perfectly within your rights not to answer any more of our questions but if you don't mind, Bill here, and I, will just be going over a few of our notes we started to make on your background. Those notes containing not only your spotless community record with local law enforcement, but also something we just found out about. It seems BILL, that our innocent little law abiding drugged up suspect here, that we just picked up with enough weight on him to book him on possession AGAIN, has had a recent death in the family.

"Seems Bobby here had a wife that died six months ago at the hands of, no, are you ready for this Bill, she died at the hands of a plastic surgeon after a botched boob job! I'm also noticing here, BILL that it wasn't just any plastic surgeon; it was at the hands of Dr. Rick Holden who, coincidently, was the husband of the first wife of the now SIX wives to have expired recently in our previously quiet little community.

"Also sitting on the corner of 'Strange' and 'Unbelievably Coincidental' are these facts," Ed paused for effect before going on as he rather irreverently tossed the post mortem photo of Allison Shaw on the table, so it spun around and winded up straight in front of him, "Aimee Holden, as well as the wives of five other plastic surgeons, had her left breast removed, just like Allison here.

"And do you know what Bill?" "I can only imagine Ed," said Bill enjoying his role of playing along.

"All six wives had a right ankle smashed, yes that would be the RIGHT ankle it says here, just like Allison's RIGHT ankle that happened to get broken when she was rushing into the emergency room burning up with fever.

"They also all had their hair cut short just like Allison's hair style in that picture right there in front of Bobby, Bill; if you can believe that coincidence. The genius that still thinks it's in his best interests to play the lawyer card is making himself look all the guiltier in my eyes Bill. I don't know about you," said Ed.

"Oh yes Ed, he's looking guiltier by the minute in my book too. That guilt is all over him like ugly on an ape about now," Bill taunted.

"Well let's just finish up our little note review before BOBBY'S lawyer gets here to straighten this all out for us dumb ass cops Bill. I think you can see in the rest of these photo's of Bobby's deceased wife that there are one or two more similarities between the way she looks in these photos," Ed continued as he tossed out the rest of the file photos, "and how we happened to have found all six murdered wives!

"There's the burn marks along the left side of their bodies, just like the red skin on Allison from her severe infection, not to mention the similarities in the eye markings. I tell you Bill; one thing that puzzled me was the little burned dots behind the right knee and in the right arm pits of all our SIX victims. Puzzled me, that is, until I took a look at these pictures of Allison and noticed the rather pronounced birth marks in EXACTLY the same spots on her body! Now that IS a FIRST class coincidence isn't it?" Ed finished up.

"That IS a coincidence Ed. Well it's either altogether the biggest cluster of coincidences I've ever seen or BOBBY here is about as dumb as he looks, sitting there thinking that we'd believe in this many flukes. Hell he'd have had to fall from the very top of the stupid tree and hit every branch on the way down to think we'd believe in a list of coincidences that long ED," said Bill.

"I can see where a fellow would be quite pissed off with a set of conditions lining up like that on his side of the fence, yes sir I can! Then there's the hard feelings probably that stemmed from not being able to pay for the surgery in the first place and to have to go to his brother for the money just like he did when he opened that flower shop of his."

"What's the matter BOBBY? Boobs weren't big enough for ya?" taunted Bill.

"THAT'S RIGHT; I didn't pay for that butch job that killed her, my brother did. That's because he was fixing her up to marry her out from under me. He always had a crush on her and thought I wasn't good enough for her. We both liked her, but I married her while he was spending his life in med school, and he always resented me for that. Being her husband didn't stop him from sleeping with her though. If I had the money, I'd do a paternity test to see if my youngest was mine or his. My brother's wife thought my youngest son was his when she divorced him last year.

"Here's me finally straightening my life out and trying to make good for my wife and kids. Through it all, he's sleeping with my wife while I'm working long hours at that damn flower shop! Everyone thinks Mark is so perfect. Well he isn't! He was the source of most of the problems in my family. The final straw between us was when he cut me off completely just because I talked her into counseling to try to save our marriage. I DID

NOT KILL THOSE WOMEN!" Bobby screamed back at the two of them, emphasizing each word by pounding on the table.

"Well bend me over and call me Sally, Ed. Bobby here must be innocent; he said so! Well how'd all that counseling work out for you BOBBY? It doesn't look like it went well at all to me. Perhaps that's why you decided to take out some of that hostility of yours on ALL SIX OF THOSE WOMEN! Sounds to me like you're so angry at 'bro-bro' that you probably have plans to cancel his birth certificate too. Is that about right, BOBBY?" Bill screamed back at him.

"I'm done talking. LAWYER!" Bobby said with utter finality as he crossed his arms and threw an icy stare at first one inspector then the other.

CHAPTER 37

"So what bugged you this time, Oh Wise Google Master?"

Monday, 10:30pm, December 3rd, 2012

Waiting across the street from the interrogation room sat the Nemesis behind his favorite listening device, taking in the entire interview.

'That's it Bobby. It's all my fault. I got you started gambling and hanging out with those losers at the factory. You know what they say little brother, "If you lay down with dogs, you wake up with fleas." And that's exactly what happened to you. They got you started down that dark path, not me. First the drugs, then the loan shark to pay for the drugs, then the crime to pay for the loan shark and all the while your wife was there to continually bail you out of jail on her puny salary. Even when I tried to get her to let you learn your lesson, she was just too kind and yes, too good for you. I encouraged you to stay in school, offered to help with your studies but no, you just couldn't stick with it and dropped out.

'You had too much Allison on your brain and not enough medicine, or your life would have turned out entirely different, and mine would have as well. The only truth you told just now was that you were not good enough for her.

'I don't think they've made a ladder long enough yet to get you out of the hole you're in this time little brother. You're just another piece of justice I've ensured for your good wife,' thought the Nemesis as he drove away once again satisfied with the successful completion of another part of his plan.

Tuesday, December 4th, 2012

Waiting for the rest of the team to reconvene, Bill reflected on their interview last night with Bobby Shaw after his arrest.

"I'll give it to him Ed. He stuck to his story like a hobo on a muffin. If it weren't for the mountain of evidence that's so big now even Pelham can't see over it, I'd almost believe him. In fact, it may not be a bad idea to learn a little more about 'bro-bro' Mark while we're at it just so we are better prepared for our first talk with Bobby's lawyer. If I'm reading Bobby correctly, he and his lawyer will try to shift the blame over to 'bro-bro' Mark when they start developing his defense. Seems to me, Bobby has a hell of an ax to grind with this brother of his and wouldn't mind throwing him square under the bus that would otherwise be taking him to Stateville Prison," Bill suggested.

"Not a bad idea Bill. Ah, here comes the rest of the team now," Ed observed as Connie, Cory, Rick, ADA Pelham, John Halifax and Lt. Gorten joined them at the crime board.

"Things are finally coming together nicely. First Cory coming through yesterday with his game winning Grand Slam on 'Black Breath' and then picking up Bobby Shaw last night.

"With any luck, this may just get wrapped up before Christmas. What have we got that's new today people?" asked Mike Gorten.

Bill couldn't wait to fill everyone in on the interrogation last night and also about his confusion at how all this evidence could possibly be pointing to Bobby since he professed his innocence so strongly and all.

Then it was Cory's turn, and he couldn't wait. He stood up at the front of the room and addressed everyone as he made his way to the white dry erase crime board.

"Well Lieutenant, if you liked my report yesterday, you're going to love what I have for you today. You see; I love a good puzzle, and I found one in the only thing that I just couldn't get out of my head. That's why Bobby changed what we thought was his pattern and went after Olivia Reed next instead of Gabriella Giovanni last Saturday. After Ed had called me with the news about the file on Bobby's wife, I played with the names a little, and this is what I came up with.

"Instead of assuming Bobby was using last summer's Sun-Times article on the 'General's' and the alphabetical listing of doctor's last names, I realized that we now have information that's much closer to our suspect. Check this out! What do we get when we use the first names of all the murdered wives in order starting with Dr. Holden's wife Aimee?

"Just look at this," he said as he began writing the wives' names on the board in front of them with emphasis on the first letters, "we have;

A imee,
L isa,
L ori,
I sabella,
S andra,
O livia and I can take a very educated guess at the only wife on the list of 'Generals' who's name begins with the letter "N" and that would have been
N atalie Kerr!" Cory concluded to a number of gasps from the team.

"Holy shit Cory, you've done it again! Now that you put it up there it sticks out like a boner in sweat pants! Ah, excuse my Texas French there Connie, but damn boy, it was right there in front of our noses and we missed it!" exclaimed Bill a bit red faced as everyone started chuckling at him.

"Well it wasn't quite so easy to see until you found out about the tragedy Bobby's wife endured at the hands of Dr. Holden. We have all been trying to tie Holden to the 'General's' for quite a while now but I'm sure Allison was the trigger," Cory concluded.

"I hope you all realize I had to let him go the first time we had him. We just didn't have enough on him, but we sure do now," added Lucy Pelham.

"Now that I have you all liking me so much, I hope you don't get mad at me for my next pitch!" Cory started out.

"Again, you see things that don't tie up nice and neatly really bug me so then I start hitting the keyboard," he continued.

"So what bugged you this time, Oh Wise Google Master?" asked Bill.

"Well actually two things. First we have the questions concerning getting that nasty drug in the beautiful north shore town of Winnetka, or Illinois, or the US of A for that matter. It just isn't prevalent anywhere here, so how did it get here from Columbia? I simply couldn't accept that Bobby, even with his drug dealer contacts locally, could get his hands on that drug here.

"Secondly, after I started cross referencing the drug with the FBI data base to see where else it may have been seen beside Columbia, I found a rather interesting case involving two local girls who were found murdered and mutilated with the same M.O. as the wives in our cases. Girls that were local to Cartagena Columbia that is. After some checking, I found their cases to be related to ours right down to the cut hair and burn marks behind the right knee and in the right arm pit! What are the odds on that boys and girls?" he had them all on the edges of their seats now.

"This occurred on November 23rd, and I checked the delivery records at SFC. Bobby was definitely in the states at that time delivering SFC bouquets and corsages to the masses on the north shore. Besides, Bobby doesn't even have a passport," said Cory as he gave this new information a chance to sink in.

"I liked you better five minutes ago Cory," said Bill.

"It gets better, or worse depending on how much you all like Bobby for being the 'Plastic Wife Killer'.

"At this point I'm sure I don't have to explain my discontent with loose ends, so I did some more digging. Both the first victim in the Cartagena Columbia crime, a Ms. Elena Sanchez, single, age 22, waitress poolside at the Occidental Grand Cartagena, and Ms. Graciela Gomez, single, age 23 house keeper at the same hotel were seen, according to local police investigating the murders, in the hotel restaurant with a man spending a lot of money," he continued as he started circulating photos around the room.

"He was later identified through sketch artists and a review of the hotel security tapes as, are you ready for this one sports fans, Mr. John Deramore. I have pictures here for everyone, and as you can see he bears a resemblance to Bobby but shorter, probably about 5'-9" tall and no mustache like Bobby's. They don't have him on camera without a hat and sunglasses, and the short, thick beard makes it more difficult to relate his looks to Bobby. He definitely isn't black, bald and walking with a limp like the John Deramore that returned the white delivery van to the North Chicago Rental Express office but somehow he has to be involved!

"I mean more than one John Deramore suddenly popping up in our investigation no matter how obscurely is too much for me to write off as coincidence. It gets better.

"Mr. Deramore checked out of the resort the next day and there are no flights out of Columbia listing him either arriving within the last month or leaving up to today's date. He seems to have just showed up and disappeared, both being equally mysterious. The local police and our Bogota FBI office have been looking for him since with no result.

"So, in a nut shell somebody killed two young ladies where Bobby's drug of choice is grown. Not only that, they also happened to be killed in precisely the same fashion as Dr. Holden's wife and all five of the 'General's' wives were here on the north shore. I'm sure it wasn't Bobby, hell I don't think he could afford a plane ticket let alone that resort, and I don't know how that drug got up here for him to use. There are still too many loose ends to tie up, but there is a good chance that Bobby is not our killer after all, as strange as it may seem," concluded Cory.

"OK, now I'm beginning not to like you at all Cory, no offense," said Bill.

"Well, on a positive home front note, Rick and I were able to confirm the Datura drug on one of the rose petals delivered to Sandra Falkland. He put a waxy substance on one of the red rose petals to keep the drug from being absorbed into the moist petal thereby allowing it to be easily sniffed up by Sandra Falkland. The tape showed that he probably suggested that she smell the flowers. In retrospect, if he had used a white rose instead of a red one I might not have seen the slight discoloration on the petal.

"I also found the drug in tissue samples of all the victims. There's no doubt in my mind that the women were not only initially drugged into submission to do the killer's will, but also given the deadly second dose that wound up killing them," concluded Connie.

"Ok, it looks like we have a motive and opportunity but we need to get a better handle on means by proving he was able to get his hands on the drug. We need to go at him hard on that one and find out who his drug channels are, and if they may have been able to get their hands on that drug.

"I'll tell you people, in a way I'm hoping Cory is right about either Bobby's difficulty or impossibility in getting that wicked of a drug locally, because if he can get that shit in the vicinity, we could be in for one hell of a crime spree on the horizon.

"Let's all hope not, anyway. Now that we know what drug was used, if we can find his source and tie Bobby to buying it we have that sucker strapped to the injection table," said Mike Gorten.

"It's time to pull out all the stops to find out how this drug got to our sleepy suburb."

*

The Nemesis was furious, 'That's it! That little shit has to go. He couldn't wait for one more body before figuring all that out? There's smart, and there's pain in my ass, and he just crossed the line.

'They'll probably be all over Natalie at the art show tomorrow now. Well I guess it's back to the drawing board to develop Plan B,' thought the Nemesis as he once again listened in.

CHAPTER 38

". . . if I could compare that experience
to something you could relate to . . ."

Wednesday, December 5th, 2012

*B*obby had a much different demeanor about him after spending a full 24 hours in the Cook County Jail. It hit him that after all the minor offenses he got caught at, he had never made it past the local lockups. The bologna breakfast, lunch and dinner menu depressed him as well. His associations with unsavory characters on the 'outside' didn't begin to prepare him for the 'inside'.

His lawyer didn't have a lot of good news for him either. He couldn't afford a good lawyer and the court appointed the councilor explained that with the evidence they had on him, coupled with the number of very high profile murders he was charged with, it was going to be almost impossible to mount a credible defense. About all Bobby had going for him was his claims of innocence.

Now it was time to face the inspectors assigned to the case, which were like a couple of sharks smelling blood in the water.

✻

"How'd you sleep last night Ed? I slept like a baby after my big juicy steak with all the trimmings and that dessert! I swear that I'm still full, and it's nearly lunchtime," exclaimed Bill.

"Yeah, I got home to the family and a warm cozy fire. Then my wife had the best meat loaf dinner I have ever eaten. I mean it was smothered in onions and mushrooms with a wine sauce and garlic mashed potatoes. We cracked open a bottle of wine that we've been saving for a special occasion. I believe we put that bottle on the shelf over six years ago now. There's just something about a cozy evening, a great meal, and the knowledge that a significant case has been cracked wide open that turns on the sex drive like nothing else to a good cop.

"About the farthest thing in the world from the bologna sandwiches we used to eat as a rookie Bill, you know that?" Ed continued.

"Sure do Ed. I guess I'll take that new girlfriend of mine; you know the one that's round everywhere, and only everywhere a woman should be, out tonight and celebrate. In fact, I don't even know why we are even wasting any time on BOBBY here. This one's all wrapped up. He has no bargaining chips anymore. From here on out, I guess BOBBY here will be waiting on the, "it's gonna be just fine because I said I was innocent" defense to spring his dumb ass out of Stateville prison.

"Yeah BOBBY, you aren't looking quite so cocky and confident today, now why is that anyway? You left yesterday, and only one day in the Cook County lockup has you thinking doesn't it? I'd be willing to bet you're probably trying to figure out what a life stretch in Stateville maximum security prison will be like about now. Well, I'll give you a big 'ole clue BOBBY. When old TY-RONE catches up with some fresh meat like you and makes you his bitch, things will get REAL interesting. For the first few weeks, you probably won't want to sit much. Let me see, if I could compare that experience to something you could relate to, it would probably be like trying to stretch a flea's ass over a rain barrel. You get my drift, BOBBY?" said Bill.

"There are other alternatives you know Bobby," Ed said taking over for Bill.

"If you cooperate with us, we could use some of that pull we have with the D.A. Hell the assistant D.A. even owes us some favors doesn't she Bill?"

"Yes she does Ed. You know; he's sitting there looking kind of sad. What's the matter BOBBY? Chevy stop making trucks?" asked Bill.

"Look you guys. I told you before. I'm not just saying this. I really didn't kill those women! Hell yeah, I'm down in the dumps. You would be too if you were being framed and had to spend the night in that hell hole with a bunch of degenerates staring at you all night like you was dinner, prey or both," he said.

"Yeah, I'd go heavy on the 'or both' there BOBBY. Oh, wait a minute Ed. How could we have missed that whole 'framed' angle?" chided Bill.

"Look, I'm being framed; you guys are never going to believe me, so let's get to it. What kind of cooperation are you talking about?" asked Bobby.

Ed tried to coax Bobby with a softer tone hoping for some cooperation, "Let's start with a list of all your drug buddies; then we'll see what we can do about some better accommodations for you until your arraignment. If you are being framed Bobby, we'll find the person or persons behind it, but we'll need your full cooperation."

"Give me some paper and a pencil. You know you guys are forcing me to give up my shop and home here with this list."

"Well perhaps a fresh start is just what you need, but we're a long way from even thinking about that yet," Bill said maintaining control over their prime suspect.

✽

With their small victory in hand, they handed Bobby's list off to vice and headed out to the prearranged remote location for their meeting with the state police to discuss stake out assignments.

✽

Sergeant John Callahan of the Illinois State Police Cook County District was placed in command of all necessary field surveillance activities until the cases involved in the string of murders were officially closed. He called a meeting to review tactics and assignments at an abandoned farm just north of Winnetka to avoid the media circus which was a steady staple at the Winnetka crime scenes, and now also at the Wilmette police departments. Meetings at this location could be joined independently by representatives of all law enforcement entities with absolute discretion.

"No offence to inspectors Cassidy and Weller or their outstanding work in apprehending the suspect Bobby Shaw now in custody, but we think that even though they have a suspect in custody, it would be prudent to keep our surveillance teams in place until the case against their scumbag is made air tight. Especially in light of FBI Data Tech Cory Seaver's growing theory that Bobby Shaw may not be our killer. So gentlemen, the order of the day is to proceed as if our perpetrator is still at large.

"Now with that in mind, and thanks to all of Cory's new insights, we've decided to keep the crew assigned to the Giovanni home in place and, in fact, make them somewhat more obvious to throw the sick bastard off if indeed he's still out there. We want him to think that we still believe Gabriella Giovanni will be the next victim.

"Meanwhile, we have some very discrete surveillance established on the Kerr residence. They have excellent observation spots with great concealment at the northwest corner of the property in front of the house and the southeast corner toward the rear. Each position has an excellent view of two sides of the home.

"Now Mrs. Kerr is scheduled to attend an art fair tomorrow which I imagine will have numerous locations and opportunities for gaining control of his next victim. We've coordinated joint rotating assignments to watch her every movement at that event."

✣

'Sick bastard? Really? Sergeant Callahan you need to brush up on your manners or maybe I'll have to demonstrate what a sick bastard I can be. I have kept my tribute amazingly on task to this point, but pointless name calling like that; well your guys may just have to pay for that one Sergeant, but first things first. Let's have that duty roster now,' thought the Nemesis as he listened in from a discreet distance.

✣

Sergeant Callahan continued, "I have drawn up a duty roster to cover both the Giovanni and Kerr residences up to and after the art show in Chicago, which we feel confident in allowing her to attend. There's a good chance a move may still be made on her at that show, but Chicago's finest are totally up to speed on our operation and will be on that event like white on rice.

"Each shift on the duty roster will contain two men from different agencies. We'll meet here again Saturday morning if needed, and I would like to go over the names in case any of you may need a change due to other pressing assignments."

At that point, he reviewed the assignments with their agency representative in attendance, received no objections, and promptly adjourned their meeting.

✢

Armed with all the information he needed, the Nemesis retired to his panic room, otherwise known as his 'planning den', which he had built several years ago once he realized the unsavory company his brother was keeping.

There he had securely hidden all aspects of his tribute preparation. Schedules of surgeon wife activities as well as those of his own, images of every conceivable angle of each home and all major participants, maps, architectural plans of all the homes, transcripts of police activities, it was all here at Nemesis planning central. The room was as secure and invisible to the outside world as it was complete, and utterly functional for his purposes.

Besides his impressive planning resources, it also contained all the make-up materials he needed to change his appearance according to various plans. It was also stocked with enough food and beverage to last him several months should he need to lay low that long.

It was here that he went to work on 'Plan B'. It took shape in part due to the inspiration given to him earlier by John Callahan's crude description of him.

'Yes this will work quite nicely, in fact, probably much better than the art show abduction would have and with much less risk!'

He examined each name on the list until he found a cop that was similar enough to his physical description in height, weight, and hair color so as not to be detected at a distance should they be checked in on while on assignment.

Friday it will be then. Right after the team rotation at eight pm.

CHAPTER 39

" . . . shit list priority numero uno."

Friday, December 7th, 2012

When special police task forces are formed, patterns begin to emerge. Important information usually starts to trickle in, then it seems to snowball as all elements begin feeding off each other. This tends to generate a flood of new relevant information that is then concentrated and collated which will usually redirect the investigation's course.

Ed and Bill were at the epicenter of this whirlpool of resources and results. The investigation was gaining a new momentum since moving to their remote location.

Regular meetings were scheduled every two days at 8:00 am and all the most up-to-the-minute progress was easily monitored from the Nemesis' rear observation position in the adjoining wooded area.

'So it looks like they will be seeing just how lovely an array of friends Bobby is regularly in contact with today,' thought the Nemesis.

He knew that on today's agenda was reviewing stake out results, or lack thereof, results from interviews with Bobby's drug dealing buddies and decisions on new tactics as a result of any recently reported intelligence.

*

The usual team was once again assembled at the remote farmhouse location where Sgt. Callahan got things rolling by inviting Winnetka vice to report on the drug dealer leads obtained from Bobby.

"We talked to all five of Bobby's drug dealing buddies and found a very specialized grouping of products offered to the street.

"Bobby had access to the following drugs through his former buddies. By the way, I use the word had because his list resulted in fifteen arrests over the last two days," he said as he posted a listing of drugs each dealer sold which included the street name and actual drug names.

The list consisted of:

Dealer	Street Name	Drug
One	Smoking gun	Cocaine
	Moon Rocks	Crack
	Green Dragons	Depressants
	China Girls	Fentanyl
Two	Bump	Ketamine
	Pink Robots	LSD
	Zambi	Marijuana
Three	G-riffic	GHB
	Black Pearl	Heroin
	Honey Oil	Inhalants
	White out	Inhalants
Four	Cactus	Mescalines
	Beannies	Methamphetamine
	Wild Cat	Methcathinone
	Chocolate	Opium
Five	Black Whack	PCP
	Silly Putty	Psilocin
	West Coast	Ritalin

"Our number five dealer also was a one stop shop for steroids of all kinds including; Gym Candy, Pumpers and Stackers but as you can see this rather extensive list contains no Scopolamine," they concluded.

"So if Bobby is our perp and his known sources don't deal Black Breath, he's either getting it straight from Columbia somehow or he's not our perp as Cory suggested," concluded Callahan.

"Let's table the drug source for just a moment, Ed you and Bill have some new clue or whatever from Dr. Falkland. What is it?"

"Since last Friday when I was at Dr. Falkland's home and we both saw the writing in frost on his window that I took a photo of," Ed said as he pointed to the 'Liv now' photo on the crime board, "he has been watching that window rather religiously and took this picture yesterday," he said now pinning up a new photo to the board that clearly showed the words 'Sorry Blake Know'.

"I sent this photo to Cory yesterday and, well Cory do you want to take over?"

"Sure Ed," Cory said as he rose to the board in front of the room with his laser pointer.

"If you pay particular attention to the spacing of the letters they once again produce a different message than the one you get at first glance.

"There is a slightly larger space between the 'K' and the 'now' and a definitely larger one between the 'Sorry Blake' and the 'Know'.

"If I'm right, one can start with assuming the message is in some way from Sandra Falkland and based on that, I take it to read 'K' 'now' after an apology of some kind to Dr. Falkland.

"K now could infer Kerr now, or Natalie Kerr is next, preceded by an apology. I know it seems like a stretch, but it was easier to extrapolate as it falls in line with what we now suspect is the killer's selection order.

"Without the insights we are working with now, the previous clues or messages left were too obscure to explain but I feel pretty confident with this analysis" Cory concluded.

Bill added, "I guess that's another one hit out of the park Cory, but I'm still not liking you for putting the stink on Bobby as the likely perp."

"Ed, what do you have on Bobby's brother? Anything new or insightful?" asked Callahan.

"Yes indeed. Let's start with the fact that big bro Mark hasn't been spending much time at his veterinary practice over the last few months. Cory was able to piece together data from several video surveillance and traffic cameras to put together a timeline of his visits to his clinic over the last two months and we found some interesting facts.

"First he was totally M.I.A. from November 19th thru November 27th with no out of town travel records from any of the airlines. However it was during this time, as you all will recall, that the murders similar to ours were discovered in Cartagena Columbia by the FBI's Bogota office.

"Before and after this hiatus of slightly over one week from not showing up at his clinic, he made only brief visits there and not on every day either. One could say the clinic was pretty much running on its own during the months of November and so far in December. He does have four other veterinarians, three vet assistants and two clerks working at the clinic. That gives him opportunity. He certainly has the means and the motive starts making sense if we believe Bobby and his assertion that Allison and Mark were actually that serious with their blossoming affair. I guess it's possible that Mark was more disturbed than Bobby about the botched surgery provided so ineptly by Dr. Holden.

"What we still can't figure out is how he could have gotten to Columbia where the 'Black Breath' drug is easily purchased. There is no video of anyone looking close to him from airport surveillance at either end or any international flight or cruise documents indicating that he traveled there during that period. The FBI ran not only Mark and Bobby Shaw but also Bobby's supposed alias John Deramore as well. As you may recall, that was also the name of the individual identified by the Bogota FBI field office as the man that had accompanied the two murdered girls there.

"Bogota FBI also circulated a photo they have of the guest at the Occidental Grand Cartagena Resort, who checked in under the name John Deramore, to the local police. They came up with a hit from one officer who claims he was directed toward a dead end after being pointed in that direction by a man resembling the Deramore photo wearing a Cub's baseball cap. He was chasing a man after being alerted to a possible assault with the typical 'Black Breath' approach down there on a young woman later identified as one of the murdered women, Elena Sanchez. He positively identified her due to the unusually striking blonde streak in her dark brown hair.

"Again, if Bobby is to be believed at all, Mark has a clear animosity for his brother and vice-a-versa. I don't see either cooperating with the other in any capacity.

"Also let's not forget, Mark has the surgical skills to pull off the field mastectomies we have been finding around here," Ed added as he wrapped up his report to the group.

✣

'Well that little shit just positioned him as shit list priority numero uno. You're a damn pain in the ass Cory. You would have been better off playing more online video games during the last few days. It might have contributed to your longevity. What's with these messages from beyond? Could these be for real? It really won't matter once I execute plan B. One more, and I'm out of here. This last one will be particularly rewarding knowing the amount of information they have and the size of the task force trying their damnedest to head me off.' The Nemesis was getting dangerously close to gloating which was an emotion he had strictly forbidden himself from enjoying just yet.

'Even with that little asshole's latest insights moving the spot light from Bobby and more towards me, I'm still too far ahead of them. If they only knew about my sitting in on all their meetings! It does rather give one a distinct advantage now doesn't it?

'Next week this will all be over with. I will be executing my escape routes to eventual obscurity and a new start. I can't wait. Events and retribution will finally be put into proper order and I will at long last be able to move on,' he thought as he reflected back on all his planning and, so far, all his successful execution with total satisfaction.

✤

"Based on all today's new information, I believe the best course of action is the one we are currently on. We will leave our decoy surveillance in place and continue with the rotating shifts on the Kerr residence. Meanwhile let's turn up the heat on Mark Shaw's clinic. Start discretely with the clerks. They may get talkative under the right circumstances. We want to confirm his schedule so let's go with the pretense of having received strong recommendations for Dr. Shaw and only wanting to work with him.

"Another go at Bobby Shaw might also be in order Ed and Bill. He's had more time to enjoy the Bologna cuisine at the Cook County lockup, and may be more cooperative today. Perhaps he might even be willing to offer up more insights to his brother's relationship with his former wife.

"Then let's review our results Monday night. The art show will be over by then, and we may get some activity at the Kerr home as well," said Callahan as he dispersed the team.

Part Five

The Cheater's Revenge

*"I found it is the small everyday deeds of ordinary folk
that keep the darkness at bay . . ."*
Lord of the Rings—Gandalf

CHAPTER 40

"Even from the grave; he's still helping us Ed"

Friday, December 7th, 2012

Waiting in the parking lot outside the 7-11 convenience store just one half block from Cory Seaver's home in suburban Elk Grove Village was a stolen red Toyota Corolla. This was his favorite car to pilfer as it was so unnoticed by the masses. Inside the Toyota was a bald headed, old looking black dude with white hair and a mustache that had been waiting in the parking lot approximately thirty minutes for the store to clear out. Once it finally does and the 'old black dude' sees not only no other cars in the lot but none approaching on the street, he exits the vehicle, limps into the store and greets the middle eastern man complete with red turban behind the cash register counter. He was intently involved in taking inventory of all the point of purchase items on the back wall. PERFECT!

"Good evening sir," said the clerk to the 'old black dude'.

"Hi 'yall doin' dis' evenin'?" replied 'old black dude' then he asked, "Sir, can you tell me if you have any Pringle potato chips?"

"Yes sir. They are at the end of this aisle facing the beer cooler," replied 'red turban' over his shoulder waving a hand and pointing up in the general direction of the third aisle from the store front as he returned to his inventory duties.

'They never pay any mind to old black men. Now, if I were a young black man he'd be watching me until I left the store!' thought the Nemesis as he limped back to the end of the snack aisle. He knew exactly where the Pringles were and also that the view of him through the store front windows was just as blocked by the magazine rack as the view from the register was by the aisle itself. He was also aware of the fact that weren't any security mirrors in either rear corner of the store. PERFECT!

His well rehearsed limp brought him inconspicuously to where he removed the plastic lid from a container of Pringle Barbecue chips. Then he removed a specially prepared syringe from his pocket. 'Old black dude' carefully penetrated the foil seal at the top of the can no more than necessary and exactly one drop fell from the syringe on to the first of a perfectly stacked can full of chips. He then carefully replaced the plastic lid and gathered up the other six cans of barbecue chips leaving the one specially prepared can as the only package of barbecue chips on the shelf.

Limping up to the counter, he found 'red turban' still so engrossed in his job that he didn't notice him arrive, so he placed the six cans loudly on the Plexiglas counter top and began pulling out his wallet to pay.

"Will that be all for you this evening sir?" asked 'red turban'.

"Yah young man that'll do 'er," said the 'old black dude'.

"Having a pa'tee?" asked 'red turban'.

"Nah, jus' a cupl' ole friends over for a lil' game of pokka. I kinda like five card stud, but its mossly Texas hold 'em. Small pots, nutin' big. We just enjoy each other's comp'ny dat's all. We genrally plays way into the wee hours of the monin' and errbody loves the Bobque chips," he continued.

"Well here is your change sir. You have the good luck tonight mister," said 'red turban' as 'old black dude' gathered up his chips and limped out of the store toward his car at the end of the parking lot.

Glancing over his shoulder on the way he waited for 'red turban' to turn his back to the store and get intently back to his inventory. It was then that the 'old black dude' dumped the six cans of chips into a trash container and returned to his car parked out of view from the cash register.

Two hours later, at exactly six forty five, a silver Volvo rolled into the 7-11 parking lot. It pulled into the same parking space it did every Friday night after work. Out popped a young red haired, freckle faced tech head in search of his usual snack before reaching home.

'Those habits of yours will be the death of you Cory,' thought the 'old black dude' as he watched the sequence unfold. 'No . . . . I mean it REALLY will be the death of you!' he thought.

It wasn't long before Cory returned to his car with the only remaining can of barbecue chips in one hand and sipping on the extra large Fanta Blue Raspberry Slurpee that he held in the other. Once in his car, he popped the top on the chips and ate exactly two chips, his usual pattern, then washed them down with a big gulp of the blue raspberry Slurpee bringing him just this side of a brain freeze. Yuck!

'What a combination. Those two items should never be brought together in someone's mouth ever! That's another favor I'm doing the world tonight,' the 'old black dude' thought as he approached Cory's window.

"Excuse me, do you have the time young man?" he asked.

"Yes I do sir, it's 6:57 pm," replied Cory.

"Would you mind picking your nose for me?" asked the 'old black dude'.

"How's this?" he said doing exactly as he was told.

"Actually I was hoping you'd go much, much deeper," replied the 'old black dude' at which point Cory dug so deep he drew blood.

It was then that the Nemesis knew he had him.

"That was just fine. I'll tell you what, why don't you drive home, put your car in the garage, go into the house, disarm your security system and leave the back door open for me ok?"

"Sure. No problem. See you there?"

"Oh yes, that you will!" he replied and followed him for the short ride home.

Cory's driveway wound around behind his house up to the garage where the Nemesis parked out of view of the street. Once inside he decided to have a little fun with the biggest pain in his ass lately.

"Hey Cory, you know what will be fun? How about you drink down that entire Slurpee without stopping and enjoy the experience?" he suggested taking satisfaction in knowing the intense brain freeze that would produce.

Once he was done, the Nemesis gave him some time to recover so he would be able to function once again. He only wished that the brain freeze could cause permanent brain damage. If it could, he would leave him like that, never to annoy his planning with those bothersome analogies again. He knew it wouldn't; which was ok because he had a plan that would be just as fitting of an end for the little techno pain in the ass.

✽

"Cory, it's Ed. Hey, I just checked my watch and noticed it's almost eight o'clock buddy, and I didn't see the final report on Mark Shaw that you said you'd post as soon as you got home. Call me, ok? I could really use it tonight. Thanks, talk to you soon," was the voicemail Ed left on Cory's answering machine admittedly a little concerned.

Cory was the kind of guy you could set your watch by once he committed to something. It wasn't like him to miss a promise like this. He sent him an email with the same message and made a mental note; try his phone again in half an hour before getting too worried.

*

When Ed picked up the phone, he heard Bill's voice saying, "Ed did our little techno squirrel send you that info on Mark Shaw yet?"

"Not yet Bill, and I'm getting worried about him not calling. It's just not like him. He's been home for two hours now, and I've called him twice, emailed him and got no response at all. It's not as if he has an active social life. I dispatched a black and white twenty minutes ago to check up on him. They ought to be there any minute," Ed related with a heavy dose of anxiety.

"Well I'm headed your way right after I check up on the second shift at the Kerr residence," said Bill as he pulled up to the night sentry site. It was strategically positioned away from the property with a view of both posted officers. Through binoculars, he could see the secluded sentinels on duty and all looking quiet, so he headed over to the Winnetka police station.

*

Having just left Cory Seaver's home to check on the Kerr residence himself, the Nemesis thought, 'Like about the most predictable clockwork imaginable! Bye, bye, Billy boy.

'Sunday night exactly one half hour after Agent Zack Jamanski hits the scene the real fun will begin.'

As usual he did his homework, and after extensive checking of police records he finally found the officer posted to the duty roster that would be the easiest to match in appearance.

He selected Agent Jamanski as he was the same height and general build. With the right make up and by the light of the silvery moon, no one would be able to tell the difference.

✻

"Ed, you'd better get over here. It looks like our little wife killer got to Cory, and it ain't a pretty sight," reported Deputy Pete Zimmerman upon arrival at Cory Seaver's house. When he got there the rear door was open, and he could see Cory hanging out of the bedroom window above the door.

✻

It took Ed and Bill less than half an hour to reach Cory's home, and they couldn't believe what they found at the back of his house.

After hoisting Cory's body back into the house, they noticed that he had been hung outside the window with several network cables wrapped around his neck. Two were tied off to hold his weight, and one was wrapped loosely around his neck to remain functional. It was plugged into the wall and still connecting his computer to the internet world. The computer screen was turned on, and Ed could see the email he sent Cory earlier, still visible on the screen, along with a crude epitaph leaning against the screen which read: "Cory won't be helping anymore. All that information was too much for him, and as you can see . . . he finally choked on it."

The letters were all different sizes and styles which were individually cut out of magazines and glued together on the paper to create the words. They knew these types of messages were meant to leave no clues and expected to find no fingerprint evidence anywhere on the note. On Cory's face was the same peaceful look they had found on all the wives so far with no indication of the trauma he had just suffered, besides the bluish-purple color that replaced his usually pale complexion. This was an all too familiar signature calling card of their thus-far elusive killer which was found at each murder scene.

Ed and Bill collapsed onto Cory's bed simultaneously staring at each other in disbelief. Stunned at what they were now putting together and at the loss of their new friend now lying on the floor of the room which served as his bedroom and computer information gathering center. Cory had been such a key part of turning the corner on solving these murders.

It took a few minutes for the numbness to settle and leave them enough to start looking around the room. After a closer look at Cory's computer, they noted that an email had been left discreetly in the draft folder which hadn't been sent yet. It contained the information they were looking for. It was the report he had promised to post earlier and was apparently missed by Cory's murderer. Whoever did this to Cory was obviously so consumed in creatively ending Cory's life, complete with the active, working cable around his neck and the computer screen showing the email to Ed, that he apparently didn't bother to search his computer.

"Even from the grave; he's still helping us Ed," said Bill solemnly as he found the unsent email with Cory's report attached. He must have initially composed the email and left it in the 'draft' box from the office before leaving.

CHAPTER 41

"Sometimes the universe shifts a bit in alignment."

<u>**Saturday, 7:00 am, December 8th, 2012**</u>

After working well into the night and grabbing some sleep, the two inspectors got an early start the next morning. They finished reading and dissecting Cory's report on Mark Shaw. Amazement at the thoroughness of Cory's work hit them all over again. It had the effect of changing even Bill's mind about Mark Shaw as he was now regretting the doubt he expressed earlier to Cory about Bobby Shaw not being their murderer.

"Our red-headed, freckle-faced little buddy was right again Ed. This is making me like Mark more than Bobby for the murders now. He's certainly capable, and it probably makes more sense that Mark was the one planning out all these clueless crime scenes.

"The more we talk to Bobby it seems like he's so dumb he couldn't pour piss out of a boot with directions on the bottom," said Bill.

Ed chuckled and said, "Based on this report it looks like Bobby's claims of Mark dipping his egg roll in Allison's won ton soup is clearly substantiated also. No wonder his wife Denise divorced him. I'm not sure what took her so long to do it.

"Look at this paper trail of gifts, local five star hotel receipts for one night stands, restaurant bills etc. Here's the charge for her boob job gone wrong too. Cory even found his plans for their honeymoon reservations. Hell he was really invested in Allison. Damn Cory, you didn't miss a trick!

"I can see Mark Shaw getting upset enough to want to punish Rick Holden for his hand in all this but I'm still confused as to why he carried it so far. Why go after the 'Surgeon General' wives? I'm missing the connection there," Ed related through the puzzled look on his face.

He continued reviewing Cory's report saying, "Something else that's now making sense is the fact that Mark is three inches shorter than Bobby. Remember the slightly weird walk we all observed on the Falkland security video as the delivery man walked up to the door? My money's on elevator shoes making it awkward to flex his ankles normally.

"The boy definitely has expensive tastes too. According to this financial report he's richer that any three of the 'Surgeon Generals' put together. Hell he could buy a new boat every time the last one got wet."

Bill wrapped up with, "We need to pay our favorite judge in waiting another visit for a search warrant so we can comb Mark's house. Cory was also thorough enough to provide us with plans to his home. We can start planning our approach to search the house while we wait for the warrant. With any luck, he'll be home, and we can kill two birds with one stone."

They noted that there was no basement or attic, and it was a rather modest three thousand square foot, two story home. It was not exactly fitting for a man of his financial means. There was a garage at the back of the house and entrances in the front and the side facing the driveway with no entrance to the rear. Having made assignments to various areas of the home in advance, their search team headed out to Mark's Kenilworth address, confident that the warrant would be granted by the time they arrived.

*

Saturday, 8:00 am, December 8th, 2012

The Nemesis had just emerged from the operational nerve center he had set up in his home. It was the panic room built two years ago when he became worried about Bobby's affiliations with known drug dealers. He had become concerned that the path might lead to his affluent door thanks to Bobby's loose lips during a beat down for drug payments.

It was built at the rear of the house taking square footage out of an enormous room meant for entertainment. He had a door cleverly built into a paneled wall; the seams of which were utterly invisible.

It was in here that he engineered most of his revenge preparations and it contained a state of the art computer system, make up/mask design area, enough food to last him several weeks if needed and of course a bed, a small kitchen area, and bathroom facilities. Here he had his plans up on the wall in sections, sequentially for each wife that was included in his grand scheme. He was spending his final preparation time in the last section devoted to Natalie Kerr when he heard a knock at his side door.

Peaking out, he saw his neighbor Paul. A real pain in the ass that guy. Paul seemed to be alarmed about something and was yelling for assistance at the worst possible moment.

'BUSY!' he thought. The Nemesis was glad he had begun to park his car two blocks away giving the house the appearance of being empty. This practice began a week ago thinking that one day he may need a quick getaway once that little pain in the ass Cory started getting too close for comfort.

'Come on Paul take a hint! There's nobody home,' he thought as he listened to him lament to an apparent empty house about his water heater bursting in his basement. He eventually left, running to his friend on the other side of Mark's house instead of simply shutting off the water himself. A real pain in the ass that Paul.

After Paul left he went back to refining his sequence for getting to Natalie Kerr. The man chosen for 'reassignment' tonight had facial features very similar to the Nemesis'. His face being so similar, would make the task of applying the facial alterations needed quick and easy. The hair color was even so close that nothing would be needed there as well. Just a simple mustache was the only other item needed to complete his Agent Jamanski transformation.

Saturday, 9:00 am, December 8th, 2012

'Now what?' he thought as he heard the front doorbell ring. This time he looked at the security camera monitor and saw a squad of policemen with swat gear on at his front door.

'Crap, time to run.' Grabbing his 'clean kit' and make-up equipment he quickly sealed the panic room and exited the rear door which emptied out into a shed attached to the rear of the house.

With no known doors at the rear of the house, Ed's team was concentrated at the front and side entrances for the initial contact giving him enough time to escape through his back yard that was bordered with tall shrubs.

As he exited the shed, he found himself nearly ankle deep in water.

'Shit, that moron Paul's sump pump is flooding my yard and all because he doesn't know how to turn off his damned water,' he thought as he sloshed through the saturated grass that extended from the back of the shed halfway to the rear of his property.

*

Saturday, 9:10 am, December 8th, 2012

With no answer to the bell, Ed's team breached the front and side doors simultaneously and began their search which ultimately turned up nothing useful. All teams reported back, finding no car in the garage or signs of recent occupancy throughout the house.

Dejected, Ed dispatched a team to search the grounds. As they fanned out, Ed headed toward the back yard and found that over half of Mark Shaw's rear lawn was partially under water. The now dead grass, which was taller than usual as it hadn't received its end of the season final mowing, was combed into one direction unlike the rest of the yard due to all the water. The water was flowing away from Paul's house. The origin of the water's path could be traced all the way back to his sump pump pipe that just burped another quick blast of water to join the already soaked yard.

Sometimes the universe shifts a bit in alignment. Once in a while, luck that has enjoyed a particularly long cohesive string of well coordinated events against you, shifts a bit in alignment.

When this happens, the new configuration will sometime provide a long awaited piece of good fortune. Also when this happens, one is apt to stumble upon things with ease that couldn't be found by teams of dedicated men working tirelessly for weeks.

This is what ultimately happened to Inspector Ed Cassidy. As he watched the water subside a bit, the Nemesis' footprints gradually started to emerge as the water level dropped in the yard.

He watched as Paul's sump pump finished its intended task. When it stopped, he traced the water's path back into Mark's yard from where he stood and found fresh footprints leading away from, but not up to, the shed at the back of the house. This would be the back of Mark Shaw's house that had no rear entrance.

"Bill, over here!" he yelled as he opened the shed door.

It wasn't too difficult to find the door concealed at the rear of the shed. Someone left through here in a hurry. Someone was in too big of a hurry to straighten up after exiting.

As Bill arrived, Ed found and opened the door to the panic room and hit the jackpot! As he did so it seemed like the entire investigation passed before his eyes in less than two seconds. They both stood there staring at the contents of the panic room in amazement before entering.

"Son-Of-A-Bitch!" screamed Bill.

"Ed you did it. You found his hidey hole! It looks like bologna sandwiches are off the menu for Bobby and on for Mark. This is incredible! We need the CSI team in here right away. This is nothing short of a gold mine!"

They both donned crime scene protective gear and started carefully looking around as the CSI unit began their work.

Saturday, 10:30 am, December 8th, 2012

In less than an hour of digging through the panic room, more information was gathered than was previously obtained by almost two months of painstaking, frustrating and often fruitless research.

"Bill, this changes everything! I'll have the arrest warrant information sent to the judge. We'll want to do this one strictly by the book. I refuse to provide even the slightest loophole for a lawyer to stretch around his client on this one.

✻

Saturday, 11:00 am, December 8th, 2012

The Nemesis checked into a roadside motel not too far from the Kerr residence because tonight was to be 'Showtime'. This was the night he chose to culminate the long road of well executed tribute to his Allison.

She had become HIS Allison. Bobby no longer held any claim to her. They were planning to be married right after she left him but, well, that turned out to not be in the cards.

After this night was finished, Andy and Barney could spend the next several years trying to find him but they never will. His exit strategy was as flawless as the taking of each wife had been so far.

☆

Saturday, 11:05 am, December 8th, 2012

"Is everyone in place?" asked Ed over their communication devices.

After a low whispered affirmative from each member of the team Ed left his car and walked up to the door. It opened before he reached the threshold.

As the door opened, Ed was greeted with, "Is there something I can help you with Ed?"

"Please step inside and away from the door," said Ed as the rest of his team arrived and spread out inside.

"I see you are all here. That's excellent. It will save us several trips.

"Doctor John Ackerman, Doctor Jim Baker and Doctor Raymond Reed you are all under arrest for conspiracy of murder involving the lives of Lisa Ackerman, Lori Baker, Isabella Channing, Olivia Reed and Sandra Falkland.

As the arresting officers began placing handcuffs on the three doctors, Ed continued, "You have the right to remain silent. Anything you say or do, can and will be used against you in a court of law. You have the right to speak to an attorney and to have an attorney be present during any questioning. If you can't afford an attorney, which in this case I sincerely doubt, one will be provided for you at government expense. Do you understand these rights as I have explained them to you?"

As they all silently nodded their heads, the officers led them to the cars to be transported back to the Winnetka police department.

CHAPTER 42

"I still have this anger inside me that isn't totally spent somehow."

<u>*Approximately two months earlier:*</u>

<u>Friday, October 19th, 2012</u>

*L*ori Baker had plans to spend time with her good friend Lisa Ackerman to discuss some of the many things they both had in common. Probably their favorite subject recently was the birth and future of the babies they were both carrying.

They were both so blissfully happy about the soon-to-be blessed events that it actually began to obscure a couple of other things they both had in common. Among those things were that neither woman's journey to motherhood had been kicked off by the men they were married to, and another was that neither husband was aware of this fact.

It was fortunate for both women that they happened to be planning to start a family soon before their respective buns began their nine month journeys in their respective ovens.

They grew fast and close friends once Lori and Jim Baker moved to Winnetka and Jim joined the 'Surgeon Generals' who all practiced in the affluent north shore suburb of Chicago. All nineteen surgeons had a lucky wife. Lucky in that, the lifestyle most women only dreamed of, was given to each of them by their husband's 'Surgeon General' success.

The lavish lifestyles weren't entirely free. They came with a price to each of them. That price was paid when the 'Generals' needed to associate and consult with each other regularly, mostly due to the rigorous schedule of surgeries and hours spent seeing patients both pre and post op. The hours kept routinely by the successful surgeons cut deeply into the husband/wife interaction time that was part and parcel of a normal marriage. This didn't include the significant amounts of time the doctors spent away from home attending seminars to remain current on all the latest surgery techniques which also contributed to the team's uncommon success.

Six of the mice regularly played while their cats were away leading to the formation and regular meetings of a social club they began calling the 'ALSOTS'. This name evolved among them from their constant references to having "a little something on the side". Olivia originally objected to the acronym as she thought it was too close to sounding like 'All Sluts' but the phrase was used so often that the other members; Lisa Ackerman, Lori Baker, Isabella Channing, Sandra Falkland and Natalie Kerr had no opposition, so the name became the inside joke they all shared.

"Lori come in, so great to see you. It is starting to get chilly isn't it? Come in. Come in," said Lisa as she invited her best friend in to warm up. She previously spent quite a bit of time getting the fireplace blazing and set to remove Lori's chill. Lori needed it, just having come in from the light snow that had recently begun to fall, painting the barren trees on their property a silvery white. This beautiful picture beginning to form outside was the only truly worthwhile aspect of the approaching winter season. Aside from the scenic postcard splendor, the other aspects of the cold, slippery weather amounted to nothing more than a sadistic sort of harassment that must be endured by all who chose to live this far north of the Mason-Dixon Line until the spring thaw.

After warm hugs, she handed Lisa her slightly wet coat and produced a bottle of sparkling apple juice which became their favorite drink since beginning their baby bumps. "Thanks Lisa. Would you mind putting this in the fridge for a while until I warm up some?" Lori asked as she rubbed both her arms for warmth.

Lori, six months along, had two months on her friend Lisa. Every new experience shared by Lori, that Lisa had yet to experience was a delight. Lori's visits provided a vision of what was coming down the path to filling the Ackerman crib with the boy they were expecting in March.

"How did your latest appointment go? Do you have any new pictures of Melissa?" Lisa asked, ever eager to see what her own baby would soon be looking like inside her.

"Of course, what kind of proud mommy would I be without them?" said Lori.

After viewing them and once the superlatives had died down, Lisa became troubled once again, as she usually did lately, asking her friend, "Lori, are you absolutely positive Jim doesn't know about you and Gabe? I know our respective timings are both just barely in line but sometimes I have trouble looking John in the eyes without just exploding with the truth," she said.

"Leese, we've been through this enough times now. Since I've ended it with Gabe, you've ended things with Pete, and we have both recommitted ourselves to our husbands; we simply must put the paternity issues behind us. We need to quit focusing on them, put them out of our mind. They must be buried as distant indiscretions that we refuse to let ruin our futures. Ask yourself, 'Do I love John and do I want to raise my child with him?' and be honest. You have been since we agreed to this path in our marriages months ago. Has anything changed?"

"No, nothing has changed and of course I love John, now more than ever. In fact since the pregnancy we have never been closer. He looks for ways to be around the house now. We haven't spent this much time together since before med school."

They had both been true 'ALSOTS' gals. Lisa conceived her precious little bundle with Pete Reynolds, one of the other 'Surgeon Generals', as Lori had done with Gabriel Shannon also a 'General'. At least they kept it in the family so to speak.

"I feel so much better and recommitted to bury our dirty little secrets when I'm around you. However, we really must decide on when we will break it to the other girls. I mean we can't just stop showing up to our little gatherings," said Lisa.

"I think we should make this month's meeting on Monday our last one. I'm sure the other girls will understand especially since we really don't contribute any new gossip to the group anymore anyway," said Lori.

"I think you're right. I mean I'll always love spending time with them, but it will help our focus to see them away from the monthly gatherings only. Their stories aren't helping my conscience lately. I realize Izzie, Sandra, Natalie and Liv have no immediate plans to stop being 'ALSOTS' gals. So we really don't need to be around those distractions and their new particulars right now," Lisa concluded for them both.

"Great, it's settled then. We tell them Monday. Now where's that bottle so we can properly toast the end of our memberships?"

✿

Not five miles from where Lisa and Lori made their decision to quit the club; coincidence was about to bring about a very different meeting that would change many lives forever. After nine long years, two very good friends and former high school football team mates just happen to be in the same bar at the same time and they both recognized each other immediately.

"Well I'll be. If it isn't my old Glenbard North Panthers quarterback 'Clutch'," said one.

"Well that's funny, you look like my old Glenbard North Panthers running back 'Ghost'," said the other.

"Jim Baker, how the hell are you man?"

"If I were any better, I'd need two of me to enjoy it all. How in the hell are you Mark?"

The two men clutched and executed a perfect double-back-pump-bro hug which started them on a trip down memory lane that would last for hours.

"Staying out of trouble Mr. Shaw?" asked Jim eventually.

"Now what's the fun in that?" he replied. "It's been an eternity Jim; we need to do some catching up here. Did you ever finish med school?"

"Yes I did. I went into plastic surgery and got hooked up with a great team of doctors here on the north shore. We had an article written on us last summer. In it they called us the 'Surgeon Generals'. I know it's corny, but it stuck, and it's been a hell of a ride since," said Jim as he filled in his old pal.

"So you're one of them? I saw that article, and you know, I skipped over the names and must have missed connecting the dots. What else have you been up to?"

"I met a great gal named Lori, been married five years now, moved to Winnetka this year, and we are expecting a little girl in January. We've already picked out a name for her; Melissa," said Jim.

"Well that's just great Jim. I wish I had as good a story to tell you on my end. Before I fill you in on my forlorn tale of dysfunctional adventure, we need a table. Have you eaten yet? This place has great pizza, and of course we'll need some appropriate refreshments. Are you still exercising that throwing elbow of yours by lifting bottles of Michelob Ultra?"

"Only on days that end in 'Y' when I don't have a scalpel in that hand. How about you? Still making trips to the end zone with a green bottle of Beck's in each hand?"

"You remembered! First round is on me," said Mark as they settled in to a table adorned with the requisite pail of peanuts in a quiet corner to catch up. On its way was the same pizza they used to order from their high school days together but that wasn't all.

According to their old tradition, they started off with one plate of loaded potato skins, mozzarella sticks and Buffalo wings with sauce so hot, they swore their heads were sweating. The bucket of peanuts remained untouched as they continued filling in their nine years apart eagerly, while waiting for the pizza. Four beers later for each of them found Mark concluding emotionally, "I loved her Clutch. Things seemed like they never had a chance to line up right. First Bobby marries her, knocks her up twice, abuses her on and off with his drug sabbaticals, then we finally start hitting it off after I get back from vet school when she decides to try it one more time with him because of the kids. That's when she heard from him; 'It's really going to be different this time babe. I'm going to make the flower shop work, get back on my feet and stay off the drugs'.

"Then she agreed to get the boob job in an attempt to show Bobby her commitment to his plan. He always wanted a Pamela Anderson chest on his wife. She viewed it as giving him that much more incentive to stay on the wagon this time, but that's when it all went horribly south!" said Mark staring blankly past the label and into the green bottle behind it.

"Damn Mark, how could she wind up dead from a boob job? We routinely perform those procedures without incident in our group. I don't, but many of the 'Generals' do with predictable results. Who was her doctor?" asked Jim.

"He's a quack that has a whole new outlook on life now that his wife is no longer at his side. Doctor Richard S. (undoubtedly for shithead . . . incompetent shithead) Holden" he said.

"Rick Holden? Isn't he the one that was just in the news today? His wife was found mutilated in their home last night," said Jim as he watched the devilish grin take over his former high school teammate's face.

"Mark, tell me you didn't have anything to do with that! Did you?" asked Jim.

"Jim, in the end I had no choice. He not only botched about every aspect of Allison's surgery and follow up care; he also wrecked our plans. Then, when I was this close to proving it and suing his ass, he pulled a team of lawyers together who had a local judge in their back pocket. Not long after that, they were able to dismiss the case before it got a chance to gain any traction. I wouldn't admit this to anyone but you Jim. I mean the shit we shared in school while on the team. I can still count on your discretion can't I?" he asked.

"Of course Mark it's me, 'Clutch'. Wow, who did you hire to do the job?"

"No one, I did it myself and it felt good to get some justice. In the midst of my depression over losing her, I began studying him, and his wife's habits in hopes of developing a plan of getting back at him but things started spinning out of control. You know me, my I.Q. for plotting and planning. It had all gone to shit, and I couldn't think straight. I decided to get out of the country to clear my head and start over. I had to if I were ever going to have a chance of pulling it off successfully and without getting caught in the process.

"That's when I made a fortuitous trip to Columbia, figuring that was about the furthest place, the most out of the norm place, I could ever go to for clearing my head. I needed to set up a distraction from constantly thinking only of her. The more I thought about her, the madder I was getting, and I was afraid I was going to do something stupid and impetuous that would wind up getting my ass in a jam. Man I had some extreme brand of hatred going at that time. I figured, 'go to Columbia, chill in the Caribbean scene a while, get a tan, score some cocaine, tap a couple of gals from the local reputable escort service, get my head on straight.' Then maybe I could come up with a plan to accomplish what I needed to. I needed a strategy that was likely to succeed. I had a burning desire to make him feel what I was feeling, and I didn't think going to jail needed to be part of it.

"I didn't trust anyone to do it for me. I kept thinking there would always be the possibility of a trail leading back to me with a big neon 'Guilty' sign pointing to my mad ass. Besides, where's the gratification in someone else doing it for me. Jim, God help me it was the most satisfying and most rewarding thing I have ever done, but it doesn't feel like enough somehow. I still have this anger inside me that isn't totally spent yet."

They talked on for several hours about what Mark was feeling, his anguish and his exquisite trip to South America as the night and the beers continued to roll on.

CHAPTER 43

"Now THIS would be a whole new ballgame!"

Friday, October 19th, 2012

*A*s their night of playing catch up continued, Mark explained, "Let me tell you, it was extremely well planned around this drug I found while down there called Datura. The locals call it 'Black Breath' because it makes your mind fall into a black hole, sometimes never to return. The thing is though, while your mind is in that black hole; a person can control it completely with any suggestion. I didn't realize it, but the stuff is very prevalent down there, and its effectiveness was easily proven. I made the right contacts, brought some back with me, and it was the perfect tool to pull off what I had to."

Jim was having a hard time wrapping his mind around what his long time friend had just admitted to him. After all, his life these days was all about helping people, improving their lives not ending them and he was quite successful at it.

Mark noticed the uneasy look in his long time friend's eyes and asked, "Aw come on Jim, haven't you ever felt as if you had something really nagging at you that needed to get cleared up?" He was attempting to erase that dark cloud he now was seeing in Jim's facial expression.

"Not to the level you had and not to the degree you did, no."

"Well what then? What was it recent? What was it, and what did you do about it?" Mark continued to badger Jim in an attempt to rekindle their camaraderie.

"Well as happy as I've become recently, there is this, this doctor's, this husband's—I don't know, feeling about Lori that I'd been having whenever I'm out of town. There was this growing tension that we had been experiencing for a while and it just kept escalating. Then things got back to being great between us again. So great, that I guess I didn't want to spoil it with any suggestions of my suspicions, and it stopped nagging at me. Besides, a short while later we found out Lori was pregnant. We had been talking about it and trying for months before that last seminar when things kind of got out of hand."

"Explain, out of hand Jim," said Mark, who was suddenly becoming very interested in this new turn in their discussion.

"Well one night after the seminar wrapped up, I returned to my hotel room and called home to check on her day when out of nowhere we got into this silly argument. It kept getting worse until it escalated from suggestion to an accusation of having a seminar escort and all the benefits that went with them.

"At the time, I wish I'd thought of that myself but I didn't. No, not really I guess. I wasn't looking for that kind of a distraction in our lives. Things were going so well with the practice. We were talking about starting a family, and I guess I've never been that type of guy anyway. I don't know what I'd do if I found out she was doing something like that to me. I guess that's what really heightened my suspicions about her. Until then they were just nagging feelings in the back of my mind" Jim speculated.

"Hey, I'm not trying to stir up the pot here Clutch, but if it bothered you to even that level, and it's that heavy of a topic don't you think you should at least know the truth? I mean if you have any doubts about her faithfulness . . . man I'd have to put that shit to sleep, if it were me that is."

"I don't know. I guess I'm just not inclined to do anything about it."

"What if I did a little digging for you? When is the next time you'll be out of town?" asked Mark.

"As a matter of fact, several of us 'Generals' will be leaving town Sunday night for a seminar in New York on Monday. We'll be gone for two days. I know Lori, and a number of the wives will be getting together on Monday night to play some cards and chit chat like they frequently do while we're out of town."

"Perfect. I will discreetly poke around a bit to see what, if anything, I can find out for you buddy."

"Describe discreetly. Ghost I can't have her finding out that I'm checking up on her. At this stage, it would be a disaster. How would you find out?"

"Let's just say I've become quite good at finding out things about people recently. Not to worry, I have a number of very hi-tech techniques. I guarantee she will not know anything," Mark insisted.

"I don't know Ghost. I'd have to-"

"Don't worry. Just put it out of your head. It won't interrupt my schedule at all, it will be fun for me and I may put a very good friend's mind to rest. Now what's wrong with any of that?

"After all, my veterinarian practice has taken off, and I have a crack crew that has it virtually running itself. To be honest with you, I've cooled off quite a bit about getting bitten by four-legged critters not getting the point that you're actually trying to help them, not hurt them. Besides, it'll give us something to get back together on."

Jim said, "Fine but please, heavy on discreet and heavy on the 'Ghost' ok?"

"You got it partner. Hey, it's almost as if we're teammates working together again huh?"

Their little reunion broke up shortly thereafter and on his ride home those obscured feelings of uncertainty and dread called 'What if' crept back, reminding him that they were never really gone.

*

Monday, October 22nd, 2012

Mark had just pulled up to a nice spot hidden from view just off Jim and Lori Baker's property when he noticed a car with MD plates in the driveway. After setting up and tuning his hi-tech listening device he found a window that would have been hidden by the landscape if the leaves had not abandoned their branches long before. The conversation was just wrapping up with Lori saying, "I'm sorry Gabe it just has to be this way from now on. It was fun while it lasted but it nearly cost us both our marriages. Jim and I are past our rough patch and I feel the need to rededicate myself to our family and our baby that's on the way. I hope you understand and we can still be friends."

"I certainly see where you're coming from Lori. We both need to get back to putting things on firmer ground at home. I kind of figured this was coming, what with the baby and all. That's another reason why I just booked a week long cruise for Bernice and me. We'll be leaving in two weeks. I really do want the best for you and Jim and yes, you're right. It was fun while it lasted," concluded Gabe who left after a somewhat formal final goodbye on the way to his car.

'Holy shit!' thought Mark who wasn't expecting that one at all and realized he hit the jackpot right off the bat. He listened in a little longer and picked up one end of a telephone conversation which Lori was obviously having with Lisa Ackerman. She was relating what had just happened. Not long into the conversation he could swear that, from what he was hearing, Lisa just went through something similar. The name Pete kept coming up as well as references to the 'ALSOTS' meeting tonight at the Reed home. He couldn't wait for tonight.

As he anticipated, the meeting he so fervently wanted to listen in on was a bonanza of information. From it, he gathered what the puzzling name 'ALSOTS' referred to and that apparently Lori and Lisa were withdrawing their respective memberships to the club. Lisa and Lori informed the rest of the group of their intentions to end the 'a little something on the side' chapter of their lives. After sufficient assurances that knowledge of their indiscretions would be safeguarded by the remaining members, they both left with confidence in the veracity of their friends promises. However they were totally unaware of the surveillance placed on their evening's activities that had concluded right after they said their goodbyes and returned to Lisa's car to go home.

Mark was certainly getting his money's worth out of his high tech listening device today. It continued to serve him well by obtaining juicy information that simply wouldn't otherwise be available.

Jim wouldn't be the only one interested in the wealth of information he had just found out. He decided sooner would be better than later, so the next morning he set up a meeting with his buddy Clutch for the next night when the Docs got back into town.

"Clutch, this isn't just a conference for you. I think it would be a good idea to bring a couple 'General' buddies of yours as well. Specifically, I have some very hard hitting information that Dr. John Ackerman, Mark

Channing, Blake Falkland, Jack Kerr and Raymond Reed will be very interested in," he concluded.

"I'm not sure that would be a good idea Mark. What information do you have for us?"

"Please Jim, not on the phone, and not while you are out of town. This is personal and I'd like to give it to you guys straight and in person. Trust me it would be best," said Mark.

"Look Clutch, why don't we all meet at the pub again on Wednesday? I found out the wives will be having another of their gatherings then. All of them except Lisa and Lori that is."

"Fine Mark, I'll see you there about seven. I think it'll probably be best to have a smaller group, maybe just me, Ackerman and Reed at first. Then we can make a decision on bringing others in if necessary," said Jim.

"I think it's going to be necessary buddy, I really do but I'll yield to your discretion for now. You know your new team mates better than I do," Mark resolved as they finished their conversation.

*

<u>Wednesday, October 24th, 2012</u>

"Are you sure Mark? You actually heard them saying all that crap?"

"Sure as I'm sitting here buddy and believe me, I wish I didn't. I hate to be the bearer of bad tidings and all but that's just the cold hard truth," said Mark as he in turn looked into the faces of first his buddy Clutch, then John Ackerman and Ray Reed. Jim consulted John and they both decided to keep this meeting just between the three doctors until they knew what Mark had that was so valuable.

Jim and John stared at each other in disbelief while Ray Reed, sitting between both of them with a hand on the shoulder of each, tried to console them.

Mark had handed each of them a sheet listing the 'ALSOTS' pairings he found on Monday night. The club members and their insignificant others were:

Lisa Ackerman—Dr. Pete Reynolds
Lori Baker—Dr. Gabriel Shannon
Isabella Channing—Dr. William Stevens
Sandra Falkland—Dr. Damien Ross
Olivia Reed—Dr. Frank Griffin
Natalie Kerr—Dr. Tony O'Connell

"If this is true, not only have our wives been cheating on us but we might not be the fathers of the babies they're carrying," John said to Jim in disbelief.

"We need to know for sure. 'ALSOTS' Mark? Really? After the lifestyle we've given all of them they felt they needed 'a little something on the side'? Not one, but six of them? How am I ever going to be able to look at Lori again without wanting to strangle her? I was working so hard on getting us past our rough patch when it was her guilt feeding it all along. That's one thing I just can't tolerate Mark. And the baby . . . ." Jim just couldn't get over this new information.

"Well there are strong suspicions Jim but we don't know for sure yet. About the babies that is," said Mark.

Ray offered, "Guys, I have that OB GYN buddy of mine that I would recommend for putting all doubts to rest. He could discreetly find your answers under the guise of a 'very thorough and painless exam for early birth defect detection'. He can knock them out safely, and do a paternity test without them knowing."

"Let's set it up for this weekend Ray. Jim and I will figure out a way to talk them into it," said John.

As he sat there watching the effect his research was having on Clutch and his new friends, Mark couldn't help but notice the partial anagram created by the random way he compiled the list of the wife names as he stared at the sheet he made for them. The first letter of the 'ALSOTS' names almost spelled out his Allison's name. In fact the name was complete when combined with that hack Holden's wife Aimee, who he set up in a permanent underground arrangement.

'I believe that's called a sign! This could have some significant potential if handled right,' thought Mark Shaw. 'This anagram is just Karma waiting to happen. What a golden tribute to Allison that would make, but no, I am getting ahead of myself here. What if? What if this could work? Could the three of them ever reach the emotional level of wanting to be a party to something like this?' He couldn't help turning over the possibilities in his head as the three distraught doctors kept getting more and more worked up. 'Striking out against Holden was necessary but now it feels like more justice could be dealt here. It was gratifying to a point-bringing that level of grief to Holden's door by mutilating his wife comparable to Allison. It hit him really hard, not seeing it coming and all but it wasn't enough.'

He thought of punishing him further by planning similar fates for other members of Holden's family but it just didn't feel right. By putting his wife in the same mutilated condition that Allison wound up in, right in his face, now that felt right. Going after relatives of his just wouldn't be as personal, but THIS! Now THIS would be a whole new ballgame!

As the discussion between the other three doctors continued to escalate, his wheels were turning upstairs and he envisioned a whole series of retribution for not only Clutch but for several of his friends. Talk about the satisfaction and the thrill of the hunt! Yes, this had significant potential but he decided to first see how this all panned out with them. Then it would be time to make a few retaliatory suggestions to appease their pain and right a whole bunch of wrong situations.

CHAPTER 44

"That's if you all agree of course."

<u>Friday, October 26ᵗʰ, 2012</u>

*B*oth Lisa and Lori, with their 'ALSOTS' membership having just ended, had no trouble seeing the logic in being tested with this new safe and painless procedure recommended by their husbands.

It was great being married to doctors that were so in tune with modern medicine.

"Lisa, we had this very interesting dinner with an OB GYN who practices locally here. Ray Reed has known him for years and trusts him implicitly. It turns out they are still a couple months away from all the paperwork being completed and the procedure being approved by the AMA before they can offer it to the general public. He's willing to make it available to us, though, because they trust our discretion. Ray vouched for us. Dr. Ainsworth is a leader in his field and there are absolutely no risks for either you or the baby, only possible rewards. In the unlikely event that anything is found, it could provide us with the head start needed to get in front of it and possibly applying any number of protocols available through him to prevent or correct an otherwise undetectable problem. The only condition of its availability to us would be, of course, the element of our absolute prudence that we would be required to maintain.

"Jim and I discussed this at length between each other and with Dr. Ainsworth before we agreed to recommend it to you and Lori," John told her as he offered a flawless case for the procedure.

The wives each gave their approval willingly as they were both anxious to jump off their guilt bandwagons and begin working on a new level of cooperation. This, they figured, was a fortuitous first step toward building trust back into their respective relationships which was something they both desperately needed to go forward.

✢

"Now please relax Lori, I'm going to give you a little something gentle to put you to sleep for a short while," said Dr. Ainsworth after she had changed into her examination gown and assumed the position in the stirrups. "The procedure takes less than ten minutes, and I'll have you alert and ready to go home in less than half an hour from now. You will feel no ill effects after the procedure. There is the possibility of a very minor soreness in your lower abdomen. This is quite normal so don't be alarmed if you do feel that this afternoon, and possibly through tomorrow."

After Lori was knocked out he actually performed a CVS or chorionic villus sampling by obtaining a sample from her uterus. Once he collected samples from her and Lisa; he would compare them to the DNA samples he had taken from both fathers.

*

The tests results were rushed through the lab, and he had them that same afternoon. The results were not good.

"Jim, I'm afraid I don't have the news you were looking for. Neither of you fathered the babies your wives are carrying. I'm sorry Jim, but the tests are 100% conclusive," said Dr. Ainsworth.

"I will, of course, issue the clear 'defect report' to you that we discussed to veil the CVS testing with your wives this afternoon. I wish I had better news for you today Jim, but sadly I don't."

"Thanks Bart. We really appreciate your doing this for us. We owe you one. I'll pass the news on to John, and if you could forward those reports to our office by tomorrow that would be great," he said dejectedly. The totality of what this meant was already taking over all his conscience thoughts and emotions. He was absolutely furious!

*

"John, it's no longer in doubt. Bart Ainsworth just called with the results which confirm our worst fears. Neither of us is the father of the babies our wives are carrying. It's only been ten minutes, and my slow burn is already beginning to rage out of control. It's a shame we had to go to the lengths we did, behind the backs of our wives, but it's a good thing we did John because it looks like they had no plans to tell us.

"We need to get back together with Ray and Mark tomorrow afternoon for a meeting. It can be at my office after three. There will be no one left there by then."

"Who did we marry Jim? If they can lie to us about a family matter this intimate, what else are they lying to us about? How can we ever trust them? I thought I knew Lisa better than this and I would have never believed she could be capable of anything close to this, this, this level of deceit!"

"Game faces John. We have to maintain our game faces, and we need Ray to weigh in on this as well. I'll see you two here tomorrow afternoon."

*

Saturday, October 27th, 2012

Once they had all arrived at his office, and the awkward silence had reached a nearly unbearable level, Jim started the meeting off with, "Well here we are gentlemen. John, I don't know about you, but I could hardly concentrate on my patients today thinking about our news. I'm so furious I can barely see straight. I don't want to be in the same house as her. I would really like to start divorce proceedings on Monday morning, but I'm thinking about the ill effect that would have on the 'Generals'. It could be significant if you, me and possibly Ray do something that rash together. It could be worse staggered through time, so I've resolved to take a breath and talk to you guys first."

Ray chimed in, "Hell guys, the way I see it once the 'club' is brought out of the closet, the other three implicated 'Generals' could get involved in the scandal which would bring it to bad publicity times six. Our practices, our lifestyle and our reputations could suffer immeasurably. If this got out it could tarnish everything the team has created to this point. I could see us needing to relocate and start our practices all over again. This stink could follow us wherever we went. We could be ruined!"

"I'm right with you Jim, I can't concentrate either. I went home last night, skipped dinner and went to bed early with a 'headache' so I wouldn't have to look at her while trying to keep this news from showing on my face all night. This really hit me like a ton of bricks guys. I'm glad I had no surgeries today because I would have had to cancel them due to my shaking hands. In all my life, I have never had anything bring me to the brink of violence like this has. The betrayal is just . . . ," John's thoughts just trailed off along with his stare as he walked to the window and just stood there unable to complete his tirade, as he looked at the barren landscape outside the window which he now related to what he was feeling toward his wife.

Ray Reed added, "I don't have the bun-in-the-oven pain that you guys are experiencing but we've been married a lot longer than you two and believe me it was just as shocking to me after everything we've shared through the years. We've made commitments to each other and shared so many things. Now in light of the way she acts toward me each and every day, like nothing else has been going on—I don't know. I just don't understand how this could be possible. I can only imagine what facing the births, and playing father to someone else's baby like you guys are in line for must be doing to the two of you. I just don't know. I'm at a loss. Their collective deceit is incomprehensible to me—simply incomprehensible. What do we do about telling Blake, Mark and Jack?"

"Well, I think we all need to take more than one breath here and clear the anger out of your heads for a bit before discussing this further," said Mark, which they all did.

Ray broke the silence with, "I want to kill her guys. I mean I really just want to kill her about now. As over the top as that sounds, that's where I'm at right now."

"I'm not thinking that's very over the top at all. I guess I'm having trouble seeing myself settling down and resuming life as usual from here out without doing something pretty drastic. Let's face it guys, this changes everything for all of us!" added John.

"Just one week ago I couldn't have imagined either of you guys talking like this. Now, a mere week later, here I am talking the same talk, right along with you. I want nothing to do with her anymore. I wish I could erase all the memories I have of her, and everything we've experienced together as a couple. In retrospect of what we just found out, it was all one big well orchestrated joke on us," said Jim.

Mark just sat there listening to the three of them spewing their venom while he tickled the edges of the idea that continued to develop in his mind. A plan which he felt could be so therapeutic for them all. It could also have healing characteristics for him. He was thinking he could help his friends and finally be at peace with his nagging feelings about evening the score. It was all about righting wrongs. These wrongs shouldn't be dealt to guys like them. They all had provided or were about to provide a life that most women only dreamed of having, and now they were all staring at losing everything or most everything they worked so hard to establish.

But how was he supposed to present this radical idea of his to this educated team of doctors?

He decided to just come out with it and started off by saying, "Ok. If I'm to understand what I'm hearing here, it sounds like some awful harsh emotions running around the room. Are you guys really at the point I'm listening to you all verbalize?"

After an uncomfortable silence, some firm, determined and reaffirming glances around the room at each other, Ray finally said, "Yes Mark, I guess we are."

"Guys, I have been thinking about the two very different ways these tests could have turned out. Mostly I've been focusing on how deeply this most unwanted of the two could affect you all because I had a feeling that was the one we'd all be here lamenting over. From what I'm hearing, you may be open to a plan that's been developing in my head. It would involve not only your three wives but the other three members of the degenerate 'ALSOTS' club," Mark began and didn't stop until he had the particulars of his as yet unfinished scheme presented to the three of them.

Once he completed the overall scope of what he was suggesting and his reasons for wanting to be involved, he began reviewing the benefits and potential complications with them.

"First off, none of you would be involved in the implementation of this plan. It would be all on me.

"Second, I'm willing to take that responsibility on, because I think this would ultimately satiate my need of wanting to right some terrible wrongs, albeit perhaps a bit selfishly. Still, after the traumatic way my own situation wound up, it isn't difficult to imagine how you three are feeling. Guys, you may not understand that totally but I know you are each feeling part of my rage right now. Even with as scandalous as this could be, and with the unthinkable potential for ruin this could have for you all; believe me it still doesn't stack up to what I saw Allison go through in the end.

"As I look back at my actions since, the thrill of the hunt that was involved, the preparation etc., all wound up being a large therapeutic part of what started turning those emotions toward Dr. Hack Holden around for me. Still, like I said before, I just can't shake this feeling that I haven't done enough, in my own mind at least. I feel like I haven't evened the score when it comes to avenging Allison's death and the suffering I saw on her face right up to the end. His wife's demise wasn't enough.

"Third, if you all don't mind, I would really be more comfortable with all of this if my involvement with not only this plan but my role in the Aimee Holden situation was not spread any further than the three of you. If this retribution we are all considering goes forward, I'd like to firmly request that Blake Falkland, Jack Kerr and Mark Channing not be informed of any of this. I know it will be tough on them, but maybe someday if the timing ever gets right, you can tell them about this after I'm long gone and no longer worried about being exposed.

"Fourth, you three need to be really sure that we all want to carry this thing this far, especially without the other three doctor's approval. I mean I know in your heads you'll have decided that we're doing them a favor and containing this mess but, please understand that as this thing progresses there is a possibility that the remaining 'ALSOTS' members may figure out they are being targeted. This could happen as their numbers systematically dwindle and no one outside the club is affected. They may come to the conclusion that, for the greater good of the remaining members, it would be best to come clean with their husbands to try to save their own skins. This could happen before I get a chance to finish. They may also reach a point of suspecting their husbands. That is, if they are even able to figure out the group that is actually being targeted."

"Good point, but you know Mark; I'm not sure how you plan to go about this exactly. I mean if we all agree to go ahead with this, in what order you would proceed that is. It seems to me you could use a last name alphabetical order selection. The names involved could work out that way for a while anyway. Mind you I wouldn't presume to tell you how you should go about any of this, again if we all consent," said Ray as he studied the names.

"I was thinking of a different approach to diversion which involves something similar. I don't want to get into too much detail. I think the less you know, the better going forward. That's if you all agree of course."

"I guess I'll be the first to throw in my hat, but I agree with Mark. The less we know about his approaches, etc., the more we will be able to pull off the shocked husband routines that will be closely watched by not only our associates, but the police assigned to investigate this," said John.

"Ok, my hat is second in the ring and I also agree that the less we know the better. I don't mean to lay it all on your shoulders Mark, but I do think it has to be that way if this is going to have a chance of working and I'm glad you offered. We shouldn't know when or how any of it is coming in order to retain our stunned responses, and to best steer the investigators away from suspecting us husbands. The husbands are always the first to be suspected and with a targeted bunch as associated and close as we all are, it wouldn't surprise me if a sharp investigator began looking for a conspiracy theory of sorts. Our distress must match those whose vote we will be effectively taking away in casting this ballot between only the three of us," concluded Jim.

"Speaking of suspecting the husbands first, has anyone made any changes to insurance policies or wills recently that could be seen as a motive?" asked Mark. His question was answered negatively by all three.

"Enough said. I realize that this idea of Mark's is the only way to make a clean break from the arrogant cheating bitches we are apparently married to. If this gets pulled off successfully, I mean when it does, because I have all the faith possible in your ability to do so Mark, we will be able to keep all of our practices intact, and be seen as the poor grieving widowed 'Generals' which could actually have a positive PR impact on the group. Maybe we'll also be more successful with finding new partners that will appreciate the lifestyle we can provide for them. I guess that makes three hats in the ring," said Ray.

CHAPTER 45

". . . . you'll need to figure out where you hid
your game faces."

<u>Saturday, October 27th, 2012</u>

*M*ark warned, "Before we get to skipping along too fast here I think we have a number of logistical things to discuss and work out first."

"I thought you didn't want us in on your particulars Mark. Really, Jim, John and I are fine with that."

"You're right, I don't, but there are a few things I've thought of that we need to touch on for now. Then we may need one more meeting before I kick things off.

"First, there may be a need for communication between us at different stages of the plan execution. For that reason, I think it would be wise to get disposable phones and keep the phone numbers hidden from all your day to day contacts, both at home and the office.

"Second, it would be a good idea to find a place where these phones will be kept outside of your homes and offices so wives and office personnel can't find them. I would suggest getting a hidden compartment set up in each of your cars.

"My degenerate brother, who I plan on framing along the way for diversionary purposes, has a number of seedy contacts that I have become aware of and one of them specializes in adding discreet compartments to high end cars. In their world it's to carry drugs. I'll have no problem getting them to install one in each of your vehicles. By that I mean, I'd have no concerns about the work being traced back to any of us.

"The way that would work is, I'd pick up your cars one at a time and bring them to a designated area, remove the plates, they'll do the job, and then we reverse the process, returning the cars to you. The phones should be kept in the compartments any time you aren't using them and checked for messages only when you drive the cars.

"I've used these people before. I can make it work with no worries about any of it getting back to us."

"Great idea Mark, what else?" asked John.

"Third, as I get this going, this is how I expect it will play out with the authorities. The first several cases will have the investigator's little brains spinning just trying to figure out how I'm able to pull them off so cleanly and absent any clues. One thing we will have going for us early is the local keystone cops have virtually no homicide experience. I know, I've checked. So after I get them initially off balance, I'm going to throw so much shit at them so fast that they'll have trouble keeping it all straight. I'm not bragging here, but they will be repeatedly blindsided with case after case in the early going. That will get them so frustrated that it will buy valuable maneuvering time as they try to sort it all out. At that point, I expect media pressure will mount, and they'll be forced to call in bigger guns and spend time bringing them up to speed. I've been seeing the first confirming signs of this theory as I watch them stumble all around the Holden case.

"I'll keep several steps ahead of them though, so don't you sweat it.

"Forth, after they try to digest the first few cases on their plates, they will start going through the painstaking protocols they always follow. That's when I will need to make a trip back to Columbia to restock my cornerstone drug. This is where having the luxury of valuable maneuvering time that I mentioned earlier will come in handy," Mark related confidently.

"If I can interrupt here a bit, and not to doubt your propensity to excel at attention to detail, but what if things start getting a little close to us with the investigation?" asked Jim.

"That's my fifth item. I think we'll need to come up with several 'clues' that need to be extremely well orchestrated to miss-lead the authorities and nudge them in the direction we want them to go, which of course is off track. They'll be strategically placed, and hell they can even be a little mystical. That will confuse them all the more, and they'll be really grasping at straws by then. If done correctly it will deflect attention away from the three of you.

"Also as we get deep into this idea, I might need a few things done so we'll need to stay flexible and I'll be in touch only if absolutely necessary.

Check your phones often but they should be seldom used. Outside of what will likely be a very rare contact from me, I plan on living up to my high school football nickname and become a ghost even to you guys. Agreed?"

Unanimously they all said, "Agreed."

At the conclusion of Mark's comments, Ray added, "One other thing guys, I'm not sure how we will be able to do this, but after what Mark learned from the 'ALSOTS' gathering, I can think of six doctors that I no longer want as part of our team of 'Generals'"

"I'm with you there too Ray. I'll have as much trouble looking them in the eye as we all will with our wives until this is all over. We're going to have to think long and hard about what we say or how we explain our wanting this course of action to the other 'Generals'," said John.

Mark got up to leave in order to begin preparing for his role in earnest giving them his last thoughts, "Well, that aside, if you guys are in, I am too. I think you may need to remove yourselves from your every day routines occasionally if you don't think you can pull off a convincing enough front. You might want to consider a mini vacation or visiting some relatives out of state. Jim you, could take an extended trip to that cabin of yours. In fact I would strongly recommend it as it would be in keeping with the whole 'grieving widower' thing.

"I want you all to know that I want this every bit as much as you do, and that I'll diligently complete this with utter discretion. From this moment forward gentlemen, it's an all for one and one for all proposition. You will witness my retribution being swift and extremely well thought out.

"Past today I will be invisible to all of you and I'm sure you're all smart enough to understand the amount of control that will be required not only amongst you three but also with the other three doctors if we are to successfully pull this off.

"When this is all done, I plan to stage my own death, leave my veterinarian practice behind, and leave the country to start over. I can't envision a life here without Allison. There are just too many memories; good and bad here. At some point after that I will get back in touch with you Clutch but not before.

"Meanwhile guys, you really need to get a grip on the anger issues and get them erased from your outward appearance. What do you say we all start that process by going out for some beers to loosen up a bit? You're all going home tonight, and you'll need to figure out where you hid your game faces. Let's not blow this right out of the box," warned Mark.

The meeting ended with them all shaking hands with firm resolve and with Mark assigning himself with the responsibility of obtaining the throw-away phones. He set up Monday as the day to have the phone compartments added to their cars with each of them explaining that their cars were being picked up from work for routine maintenance and interior detailing. Mark assured them that the phones would be there when they got the cars back with directions under the front floor mat explaining where the compartments were located and a listing of the other phone numbers.

The three doctors each phoned in explanations for their late afternoon meeting to the home fronts, then proceeded to relax their dispositions through several beers. It was at that point that each willing participant dove head first into a totally out of the norm late afternoon of playing pool, pinball and throwing darts like none of them had in years. It was just what the killer ordered.

It wasn't long before the three doctors found that they had totally shifted their mental gears. They found themselves relaxed, in a new frame of mind and ready to face their wives. In fact, they invited them down to the pub to join them for pizza, nuts, beer and sparkling whatever for the two mothers to be, figuring it would initially be easier to get the facades going in public with friends.

Mark had left them before the wives were to arrive. He seriously and systematically began to hone the perfect plan that would accomplish what they all had agreed to on that memorable Saturday afternoon.

He set off to begin his research. There would be significant information gathering, observing patterns of the targeted spouses and learning everything he needed in order to get as close to each of them as he must.

The wheels were in motion.

CHAPTER 46

"Consider it a bit of early insurance . . . ."

Friday, November 16th, 2012

*H*e certainly wasn't kidding about throwing a ton of crap at the investigating officers! Within a mere five days after the Saturday meeting with John, Jim and Ray, Mark had added the first casualty from his list in the form of Lisa Ackerman. The three doctors were shocked at how fast it had come as they braced themselves for a barrage of others. True to form, their new partner 'Ghost' remained not only absolutely hidden, but unpredictable as well. They had no idea what would happen, when it would be, or in what order they would be. When there were no new developments from him in the following week, Jim decided to stay with the course of action agreed upon that fateful Saturday by not looking over his shoulder. He felt that taking Lori up on her trip to the cabin would be a good idea. He had a feeling that it would probably be their last time up there together.

He wasn't wrong. Shortly after they got back, and two weeks after Lisa was found, Lori was made the second 'Generals' victim by Mark as his strategy continued to unfold.

"Good morning Ray, its John, how have you been." This was the first any of them had used their throw away phones. They implemented a system of leaving each other messages with a time for the planned phone call. John felt he needed some updates from the home front before he came home.

"Hey John, how's Florida?"

"Actually it's just what I needed. I'm still struggling with my face time with the in-laws but the sun and swimming smoothes that all out just fine. There have been a lot of new developments along the cold Lake Michigan shores I see. It's been making all the papers down here, but there aren't a lot of specifics, mostly conjecture. I thought there might be some time after Lori Baker was taken, but there was scarcely enough for a pizza and a beer before the news about Isabella Channing hit the papers the next day. I believe the inspectors back home must be reeling about now."

"We're developing quite a display of yellow crime scene tape up here John. The local news channels have been all over the police departments pressing them for results. The local cops simply aren't used to dealing with murders in our sleepy north shore suburb. So far the ghost has been right on the money. Ed Cassidy and Bill Weller have been assigned to all the new cases that have been developing and everything they keep telling us is 'they are clueless' so far.

"Including the Holden wife, they are now trying to connect four dots and all they have to talk about are the effects of the crimes. They have no leads or suspects at all.

"It's all going just as our invisible assassin had predicted. Jim and I were speculating that he began planning Lori and Isabella's demise simultaneously as they were both found so close to each other and two weeks removed from Lisa. Unpredictable remains the word for Mark. Everything is just as he said he would be thus far. His rhythm and the methods he's using to execute his plan are truly confounding the investigating team up to now. That's why you aren't seeing a lot of details in the news down there."

"Thanks for the hometown perspective Ray, but we'd better cut this short. I still plan on staying down here for the entire two weeks so if my patients can be covered until then, I'll owe everyone a night out on the town involving some thick steaks when I get back."

✻

The self proclaimed Nemesis observed the doctor's performances and was satisfied with how each of them were handling what he was throwing at them. He was pleased with how they had managed to not only totally shield their true feelings from their spouses, but also to keep the spotlight of suspicion from being aimed at any of them, so far. He assumed that their splendid acting skills stemmed from their near daily performances in keeping thoughts from showing on their faces as they executed 'a professional bedside manner' for their patients. They had mastered looking hopeful and optimistic for even the most terminal of patients, and it was coming in handy for their nefarious purposes of late.

He bought the 'valuable maneuvering time' as expected, which gave him the opportunity to replenish the stock of drugs needed to take him through to the end of his tribute to Allison.

It wouldn't just be a shopping trip, though. He was looking forward to the cool Caribbean breezes and warm tropical sun on his face as he cashed in on some much deserved down time. Nothing like really fine tuning the new direction he needed to take in light of the heightened security that would surely be there when he got back down to business.

*

Monday, November 19th, 2012

Once Lori's mother and sister left for Florida after the funeral services, Jim decided that a trip to the cabin to clear his thoughts and get ready for the next phase of Mark's plan was his best move. Getting back to the clean crisp air of the wooded area where the cabin was located would be the perfect recipe for refocusing after all the funeral service drama.

He was thinking, 'I just need time to think through my emotions and prepare my responses. I must avoid arousing suspicion not only from the inspectors, but also the 'Generals'. They have got to remain blissfully unaware of what's coming. I have to portray how close Lori and I were at one time with every facial expression, and with everything I say and do."

The cabin's serene setting would be perfect. With John in Florida, he and Ray had to keep things going smooth on the home front, until the focus turned to Jack Kerr, Blake Falkland and Mark Channing. There would be no 'keeping it real' issues with any of those three.

Initially his feelings were very melancholy as his trip to the cabin, stops along the way and visiting all their favorite places on his property like the beach, the cave and the numerous hiking trails consumed his day and early evening.

After his shower though, the message about seeing 'The Flowers' on the mirror genuinely shook him. At first the thought of a practical joke by either Ray or Mark crossed his mind ever so briefly but after confirming that all entry points of the cabin was secured he dismissed that idea and went back to being freaked out over what he saw for a short time written on the mirror's steam in what he swore was Lori's handwriting.

On the next day, as weird, unexplainable things continued, he found himself thinking, 'All right, I know that was Lori's voice on the answering machine message. I'm not sure how it could have gotten there, but it's gone now, and I didn't erase it. What's happening and what kind of message is, "Jim, it burns but I can't cry. I'm . . . . ," that ends in static?'

After one very supportive telephone conversation with his friend Ray Reed, he felt grounded again. Still confused, but at least somewhat grounded again.

✻

Ray Reed, on the other hand, was quite confused after fielding Jim's call. He wasn't quite sure how to take what he was being told by his good friend. To him it sounded as if Jim had decided on using the 'clues' technique that the four of them discussed in their last meeting together, but Ray wasn't sure why Jim chose to do so now.

That strategy was supposed to be held in reserve in case they needed to throw the authorities off their scent. It seemed definitely premature at this juncture. With as smoothly as everything had been going so far, it seemed like a waste of a great tactic that was better left at the ready.

'Wait a minute!' he thought. 'Maybe Jim came across something that I don't know about and felt that he needed to use it now. His phone call could have been a discreet warning to me in effect saying he's worried that the phone lines are being monitored. He did call me on a regular land line and not our throw-away phones so maybe this whole thing was a deliberate message from Jim. If that were the case, it was a good thing I played along.

'Note to self; discuss this possibility with Jim, ASAP. We did discuss his going to the cabin but not using the 'clues' just yet. I just hope he's not panicking and going with them too quickly.'

'I guess the sneak could have also been using me for a dress rehearsal. He could be planning an interview with the inspectors once he gets back.

'It's definitely going to be time for a beer as soon as we can get together.

❋

Thursday, November 22nd, 2012

The last few days he remained at the cabin; Jim found himself sheepishly exiting the shower and checking out the mirror. Every time that he did wound up being uneventful and stress relieving for him. He was finally able to gain a semblance of what he went there for in the first place which was to strengthen his game face resolve. He actually began to wrap his mind around Lori's death.

When he got home, his nerves were once again shattered by the answering machine message that disappeared like the message on the mirror and the 'It burns' message from the cabin trip. That's when he decided that he needed more than another friendly 'Ray Reed affirmation' of his sanity, so he called Garrett Heaton, the one 'General' with actual psychology training and practice.

After he heard what he knew he would from Garrett, he arranged a casual meeting with Ray at his favorite watering hole for a beer and some catching up.

His account of the latest answering machine escapade was cut short by Ray asking, "Wait a minute; you mean the incidents at the cabin, and this one really happened? I thought that, for some reason, you started with the 'clue' tactic we all discussed at our last meeting together. You really had me worried because I thought you picked up on some heat and needed to begin with the mystic crap Mark proposed to deflect it. I had this feeling fed by the way you presented it to me and the fact that you used a land line instead of our throw-away phones."

"That's what I've been trying to tell you Ray, they ARE real unless either you or Mark is messing with me, trying to freak me out.

"First, if it is him, I can't imagine how he got into the cabin which I kept securely locked from the inside at all times. I don't know why I did it, other than wanting the feeling of total isolation. Second, if it isn't him, whatever it is; it's really working. I'm about as freaked out as I can be. John is still in Florida, so I know it isn't him," said Jim.

"Crap," said Ray, "now I don't know what to make of it. You're really not messing with me Jim are you?"

"No Ray, I swear! Well let's look at this in a practical light. It is early and unintentional but since I have these very real experiences fresh in my mind, I'm going to use them on the inspectors. We might as well take advantage of them. Consider it a bit of early insurance for our stories," Jim concluded.

"That's fine Jim but I think it's also necessary to keep up with appearances and to keep the others at ease. Normally we would all be trying to comfort you after Lori's loss so let's make some dinner plans toward that end."

Saturday night Chinese dinner in at Jim's house with the Reeds and Sunday night dinner out with the Reeds and Falklands were both decided before their meeting at the bar concluded. Afterward they had a very reflective ride home as both tried making sense of what Jim had just related.

CHAPTER 47

The universe shifted in Ed's direction . . . .
but not enough . . . .

Saturday, November 24th, 2012

*I*t certainly was a great idea to invite the Reeds over for dinner even if it was only going to be Chinese delivered in. Jim needed to get back to socializing with other close acquaintances. What better way to start than with Ray helping and only one other person to face?

They had all found comfort in each other's company at the pub the other night, and with all the distractions of that public setting it turned out to be an easy first meeting with the wives. This was to be the first time in a setting this intimate. Expressions would be closely watched, and conversations would be much more focused and specific than they were at the pub. Two game faces tonight would definitely be better than one. It started off great with Olivia giving him a warm hug but before the conversation could get very far he experienced that damn blackberry ringing episode.

The one with the blackberry that had been retired to a remote closet upstairs which began operating without a battery. It came back to life long enough to give the three of them a shocking verbal message apparently from Lori before going silent for good.

'Black Breath' was the totally unexplainable message they all heard and each of them swore it was Lori's voice.

After the evening settled down and they finished their dinner Jim arranged a phone call for the next morning with Ray when he was out of Olivia's range of hearing.

✶

Saturday, November 25th, 2012

"Jim its Ray, Olivia is in the shower now and I can talk for a while. What's going on? What the hell was that with the no battery phone last night?" Ray asked Jim.

"Ray I haven't any idea how that could have happened. I know we have been suspecting Mark being involved in these incidences, but I guess I'm not sure how this could be possible, even for him!"

"Well Jim we know he's resourceful. Is it possible that he did some tinkering with that phone while you were up at the cabin? I mean, could he have done something like adding a tiny battery component somewhere besides the battery compartment that lasted just long enough to freak us out?" Ray wondered.

Still having difficulty imagining this could happen, Jim said, "I suppose anything is possible, but I'm having trouble believing all of these very different things hitting all at once. How could he get her voice to give us that message and the ones I heard at the cabin?"

"Believe me Jim, I'm not trying to convince you, and I'm not the technology wizard of the group here by any means. I wish we could get Cory involved here but obviously we can't. I swear I heard somewhere that it's possible to use a sampling of a person's voice to create complete messages. In this case, maybe the sample was Lori's voice from your answering machine message. It makes sense that a software program could exist that was able to generate a synthesized voice model from a sample like that. I'm not saying that's what's happening here but man, what is the alternative to that theory? Maybe we should try to reach Mark to straighten this out for our peace of mind," Ray suggested.

"I don't think that's a good idea Ray. Mark said to contact him only in an extreme emergency, and our peace of mind doesn't qualify. If he's behind this then all I can say is, damn he's good. None of us know what his plans entail, but I guess this could all be intended to produce a desired result. If it's not him Ray, I don't know what to say."

"I guess I agree. This isn't an emergency, so we need to keep it between us. You should probably call Ed and Bill with this though and get it on the record while it's fresh."

"I will on Monday. I think it's time to cut this conversation short for now. I'll see you and Olivia at dinner tomorrow with Blake and Sandra."

✧

It was also the right call to step things up to a slightly larger social gathering on Sunday night with Blake and Sandra. Everything went very well with Jim and Ray finding their groove. They were getting good at regular interactions with the other 'Generals' while keeping the big plan from them.

After calling Ed and Bill on Monday with the news about the 'Black Breath' message, things didn't get much of a chance to calm back down. It turned out to be a very eventful week.

The next morning was when Jim got upset all over again with the 'Sun Dancer—Sandra' message on his steamed up mirror that he was able to photograph.

'Mark, if you're messing with me . . . .,' he thought to himself as he tried to imagine that creating these situations was all his doing. It was impossible to ignore the precautions that were in place, both here and at the cabin that should have prevented Mark from being able to do any of them.

✧

Tuesday, November 27th, 2012

Later that day, Jim and Ray met John Ackerman for lunch. John had just returned home from Florida and couldn't wait to get all caught up. John, having been mostly out of communication with them, was aghast at all they told him regarding recent events on the Chicago north shore. Finally as he was told the details of the latest things, John agreed with the consensus that Mark was more than likely behind them.

"Ray, here we are again. There's been so much that happened this past week that I don't know where to begin. I guess I'm leaning toward agreeing with John. I guess I'm still struggling with accepting that Mark could be pulling these 'messages' off. I'm really having trouble coming up with anything that makes sense for that 'Sun Dancer' message I found on my steamed mirror this morning. Ray the house was locked up tight as a bank vault. There's simply no way I can see that anyone could have got in to do it."

"Jim I'm right here feeling the déjà vu with you. Maybe you weren't supposed to be able to see. We can't break protocol over it though. If we dismiss the locked houses and permit our minds enough latitude to accept the fact the Mark may have been able to do all these things, we have to admit that he is a genius. Don't forget, he has your alarm system security codes by now.

"Just look at the pattern of it all Jim. It just keeps escalating. He, and I'm going to use 'He' here, is utterly brilliant with how this has been unfolding and how Ed has now been ultimately involved.

"This all has been orchestrated beyond my wildest imagination. It's just so cohesive. Jim it has to be Mark. It just has to be. He probably dropped the hint that we may need to do something like this at our last meeting together so it would be in the back of our minds when it actually happened. It might just be his way of cluing us in on what he planned to do. Then when his big plan, the one that we all know nothing about, called for introducing the 'messages', we wouldn't totally lose it," Ray speculated.

"Ray I hope you're right and I'll tell you, I'm at the point of wishing this was all over with real quick about now."

"I'm wishing the same thing Jim but you, me and Ray need to ride it out a little longer."

They all agreed to remain patient as long as things continued to play out successfully. Hell at the clip Mark was going it couldn't be much longer before he was done anyway.

✻

The next day, Wednesday, was when Sandra went missing and the 'Sandy don't go' message was heard by Blake on his answering machine only once as was the norm lately. It wasn't until the next day that her body was found mutilated on the beach.

During Ed Cassidy's visit with Jim on Friday to bring him up to date with the investigation, the answering machine picked up and they heard the 'More Tests Connie' message that froze them both. This was the first time Ed personally witnessed one of the 'messages' that the others were relating to him recently with regularity.

Now it was Ed's turn to be personally hit with the weight of the 'messages', as the doctors had been. For the first time, they were more to him than barely believable hearsay from the doctors. It was especially disturbing because Jim Baker couldn't relate to this message as he didn't know Connie Bristol, the M.E. who was working on the case with Ed.

Later that day when Ed went to Blake Falkland's home to update him was when he got his second shock. It was way more than he needed to see as they both found themselves staring at the 'Liv now' message on the inner steamed up window. It was something that neither Ed nor Blake was ready for and something that neither could explain.

"This shot picks up the words Blake," Ed told the bereaved Dr. Falkland as he was eventually able to get the message to show up in a cell-phone photo at just the right angle for Bill's benefit.

Why the 'messages' themselves couldn't be clearer never entered his mind. He was too frustrated and consumed with trying to pull out any content from the 'messages' that might lead to a break in the cases.

*

Ed was at the height of his frustration when things started to break in the case. Once their meetings at the remote farmhouse began, the synergy of the team they assembled began taking bites out of the shroud of mystery that had hung over the murders since they began.

Before his unfortunate demise, Cory became the cornerstone of their discovery barrage that ended with the report found by Ed and Bill the night Cory was killed. So many things suddenly started pointing in the same direction for them, and it was no longer at Bobby Shaw. Their newfound interest in his brother led by Cory's comprehensive investigating was what brought Ed and Bill to Mark's home with a search warrant in hand.

As they approached his door, Mark's tiresome neighbor Paul called out to them, "I think he's home but he must be hiding from the world. I was there not five minutes ago asking for help and he wouldn't answer the door. I've seen him moving around in there this morning, but he's not very neighborly that one."

With that Ed's team did the math and decided to break in the door if necessary. They would not be denied a search of the house. Unfortunately delaying the forced entry brought on by talking to pain-in-the-ass Paul bought Mark just enough time to gather up his plans, the other things he needed for Natalie and the FBI agent guarding her that night, and allowed him to escape.

On his way out, he grabbed the bag that was already packed and ready with items essential for his escape later that night. In it was everything he needed from his makeup kit and the clothing required for several different changes in appearance, to the passports, tickets and paperwork which supported those separate identities. There were a number of different escape contingencies set up in that bag which would enable him to respond as needed, depending on how the night went.

The universe shifted in Ed's direction that day, allowing him to find the panic room full of goodies, but not enough to discover everything that would thwart Mark's plans for Natalie Kerr and Agent Jamanski tonight.

It shifted enough for them to discover the wall that was divided into sections of information that the Nemesis devoted to each murdered wife. All the details they had previously only dreamed about uncovering were within each section.

Here, everything needed to build air-tight cases was laid out for them. Everything that they had been searching for since Aimee Holden was found in her nursery. They even found the list of phone numbers that he kept handy in case he needed to contact the three doctors on their disposable phones. The phone numbers and various other items contained within this bonanza of data were the first bits of evidence that implicated the victim's husbands.

"Son-Of-A-Bitch!" screamed Bill. "Ed you did it. This is a 'hang-his-ass-for-sure' goldmine! Just look at all the stuff collected here in one spot! Our little murdering bastard must have been throwing his baby brother Bobby under the bus after all. Meanwhile looks like old bro-bro has been busier than a two dollar whore on nickel night!" exclaimed Bill.

As Ed and Bill joined their team in carefully gathering everything in sight, they kept Mark Shaw's propensity for organization intact. A detailed analysis would be next as they collected most of it for their trip back to the police station. This left the CSU team there to tear the house apart looking for more. Besides the phone numbers, some of the other things that incriminated the good doctors were notes from their meetings together, specifics on the vehicle modifications and notes on how they all approved of the murders.

They were involved all right. Ed called ADA Pelham to get the arrest warrant paperwork ready so it could be there when they got back with their new damning evidence. Many gaping holes in their investigation of Mark Shaw were suddenly filled in as well. It was all there, from his travel arrangements to Columbia right down to his final escape plans after completing his list with Natalie Kerr's murder tonight.

CHAPTER 48

"Now where were we Natalie, oh yes, please lie down on the floor . . . ."

Saturday, December 8th, 2012

O nce they got back to the station with the evidence, ADA Pelham was personally waiting for them with four arrest warrants; one each for Mark Shaw, John Ackerman, Jim Baker and Ray Reed.

Knowing that the CSU team was still at Mark Shaw's house, they decided to serve the warrant on Jim Baker first.

Upon arrival at the Baker estate, they hit the jackpot. Not only was Jim Baker home, but they noticed two other familiar cars on his driveway. One car belonged to Dr. Ackerman and the other to Dr. Reed. Before they left their own cars, Bill said, "Well isn't this our lucky day. I have an idea! Let's see what their faces look like when we dial their burner telephone numbers. You call Jim Baker, and I'll call Ray Reed when we get to the front door," which they did.

This meeting at Jim's house was the first opportunity the three doctors had to discuss the recent 'messages' they became aware of, and how they would respond to them.

As the door opened, Jim Baker's warm smile and greeting were both cut short as the two phones, one in his pocket and one in Ray's, rang simultaneously. As the expressions and color left the faces of the three doctors, Ed and Bill took their cell phones out of their own pockets and held them up by their heads with only a thumb and forefinger. Then they began twisting them in the air with a 'Gotcha' look on their faces that said more than what the doctors needed to hear. The three of them scarcely heard the Miranda rights that were read to them as they silently watched their fantastic lifestyles, their futures and their freedom vanish before their eyes.

They went without protest, without a word being said between the three of them, back to the Winnetka police station to call their lawyers.

The inspectors allowed them have plenty of time for reflection as they went back to organizing the data found earlier that morning, with ADA Pelham.

In a matter of hours the most baffling case of their careers had turned into the biggest slam dunk they could imagine.

After hours of pouring over the material they took a well deserved lunch break and began speculating as to where they might find the subject of their remaining arrest warrant. That was the one thing missing, but each of them knew he was destined to show up at the Kerr residence.

"I say we just keep to the duty roster as established and don't over react by placing an increased presence at the Kerr estate. The guys are very strategically placed, and no one is getting near that house without one of them spotting them first," Ed suggested.

"I agree," said Bill. "I think it would be wise to have them report in every half hour though, based on how sure we are now that our nasty veterinarian will be making a house call on the lovely Mrs. Kerr. If something did go south, we don't want it to go unnoticed for too long."

"I couldn't agree more Bill," added Lucy Pelham as Ed called in Officer Zimmerman to relieve him of all responsibility, except for maintaining constant communication with the field agents and reporting back to them immediately if there were any developments there.

✼

At the same time, not five miles away, Mark Shaw was checking into a hotel very near the Kerr estate.

He needed a new base of operation to prepare for what could be his last performance of the night. The one in which he would take on the outward appearance of FBI field agent Zack Jamanski, who was currently on duty, per the duty roster assignments, at the rear southeast corner of the Kerr home. Winnetka's officer Nick Paddock was at the other assigned observation point located on the northwest corner of the estate. They were visible to each other only through their night vision binoculars as darkness had fallen on the north shore by that time.

✼

Saturday, 4:00 pm, December 8th, 2012

When they were almost finished sifting through all the data they had for any clues to the Nemesis' whereabouts, a call came in from the CSU team at Mark Shaw's home relating that yet another prize had been found.

It was the very organized personal journal that Mark Shaw maintained on all his activities since he began the reign of terror he directed at the wives of the north shore plastic surgeons. They were fortunate enough to find the mechanism that opened a hidden compartment where it was kept. It was immediately brought back to the station for their analysis and less than a half hour from its discovery, they were dissecting the information it contained.

The Nemesis kept exceptional records on all aspects of his plan execution as well as the details collected through his extensive research on each victim. Also, every aspect of each step that went right and wrong was captured here to further tweak his ongoing reign of terror. This was the key that allowed him to stay on track as he executed this very intricate plan with all the details and contingencies clear in his mind. The total 'ALSOTS' layout of partners, hook up dates, meetings, conversations, etc. was all there as well.

✽

Saturday, 4:30 pm, December 8th, 2012

As they started to disseminate the journal's information, it became 'Showtime' at the Kerr stakeout. Natalie Kerr was home alone. Her husband was at work tediously reviewing patient consultations with other 'Generals' for upcoming surgeries.

The setting was perfect for disrupting the plans they made for him. Unfortunately, the good guys were unaware that Mark knew everything he needed to through his spying efforts at their farmhouse meetings.

He snuck up on the unaware FBI Agent Zack Jamanski, who had the build and appearance so very close to his own, with a mist sprayer positioned at the end of a long nozzle. He was able to dispense a slight mist containing his drug of choice just to the side of Agent Jamanski's head which produced the desired effect of causing him to turn toward the sound and quickly breathing in, surprised by the sound.

Zack Jamanski's mind was instantly blanked of his assigned task, and became a clean slate that was immediately open to the suggestion that filtered quietly to him from the other side of the bush.

"Zack set down your binoculars and toss your weapon to me over here in this bush," which he did without a second thought and the Nemesis knew Jamanski was under his control. From there he decided on some retribution for the task force that collectively called him a 'Sick Bastard' at their last meeting.

'Payback is a bitch gentleman,' he thought as he gave Agent Jamanski his new assignment.

"You know Zack; your little red-headed, freckle-faced-pain-in-my-ass Cory Seaver turned out to be not only great at gathering information that has recently caused me grief, he also proved to be quite the nose picker!

"Now, I'm going to bet that you're not only a better nose picker than freckles, but you can probably scratch your ass with the best of them. As a matter of fact, why don't you quietly go home, right now, without being seen mind you, and show us all just how vigorously you can pick your nose and scratch your ass at the same time? Also, I don't want you to answer any of your phones should they ring."

"No problem. I'm on it," was all he whispered as he quickly used his best stealth training from Quantico and vanished without a sound on his way home to carry out his new assignments.

✻

Saturday, 4:45 pm, December 8th, 2012

"You have got to be kidding me! No wonder he has been so hard to catch up with Ed, he's been listening in on our meetings all this time!" said Bill as the Nemesis' journal revealed to them that juicy fact.

"That means he's on to us and our stake out at the Kerr home which means he has his usual decided advantage over our feet on the ground there," Ed added.

Saturday, 4:50 pm, December 8th, 2012

The Nemesis had no trouble entering the house through the rear entrance after dispensing with Zack Jamanski. With Natalie being home, the alarm system was not set and his lock picking skills proved to be better than the lock he applied them on. Once upstairs he was able to creep behind Natalie Kerr who was intently involved in reading a book and again made use of his latest long nozzle spraying technique.

She fell for it just as Agent Jamanski did. That sound was a head turning magnet. It was a magnet that unconsciously commanded the requisite quick breath of surprise.

"Natalie, look at me as if you see forever in my eyes and smile for me," he said.

She instantly obliged with a dreamy expression of love and her warmest smile. Then he knew he had her. She was his to command as the others had been!

He began his instructions for her with, "Now, we need to do this rather quickly my dear so let's start by taking off all your clothes and folding them neatly on that chair by the window there."

The chair, he knew, would be on the side of the house most easily seen by the now abandoned FBI agent's post and couldn't be seen by the unsuspecting Officer Paddock, who was stationed out front. What he didn't realize was, by that time, officer Paddock had made his way to the FBI agent's deserted post and was now getting quite the show.

✱

Saturday, 4:45 pm, December 8th, 2012

'Where did you go Jamanski? We're not to leave our positions for any reason. Nature can't be calling already we haven't been here an hour yet.

Something just doesn't smell right here,' thought Officer Nick Paddock as he made the decision to take a secluded route to check on the other corner of the house.

Once he got to Jamanski's observation post; he found the agent's weapon on the ground along with his binoculars and knew they had a problem. A quick glance at the house confirmed his suspicions as he looked up to the bedroom window and saw Natalie Kerr standing there buck naked.

He immediately called Zimmerman for backup and headed for the house.

✻

Saturday, 4:50 pm, December 8th, 2012

Ed and Bill agreed that this new information warranted a visit to the Kerr estate. They were burning up the short distance to the Kerr home when Zimmerman called and gave them the news from Paddock.

A few minutes later they were headed up the Kerr driveway.

✻

Officer Paddock wasn't nearly as stealthy as Mark had been when he entered the house and it didn't go unnoticed. Mark gave some last minute instructions to Natalie which she followed to the letter.

As Nick Paddock slowly peeked around the corner of the bedroom door frame with his gun preceding his approach, he froze at what he saw.

Natalie Kerr was doing her most seductive dance, rubbing everything her mamma gave her and beckoning him to her with an index finger. That hesitation was all the Nemesis needed to direct his third spray of the night into the air, this time triggering the reflexes of Nick Paddock and capturing his undivided attention.

"Well Nick, you are in for quite the show tonight. You get to be the one and only witness to the entirety of any of my masterpieces before you die. I have to be quick about this, so it's a good thing I've had so much practice at it by now. Not only did you get to see the incredibly beautiful Natalie Kerr doing her last vertical dance tonight, but you are about to witness her very last horizontal dance of any kind as well. Take a seat on the floor by the window there Nick, set your gun down, not another word and don't make a sound. Oh and Nick, you won't remember a thing about any of this after tonight," was all he needed to say as Paddock quickly complied.

"Now where were we Natalie, oh yes, please lie down on the floor here by me and enjoy everything that we are about to do together," he told her as he dove right into his goodie bag, no longer needing to don his 'clean suit'. This would be his last performance and in about fifteen minutes, he would be on his way to his new life so DNA evidence left behind was no longer significant. What good would DNA evidence of a dead man be?

He was sure that the recent challenges he faced in pulling this one off along with the thrill and spontaneity of it would definitely satisfy his last remaining desires for revenge. He would finally be able to move on to starting his new life and be free of the need for dishing out any more pay back that had been nagging at him since Allison's death.

✡

Saturday, 5:00 pm, December 8th, 2012

He had just removed the hammer and was about to take aim at Natalie's right ankle after a long reflective glance at her nearly perfect body, a body that was about to be changed forever, when he heard the sirens blast right outside the window.

Ed Cassidy waited until he was right at the house to maximum the surprise effect and it worked. He didn't want to give the Nemesis any undue warning if he were there. He wanted to do everything possible to capture him.

Mark's reflexes and sense of survival made him instantly abandon his plan, grab his bag and the gun from Nick Paddock; then he quickly took flight. He narrowly made it down the rear stairs and out the back door as the two inspectors burst through the front door, running up the front stairs to the bedroom according to the report Paddock had called in.

What they found there both relieved them, and frustrated them once again. Paddock was safe and Natalie was still alive. On the relieved side, both were displaying the most carefree, mindless expressions they had ever seen on two human beings. On the frustrating side was the absence of Mark Shaw who remained one step ahead of them and had once again avoided capture.

CHAPTER 49

Mark wasn't the only one that didn't hesitate.

Saturday, 5:30 pm, December 8th, 2012

The three squad cars that followed Ed up the Kerr driveway early that evening; emptied and immediately began their search of the Kerr estate. Meanwhile, upstairs, Bill was finally able to tear his eyes off Natalie, who was lying there on the floor oblivious to her nakedness and perfectly content to answer Ed's questions from there. This was the first time that the two of them got a chance to witness just how completely effective the drug was as they observed its two most recent victims. Both were totally mindless, but still alive.

"Yes officer, I'm fine and how are you?" she asked him remaining right where she was.

"Nick we're all glad the two of you are ok but where's your gun?" Bill asked officer Paddock.

"Oh, I gave it to Mark Shaw when he asked for it. He said he needed it more than I did tonight," was the explanation they received from the very emotionless and cooperative Officer Paddock.

"Natalie, please get up and get dressed ok?"

"Sure," was all she said as she popped up and quickly began getting dressed as if there were no one else in the room with her. Once she finished dressing, Ed was amazed as she turned to him with a totally hopeful and expectant look on her face in anticipation of his next instruction for her. She stood before him almost hungry for direction. It was as if he suddenly had his own voice controlled totally obedient real live party doll.

That was when Connie arrived, having been summoned by Ed on his way to the Kerr residence with the caveat, "Just in case you're needed."

After hearing about the Nemesis' newly acquired weapon, Bill added "Suspect is armed and dangerous. Please proceed with caution," to the end of the APB description he sent out.

✤

Saturday, 5:45 pm, December 8th, 2012

After Mark Shaw ran out the back door he retraced his steps through the Kerr landscaping to his car that was hidden nearby and discreetly sped off to his hotel. It was now time to exercise his well rehearsed escape plan, and one of its contingencies. He decided long ago that this was obviously the most crucial element of the overall scheme. It commanded more thought and more contingencies than the murder of any two sluts from the 'ALSOTS' club combined.

Even though he was so comfortable using his alter identity of John Deramore, and as such was less prone to mistakes, he figured out early that Cory's discoveries could make it necessary for the new alternative personality that he developed in the event things went as far south as they just did.

From listening in on many of the meetings Andy and Barney had with that techno nuisance Cory recently, actually that recently-deceased-for-discovering-too-much-of-my-plans techno nuisance Cory, he found that the John Deramore name had been exposed. The name being uncovered combined with the heat brought on by tonight's turn of events meant that both the 'old black dude' and the Columbian playboy disguises that he took with him were now useless.

Scratch them and the ticket/passport packages that went with them.

He was totally prepared to give birth to Jerry Bostwick—which would be his name until things cooled down. He had a second ticket, passport and identity documentation, and was well practiced in applying makeup to complete this disguise.

As the visual elements of the Jerry Bostwick identity slowly came together, he reflected on the fact that he was unsuccessful in checking Natalie off his list. This didn't bother him for the moment. There would always be tomorrow. Correction, if he got out of dodge fast enough there would always be a tomorrow.

Like all other components of his grand tribute to Allison, this escape was a well rehearsed play in his head. It wasn't necessary to think or refer to notes to complete each critical step. It was like his body was suddenly switched to automatic pilot.

There would be no second guessing, only mistake free execution. This is what came of the hours of going over literally hundreds of possible scenarios which might keep him from not only starting his life over again, but also from ultimately catching back up with Natalie Kerr. He would never lose sight of the fact that she needed to be ultimately terminated.

It was now forty five minutes until his flight took off. He would have had plenty of time in his original plan to finish off Natalie and reach the terminal for his flight. Everything he brought with him would now be left in his hotel room except the Jerry Bostwick identity package, and nearly empty carry-on, designed to minimize airport hassles.

As it turned out, he thought of everything but failed to realize that it was almost impossible to out run a universe that had shifted this far against you. Taking his plans for Natalie with him but leaving the photo and description of his recently developed crisis identity in his journal, would be his ultimate undoing.

When the journal was brought back to the police station for Ed and Bill to review, they had to give him credit for coming up with such a brilliant character for his escape. The outward appearance of the face in the picture used by him for makeup rehearsals was so nondescript that, at the time, Bill commented, "This 'Joey Bag of Donuts' face could melt into any crowd without being noticed."

It was a description of the 'Joey Bag of Donuts' face that accompanied the other details of Bill's 'Armed and Dangerous' APB.

⋇

Saturday, 6:15 pm, December 8th, 2012

The team of officers finished searching the grounds but couldn't find a trace of Jamanski except for his pistol and binoculars which were discovered near his abandoned post. They tried to call both his cell and home phones to no avail, so the search moved to his apartment to look for anything that might help find him.

As they arrived there, they found that the front door was left ajar. As they peered inside past the door, they found the one they were looking for, but weren't prepared for his condition. There in the dining room facing the front door Ed and Bill found what was mentally left of Agent Zack Jamanski.

Fortunately, they found him within an hour of being missed by Nick Paddock, because any longer, and he might have bled out due to his current condition.

Ed turned to the officer on his left and said, "Wilson, get and ambulance up here right away. I'll try to stop this madness."

His shirt and Kevlar vest were both soaked in blood which was now pumping freely from the massive facial injury caused by his strict obedience to Mark Shaw's last instructions to him. His right nostril was torn and basically missing as was half his right cheek. Picking what was left of his nose with his right hand had progressed to within millimeters of his right eye. In as little as ten more minutes he would have happily destroyed his eye as he mindlessly continued his compulsion to complete his assigned task. That is, if his body still had enough blood left to keep functioning.

The puddle of blood on the floor beneath him was significant and growing as it was also being fed by the now massive wound to his left butt cheek as Zack had worn through both pieces of clothing and approximately an inch and a half of his left rear cheek as he continued to scratch vigorously as instructed since he arrived home, oblivious to the ringing phones around him.

"That's just cold man," was all Bill could say. He was in no mood for levity having walked in on such a gruesome sight.

After providing Zack with a new set of instructions, stopping him from further damage to himself, Ed commented, "That has to be the cruelest abuse of an individual's dignity I have ever seen."

"I know just the team of good doctors to recommend for his recovery," offered Bill.

*

Saturday, 6:50 pm, December 8th, 2012

The Nemesis was spotted by airport security as soon as he walked into the terminal. The terminal that was listed for the escape flight found among the other meticulous details in his journal. It was at the Chicago Executive Airport. All police and airport security personnel at the scene were given orders to discreetly observe and report the suspect if spotted, but stand down as Ed was only five minutes away. He and Bill knew there was plenty of time before Mark would use his preprinted boarding pass to walk onto his flight fifteen minutes from now.

Once Ed and Bill arrived at the airport, they split up with Ed maneuvering to a point in front of Mark but still out of sight. Bill took up a position to the rear covering the only other way out of that part of the terminal. Both had Sig Sauer 1911 Nitron pistols with silencers to minimize panic in the airport should there be any shooting.

'Let the show begin,' Ed thought as he walked out between Mark and the boarding gate wearing a Kevlar vest under his clothing. His gun was drawn but held out of sight at his side.

"I think it would be best if we go outside for a chat Mark," he said as he approached the Nemesis calmly.

There was no hesitation, not time for the blink of an eye as Mark stared Ed in the eyes, recognized him and started to raise his left hand, which was holding Nick Paddock's service weapon covered by a jacket. As he did so, he simultaneously began reaching his right hand out for the eight year old boy seated to his right. He had selected the child as a possible human shield while sitting there waiting for his flight. His mind never rested.

Mark wasn't the only one that didn't hesitate, however. Bill, noticing the Nemesis' initial movement, instantly fired his Sig twice hitting the target that was already in his sights. The bullets found their mark as two near side by side entrance wounds began flowing on the killer's forehead with no more noise than two mild coughs.

Having formulated his last destructive thought, Mark looked as if he suddenly decided to take a nap as he simultaneously stopped reaching for the eight year old, dropped his left hand back down and let his head simply fall back to the high rise seat complete with headrest. His body slumped, thankfully absent any further movement, and finally was no longer a threat to anyone. That was the way that Connie found him once she arrived, and she was never more content to pronounce a body dead on arrival.

The eight year old boy, still sitting next to Mark's now motionless body, was too involved in the game he was playing on his phone while listening to music with his headphones to notice what just took place less than three feet to his left.

Immediately all officers on the scene had sprung into action containing any potential panic as they calmly and professionally cleared the terminal. With all the potential passengers gone from the area, Ed suddenly realized that he didn't need to serve the last arrest warrant after all.

Bill approached Ed slowly with a remorseful look on his face and said, "I'm so sorry Ed."

Ed replied, "What are you talking about Bill? He was drawing down on me and shamelessly about to pull that kid in for a shield."

"That's not it. What I mean is, I cost the tax payers fifty cents, not twenty five as planned, instead of the trial."

Ed merely shook his head placing his arm around Bill's shoulder as they left for the station to let LT. Gorten know that it was finally time to sign his retirement papers.

✲

Saturday, 8:00 pm, December 8th, 2012

Sufficient details of the airport shooting were picked up on the police channel chatter by all the news vans camped nearby and waiting for the next development in the 'Plastic Wife Murder' cases. They were waiting at the Winnetka police station when Ed and Bill got back. The inspectors' only option for entry was through the one driveway still kept open which was reserved for official business.

With no more suspects at large, Ed was finally glad to freely answer any questions the reporters had for him. At long last, this was no longer an ongoing investigation.

As questions were answered, they all became fodder for the countless newspaper and TV headlines that would soon materialize to satisfy the Chicago area, and national interest in the north shore murder cases.

✿

"Tonight, the man responsible for seven murders recently discovered in and around Winnetka Illinois, was killed by local police in a near shoot-out. The take down of the 'Plastic Wife Killer' took place in a terminal building at the Chicago Executive Airport in nearby Palatine.

"It has been a harrowing past few months leading up to the Christmas holiday season, as members of the local and state police, as well as the FBI agents assigned to the case, finally got their man. As it turned out, he didn't act alone. Details are still sketchy, but it appears that husbands of three murdered wives were involved in a plot of revenge that came very near completion before the team of investigators headed up by Winnetka's Ed Cassidy and Evanston's Bill Weller cut it short before claiming it's final victim.

"We will have more details on our 10:00 broadcast later tonight as this story continues to develop.

"This is Susan Peterson reporting live from Winnetka for Channel Seven News."

In the next few days, stories born from that night's developments detailed everything from Jack Kerr's filing for divorce from Natalie to all the juicy details of who was shacking up with who in that 'all too wealthy for their own good' crowd of doctor's wives. All were viewed as woefully short of morals in most reader's eyes.

✿

Tuesday, March 5ᵗʰ, 2013

After passing the letter back to the jury's foreman, the judge asked, "Will the jury foreman please stand? Mr. Forman, has the jury reached a verdict?"

"Yes we have your honor."

"Ladies and gentlemen of the jury, in the matter that has been before this court involving the deaths of Aimee Holden, Lisa Ackerman, Lori Baker, Isabella Channing, Sandra Falkland, Olivia Reed and Cory Seaver, and in response to the charges of conspiracy to commit murder in each of these cases by the defendants; John Ackerman, Jim Baker and Raymond Reed, how do you find?"

"Your honor, we the jury, find the defendants guilty as charged," was the jury foreman's response to the court. The verdict didn't elicit a single sigh of shock or surprise from anyone in the courtroom due to the overwhelming evidence presented. The expected murmurs confirming the expected verdict was all that was heard. It was the most one sided case tried in Cook County Illinois for quite some time.

"Ladies and gentlemen of the jury, this court hereby dismisses you and thanks you for your honorable service.

"As there can only be one sentence issued in this case, I will deliver it now without delay.

"John Ackerman, Jim Baker and Raymond Reed, please stand. You are hereby sentenced to serve prison terms the Stateville maximum security correctional facility for as long as you each shall live.

"This sentence is to commence immediately. These crimes were so heinous and premeditated that I am also removing the possibility of parole for the term of the sentence for each of you.

"Gentlemen the state of Illinois doesn't allow me to assign the death penalty any longer but if it did, I wouldn't hesitate at applying it here. I don't have anything else to add. Enough has been said regarding the sad matter that has been decided in this court. The court is adjourned."

Part Six

Beyond's Justice

*"The only ill will to be found in this valley
is that which you bring yourself."*
Lord of the Rings—Gandalf

EPILOGUE

They all only hoped that it was going to be the last.

<u>Monday, March 4th, 2013</u>

*T*heir first day in the general population at Stateville, a level one, maximum security, adult male only prison was as dismal as each of them had envisioned it would be. John Ackerman, Jim Baker and Ray Reed were each assigned to the same cell block but were several cells removed from each other, and each had a cell mate that was also recently imprisoned and just as depressed as they were. The first day's routine sucked. They were each reflecting on the waste that their lives had recently become since their life long prison sentences without the possibility of parole were handed down.

All the years of medical school, all the seminars, all the successful surgeries, the lifestyle that other's only dreamed of, all of it out the window. The judge reminded them of how lucky they all were that the death penalty was abolished in Illinois. Somehow the three of them weren't feeling quite as lucky as the judge portrayed. It might have been better if they did receive the death penalty for all the good they would be able to do themselves or anyone else from this point out.

It was truly depressing. From the new wardrobe they had each been given with their new numeric names affixed to them, compliments of the tax payers of Cook County, to the oh-so-flavorless meals they had received today which were high in soy content and difficult to process successfully for many digestive tracts that weren't used to it.

Orientation day was a real treat for the three of them as they received their schedules for recreation periods, healthcare passes, religious services and work routines. They also picked up several helpful tips from other inmates on their first day as convicts, about avoiding the gang systems that were in place. They were also advised to claim the title of 'Neutron' quickly, which was the status of non-association with any gang that tended to enhance their chances of survival.

They had just finished their first day of incarceration and were resigning themselves first to showering, then to laying their heads down on the uncomfortable beds that were confirmed as such by each of them earlier when they first arrived. They each got a taste of what sleeping in Stateville would be like when they brought the meager possessions allowed each inmate to their newly assigned cells. Each of them knew that there was sure to be a long reflective period of time lying on those uncomfortable mattresses tonight before the bliss of sleep would rescue them from that first day of depressing change for all of them.

The conversation in the shower was brief between the three former doctors. As they left, they couldn't help but be concerned by a gathering of inmates that had formed just in front of the sink area where they all needed to pass through.

Was this going to be their first confrontation, naked and about as defenseless as can be? Was this what their new way of life was destined to throw at them so early in their lifetime prison sentences?

As they cautiously approached the cluster, the three of them noticed that the group wasn't gathered there for hostilities at all. They were staring at a steamed up mirror. It was a steamed up mirror that had a message written on it. They were all a good distance away from the mirror with none of them having had a chance to do the writing.

All of them were just staring at it with puzzled looks on their faces as if to be questioning each other to find out who did write the message there. The first ones out of the shower began making way for the new arrivals as deciphering the message's meaning was attempted by each of them.

The three former doctors stood there, becoming one with the gathering crowd. They were wearing nothing but their shame and remorse as they stood there with towels hanging from the hand at their side as each read the message on the mirror. If shame and remorse were all it took to get their prison terms commuted they had enough between the three of them to get it done, but it didn't work that way. It was too late now. They should have taken the possibility of this ending to their story much more seriously when they all threw their hats one at a time into Mark Shaw's ring of destruction.

They were the only ones in the group of inmates standing there that understood the meaning contained within the message written on the mirror. It was at that moment that they finally got the answer to the only remaining question which had eluded each of them until now. Answers to the last question they had about Mark Shaw's involvement in providing 'clues' to them all during his execution of the 'ALSOTS' members that they had all chosen to target. They had been denied a final conversation with him at the moment he lost interest in obtaining the human shield in that Palatine airport terminal three months ago. Those damned 'clues' that had been dropped in front of the inspectors and the 'Generals' like so many bread crumbs to a bird which ultimately helped lead Ed and Bill down the trail of discovery and to their eventual demise.

Mark Shaw was now dead; their trials were now over, and here was another 'message'. They all only hoped that it was going to be the last.

This message was slightly different from the steamed mirror messages Jim Baker used to receive from Lori at the cabin, which was now sold along with his estate in Winnetka. This one had an eye, a wide open eye, drawn in the upper left and lower right corners of the mirror. In between the two eyes, they found a set of initials that were all too familiar to them.

A
L
L
I
S
O
C

Slowly the three doctors took their towels, approached the mirror and slowly started to wipe away the message. All three of them struggled to overcome their urges to destroy the mirror as they did.

It was soon gone from the mirror, but none of them would ever be able to remove that image from their minds.

THE END

CPSIA information can be obtained at www.ICGtesting.com
Printed in the USA
LVOW06s1108191213

365993LV00001B/1/P